QUEENDOM COME

JORDAN H. BARTLETT

The
Frean
Chronicles

QUEENDOM COME

She ascended the throne a war too late.

CamCat
Books

CamCat Books
2810 Coliseum Centre Drive, Suite 300
Charlotte, NC 28217-4574

Hardcover ISBN 9780744310764
Paperback ISBN 9780744310788
eBook ISBN 9780744310795

Library of Congress Control Number: 2024941158

Book and cover design by Maryann Appel
Map illustration by Andrew Martin

5   3   1   2   4

For those who have fallen,

those with the strength to get back up,

and those who keep trying.

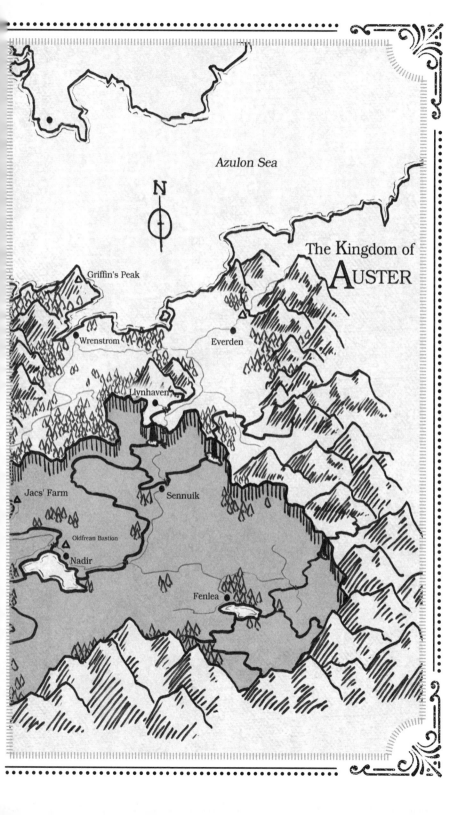

In times the realms have long forgotten,
when the age of woman was but a seed in history's soil,
the Court of Griffins ruled all.

With talon, beak, and wing, they ruled the skies, and
all beneath the clouds fell under their domain.

Had women accepted their place
alongside the beasts of the land, there need not
have been as much bloodshed . . .

1

NOT BAD NEWS

The Griffins were furious. Sounds of their displeasure tore through the throne room, reverberating from pillar to pillar and rising high into the vaulted ceiling. A sound of thunder, the perfect blend of eagle cry and lion roar, echoed inside Jacs's chest. It thrummed like a second heartbeat, consuming her mind. Jacs couldn't blame them, and knowing the true power of what a Griffin's grief could do to the minds of others, she was grateful that their cries were the only things filling her thoughts.

"I understand." She tried to make her voice heard above their crashing screeches. Kneeling at the base of the throne dais, she lifted her head, catching a glimpse of the snow-white monarch of the Court of Griffins, Altus Thenya, and two others: Altus Hermes, the messenger with its gray eagle head and tawny lion's haunches; and Altus Riesa, the monarch's mate, jet-black from beak to tail. Each shone with gold-dusted feathers and fur. The trio stood above Jacs on the dais, in front of the Griffin-shaped golden throne she only ever vacated when holding council with the Court.

Altus Thenya's eyes flashed. Altus Riesa stamped its taloned foreleg and roared again. An echoing chorus came from the open-bottomed temple in the ceiling high above their heads where nine other members of the Court looked on in outrage. The beautiful mosaic rim of the oculus in the ceiling was surrounded by a dozen stone pillars that created viewing windows for the Griffins to stand in as they peered through the hole into the throne room below. The pillars were topped with a roof that extended far enough to shelter the Griffins in times of poor weather. Curiously, only Altus Hermes had been silent, head bowed, eyes closed.

"Please, I understand your pain." Jacs blinked away the memory of the chained and bleeding Griffin she had met in the bowels of Alethia. The Undercourt Griffin had ripped her worst memories to the forefront of her mind before forcing her to feel the depths of its own grief. She understood their pain exactly. "It's monstrous what Celos has done to the Undercourt, and nothing will ever make it right, but we know where they are now. We know who has them. If we work together, we can free them."

The screeches subsided as the gold-dusted trio scrutinized her. After a moment's pause, Altus Hermes stepped forward and placed its beak and forehead against those of first Altus Thenya, then Altus Riesa. Jacs did not know what thoughts passed between the Griffins, but whatever they were seemed to settle their ire.

At a nod from Altus Thenya, Altus Hermes stepped down from the dais and approached Jacs. Her muscles tensed as the magnificent creature drew near. She tried to remain composed, but the memory of her last run-in with Griffins caused sweat to prickle her palms and bead her forehead. Altus Hermes motioned for her to rise and, after a moment's hesitation, softly pressed the dorsal portion of its beak against her nose and forehead. She felt its breath huff across her lips and down her front. The tiny feathers outlining its beak tickled her brow.

After her many dealings with the Griffins' powers, Jacs had built a wall of protection around her mind as a way to control what thoughts could enter, what thoughts were pulled from her, and when. It was against this wall that Jacs now felt a gentle pressure, an invitation. She took a breath and nodded, lowering her mind's defenses and allowing Altus Hermes in. This was new. When it came to her communications with the Griffins, they had typically pushed their way in regardless of whether she was ready or not. Some of the tension eased from her shoulders.

A vision filled her mind that was so vivid, she could almost feel the wind in her hair. She was riding on the back of Altus Hermes. To her left and right she saw the rest of the Court slashing through the air with knights of the Queensguard perched on their backs. A giant V formation cut like a dagger through the sky. Ancient eyes blazed. Griffins roared with wings beating, talons flashing, beaks gnashing. Cries of war filled her ears as they struck out with purpose. Far below, the land rushed past them. Forest, lake, and plain sped by, marking their progress. To the north, the Azulon Sea stretched toward the horizon.

The vision shifted; the Court and its riders now entered the catacombs. The once graceful rulers of the skies crashed through the caverns. Wings tangled, talons tripped, and frustrated roars of pain filled the air. A rumble came from overhead and Jacs looked up just in time to see stalactites break free and rain down on their fleet. She looked ahead. The narrow tunnel now held multiple purple-hooded assailants, all with nets and nasty-looking swords. An ambush.

With a metallic clang, chained bridles were hammered in place around the Court's necks. Her knights were manacled together and forced to march through the labyrinth while Jacs watched helplessly through iron bars. Her crown, now a barbed circlet, pierced her temples.

Trickles of blood dripped down her forehead and into her eyes, blinding her. The images faded and she blinked furiously, wiping at her eyes, but her vision was obscured by tears, nothing more.

Swallowing hard, she nodded. "I agree, it would be foolish to think we could free them by attacking Alethia head on. Griffins aren't meant to be underground, and I couldn't ask that of the Court." Altus Riesa huffed loudly in agreement. "But the Queendom's military is filled with the most lethal women in the two realms. Their skills make them powerful weapons in the catacombs' confined tunnels. Let me speak with Chivilra Amber Everstar—she's filling in as head of the Queensguard while we wait for Masterchiv Rathbone to return, and we can discuss strategy and devise a plan. We've both been in the Catacombs of Lethe twice now and have each visited different parts of Alethia. We have more knowledge of our enemy than we did before and can use this to our advantage.

"Once we know our next steps, I will let you know what part, if any, the Court will be expected to play, but know that you will not be forced underground without good reason."

Altus Hermes turned to look over its shoulder at the other two Griffins. While still obviously outraged, the griffins bowed their heads, accepting her plan.

"Because speed is of the utmost importance, I've installed a signal torch on the top of your temple." She pointed a forefinger up toward the circular, pillared structure the other Griffins were perched in to observe the throne room. "If we need to speak with you again, I will light the torch and await your presence. All I ask is you have a member of the Court watching for it." She scrunched her brow as an idea hit her. "During the day though . . ." she said hesitantly, half to herself, mind whirling. "During the day, you likely won't see the flames. I'll speak with the palace alchemists . . . I know there's something we can add to the fires to make the smoke more visible, or maybe a different color. Yes, let's do that. During the day, watch for smoke."

The Court agreed. Like Jacs, they seemed calmer with a plan in front of them. She bowed to each of the three Griffins to receive a farewell preening. Their sharp beaks ran through her auburn hair. Altus Riesa was more vigorous than the other two and seemed the most displeased after their council, whereas Altus Hermes lingered a moment. Jacs had the impression that the Griffin had more to share but must have thought better of it, because in an instant its beak had vanished from her hair, and it followed the other two out of the oculus in the ceiling. In a flurry of wingbeats, the Court vanished.

Jacs let her breath out slowly. That had gone much better than expected. For a moment she had worried that the enslavement of the Undercourt would make the Court distrust not just Celos, but all humans. Thankfully, the treaty held true, and the peace between their two species, between Court and Crown, remained unbroken.

With split skirts flaring around her, she strode boldly down the long indigo carpet that striped the center of the throne room, pillars marking even intervals on either side. Jacs twirled a strand of hair around her finger anxiously. Her green eyes were shadowed with the mess of thoughts that raveled and unraveled in her mind. There was so much to do, so many unanswered questions, and since removing the corrupt members of the Council of Four, so many additional duties had been laid on her plate. While she knew it had been the right choice to remove the Councilors—after all, their crimes against the Crown included assassinating her predecessor, Queen Ariel, and kidnapping her mother and Master Leschi to blackmail Jacs and manipulate her actions as Queen—it still meant Jacs was now picking up the workload of four competent women. Not to mention, she didn't even know the half of what they did to help the Queendom run smoothly.

Jacs shoved the large throne-room doors open, and a snippet of conversation met her on the threshold.

"Flent, I swear on my sword, you are crossing a line that will get you demoted, do you understand?"

Guard Dyna Flent, Chivilra Amber Everstar's current partner while Chiv. Andromeda Turner healed, jumped back as the doors opened, and Jacs saw her umber cheeks flush darker with an emotion that was hard to read.

With the speed of a pickpocket, Flent quickly tucked away a grin, her face cleared, and she stood to attention, whisking a black curl up into her silk headband. Her gaze darted swiftly back to Amber for a moment, then returned to face forward.

The look on Amber's face was much easier to decipher. Jacs had experienced that look firsthand in the early days of their training sessions: disappointment at a mistake she knew you were smart enough not to make. For such a short woman, Amber had an incredible talent of making others feel small when she felt they were not living up to their potential.

In an instant, Amber's crooked grin smoothed her features, and she flicked her long tail of brown hair over her shoulder. Chin jutting forward, she looked up at Jacs.

"You look like you have good news. Or at least not bad news," Amber said, taking a half step away from Flent.

They began walking down the deserted corridor, Amber falling in step beside Jacs, Flent walking two steps ahead of them. Not the usual formation. Jacs looked from guard to knight; Flent walked with a definite spring in her step and Amber looked perturbed. Jacs raised her eyebrow at Amber, who frowned and shook her head sharply. Later, then.

"Not bad news," Jacs agreed. "Obviously, the Court was outraged to find out about their captured kin, but we started discussing next steps, and actually, that's where you come in. Can we gather the Queensguard? We need to talk strategy."

"Of course. Flent, send a messenger to gather the Queensguard at once, we'll meet in the—" She looked at Jacs for confirmation.

"Battle room, we'll need the maps."

"Battle room it is."

"But shouldn't I stay—" Flent began. Jacs understood. Knights and guards always worked in pairs. It was a risk to separate a guard-pair, especially the pair protecting the Queen.

"Make quick work of it and you won't be five minutes, I think Her Majesty will be safe until you return," Amber said curtly.

"Understood," came Flent's clipped reply. She bowed quickly to Jacs and, without a second look at Amber, spun on her heel in search of a messenger.

Once she was safely out of earshot, Jacs commented mildly: "Bit harsh."

Amber forced an exhale through her nose. "Necessary. She forgot herself."

"Oh?"

"It's nothing. Of no concern to the Queen, at least. It has no effect on your protection, nor on the performance of your guardpairs." She walked briskly, eyes sweeping left and right as they moved down the corridor.

Adopting her tone of professionalism, Jacs said, "Of course not, Chiv. Everstar. I expect nothing less from my Queensguard. But Amber . . ." She paused and studied her a moment. "What if it's of concern to a friend?" she finished softly and stopped in her tracks, forcing the knight to do the same. "Is everything okay?"

"Fine."

"Are you sure?"

Amber looked around to ensure they were alone in the corridor. Seeing the coast was clear, she sighed and admitted, "It's Flent."

Jacs waited.

"Nothing I can't handle," Amber said with forced bravado. "I'm just trying to navigate it. She's an unpredictable variable, that's all."

"An unpredictable variable?" Jacs teased good-naturedly, hiding a smile. "You're starting to sound like Andromeda."

Amber barked a laugh and shifted her weight from one foot to the other. "She just, I just find I don't know what to, or how to . . ." A blush crept up her neck.

Realization dawned and Jacs remembered a comment Andromeda had made in the infirmary over a week ago, "Oh. My. Goodness." Jacs pressed into each word as Amber's head snapped up, confusion blooming on her face. "You like her."

"I do not! I mean of course I do; we're partners."

"No, I mean more than that. As I live and breathe, this woman has you smitten."

Amber crossed her arms. "What? No, she hasn't. If anything, I've smittened her. I don't have feelings either way. Except professional ones. Because we're partners. Until Turner heals. Then she'll be someone else's partner. And that will be fine too."

"I see," said Jacs, a knowing smile spreading across her face.

"Truly."

"No, I believe you. *Truly* I do."

Amber stood still while Jacs composed herself around a rogue smirk.

"Oh, shut it," she snapped.

Jacs feigned offense. "Is that any way to speak to your Queen?"

"Sorry," Amber said, rolling her eyes with a grin. "Shut it, Your Highness."

"Better."

They resumed walking down the corridor. Jacs nodded a hello to Dame Shane Adella as she passed by.

"So, what are you going to do?" Jacs asked in a low voice once they were out of earshot.

"I'm not sure. But don't worry, I'd never jeopardize my position. If something has to go, it'll be Flent."

As if summoned, Flent rounded the corner, her lips pressed in a thin line. "The Queensguard will be waiting in the battle room in half an hour. I sent for refreshments to meet us there, as Chivilras Fayworth and Pamheir were sparring."

Amber cleared her throat. "Excellent, Flent. Lead the way." The group fell into formation and an uncomfortable silence. Jacs wasn't sure how much of their conversation Flent had heard, but she had a sinking feeling she'd heard the last comment.

"Your Majesty!" a simpering voice called from behind and cut across her musings. Jacs turned to see the blue-eyed, doll-faced, golden-curled Lord Hera Claustrom float toward her. Full skirts of powder blue swirled about her ankles.

Hitching up a smile, Jacs greeted her warmly. "Good morning, Lord Claustrom. To what do I owe this pleasure?"

"Well, that's just the thing, I bring news of great pleasure! I've just received a letter from my dear little brother, Lordson Theo Claustrom. You remember inviting him to join you in the palace?" Hera spoke loudly, as though inviting perked ears to listen. The last piece of information was most definitely for others, as Hera had not let Jacs forget her invitation since she had made it.

"Of course I remember, Lord Claustrom."

Hera flashed a smile. "He wrote to say he was thrilled to receive your summons and will be arriving within the next few days. Is that not the most wonderful news?"

"Truly wonderful," Jacs said.

"And of course, you have something special prepared for his audience with you? A certain question you must be dying to ask?" She paused expectantly, a wicked glint in her eye. "Oh, but I wouldn't want to ruin the surprise prematurely! I guess we shall *all* simply have to wait to find out."

Hera's words fell heavily on Jacs's heart. It had now been over a week since she had last seen Connor. A week since she had made her deal with Hera. A week since her heart had stopped, and she had shattered it at the feet of this vapid plip. All for what? Power she desperately needed to overthrow the corrupt Council of Four. The price? She must marry Hera's brother and forever destroy the life she and Connor could have built together.

Without Hesperida's support, the Council would still be at large and pulling the strings of the Sons of Celos. Jacs needed to remember that this was what she wanted. Harder to do, given that she was now taking on all four Councilors' roles.

Hang on. Jacs's thoughts derailed as a new idea took their place.

"That you shall, and I promise it will be worth the wait," Jacs said with a sweet smile. "I'm glad you found us, actually, as I have a task for you."

Hera's eyes betrayed a wariness that her smile and tone denied. "How wonderful, what is it?"

Jacs weighed her next words carefully. "As you can imagine, the Council of Four did a great many things to keep our Queendom afloat. Each position holds incredible responsibilities. I myself find I am unable to keep up with all that they used to do, and I worry that I don't yet understand the exact scope of their roles. Since you are my sole Councilor until the other three are chosen, I wonder if you could compile a document outlining each of the previous Councilor's roles, responsibilities, and duties. I work much better with lists, and I know of no other person who I would trust with such a task.

"From there, we can begin to delegate some of those duties to your capable hands. Until then, I will have Edith—who has been desperate for a distraction since Cornelius went missing—act as your assistant."

Jacs finished her command with the satisfaction of placing the final gear in a mechanism and seeing the cogs whir. If she could only keep Hera's time occupied, she may not have any left to spend opening her mouth. As a potential bonus, she may even prove herself useful.

Before Hera could respond, Jacs waved over a nearby serving boy and said, "Barlow, please fetch Edith and let her know I have a new position for her until Cornelius returns. She is to watch over Lord

Claustrom's progress as she prepares a comprehensive list of Councilor obligations."

Barlow hurriedly noted down her instructions and bowed before rushing off to find Edith.

Jacs turned back to Hera, hands clasped happily in front, and beamed. "Oh, it's such a relief to have someone so competent on my Council."

Hera replied through a barely concealed grimace: "I'm happy to be of service, Your Highness." As if to avoid Jacs's adding more tasks to her now extensive to-do list, Hera bowed low and excused herself.

"And do keep me updated with news of Lordson Claustrom's arrival!" Jacs called after her.

Amber shared a subtle nod of approval with Jacs as they watched Hera retreat down the corridor. Although it was a victory, Jacs had to concede it was a small one. Hera still held the power. The nobility still listened to her, not their Queen. Theo was still on his way. All Jacs had done was the equivalent of a rough patch job on a leaking bucket. The water would drain eventually; she had just slowed the inevitable.

They passed through to another corridor, this one much busier than the last. The portraits of former Queens gave way to large windows overlooking the grounds. Several members of the nobility were seated or standing in front of the windows, admiring the view, while the serving staff floated about with refreshments. Jacs suppressed a shudder. While much more cheerful in the daylight, this corridor had been the scene of her ambush, when nine hoods had kidnapped her guard and closest friends and left her in a panic.

As if sensing her mood, Amber introduced a new topic. "How's your mother doing?"

"She's doing well, some of the time. Still in the infirmary under observation. Master Epione is worried she'll continue to slip in and out of lucidity for a while since she was in Alethia for so long, but I see her for an hour or so every day, and every day she seems . . . brighter."

Amber nodded curtly.

Everything seemed brighter outside that city. But they would have to go back, and soon. Jacs pushed that thought away.

"She plays a fierce game of chess, your mother." Flent piped up, only half turning around. "So far, she's beaten me three games in a row. I thought I'd let her win the first one, you know, boost her mood, but she wiped the floor with me, no problem."

Jacs laughed. "I'm glad I'm not the only one. I haven't won a game against her in years. I think, growing up, when she was teaching me, she held back to give me a chance. Now it's a bloodbath. Who taught you to play?"

Flent hesitated before replying. "My . . . aunt. Chess is actually what got me interested in the military. I liked the poetry behind the different plays and became obsessed first with chess, then military strategy and formations."

"Very noble," Jacs said quietly, understanding Flent's hesitation. Her aunt was Councilor Beatrice Fengar.

Flent stopped short. "Your Highness, forgive my forwardness, but I have to ask." Amber visibly bristled as Flent continued. "May I visit my aunt before she's relocated? I know she is guilty of a long list of crimes, but could I see her, just once?"

Jacs frowned. She had moved the Councilors to isolated rooms in a location known only to a few and strictly forbidden any contact between them as well as with their guards. Unsure as to who was still loyal to them, she had decided to assume any contact could be dangerous. But Flent was Fengar's niece and had proven herself to be loyal to the Crown.

As she took a moment to consider, Amber interjected: "Your Highness, I could . . . I could accompany Flent during this visit. To act as witness if Councilor Fengar attempts any foul play?"

Flent flashed Amber a smile that could have melted even the most stoic of knights. Without any further reason to deny the request, Jacs nodded. "That sounds reasonable. But I would like a full report about what transpires between you."

"Of course, Your Highness. Thank you."

"And Flent," Jacs began, adding an edge to her tone. She cast her gaze around the sunlit corridor and noted the pockets of nobles and serving staff milling and bustling about. Lowering her voice, she said, "Next time you have a request of as delicate a nature as this, please wait until we are in a private room to ask it. Or else request an audience."

Flent paled and said hastily, "Understood, Your Highness."

"Good, now I need to find the palace alchemists quickly before we head off to our meeting with the Queensguar—oh! Cyrus, please tell me you have news." Jacs cut off as a palace scryer hurried over, bowing preemptively and stumbling over his feet.

Straightening his doublet, he bowed again and reported in undertones: "Good afternoon, Your Majesty. I regrettably have nothing new to report. Royal Advisor Cornelius has not yet appeared in our scry glasses, and regardless of what mirror we are using, it continues to buzz sporadically. We have brought in the court composer to see if there is any musical significance to the buzzing, but so far, she has found nothing of note. Pardon the pun, that was . . . entirely unintentional." He looked mortified as he hurried to continue. "The rest of the missing persons continue to elude our scry crystals; however, their names do not cause the mirrors to buzz. Also, we have confirmed that Masterchiv Rathbone is not currently registered, so her name is no longer on our list of recitation."

Jacs nodded her understanding, mind caught on the new theory. "A musical significance," she said. "Is there a rhythm to the buzzing, then?"

"That's what we are trying to figure out, Your Majesty, and I'll report back with any updates, or else I will find you again in an hour for the next one."

"Excellent, thank you, Cyrus. I will see you soon."

As the scryer departed, Jacs could feel Amber's eyes on her. Their weight made battling the lump in her throat much more difficult.

"I'm fine," she said to the knight's unanswered question.

"We'll find him, Jacqueline," Amber said gently.

They walked the rest of the way to the battle room in silence.

2

HEALING THE RUIN

He was burning. Fire erupted from his skin. Flickering and growing, consuming him whole. Scorching its way through vein and artery until he could almost feel his blood boil.

No, never mind.

He was freezing. Ice stopped the fire short, plunging him into glacial depths. Wild shivers wracked his frame as though his joints sought dislocation. His lungs ached, throat felt scraped raw, and ribs were bruised from what must have been a lifetime of coughing.

Wait, he was definitely burning. Or was his skin burning and his blood freezing? To be all at once too hot and too cold was maddening. Surely an equilibrium would have been reached. Instead, he was stuck in a paradoxical state of living both extremes at once.

He groaned.

"Your Grace, with all due respect, you need to keep quiet, or I will be forced to gag you again," a voice whispered. Who was that? He didn't like their tone. No, he wanted soft blankets, a cold flagon of water, and gentle voices only. He definitely didn't want that nasty rag shoved in his mouth again; he'd only just gotten rid of the thing. He groaned again and felt a coarse fabric force its way between his teeth.

Indignation sparked in his burning, freezing, aching chest. He was the former Crown Prince, current royal advisor to the Queen, likely to be King . . . He shouldn't be chewing on crusty linen. Opening his eyes a crack, he tried to make sense of his surroundings. His vision vibrated as his body convulsed in another coughing fit. How do you stop your lungs from escaping when they clearly want out?

Everything was eerily blue. A face swam before him, blonde hair surrounding blurry features. "Mother?" he croaked into the ball of fabric. His throat was so dry, and now this rag was sucking up all his extra saliva. What a waste. He frowned and lifted a hand to remove it. A thousand needles assaulted his joints with each minute adjustment. Groaning again, he abandoned his mission and let his hand fall back to his side. Fear tiptoed its way into his mind.

He was glad his mother was here; she would know what to do.

But the hand that felt his forehead was rough and callused, not the soft touch he remembered. His heart sank as Masterchiv Cassida Rathbone's features swam into focus.

"Your Grace, you still have a fever. We need to get you some water, and we need to get out of these tunnels. I'm going to try and carry you. You need to keep quiet."

"Yes, Chiv!" Connor said into the fabric and attempted a guard salute, again forgetting that it hurt to move his arms. Masterchiv Rathbone grunted as she tried to hoist him onto her shoulders, then onto her back when that didn't work, then into her arms when that failed, until she finally returned him to the ground with an *oof*. Connor tried not to take offense. He couldn't blame her grumbling. His limbs didn't seem to want to do anything but hang uselessly from his torso. That made him very awkward to carry.

"New plan," she said. "You're going to have to try to walk a little. I can support you, but I can't carry your dead weight."

Connor curled up into a ball like a child requesting five more minutes of sleep.

"If we stay here, you'll die," Masterchiv Rathbone snapped. "You have to try."

Reluctantly, Connor unwound and attempted to sit up. His head throbbed and everything hurt. Was dying really such a worse alternative? The thought briefly entered his head and caused him to giggle. He couldn't die yet. Not in a tunnel.

Slowly, he allowed Masterchiv Rathbone to pull him to his feet. He knees buckled and she caught him swiftly under the armpit, throwing his arm across her shoulders.

"Easy does it, Your Grace. Keep your eyes closed if it helps. There we go. Now take a step. Good. Another. Excellent, now keep going just like that."

While Connor wasn't a fan of the patronizing tone the knight had adopted, he did feel a quiet satisfaction that his hard work was being acknowledged. Walking was difficult when you were freezing hot. Boiling cold? Curious.

While Connor swam in and out of consciousness, he marveled at his ability to jump across long distances in seconds. A bend in the tunnel ahead would be behind him with a single blink of his eyes. He must have developed a magical power in these caves. One that would come in handy in the future when wanting to avoid taking the stairs. Or maybe he could have gained Alessi magic? They were forged by Griffins after all. Legendary golden-winged women who bridged the Griffins and humans to bring peace to the Queendom, they must have special powers. But Griffins only forged *women* who were deemed worthy into Alessi . . . and he was Connor. Just Connor. He'd never get wings. So where did his newfound magic come from? He stumbled and a strong pair of arms pulled him upright. Maybe those arms belonged to an Alessi. Maybe it was her magic blinking them through the caves.

"I see an opening, Your Grace, I'm going to leave you here for a moment and check if the coast is clear," his Alessi whispered. Hopefully she would be able to fly them out soon. His legs were so tired. She set him down gently, and he felt the poke of rocks and stones along his back. Rude little things. He was already sore; there was no need for added insult to injury.

In no time at all, he was being lifted again, this time by two sets of hands. His back landed on canvas, and he was hoisted into the air. He knew she could fly! How clever of her to bring him a bed to make the journey smoother. Such a thoughtful Alessi. He let the darkness take him then. His giddy fear flickered and died. An Alessi could find anyone in the dark.

The first thing he became aware of was the smell of roasting meat. For a moment he worried he really had burned in the caves, but there was a warm buttered-herb scent that suggested a meal, not flesh. He scrunched his eyes and gingerly pried them open. The light blinded him, forcing his lids shut before a successful second attempt. Coughs convulsed his weak frame. Rolling over, he shifted the weight of his blankets. He looked around the space curiously, trying to sweep the fog from his mind. His skin felt clammy, and his tunic was soaked through with sweat.

He was on a bedroll on an earthen floor surrounded by crumbling stone walls. It appeared to be the ruin of a cathedral or a military barracks, maybe a fort of some kind. The room was very simply furnished and had a makeshift thatch ceiling that had obviously been added after the place had begun falling to ruin. The walls held the rounded and lichen-covered signs of age, and some areas were pockmarked where ferns had dug their roots in and fallen once they had outgrown their perch, pulling a section of stone away with them in the process. Other sections looked like they had been ripped apart with giant angry fists. Where was he?

He shivered in the damp, cold air and pulled the blankets up around him. Blankets? Where had they come from? He'd only had his damp clothes and purple cloak with him in the catacombs.

Suddenly, memory caught up with the moment and he sat bolt upright. The catacombs, Alethia, the Undercourt! He needed to find Jacs, he needed to know she was okay. Taking a couple deep breaths, head clear of Griffin and fever, he collected his thoughts, thankful that they were now entirely his own.

Where was Masterchiv Rathbone?

Stumbling to his feet on legs not prepared for movement, he fell toward the ruined doorway. The murmuring in the next room stopped as five women turned to look at him.

"Your Grace! Welcome to the land of the living, I was just about to check on you," Masterchiv Rathbone said cheerily, relief etched into her features. Her blonde hair was braided in its usual tight swirl at the base of her skull, but the strands around her temples were loose and frizzy from frequent rubbing, a sign that typically meant she had been worrying.

"Where?" Connor croaked and cleared his throat. Air scraped sandy fingers up his windpipe, and he gripped the door frame to stave off a wave of dizziness. Concern flickered across Masterchiv Rathbone's face, and she hurried to his side, took his arm, and helped him to a seat around the cook fire with the other four women. Each, Connor now noticed, wore the distinctive uniform of a guard: oiled leather armor with a dagger and restraining strap on their belts. Masterchiv

Rathbone stood apart as a knight, with her shortsword sheathed at her hip in place of a dagger.

Wincing as he lowered himself onto a wooden stool, he looked around at the others. All strangers except one who he recognized with a start as Iliana Dryft, a former guard of his mother's. He'd been infatuated with her when he was a kid. Back then she'd had long, dark hair; it now curled around her ear and barely grazed her jaw.

Masterchiv Rathbone shoved a mug of something warm into his hands, and he took a tentative sip. Bone broth. His stomach growled in approval, and he forced himself to drink slowly.

"Where am I?" he asked, suppressing a shiver. One of the guards got up and retrieved his blanket, draping it over his shoulders gently. He nodded his thanks. This room was bigger than the first, outlined with the same ruined walls. One wall held an alcove and a collapsed chimney where a large fireplace might have been in the past. Now the fire crackled happily in a pit in the room's center with a metal frame set up sporting a spit and a hanging cauldron. This room had no thatched roof and the smoke wound a lazy path above their heads. Every so often, a guard rotated the spit and pig fat dripped into the flames below with a hiss.

"SouthGate battlement, in the Lower Realm," Masterchiv Rathbone replied.

"How long have I—"

"Three days you've been out with fever. You must have picked up an infection in the caves, because you started going downhill fast. It only just broke last night after we arrived here."

"Wet clothes, stress, no sleep, and bad ventilation, it was a recipe for disaster, Your Grace," a guard said kindly.

"It's been over a week since we were separated from the Queen," Masterchiv Rathbone finished.

"Right, over a week . . . have we been able to send a message to her?"

"Not yet. We were just discussing options. Our best bet seems to be heading for Bridgeport and taking the Bridge back to the palace. SouthGate gets a steady stream of people through so we could find someone to run ahead with a message for us, but I'm reticent trusting a Lowrian stranger with the knowledge that the royal advisor and head of the Queensguard are vulnerable and separated from Her Majesty."

Connor nodded slowly. His head throbbed, and he took another sip from his mug.

"How many days' ride is Bridgeport from here?" he asked, trying to remember his geography lessons.

"Five days at a breakneck pace. Given your condition, I'd say eight, comfortably," Dryft answered from across the fire. Her voice had a lilt to it that was much more pleasant than Masterchiv Rathbone's staccato. Brow furrowing, Connor waded through sticky slow thoughts and tried to think clearly. He was still registered in the scry crystal memory bank; he'd never had the chance to unregister himself before the gala, before it all went sideways.

"Do we have any scry crystals here?" he asked.

The guards looked at one another and shook their heads. One said, "No, the last were rounded up a couple weeks ago and taken up the Bridge."

Connor cursed and ran his fingers roughly through his hair. Not knowing was always the worst part, and there seemed no quicker way to find out if Jacs was okay. No quicker way to let her know that they were okay. Again, that blasted Cliff separated them. Only this time, he was stuck below.

"Would it be quicker going up the way we came?" Connor asked Masterchiv Rathbone.

She shook her head decisively. "That's not an option. Unobstructed, it might save us a week, but we can't assume we'll be so lucky the second time entering their lair. No, I won't put us through that again."

Relieved, Connor took another sip and stared into the fire. He was glad he hadn't had to make the call, and glad Masterchiv Rathbone was of a similar mind about revisiting the Undercourt of Griffins. He would happily scale a hundred Bridges before crossing paths with them again.

"Right," he said abruptly as he rose unsteadily to his feet, "then let's get going. We might as well cover some ground before dark. Jacqueline always said the twilight descends early in the Lower Realm, so we don't have as much daylight to work with as it is."

The guards stared. Masterchiv Rathbone surveyed him warily. "Your Grace, you're still not well, it might be best if we wait until morning."

"No, we need to leave now. I need to know she got back all right."

"We know she's alive," a guard said helpfully. "There'd be a Goddess-awful ruckus of bellringing if she died."

Connor glared at her and did nothing to keep the venom from his voice. "But not if she's missing, captured, injured, or any other terrible outcome I'll be envisioning for the next eight days. I doubt there's a bell ringer for those scenarios. So, we have to move." His command was weakened slightly by another bout of coughing, but he motioned impatiently for Masterchiv Rathbone to stand and was satisfied to see her rise slowly to her feet.

"Okay, but if your condition worsens—"

"It won't."

"But if it does—"

"It can't. We have to get to her. Thank you all for the broth and the hospitality." He directed the last comment to the four guards before spinning on his heel and returning to the room he had slept in. There wasn't much by way of possessions—the blanket and bedroll belonged to one of the guards, but he packed that up anyway, and after a moment's hesitation, he reluctantly retrieved his purple hooded cloak, one of the disguises Master Moira had made to help Jacqueline's team of friends, soldiers, and that smug dancer Yves blend in with the Sons. It seemed like a lifetime ago. As he picked it up, a glowing blue crystal rolled out of its folds. He'd taken it from the waterfall cave to light their way through the catacombs. An eerie blue glow illuminated a small halo around it. Connor suppressed a shiver, unsure if it was a fever aftershock or something more. Amelia the Daring had always been resourceful with her supplies before any of her big adventures, and a flameless torch was useful, regardless of the heebie-jeebies it evoked, so he wrapped it up in the cloak and returned with his bundle to the cooking area.

In his few minutes of preparation, Masterchiv Rathbone had been busy. She'd packed her own possessions, gathered a small bag of provisions, and ordered the guards to saddle two horses. As Connor reentered the room, he heard her say, "We can send provisions and extra horses back once we reach Bridgeport. I know you have limited personnel out here, but I'll need at least one guard with me. This is more important than guarding these battlements, but I hate to leave you shorthanded." She looked up sharply as Connor entered the room and said, "Give us fifteen more minutes for the horses, Your Grace, and we'll be ready. I recommend you sit and rest in the meantime, have some more broth, as you'll need your strength."

A deep crease had formed between her brows, and she continued to snap orders. Rather than stay and get underfoot, Connor refilled his mug with a ladle from the cauldron and took himself out a side door to the outer wall of the battlements. With the ruined ceiling boasting more holes than coverage, there wasn't much difference out here than there had been in the cooking area when it came to light, but somehow it felt brighter in the open. The promise of action sparked hope in his chest.

Restlessly fidgeting in place, he swatted at a few gnats that hovered overhead and decided movement would be less maddening. With his warm mug clasped between his palms, he picked his way through the ferns and bracken around the ruins. The building must have been spectacular in its day. Domed arches, pillars, and twisting spiral staircases were exposed to the elements like the ribs of a long-dead great beast. Despite his worry, he couldn't deny his awe. What had caused this place to fall into such disrepair?

As if in answer to his thought, Dryft spoke from behind him. "It's incredible, isn't it?"

He spun around, making his head pulse painfully, and replied, "Incredible. What happened here?"

Dryft shrugged. "The SouthGate battlement guarded one of the Bridges before the Great Divide, over fifty years ago." Following her pointed forefinger, Connor craned his neck and looked up at the Cliff stretching off to the left and right of him. It rose like an immense stone wall stretching toward the clouds. The broken and dangling remains of the Bridge, which had once spanned the two realms, littered a stretch of the Cliff's face. Dryft continued: "Once Queen Frea the Third cut the Bridge, the Lowrians ambushed the remaining guardpairs here and seemed determined to destroy the battlements. A lot of lives were lost on both sides. Eventually, the mayor of SouthGate stepped in and called an end to the bloodshed. Once she lost her daughter to the cause, her grief took the fight out of her. Now SouthGate guards the one road connecting the Lower west to east, from the Salt Pits to Bridgeport.

"After the truce, the building was as it is now. There've been Upperite guards stationed here for the past fifty years to remind Lowrians of their place. Our numbers doubled after Queen Ariel's . . ." She trailed off only to pick back up. "Although I feel like the memorial is a better reminder by far. Apparently, after the feud ended there was a mass pyre on the other side of the building for all the bodies. A memorial stands in its place now. You can see it from the road. It's beautiful: a thick ring of poppies grows around the base."

Connor remained quiet for a moment; he never knew. The Upper Realm had very few remnants of the Centennial Feud as most of the battles had come to a head in the Lower Realm. He realized how ignorant he had been of his Queendom's bloody history. "That's . . ." but what adjective would encapsulate *that*? "Can we see it?"

"Of course, Your Grace. Do you need a hand or are you okay to walk?"

Connor accepted her arm gratefully and together they made their way around the battlements. Dryft had not exaggerated; the radius of the thick blanket of poppies surrounding the base of the memorial tree extended several meters. Autumn's chill was sapping the heat from the summer sun's rays. Many of the flowers had faded with the cooling weather. Wading through the remaining ruby blooms, he picked his way carefully to the center.

As was customary, the memorial comprised six bleached-white sycamore maples that had been woven together over time to form one tree. Little diamond openings checkered the fused trunks, through which mourners slipped letters and trinkets to their departed loved ones. Hanging from the junctions of each fused trunk and branch were dozens of stone plaques. As Connor drew close enough to inspect them, he saw each had a name of a Lowrian citizen or an Upperite guard etched into the weathered surface. As the years had passed, each name had grown with the tree, the memorials grafted into its bark. A larger plaque had been erected at its base, a few lines of a poem that had long since faded from the number of fingers brushing over its words, the stone polished to a high shine. Its last line had been freshly re-carved:

All are level in death. May we one day understand this in life.

Connor bowed his head and sent his thoughts to the lost souls who had fought in the war of his mother's predecessors. A winged seed spiraled down from above and landed near his feet. He held out a hand and another landed in his palm, its paired wings so thin as to be almost transparent.

Stepping forward, he ran his fingers over the memorial plaque. The polished stone sent a barbed splinter through his heart. He had witnessed firsthand how bloody the fighting between Lower and Upper Realms could be. The riot after his mother's murder had left many slain in the streets. His father had denied Bridgeport the right to plant a memorial tree, saying that the destroyed fountain and clock tower were all the memory their town deserved. Connor had agreed with his decision at the time, but now he saw the malice in it. To deny the town the ability to tend to and nurture a memorial tree, to deny the promise of life after so much death—what a cruel punishment to an already hurting people. This was yet another wrong he had to make right.

"Your Grace!" Masterchiv Rathbone's voice cut across his reverie. She stood by the battlement's entrance with two saddled horses. Dryft touched his shoulder, and they crossed the poppies together.

Seeing the two horses and knowing there'd be three riders, Connor turned to Dryft and asked, "Will you not be coming with us to Bridgeport?"

She nodded the affirmative and smiled. "You're riding with me today, Your Grace. Masterchiv Rathbone thought it best you ride with someone, just until your strength returns."

Connor frowned. "I can manage a horse by myself."

"Of course you can, just not today."

"Won't it slow us down?"

Dryft cocked her head to the side and reassured him. "We'll get you there as quickly as possible, Your Grace. Careful!" She grasped his elbow as his foot caught on the uneven ground and sent him stumbling. "Here, hold my arm."

Connor straightened and pushed down his frustration. He didn't have time to be unwell. He thought of Jacs. Where was she? Was she safe?

With the help of another guard and Masterchiv Rathbone, Connor found himself in the saddle in front of Dryft. His joints still ached, and his muscles felt sore and weak, but he hid his discomfort and sat up straight. Eight days. They could make it in eight days.

3

THE RIGHT TO FIGHT

Amber stood at the head of the oval table, a large map of the
Queendom spread out before her. The battle room was awash
with the midday light and a soft breeze filtered in from one of the
high windows. Apart from the stone fireplace, doorway, and six stone
pillars, the entire room was made of glass. Since they were four stories
up, the views from this room were spectacular. The entire barracks
spread out around them as though they were the center of a compass.
Despite looking incredibly impressive, this room would be a nightmare
to heat in the coming winter. But the metaphor of the room must be
preserved. Transparency in the military was what kept the plebeians
happy. Seated around the table were three knights: Chivilras Lerin
Pamheir, Claudia Fayworth, and Michelle Ryder; three guards: Miera
Jaenheir, Faline Cervah, and Dyna Flent; and the Queen, with Amber

to her left. The seats for Masterchiv Rathbone and Chiv. Andromeda Turner sat empty. Two staff members stood by the door, and a scribe sat at her own table, inked quill poised and ready.

Amber cleared her throat. "So it's agreed, we will gather an attack force to infiltrate Alethia and free the Undercourt of Griffins. We will depart in eight days. We maintain a no-kill order. All hoods we encounter will be contained and restrained. Equip extra straps. The leader, Celos, is our most dangerous adversary. We have no physical description as of yet, but—"

"Wait," Jacqueline stood up and all eyes snapped to her. "We might." She turned to address her valet by the door. "Adaine, go find the dancer, Yves, and bring him here." Adaine bowed her understanding and hurried to follow the order. Jacqueline sat back down and nodded for Amber to continue.

"The hoods are easy to subdue. Their training is minimal, and their cloaks are a hindrance. Recent experience suggests a number of them are proficient with the bow and with swords. Many did not appear to carry weapons with them." Amber took a breath, glanced around at the women who had experienced Alethia firsthand, and said, "I want to avoid heightening superstitions and creating attercoppes out of shadows. There's no fabled creature whisking boys from their beds. This is an organization that targets the vulnerable and lures them away with the promise of a better life. As those of us who have been there know, the Catacombs of Lethe are a miserable place. From there, once we get into Alethia, it will only get worse. It appears the Undercourt Griffins have weaponized their grief and have the ability to use your sorrow against you. Any woman would be forced to relive her darkest thoughts, memories, and nightmares. They do not discriminate. The visions and voices get stronger the closer one is to the source, so it will get worse before it gets better."

A ripple of unease spread around the table, but all kept their composure. The door squeaked open and Adaine ushered Yves into the room. He strode past her with the confidence of a genteel and swept an elaborate bow in the direction of the Queen. His dark hair was slightly damp and freshly combed, a little curl forming at the nape of his neck. His olive skin glistened and he smelled faintly of the cedar and geranium oil from the bathhouse. He wore cream linen trousers and an embroidered burgundy vest without an undershirt, likely to better display the toned muscles of his arms and shoulders. Amber noticed Adaine's frequent blushing glances toward the dancer and had to concede the man knew what he was doing.

"Greetings, Your Majesty," he said in his honey-toned timbre. "How may I be of service?"

Jacqueline invited Yves to sit at the end of the table. He sat with a flourish and inclined his head to each knight in turn, flashing his dazzling smile.

"I was hoping you could help us with information about Celos," Jacqueline said.

Yves, a glimmer in his eyes, ran his thumb down one corner of his mouth and said smoothly, "Of course, Your Majesty. As you well know, I am always generous with the information I provide the Crown. And I've come to understand the Crown generously rewards generous subjects."

Jacqueline arched an eyebrow.

"For example, Your Majesty's threefold gift of cottage, title, and concert hall in exchange for my services in Alethia was the very picture of generosity. I just know the information I have will further your cause for peace and justice. Yet, alas, these boons and the knowledge of a duty well fulfilled all ring hollow without someone with which to share them. Specifically, a well-bred, high-ranking spouse? Failing that, I would be similarly content with a ship that I could moor in front of my seaside cottage. The provision of a ready crew goes without saying. I'm sure Your Majesty has the means to fill this void that lies in the heart of a generous subject such as myself."

After a moment's hesitation, Jacqueline replied, "I'll see what I can do."

Yves inclined his head in thanks, and Jacqueline, the ghost of a smile tugging at her lips, indicated for Amber to proceed.

"We need a description of what Celos looks like, any information you can give us about Alethia, and where he might be within the city. Also, anything to do with Alethia's defenses, military, and weaponry," Amber said.

Yves appeared deep in thought, his dark eyes focused. He tented his fingers on the table in front of him and leaned forward. In a voice fit for the stage, he began: "What you must understand about my experience within Alethia is this: I was welcomed as Celos's son when I was a boy of sixteen. I spent a year within the walls of that city before Father determined I was made for a larger audience. He allowed me to select the members of my troupe, and together we traveled the Queendom doing Celos's work. I would report back once or twice a year, but messages would find me in each town I visited. He has a reach that extends farther than you can imagine, and claws that sink deeper than you—"

"Yves," Amber cut in. "What does he look like?"

Deflating only minutely, Yves broke off his monologue and replied, "He is a being void of color. Years spent in the dark have turned him into a specter, a ghost. Some hardly believe blood runs through his veins—"

"Hair color?"

Yves sighed. "White."

"Skin color?"

"Very pale."

"Eye color?"

"We were never that close, and direct eye contact was not the sort of blessing I was ever—"

"Height?"

"He looms over most men, he—" Yves caught Amber's look and amended, "Maybe six foot four?"

"Age?"

"Ageless and ancient, he is a being from the dawn of—"

"Yves!"

"Fine, half a century at least, maybe more?"

"Good. What about the city's defenses? We've seen the bridges and the gates. Any fail-safes? Anything set against intruders?"

"It is said that the entire city has a lockdown mechanism in the case of an invasion. Many believe that the city is protected by a series of wards—"

Amber pinched the bridge of her nose and said, "I need facts, not stories. Do you know if there is one or not?"

"Not that I've seen, but the main bridge can be locked off with the gates."

Amber nodded. She and Andromeda had passed through those gates and seen their size. Once closed, it would be almost impossible to break through.

"Any scouts?"

"Possibly. Bear in mind, I've not lived within Alethia for more than a decade. I urge you not to do the math, it will age me horribly!" He flashed his smile around the room.

"Weaponry and military training?"

Yves crossed his arms, clearly annoyed by the artistic restraints around his storytelling. "Most are trained with the sword or the bow if they are able. We spar with one another often; it's one of the few times a day that sound is encouraged within the silent city."

"So, the best bet seems to be to hit them hard and fast, before they know we're coming. Stealth will be key, and any scouts should be swiftly dealt with."

"And my troupe and I will be happy to assist your cause," Yves offered magnanimously.

The table was silent for a beat. "What do you mean?" Amber asked.

"You'll be recruiting soldiers for this ambush, I presume? I'm saying my troupe and I are ready and willing."

"Your boys are wanting to fight?" Amber asked incredulously. Jacqueline studied Yves with a look in her eye that made Amber uneasy.

"My *men*? Of course. Who better to help overthrow our dear father? I know we are all grateful for the treatment we have been shown since our disappointing performance at the gala. None of them have any interest in returning to the service of such a cruel father, and they would follow me most anywhere. So, we lay our skills humbly at your feet and ask you to put them to use."

Amber reeled. Trusting boys, especially this group of boys, to fight in this mission was out of the question.

"Chiv. Everstar, that might not be a bad idea. We've been discussing introducing men into the military since I was crowned, and Yves's group might make a promising first attempt. If they're willing, why deny them?" Jacqueline said. Yves beamed and inclined his head to her.

Amber felt trapped. Her head told her sternly that this was a terrible idea. It put her women at risk. Stalling for time, she said bluntly, "I will think on it. This needs proper deliberation, and I don't want to make this kind of decision without first considering all the options." Yves opened his mouth to interject but she talked over him. "It is a noble gesture, Yves. We have eight days until departure, I can let you know tomorrow."

"Would a demonstration of our abilities be helpful?" Yves asked innocently.

"We saw you at the gala. Surely that is enough."

"No, not nearly enough! That was mere child's play—no offense, Your Highness, of course we reserved the very best for you—but what we can do when no royal censor is shackling our performance! Well, why don't you oversee our training session this afternoon? Then I can show you what my men can do when pushed to their limits. You will be able to make an informed decision after that."

"That sounds like a fantastic idea!" the Queen said.

Unsure how to avoid it, Amber conceded, nodding reluctantly. Jacqueline looked delighted. The knights looked uneasy, and Flent looked beautiful. No, not beautiful . . . she looked concerned. That was it.

"Fabulous, our troupe will be practicing at two this afternoon in that sandy pit you call a training ring, I encourage you to stop by."

After Yves had been dismissed, the Queensguard jumped back into discussing the minutia of their attack on Alethia. As they were wrapping up, Amber felt the exhilaration of their upcoming battle tease her peripheries. Her fingertips tingled, and her heartbeat anticipated the steady rhythm of war.

"As I've visited Alethia before, I am happy to help lead the first battalion. That way we can sneak in and nullify their scouts, leaving the way open for the remaining battalions to follow," Jacqueline said.

Amber gave a start and shared a look of surprise with Chiv. Ryder. "You mean to join the ranks, Your Majesty?"

"Of course."

"Surely you can't be serious?" she asked, abandoning formality in her moment of shock.

Again, Jacqueline arched an eyebrow.

"What I mean to say is, this mission is incredibly dangerous. With your royal advisor and head of the Queensguard still missing, four empty seats on the Council, the dowager King a reported recluse—no judgment, just stating the facts—and a Queendom still reeling from the loss of their last Queen, I must insist—no, I beg you to remain in the palace. If we were to lose you, the Queendom, unstable as it is, may fall. I just pray our neighbors to the east haven't caught wind of our vulnerability."

Jacqueline frowned and studied the map on the table before her. "You're right. I admit I got caught up in the action of it all, but you're completely right. I'll woman the helm from here." She paused, and Amber could see her trying to hide her disappointment and recalibrate before continuing. "Since I won't be on the frontlines of this battle, it goes without saying that Chivilra Everstar will remain behind as well. I'll need your guidance as we watch the battle from afar. If hands are needed, I would be selfish to keep my entire Queensguard out of the fight, are there any of you who are willing to go?" Jacqueline asked the table. Amber's heart sank as her recommendation became her leash; of course her first priority was the Queen. She had forgotten herself for a moment.

The knights looked at one another, but Flent stared at her hands, clasped loosely on the table.

"Your Majesty," Chiv. Ryder said. She had a long, thin nose and tight brown curls smoothed back and tied in a bushy tail at the base of her skull. "I still think an adequate guard is required. We saw what happened at the gala. If we dilute our forces and you are left vulnerable . . ."

"Agreed," said Chiv. Pamheir. She had red hair cut short to display her right ear, which was missing a large chunk from the top of its pinna. She wore the old injury like a badge of honor. Others nodded along. Jacqueline looked torn, and Amber knew why: Jacqueline worked best in the middle of the problem. *It must be hard enough for her to know she can't be in the thick of it herself. It must be harder still knowing that she is the reason the Queendom's best fighters won't be on the front lines either.*

"Well," Jacqueline said, "in any case, I have one last point of order; we still have missing people down there. We need all guards to be on the lookout not only for Cornelius and Masterchiv Rathbone but also my dear friend Phillip Leschi. He accompanied us into—"Amber grimaced. "What's that face for?" Jacqueline broke off, looking at her expectantly.

"What face?"

"I mentioned Phillip and you flinched."

Amber hesitated but chose honesty. "I have reason to believe Phillip is a traitor."

Jacqueline blanched. "No, he's not. I mean, he was feeding the hoods information about me, but he didn't mean to betray me."

"He *what?*"

"Wait, then what were you talking about?"

"Chiv. Turner and I saw him running around Alethia. We ran into him near the prison where they kept your mother. He was with the hoods."

Jacqueline shook her head slowly. "He's one of my oldest friends. He wouldn't betray me."

"But you just said—"

"I know. That was different."

Chiv. Pamheir cleared her throat, and Jacqueline, who had appeared to lower her defenses momentarily, gave her head a little shake before resuming in a brisk, formal tone: "Never mind that. He is not to be harmed. The no-kill order extends to Phillip regardless of where his loyalties lie."

"Understood," Amber said.

"Right. Let's get preparations underway, and we can meet again before we launch the attack and make a final decision regarding who from the Queensguard will remain behind." A flush had crept up Jacqueline's cheeks and Amber noticed a slight quiver of her lip. Nothing more betrayed whatever thoughts whirled inside her mind.

Amber bit the inside of her cheek and looked over at the scribe. Checking the clock on the mantel, she said, "The Queen's right, we've covered a lot of ground. Copies of the transcript will be delivered to you all within . . ."

"The hour, Chiv," the scribe squeaked at an expectant look from Amber.

"The hour. We all have our points of action. Let's reconvene tomorrow with updates and progress reports. Flent and I will finish our shift with Her Majesty, then Chivilras Pamheir and Fayworth, you'll be taking over this evening. Any questions?"

A chorus of "nos" rippled around the table and Amber dismissed the meeting. A few of the knights lingered to share parting words with her, but soon the room was empty save the Queen, Adaine, Amber, and Flent. Jacqueline had pulled Adaine aside to share a private instruction, and Flent stood at ease near the door.

Amber took a couple of breaths to fully live in this moment. She, the head of the Queensguard, had just held her first meeting in the battle room. She had led the discussion on the invasion of Alethia, and her name would be the first mentioned when any spoke of the military force that freed the Undercourt of Griffins and brought the infamous Celos to justice.

She'd imagined filling Masterchiv Rathbone's boots would be more daunting. It was likely that the reason for her temporary status made the position feel less real, as though she were a child playing dress-up, but in her case, the costume fit perfectly, and she couldn't imagine taking it off.

She shouldn't be so happy that Masterchiv Rathbone was still missing, and she was eager to find the knight safe and sound, but she had to admit this felt good.

Gripping the back of her chair, she studied the map. Lost in thought for a moment, she turned when she felt a presence by her shoulder. Flent had sidled up beside her.

"You spoke well today, Chiv. Everstar," Flent said.

"Thank you."

"And about your offer . . . to join me to see my aunt . . ."

"It's only proper. I wouldn't want your loyalties questioned. This way you're covered."

"I know, but"—Flent took half a step closer—"I don't think you realize how much that means to me." Her hand rested lightly next to Amber's on the back of the chair; a hair's breadth separated them. An impassable no-woman's land.

Amber cleared her throat and met her gaze. "Flent, I . . ."

"I shouldn't have teased you earlier, outside the throne room, I mean." Crossing the chasm, Flent's pinkie lifted and shifted to rest on top of Amber's.

Amber shot a look to where Jacqueline stood with Adaine, still deep in conversation. "Let's not discuss that here," she said, reluctantly pulling away.

Flent nodded and turned her attention back to the map. Following today's meeting, the area around the Catacombs of Lethe's entrance was now surrounded by military tokens.

"It's wild to think Alethia has been under our feet this whole time."

Amber picked up the subtle scent of Flent's perfume—jasmine and orange blossom—and wrinkled her nose to keep her head clear. "I guess no one thought to look for it," Amber replied, shifting to face the guard and, finding her closer than anticipated, immediately taking a step back, and colliding with her chair. Flent stood her ground, a single eyebrow arched as she lifted a hand to idly twist her earring.

"Some people can be blind to what's right in front of them."

The back of Amber's neck grew hot and, in an instant, she clocked Flent's green-gray eyes as the sun lit the flecks of yellow around her pupils, the way her lower lip hesitated to release the *m*, and the relaxed curve of her pinkie finger while her forefinger and thumb moved the golden stud clockwise.

Jacqueline cleared her throat, and Flent spun smoothly on the spot to join her by the door. Amber shook her head and followed.

Shoulders back, mind focused on her duty, and following the scent of jasmine, Amber opened the door to the tower and took the lead as the group descended the staircase.

The afternoon saw her off the clock and spending her well-earned downtime watching a bunch of boys leap about. Amber sighed and took a seat in the stands around the large sand training ring. Early autumn sunlight filtered through a smattering of clouds, withholding its promised warmth and illuminating the huddle of dancers in their pocket of the ring. Knights and guardpairs sparred around them. Grunts and groans filled the air, punctuated with the sound of each landed strike.

Yves stood confidently, one hand at the small of his back, the other performing short, sharp gestures as he spoke with the dancers. All heads leaned in close to catch his rapid-fire instructions. Each boy wore loose-fitting indigo linen trousers and a rose vest with a silk sash of deep burgundy. They were hard to miss in the sea of navy blues, blacks, and browns of the guards' uniforms. With a sly grin and a wink over his shoulder at Amber, Yves clapped his hands once and the troupe sprang into motion.

Feet swept slow circles in the sand then left the ring as the boys threw themselves into the air. With a half twist, backs arched, hands reached then caught the earth below. Elbows bent to absorb the momentum, then snapped straight, propelling the dancers back into the air. The amount of time spent on the ground was minimal. Boys rolled and dove, tossed one another into the sky, and caught brothers thrown by others.

Amber felt herself leaning forward on the bench and stifled a gasp just in time. The trust they had in one another was undeniable. Their strength . . . she watched their muscles bulge and ripple with each catch and throw. Yves barked an order and the formation changed. The troupe parted down the middle and squared off, stances wide, heads high. One blew a kiss to his counterpart, who winked a reply. The left side crouched low and charged; the right side stood their ground, knees bent, fingers flexing. At the last moment before impact, the dancers on the right leaped as one, torsos turning in midair, palms planting on the backs and shoulders of their charging companions, and they were over. The airborne group landed and spun around to face the rushers, who had somersaulted mid charge and matched them now, nose to nose.

A moment of heaving chests passed; then, as though answering a silent call, each group settled into a ready stance. At a command from Yves, the two sides collided. By this point, the surrounding knights and guards had ceased their own drills to watch the faux battle unfold. The dancers grappled with one another: parry, block, thrust. Sand sprayed as heels dug in and bodies landed with thumps and rolls. One boy was thrown to the ground, his opponent towering over him, then with a sweep of his legs the tides turned and his opponent came crashing down beside him.

Was it all just carefully practiced choreography? Yes. But wasn't that the same as running through the various fighting drills and formations?

Both dance and combat involved practicing the movements, poses, and stances, and memorizing the forms until they became second nature in your skin. Amber furrowed her brow.

Another command from Yves, and the battle stopped as quickly as it had started. The disorganized jumble of bodies smoothly floated into a precise and perfect diamond formation. Every muscle stilled and they waited, heads bowed, hands clasped behind their backs. A smattering of applause skittered around the ring and Amber rose to her feet to join Yves in front of his troupe.

"Impressive," Amber remarked.

Yves bowed his thanks.

"And clearly well practiced. But I wonder how the boys would handle an unpredictable opponent?"

Yves straightened slowly and raised an eyebrow. "I suppose there is only one way to find out."

A knowing look passed between them, and Amber felt the pre-battle calm wash over her. "Shall we dance?" she said with a grin.

Yves's face split into a dazzling smile and he clapped his hands together, dispersing his troupe and clearing the field. "You do me an honor, Chivilra Everstar. But know that I won't go easy on you."

"I'm counting on it," Amber purred, settling into her stance. Yves mirrored her with additional flourish, rolling his wrists and delicately arranging his hands.

The heartbeats stretched out between them, and Amber noted three things. His hair had fallen slightly over his right eye, a finger appeared bent as though it had been broken in the past, and he was favoring his right foot ever so slightly. Possible injury to the left ankle? Either currently healing or had healed poorly. Her eyes snapped into focus, and he sprang to meet her.

Their bodies whirled, fists struck air, and knees narrowly missed contact. Seconds grew into minutes as they parried back and forth across the ring. Amber hadn't had this much fun with an opponent in a while, and she found herself grinning. Flashing a fist forward, she caught his right side and heard the wind force its way out of him. Dropping low, she swept for his left foot, but was caught mid strike as he threw his weight into the supposedly weaker ankle and launched up and over her.

A feint, she thought, cursing. *Of course, the dancer can act.* She spun quickly to face him, but a heartbeat too slow. He struck her square in the sternum and sent her reeling. Now she was on the defensive, blocking and dodging his movements, trying desperately to find a break in his barrage.

Their eyes met, his widened for a moment, and he must have read something on her face, because he paused for a fraction of a second. Anyone watching would not have noticed anything amiss, but Amber did. She saw the pause stretch out like a lightning flash in slow motion. Saw her opening and took it. Struck him hard behind the knee and watched him crumple. Watched his hands come up in surrender and she knew. Knew without a shadow of a doubt. He had thrown the fight. She had won because he'd let her.

Too stunned to speak, she let her hands fall to her sides as Yves rose to his feet.

"Well matched, Chivilra Everstar. Very well matched. A glorious display of what years of dedicated training will get you, right, men?" he said with a voice that boomed across the ring. Sound returned to Amber's ears, and she heard the cheers of her fellow knights and guards, heard too the applause of the troupe.

Yves held his hand out to her. She looked from it to his face, then shook it.

"A good and *fair* fight, Chiv.," he said in an undertone. Amber studied his face and nodded, unsettled. "Right, men! I feel our honorable head of the Queensguard has seen enough of our sweaty mugs for one afternoon. Hit the baths and take the evening off!" A cheer went around the troupe, and they slowly dispersed. The surrounding guardpairs resumed their drills; knights turned back to their sparring partners.

Yves lingered.

"Why did you do that?" Amber demanded, voice low.

"Do what?"

"You know what."

Yves ran his fingers through his black hair, coiffing it in a way that it fell just so. With a languid air, he studied the proximity of those around him, then stepped toward her.

"Let them fight," Yves demanded, suddenly serious.

Amber froze, a snarky comment died on the tip of her tongue, and she surveyed the dancer. "No."

Yves crossed his arms. "Why not?"

"You're a liability. It's nothing personal, Yves, but I can't risk my women for the sake of your troupe."

Yves arched an eyebrow.

"You have no military training," Amber added.

"That may be, but my troupe and I have trained just as hard for years."

"As *dancers*, not fighters."

"Semantics. You saw what we can do. Or will you ignore that a mere dancer could have beaten you? We have the discipline, we need technique. If my men can learn a new choreography in a few hours, I'm sure they can pick up a handful of ways to hit someone in no time. If given the right instruction."

Amber huffed and chose a different angle. "What if one of your boys lost their temper? We'd have a raging bull to deal with on top of whatever the enemy has to offer."

Yves shook his head mirthlessly. "Chiv. Everstar, with all due respect, men aren't some rage-fueled time bombs waiting to explode. Everyone gets angry, men are just penalized for it. I can't promise they won't, but I can promise that they'll have the wherewithal to keep their heads if the fire takes them. Again, they've trained with me for years, they have the discipline, they have the fitness and the strength. I shouldn't have to argue with you over their right to fight for their Queen."

"It's just not done. Women are the creators of life; only we can be entrusted with the burden of extinguishing it. You have to make life to take life. That's how it goes."

Yves scoffed. "Oh please, you don't even have children. Just because you can doesn't mean you will, and that's a ridiculous ditty regardless. I'm not advocating for my men's ability to start *extinguishing life* willy-nilly. If anything, I'm advocating for their right to protect it. Need I remind you that men have an active role in the life-making business? Let them have an active role defending it too."

Amber bit the inside of her cheek, Andromeda's words coming back to her in a flash. *If we don't harness their strength, someone else will, and then we would be on the wrong side of progress. It could cost us in battle.* "How do we know they won't betray us the first moment they get?"

"The Queen has saved them from a fate serving a mind-twisting brute like Celos. They owe her their lives. Let them show their gratitude. They at least deserve the chance to liberate their brothers. Let them fight."

"And you? Will you fight with them?"

A wry smile cracked Yves's face. "Goddess, no. I have a cottage to furnish, a ship to learn how to sail, and a set list to finalize. That is, I will once His Grace sees fit to return to sort out all of the finer details."

"Then why are you advocating for them in this?"

"I'm their leader. They look to me to book their next show."

"You're a fool."

"Perhaps. But I'm not the one refusing ready hands before a war."

Glaring up at his self-satisfied smirk, she slowly unclenched her fists. Her face softened and she looked away. "I hate that you're right."

"Understandable."

"There's not enough time to train them before we take Alethia. I don't want a troupe of loose cannons interfering with formation and strategy."

"Let them—"

"But . . ." Amber cut him off, and Yves shut up faster than she thought possible. The wheels in her head began turning quicker than her denial could slow them. Yves was right. To refuse them would be an act of stubbornness that might cost lives.

There was no use arguing about *if* boys should join her ranks now she had to focus on the *how*.

They had sent a number of knights into the Lower Realm already to recruit Lowrian women into their ranks. That left far fewer training officers, and none that she would trust with this particular batch of new recruits. This was going to be complicated. She needed a knight who could work with the natural strength of boys, a knight who was used to working with people much bigger than her. A knight skilled enough in battle to know how to prepare the troupe for the front lines. A knight like—

"I will train them," she said, shocking herself and, by the look on his face, Yves. "They won't be ready in time for the ambush of Alethia, so do not promise them the right to fight in the catacombs. I'm sorry, it's too short notice, and this mission must succeed. But I will train them. If they are willing, I will make sure they are equipped to fight for their Queendom. Who knows, our battle over Alethia may extend longer than expected. They may even have a chance to right their wrongs personally. But I will not send them in until I know they are ready."

Yves's eyes sparkled and he barked a laugh. "Excellent! You won't be sorry, Chiv. Everstar."

Amber felt the thrill of the challenge pulse through her, and she forced herself not to return Yves's smile, as infectious as it was.

"I will run this by Her Majesty and will meet your troupe tomorrow morning at cock's crow in this arena. We will start immediately. Anyone late will be excluded from all future practice. I understand they are in temporary lodgings in the contestants' wing of the palace?"

"That they are."

"I'll talk with the guards and organize a wing in the barracks for them. If they want to train as guards, they will live as guards."

"Understood."

"They will also be held to the same standard as the women in the barracks, likely an even higher one, so note that any slipup will be severely punished."

"Absolutely. They will be the picture of obedience."

"And Yves?"

"Yes?"

"Don't make me regret this."

"Wouldn't dream of it," he said with a wink, and she dismissed him. Sighing at the thought of her lengthy task list, she waved two staff members over and began relaying her messages. She broke off midstream when she spotted Flent making her way over to her from across the training ring. Hurriedly she repeated her previous instruction to the messenger and continued. It was going to be a long afternoon.

4

BED REST

"You're awake! No, don't get up. Easy does it." Anya's voice tiptoed through the barbed mist in Lena's mind and allowed her to finally focus and open her eyes.

Lena should have felt terrible, but there was a cheerful opaque cloud cushioning all the sharp sensations in her side. She felt like she was floating in a soap bubble. The room was bright, everything white, and for a moment she worried she'd found herself in the Eternal Realm, but Anya's hand in hers felt warm, and the glass that was pressed to her lips dribbled cold water down her chin. She was in the infirmary. White walls, white furniture, white sheets. But on every available surface was a vase filled to bursting with a vibrantly colored bouquet.

She breathed a laugh. "Oh! They're beautiful." Catching her fiancée's hands in her own, she brought them shakily to her lips and kissed her knuckles. Anya flipped her palm and cupped Lena's cheek, brushing her thumb along her cheekbone.

"How are you feeling, Lee?" she asked softly.

Lena took a moment to truly see her. The warm tones in her dark skin caught the late-afternoon light, and for a second she seemed to shine. Her thick black hair was pulled tight into its usual delicate plaits, the ends left free, and Lena guessed that Anya must have been fiddling with them in her nervousness, as they were much frizzier than normal. A delicate golden ear cuff twisted like ivy down her left ear, and a diamond engagement ring stood out on the fourth finger of her left hand. She had a soft crinkle between her brows and was watching Lena now as though she were a porcelain vase perched too near the edge of a mantel.

"I feel——" memories battered her into silence. Bloodstained hands, a blade's hilt digging into her palm, and the flickering pulse at Cllr. Perda's neck filled her mind. She hurriedly checked her hands, turning them over to be sure. "What happened?" she asked.

Anya cleared her throat and smoothed the sheets. "You were stabbed."

Lena's hand flew to her side, and she winced. The soft bubble shielded her from the sting.

"By Councilor Perda," Lena said quietly, remembering the blood dripping from the tip of a lethal ruby pendant. Her blood. "And I . . ." she trailed off, too scared to voice the question, but desperate to know.

"You didn't hurt her," Anya whispered.

"But I was going to. I wanted to."

"But you didn't."

"I didn't." Again, she felt the weight of the blade in her palm. Saw her bloodied fingers wrapped around its hilt. Against the stark white sheets, her hands were spotless. Relief washed over her, and she looked up at Anya, smiling, and repeated, "I didn't."

Anya smiled back, but a sadness lingered around her eyes. "Lee, that was really scary."

Lena took a breath.

"What did you . . . *why* did you . . . I want to understand," Anya said.

"I don't know."

"But you almost . . ."

"I know. I guess . . . I guess I was tired of being helpless," Lena said bitterly. She heard the words and knew they didn't come close to describing the feelings she'd felt in the chamber with Cllr. Perda. They rang hollow. Reason's vocabulary fell short as it so often did with matters of the heart, of passion, of whatever fire had burned through her that day. What day? "How long have I been here?" she asked suddenly.

"Just over a week. You've been in and out of consciousness, but you lost a lot of blood," Anya said distractedly. Her gaze had turned inward.

"A week? Where's Jacqueline? I need to speak with her, the Councilors! They're—"

Anya made a shushing motion with her hands, pushing her gently back down onto the pillows. "They've been taken care of. Tried for high treason. Hera shared your information and provided some damning evidence of her own. Jacqueline locked all four Councilors away and few know where they're being kept. She will want your account of the night though. When you're ready."

Lena nodded. Some good had come from her actions, then.

"Lee?" Anya asked, hesitantly. Her hands hovered in the middle of adjusting Lena's sheets. "You know you can tell me anything, right? If something happened, no matter how awful . . . I could maybe help?"

Lena's insides went cold. "What do you mean, something awful? You said so yourself, I didn't hurt the Councilor. Everything is fine."

"I'm talking about the catacombs."

"What about the catacombs?"

"They affect you more than most, Lee," she said carefully, watching Lena's expression.

"So, you're saying I'm weak?"

"Of course not."

"Then what? I wasn't trying? I was faking it? You think I'd—"

"Lee, hold on, slow down. That's not what I'm saying at all. We don't have to talk about it now, I shouldn't have brought it up. I just need you to know, I'm on your side. Whatever it is—"

"There's nothing."

"Okay," Anya said in appeasement. "Okay." She smoothed the corner of Lena's bedspread gently.

Suddenly, Lena wished she were alone. Wished Anya would leave. Her heart raced painfully, evoking a wave of dizziness that only increased her frustration. She wasn't weak.

"It's okay," Anya said softly and reached to hold Lena's hand. As if in reflex, an aversion washed over Lena so severely that she tucked her hands beneath the bedsheets before she knew what she was doing. Anya froze. The moment rang out between them as though Lena had screamed at her.

The door squeaked open.

"Message for Courtierdame Lena Glowra," came the clipped declaration from the doorway. Tearing her gaze from Lena's, a crinkle between her brows, Anya stood to retrieve the letter. The messenger bowed and departed. One of Master Epione's apprentices slipped through the closing door with a small crystal glass on a tray.

"Good, you're up," the apprentice said to Lena. She was short and wiry with a voice too loud for her stature. "Take this."

The glass was thrust into her hands. It was warm to the touch and smoked ever so slightly. The apprentice watched as Lena swallowed it down with a grimace, then retrieved the glass and departed. It was faintly minty with a sour slap of an aftertaste. Anya hovered with the letter clasped in her hands.

"Who is it from?" Lena asked, eager to move past their prickly moment.

Anya turned the letter over and frowned. "Your mother."

"Oh."

"We can wait to open it if you want. I suppose word of our engagement has reached her by now. And likely word of your injury. She'll have a lot of opinions."

Lena shook her head, sitting up and dabbing her mouth daintily with a kerchief. "It's all right, read it to me."

Anya broke the ornate wax seal and unfurled the letter. Clearing her throat, she read:

My Darling Lena,

A mother should not receive important information concerning her daughter from the town's gossipmongers. I have since discovered that you are not only engaged but have suffered near-fatal wounds at the hands of a most trusted Councilor. Our allegiance to the Council of Four should have protected you from such violence and I am enraged to learn the name of the beast responsible. I have been wringing my hands over both pieces of news and will require new gloves for the winter at this rate.

Come home.

Lord Ava Glowra

P.S. Your father sends his love.

Anya handed Lena the letter and muttered, "Goddess forbid she need a new pair of gloves."

Lena looked over the letter, eyes widening with understanding. "She's scared."

"What do you mean? Lord Glowra doesn't know the meaning of the word."

"No, look, her hand was shaking when she wrote this. I know my mother, when she's in a rage she becomes cold as ice and steady as iron. She's afraid, and I bet it's because this"—she indicated her side— "is evidence that she's not as powerful as she thought."

"That explains the summons home."

"Exactly."

"Will you go?" Anya perched on the edge of her bed so lightly she might have been hovering above it. Looking up, Lena stretched out her hand, tentatively offering it for Anya to hold.

"No. At least not now while I'm healing."

Anya looked relieved. Her fingers encircled Lena's gently. A warm comfort.

A new soap bubble formed around Lena, freshly numbing the sting in her side and fuzzing the edges of her thoughts. She felt giddy, floaty, fluffy. She giggled. "It's kind of sweet. Wringing her hands . . . You know how she loves her gloves."

"But they shouldn't be her priority with all that's happened. She didn't even ask how you're doing."

"If we ink over *come home,* we could make it say *love from* and then I wouldn't have to go," Lena said mischievously. "We better be careful, or all this time in bed shall make me a scaster me . . . a masker steam . . . a master schemer."

Anya's gaze shifted between Lena's eyes, and she said, "Okay, Ms. Loopy, I'm going to get you something to eat and just have a quick chat about your medication."

"I love when you take charge," Lena said in a low voice.

Anya rolled her eyes. "Then do as I say and have a nap while I'm gone. You need rest. I'll be no more than an hour."

"Wait!" Lena said playfully, making Anya turn. "Call me sweet pea, please."

"I'll be back soon, sweet pea," Anya said with a laugh.

"Now snapdragon, because they are much fiercer."

"As you wish, my fearsome snapdragon." Anya obliged, plucking one from the nearest vase and flourishing it like a ceremonial sword before handing it to her. Lena accepted it warmly and waved it under her nose. It smelled faintly of vanilla. With the flower dancing in her left hand, her engagement ring caught the light and she smiled to see the little daisy embedded in the crystal.

"Now call me your daisy, because I love you."

Anya lowered herself to sit on the edge of her bed and cupped Lena's cheek in her palm again. Leaning forward, she paused before softly saying, "I love you, my daisy."

Lena closed the distance between them. She noticed with fuzzy disappointment that Anya broke away first. Her eyes shone and soft creases lined their edges, but a cloud of apprehension hung around her. Lena wanted desperately to dispel it.

"Thank you, Flower Girl. I'll need more kisses soon so hurry back. Wait, wait, I'll need tulips soon. *Two-lips*, get it?" Lena almost didn't manage her explanation before she dissolved in a fit of giggles.

Anya smiled indulgently, chastely pecked Lena's cheek, and departed.

With a giddy warmth engulfing her and a cherry sunbeam streaming in through the window, it wasn't long before Lena found herself nodding off. She was vaguely aware of Anya entering and leaving again, and the movement of others in the room, but no one seemed to need her, so she floated in and out of sleep. A gentle knock at the door woke her.

"Come in," she said.

"Hi, Lena. I was just visiting Andromeda, and Anya told us you were up," Jacqueline said. "I'm so glad to see you!" she added feelingly, and pulled a wicker chair close to Lena's bedside, clasping her hands. Her green eyes sparkled with relief. "How are you feeling? Does it still hurt?"

Lena squeezed Jacqueline's fingers. "I feel just fine, they've given me some medicine, I'm not sure how long ago. I've been dozing." The fuzziness had most definitely lessened, and Lena felt far less giddy than before, but her side was still deliciously numb. "It's good to see you, Jacqueline. Are you well?"

The two friends wasted no time in catching one another up with all that had transpired since Jacqueline had watched Lena's boat sail toward home. Lena shared all that had happened between her and Clr. Perda, glossing over some of the more brutal aspects, and Jacqueline shared her discovery of the Undercourt, losing Cornelius, finding her mother, her deal with Hera, arresting the Councilors, and the upcoming invasion of Alethia.

"A lot has happened in a few days," Lena said quietly.

"You can say that again."

"How's your mother?" Lena asked, seizing one aspect of their conversation that seemed the safest.

"She's doing well, she was sleeping when I went to check on her this afternoon, but I'll pop back in after this. We've been taking things very slowly as she heals. Talking, playing a lot of chess, although I've a mind to take a break from my losing streak and teach her Pantheon. And hopefully we'll be able to try a walk in the gardens soon."

"A lot has happened," Lena repeated, squeezing Jacqueline's fingers reassuringly. "You have a lot on your plate. Don't think you have to do it all at once."

Jacqueline laughed and looked away. Another knock came at the door, and Anya returned with a tray laden with food and a new vase of flowers. This one contained three pink tulips. When Lena spotted them, she felt her cheeks grow warm and knew she likely matched their hue.

Jacqueline rose to greet Anya and help her set the tray up within Lena's reach. While most of the dishes looked delicious, Lena wrinkled her nose to see another plate full of cubed meats. Apparently, it was important after all the blood she'd lost, but she was not the biggest fan of liver. At Jacqueline's insistence, Anya took the seat by her bedside, and Jacqueline selected another chair by the window.

"Thank you, Flower Girl," Lena said sweetly, kissing Anya on the cheek.

"What did I miss?" Anya asked, passing Lena a bowl of chocolate mousse topped with raspberries.

"Jacqueline has just finished filling me in."

"Excellent, you've saved me a speech," Anya said with a nod of thanks to Jacqueline.

"Is there anything I can do to help?" Lena gestured down at her bedridden state. "I mean, when I'm able."

"There is actually something I wanted to talk to you about."

Perking up, Lena shifted to a more upright position. Anya retrieved her bowl and exchanged it wordlessly for the cup of tea she had just finished stirring honey into.

"I wanted to offer you a seat on my new Council of Four," the Queen declared without any pomp or ceremony. "You're one of the few people I trust, and you've already taught me so much. I would be honored to have you by my side as Councilor."

Lena looked quickly at Anya, who glowed with pride. "You would make an excellent Councilor, Lee," she said excitedly.

"There's a minor downside that I should mention," Jacqueline said hurriedly. "You would be working closely with Hera."

Anya's face fell. Lena thought for a moment before replying mischievously, "Every silver lining needs its thunder cloud, I suppose."

Jacqueline looked hopeful. "If you need time to think, that is understandable, there's no immediate rush, as your duties wouldn't start until after you are fully healed."

Smiling, Lena nodded. "I would be honored to serve alongside you as Councilor. Altus knows you'll need all the help you can get with Hera there too."

"Excellent!"

"Congratulations, Lee!"

Lena beamed but turned swiftly to Anya as a thought struck her. "Oh! This means we'll be staying on at the castle. We need to talk to Master Caldriene and get you a permanent position with the florists."

Anya took back the cup of tea and deftly replaced it with a fork with three chunks of either liver or kidney speared on its tines, a bowl of fruit ready and waiting. "In due time, my love, in due time."

5

ALETHIA

Phillip walked with muted footsteps, hands clasped within heavy sleeves, eyes down. *Speak softly. Breathe shallowly. Think carefully, for others may be listening.* He was learning. He'd thought the voices had been bad, that they were the worst it could get down here. That was before Celos and his ring. That's when the pain started. The whispers had been a blessing compared to the pain. He would give anything to have those instead.

On the first day beneath the hood he had been loud, clumsy, a buffoon. Scared too. It had helped a little when he had found his ma, but then the pain came.

On the second day he had been quieter. His footsteps still fell heavily, and his sobs were still too loud.

So, the pain came again.

It had now been over a week and the pain had come like clockwork every day since, no matter what he did. He would try harder today. Maybe if he was quiet enough, the pain would stay away. Father didn't mean to hurt him; it was the only way. He was starting to understand. Father knew everything, it had been foolish to try and hide things from him, to hide his thoughts. Father . . .

But Celos was not Phillip's father. He had to remember that. It was hard to remember things outside of Alethia's walls. Outside of his own dark thoughts. No, Celos was not his father. Florence was his father. His pa. His pa had been a kind man. A funny man. A loud man. He had been a builder. A good one too, and his workers liked him. This was back when Ma only built smaller inventions. They made a good pair. Pa always said that she was the tools to his toolbox. "I make the houses, and my wife fills them with useful things!"

He had loved building and took pride in pointing out all the houses and shops in Bridgeport that he'd helped create. The greatest crime, he said, was sloppy carpentry. It was one of life's cruel jokes then, that a poorly constructed building killed him. Phillip had been five. Old enough to remember a life with his father in it, but not yet old enough to understand he'd have to live the rest without him.

He walked through the cold tunnels with two other new sons and an older brother. The older brother, Hemway, was kinder than yesterday's. He made sure Phillip, Mallard, and Oliver followed the flow of the day without incident but wasn't a brute about it.

They made their way to the Connection Room, winding through the cobbled labyrinth. The amount of purple-hooded brothers increased the closer they got to the room, and Phillip felt nervous excitement nuzzle itself within his rib cage. The Connection Room was one of the few places within Alethia where noise was encouraged. If he was lucky, he might even see his ma.

The slate archway came into view, two statues of stone brothers flanking the doorway, hoods thrown back to reveal their faces. Both calm and serene, sickly so. Phillip arranged his features into a close imitation, and as he passed through the archway, tentatively lowered his hood. All brothers before him had done the same. He shared a look with Mallard. The poor lad was white-faced and shaking. He'd been down here longer than Phillip, and apparently the pain still came for him too. Mallard's eyes darted around, searching. Phillip kept his eyes forward.

They entered a large domed hall, scooped out of the rock as if by a giant's hands. As soon as feet crossed threshold, footsteps became amplified, and whispers grew.

Phillip leaned close to Mallard's ear. "Found him yet?"

Mallard shook his head sharply. "Nah, Father tells me I'm not ready to meet him. He's promised Gad is here though. So, it's only a matter of time."

Phillip grunted.

"Have you talked with your ma?" Mallard whispered so softly Phillip almost didn't catch it.

"Yeah, I get five minutes every evening. Guarded though, can't say much."

"Figures."

Another grunt.

"Is she trying to escape?" Mallard asked lightly, and something about his tone made Phillip pause. He eyed him warily. Mallard had chosen to come here. He may not have known what he was signing up for, but he had chosen this path.

Hesitating, he lied: "No, too risky, she's worried about what'll happen to me."

Mallard nodded, gaze still darting around the faces of their brothers. The hall was now filled with men. All cloaked in purple, all with hoods thrown back. Many wore expressions of serene bliss; many were as white-faced and shaken as Mallard. Phillip saw Oliver standing nearby and attempted a smile. Oliver smiled cheerfully back and nodded, sandy-blond curls flopping over his eyes for a moment. He was from Salmyre, a town in the far west of the Lower Realm, and was so happy to be here it made Phillip's teeth hurt. The pain had stopped coming for him on day two. Lucky pitstain.

The buzzing whispers made Phillip feel like he had stepped into a beehive. Whispers shifted to talking and soon conversation floated around the room. It felt good to *hear* again, to have things to listen to outside of his own blasted thoughts.

"Praise be Celos." A voice near his shoulder caused him to turn.

"Praise be," he hurried to reply. The speaker was a shorter man made taller by the height of his hair. Phillip wondered idly if, when the man wore the hood, it flattened his hair down or perched on top of his locks.

"You must be new, brother. Welcome. I'm Eric."

"Phillip."

"Thanks be to Celos for this meeting."

"Um, yeah, thanks be."

Eric regarded him shrewdly, and Phillip shifted his weight from one foot to the other, feeling suddenly as though each breath were being measured. Without warning, Eric clapped him hard on the shoulder, gripping just below the socket, and smiled warmly. "Ah, brother, rest easy, you're with family here! Have you found bliss yet, or are you still in the pits?"

Phillip looked at him, confused, and asked, "The pits?"

"You're *very* new then?"

"Yeah."

"That explains the white knuckles. Never fear, lad. That passes right quick. Once you're through, you'll really get the full Alethian experience."

"Oh?"

"If I had paper, I'd draw you a map!" He laughed. "But I can paint you a picture." He mimed sweeping brushstrokes in midair. "Close your eyes and allow me to—I said *close them*." The last command came out as a growl, deep and distorted. Eric's fingers gripped Phillip's arm painfully, shocking him into obedience. "Good. The black of fear will soon fade to the grays of despair but linger not! For next your palette will be filled with apathy's cream and beige. You see how the shades shift? Once we've added those to our canvas, the piercing white of bliss smothers all! It is said that if you stare long enough into bliss's brilliance, you'll see all colors, all shades. Only a few brothers have made the final shift though. Open, I obviously have no more paint."

Phillip hurried to comply.

"If you can hold out till then, brother, I promise you it is worth the wait. Any good journey needs its struggles, or else you have nothing to talk about!" And he boomed a laugh so loud and so forceful, Phillip found himself laughing with him, first with alarm, and then in a hysterical giddiness that washed over him. It felt good to laugh.

Wiping a tear, Phillip asked, "Where are you from?"

Eric's easy smile immediately froze. "From Alethia. I'm happy to be here, brother. I do not have a life beyond this fair city." There was a warning in his tone.

"No, I know . . . P-praise be Celos."

The smile returned. "Praise be! You're a quick learner, brother. That will be important down here. Father loves his clever Sons."

Shaken, Phillip could only nod. Eric's fingers were still squeezing his shoulder painfully. Phillip reached up and clasped them, thinking to pry them free. At his touch, Eric's face spasmed and the smile slipped; he stared at Phillip's hand on his with a look of wonder. Eric's grip tightened; like claws his fingers dug into Phillip's flesh. He leaned close to Phillip's ear and said almost tenderly, "You know what I miss most?"

"W-what?"

"Warmth. Of sunlight. Of . . . my little sister used to hold my hand walking the fence. It fit in mine just so."

He let go and with a quick twist of his wrist, held Phillip's hand in his, gently now. His thumb brushed across his knuckles. Alarmed by this sudden change, Phillip stood frozen in place, unsure what to say. Eric's face had softened, and he looked five years younger. The hair stood up on the back of Phillip's neck.

"Do you miss her?" Phillip asked, searching for something to fill the silence, fighting the urge to step away.

"Who?"

"Your sister."

Eric slapped him hard across the face, causing Phillip to yelp. "I have no sister, only brothers. Silly boy, not as clever as I thought!" He waggled his finger playfully and winked. Before Phillip could re-calibrate to this change, Eric reached up and placed a tender kiss on Phillip's now stinging cheek.

"Seek bliss. Forget."

"Eric! Who's your friend?" a new voice called. Eric wrapped an arm around Phillip's middle and whisked him toward a man with a wide, flat nose and thick beard.

"Jacob! We have a new brother. This is Phillip—he knows the inventor."

"Wait . . . how did you know—" Phillip began.

Jacob's eyes lit with interest. "A gift. Praise Celos."

A sudden hush fell over the room like the snuffing of a candle. Phillip, still clutched at Eric's side, turned his eyes to the balcony at the far end of the room.

Celos stood, waiting. Tall and thin, he looked almost skeletal in the white, ghostly light of the hall. His jet-black cloak hung from his shoulders, more shadow than fabric. As the last echo died away, he lifted his arms and his cloak slipped to the floor, revealing a pure white suit. The one splash of color on him was a rose-gold ring. Its thick band, wrapped around his right forefinger, drew every eye as he rested it on the banister.

The ring was pain. Phillip didn't know how, but he and every Son within Alethia's walls knew that Celos's ring was the source of the pain that came for them every day. It was Celos's gift, he said. He gave them each a new life and he could take it away, just so, he brought pain and he could take that away too. Every light source brought a shadow. Only those who had reached Celos's inner circle could enjoy life without pain.

"My Sons," he said lovingly, "are you well?"

"Yes, Father," their voices replied in unison. A proud smile split his face.

"Sound is a gift; its vibrations connect us all. Misuse and abuse cloud its purity. We savor it now as we have for decades and come together as one!" The entire room erupted with the word *one* turning into a rolling chant. An ongoing repeated vowel flowed through the hall in waves. It swelled within the room, filling spaces between people, filling the space within Phillip's chest. He hated to admit, even to himself, that he enjoyed this part. He felt like a stone worn smooth in a river, and for a moment, he opened his mouth and added his voice to the call. Celos held up his hands and began shaping the sound around him. Tones became words, and the Sons eagerly awaited their turn to reply.

"Who saved you from your wretched lives?" Celos called.

"You, Father," the room answered.

"Who gave you freedom?"

"You, Father."

"Who protects you?"

"You, Father."

"Who loves you?"

"You, Father."

"Who brought you life?"

"You, Father."

"And who will free your minds from pain?"

"You, Father."

"Are you grateful?"

"Yes, Father."

"And how do you show your gratitude?"

"We obey."

Celos tapped his finger on the banister and a wave of movement rippled through the crowd. Each man flinched, buckled, or bowed for just a moment before standing upright again. As the wave reached Phillip, he felt the pain pierce his mind. He gasped and doubled over. Then the pain vanished. Eric hauled him upright.

"Good," Celos said softly. "I have exciting news. Despite the delay, the first stage of our plan is ready to move forward. We will commence Operation Palimpsest two nights hence. This is a trident attack with three important tines. Tabula, Rasa, and Ortus. Those of you who have been trusted with a role in Tabula will need to meet in the weapons store this evening for equipment, explosives, and targets. Those with the honor of serving in Rasa will join me in the crystal chamber to load mirrors into wagons. Those select few in Ortus must wait. We owe a certain inventor thanks for the delay. Once the bridles are complete I will have tasks for you."

Phillip had no idea what most of Celos's instructions meant but noticed a large group of brothers stand up straighter at the mention of each tine. It seemed not all men were included in these plans, but Phillip wagered a guess that each group involved a small battalion.

"We draw ever closer to our goal. Vigilance and loyalty are more important now than ever before. Be on the lookout for traitors among us. Any Son who is guilty of treachery will be forever barred from our promised land. Any Son who discovers a plot of disloyalty will be greatly rewarded." A ripple of unease passed through the crowd. Phillip stared straight ahead and avoided making eye contact.

Movement stirred to Celos's left, and two Sons hauled in a gagged and squirming woman between them. Entwined in the horror he struggled not to show, Phillip felt a surge of pride to see his ma still fighting the hands that bound her. If looks could kill, she would have murdered the lot of them. Phillip had never seen her so furious; her features were contorted with hatred. Her graying black hair, piled in a mess of a bun on the top of her head, almost crackled with electricity. Anger was a fire, and fire was catching. A spark of rage ignited in Phillip's heart. The embers flared to life as a brother's fist collided with her side and she doubled over, cursing and wheezing.

Phillip felt both Eric and Jacob steal glances in his direction, watching for a reaction. Forcing his features into a neutral mask, he clenched his jaw. He would not give them the satisfaction.

"My Sons, welcome the inventor, Bruna Leschi. She has designed our fleet and inspired the vessel for our message. Without her, we could not make it off the ground nor into the hearts and minds of my future subjects, so let us thank her now."

An eerie chorus echoed around the chamber. "In Celos name, we thank you."

"I'm sure Bruna has a few words too," Celos said. Phillip felt the muscle move along his jaw as he contained his fury. His mother was a master and should be honored as such. "First and foremost, she will be apologizing for the delays and dead ends that have impeded our deadline. Clever though she is, her reluctance to obey has set us back. For this she must now beg forgiveness."

At a nod from Celos, a brother reached up and removed her gag. Wasting no time, she arched her neck and spat. The wet gob landed on Celos's cheek and slipped down to his chin. Phillip hid a smile; the congregation held its breath.

"Women are such base creatures," Celos said softly. "Apologize." His ringed hand curled into a fist and Master Leschi cried out, knees buckling for an instant. With teeth clenched in a fierce grimace and eyes never leaving Celos's, she stood tall on shaking legs.

"No," she whispered.

The seconds lingered. The two stood, locked in a silent battle of wills. Finally, Celos relaxed his fist, and with a shuddering gasp, Master Leschi collapsed into the waiting arms of the two purple-cloaked Sons. Phillip did nothing and felt a wave of self-loathing wash over him. Back rigid and fists clenched, he registered a muted sting across his palms where his nails had cut into flesh.

"This will not do," Celos said and turned back to the room. "Phillip, my Son. Step forward."

Phillip's insides went cold. With a helpful shove from Eric, he felt his body lurch into motion and move through the parting sea of purple.

When he was standing directly below the balcony, Celos addressed him. "This woman holds many delusions. She claims to be your mother. This is a lie. Tell her who gave you life."

Phillip looked into the terrified eyes of his mother and whispered, "I'm the son of Master Bruna Leschi and Florence Le—"

With a tired gesture, Celos pointed his ringed finger, and white-hot needles raked themselves through Phillip's mind, cutting off his speech. The pain summoned faces from his past, distorting them into grotesque masks of ridicule. Celos lifted his hand and the pain vanished.

"Who gave you life?"

"Master Bruna Le—"

He was cut off again as Celos angled his ring at him, and his knees gave out. He fell to the floor. Trembling on all fours, he cowered as the pain returned, caressing his mind, igniting all it touched. This time it drew forth shame. Shameful memories swirled around him, and even the smallest instances became overwhelming burdens. A mistimed comment, a poorly performed task, a forgotten promise, all now heightened, barbed, and unbearable. As quickly as they came, they disappeared.

"No more, please, Celos. I'll apologize, leave him be." His mother's voice reached him as if from far away. Still shaking, Phillip pushed himself up to standing, wishing for the hundredth time that he were a stronger man.

"Then say it," Celos commanded.

"I'm sorry," his mother breathed.

"There now, that wasn't so hard, was it?"

"No, Celos."

"But insolence must be punished. You have delayed our goals and must pay for your defiance. Don't you agree, my Sons?"

Phillip heard the voices around him answer as one: "Yes, Father." A rushing filled Phillip's ears, and he looked around wildly. Dozens of hungry eyes stared at him, smiles flashing.

"Please, Celos—" his mother begged.

The pain came for Phillip a third time.

6

THE BATTLE WORTH FIGHTING

"You worry too much, that's supposed to be my job, Plum," Maria protested lightly as Jacs draped a shawl around her slim shoulders and tucked the ends around her. Noticing her mother's contented little wiggle, Jacs hid a smile. She was seated at Maria's bedside in her private room in the infirmary. Her mother sat upright with a distant look in her eye and a vacant smile on her face, but Jacs was pleased to see she had caught her in a moment of lucidity. In the days since escaping the catacombs, these moments came more frequently, but they were still few and far between. Jacs chose not to look at the wrist and ankle restraints half hidden by blankets and hoped her mother would not need them today. A hulking, hawk-eyed attendant stood just inside the door, arms folded and brow creased. Jacs ignored her for the moment too.

Maria still bore the marks of the Council's brutality. Her face was mottled with various bruises in shades of purple and yellow, two fingers were splinted and freshly bandaged, and Jacs knew there were cuts and bruises hidden by her loose-fitting robe. But she was eating well and sleeping through the night. If only her mind . . . No, focus on the positives. Soon she would be her old self again. All Jacs could do was remain optimistic, help where she could, and thank Master Epione.

The room was calm with windows overlooking a small water feature in the garden beyond. Its gentle tinkling sound tickled the edges of her ears. Jacs sat in a comfortable chair next to the bed, and vases filled with lavender perched on the windowsill. Their soothing scent hung languidly in the air. An assortment of stained-glass forget-me-not ornaments hung from the ceiling near the windows. Blue and green dappled light filtered through their softly twisting panes and onto the two women. A chess board was perched on a table across Maria's lap, and steaming cups of tea were close at hand. The late evening air had cooled the grounds outside, and a light misting of rain speckled the windows.

"I wouldn't dream of giving you my worries, Mum. You need to focus on getting better."

"I can focus on that and listen. You seem distracted. What's on your mind?"

Jacs sighed, eyeing her warily. "Well . . . Between searching for Connor, his buzzing mirrors, the attack on Alethia, my impending betrothal, Phillip possibly being a traitor, keeping the peace with the Griffins, organizing a new Council, and . . . and . . ." suddenly she was a little girl again, coming to her mother after Mal and Casey poured pepper powder down the back of her shirt. She paused to breathe, and her mother reached across their game to place a hand on hers. The simple gesture made Jacs's eyes burn, and she looked away.

"You are strong enough for this, sweetheart," Maria said softly.

"It's just, there's so much."

"I know." Maria gave her hand a little squeeze and a wiggle, eyes kind and voice soft. Her gaze darted to the chess pieces between them. "Do you know why I always beat you in chess?"

Jacs fought a smile. "Because you're ruthless?"

"No," her mother laughed. "You can be ruthless and a terrible chess player."

"Because you have more experience?"

"Partially," Maria conceded. "But mostly it's because you treat each piece as an island. I attack your pawn, you defend your pawn but fail to realize that my initial attack was a setup with two other pieces for a larger attack. My pieces work together. Your pieces react in isolated pockets."

"What do you mean?"

"Okay, think of it this way. You're the Queen. Just like in chess, the queen is the most important piece on the board. If you lose the queen, the game—or the Queendom—is lost. However, the queen is not the most powerful piece on the board. She's actually quite limited in what she can do, only moving one space per turn. The genteel, as her second in command, has run of the board, can dart in all directions for as many spaces as it wants, backward, forward, and diagonally, but despite this, it is not the most important piece. The queen's power lies in the fact that this is her army. Half the board fights for her. She doesn't have to move far because other pieces will do that for her."

Jacs looked at the board. "So I need to stay put while everyone else does all the work?"

Maria shook her head gently. "No, Plum. You need to recognize your limitations and take control of your strengths. You can't move across the board like the genteel, you can't hop over enemies like the knight. But you are the Queen, the commander of those that can. *That* is your role. *That* is your strength. So, stop trying to do it all yourself and put your other pieces to work."

Maria patted Jacs's hand again and Jacs felt the tightness in her chest release. With a wink, Maria delicately lifted her castle with bandaged fingers and, taking Jacs's knight, announced, "Checkmate."

"Ha! See? Ruthless!"

"I mean, that helps too . . ." Maria agreed. "Just . . . don't think you have to do this alone. Use your army."

Jacs frowned and looked out the window, chest constricting again as another wave of doubt washed over her. "I'm so worried about Connor," she whispered. "It's been over a week."

"Oh, sweetheart," Maria said.

"Mum, what if I've lost him?"

"You can't think that. I'm sure he's—"

"It's my fault he was down there. I didn't think it through. He watched his mother die in front of him; of course those catacombs were going to mess with his mind. I took them all down there without warning them. Phillip's gone, Masterchiv Rathbone's gone, and Connor. Connor . . . I never got to tell him . . . I mean he knew how I felt about him, but I never said it. And now I may never have the chance." The words scraped through Jacs's throat. "And what if, when he does come back, I'm married to someone else? How could I face him?"

The light drizzle outside shifted into the pitter-patter of steady rain, and the two women sat silently for a moment, watching the sun linger on the horizon.

"We give the people we love the power to hurt us the most," Maria said in a soft, eerie singsong voice, almost to herself. "But in this life, a heart is too heavy a burden for one person to bear alone. It's a gift to find someone to share it with. Someone worth the risk of a heartbreak."

Jacs searched her mother's eyes and saw them lose focus. The beginnings of dread settled in the pit of her stomach and she fought to keep her mother with her for a few more moments. "Like Dad?"

Maria smiled sadly. "Like your father. I was so lucky to have found a love like his. To have had it when I did, for as long as I did. Even though . . . even though it wasn't for as long as I'd hoped." Jacs quietly watched her mother pick idly at the fringe of her shawl, too afraid to speak lest she break the spell that had settled around their shoulders. "He helped me shine. He was gentle and kind. Took the good days with the bad, and that was important. It's all well and good to find someone who'll bask in the sunlight with you, but it's when life's storm hits that you want someone by your side who can brave it with you. He was the person I trusted above all others, and he's the only man I'd trust to help me raise the future Queen of Frea." She laughed shakily. "A love like that needs to be protected. Cherished." Maria looked up and held her daughter's gaze. "Is that the kind of love you have for Cornelius?"

Jacs balked at the question, floundering for an answer.

"Is it?"

"Yes."

"Then you need to find another solution to your problem with power, because from what you've said, you are to marry a man you don't know to fit yourself more snugly in the pocket of a woman who holds the Queendom's power already," Maria said seriously, picking up Jacs's defeated queen from the board between fingers still too thin for Jacs's liking. She closed her fist over the piece, obscuring it from view.

"Mum, it's a bit more complicated than that."

"Is it?"

"Yes . . . well . . ."

"You are giving this Hera woman your place on the board, and you're doing it at the cost of love, Jacqueline. You pay too steep a price."

"B-but I . . ." Jacs stuttered, "I couldn't see another way."

"Sweetheart, you invented a hot-air balloon to compete in a contest a world away. You are the first woman to ride with Griffins in centuries. You won the Crown with a broken wrist and half the Queendom against you. If you can't see another way to solve this problem, it's because you've stopped looking."

"I have not!"

Maria simply looked at her. Jacs felt her indignation flare and die. Deflated, she sank into her chair. "Keep looking, you'll find it," her mother said as though helping Jacs locate a lost sock. "Remember"—she cleared her throat and frowned—"remember what your father used to say whenever you'd come to us upset over a failed project?"

Jacs huffed a laugh. "That he was proud I'd found exactly how *not* to do it."

Maria beamed. "Exactly, 'now you're one step closer to the right way,' he'd say."

"I miss him."

"Don't worry, he'll be along shortly, he's just taken my Plum skating."

"Mum?"

Maria's hands began to shake, and a grin spread slowly across her face. "They'll be back any minute now. You should have seen her, all dressed up in her new winter coat, she looked proud as a peach, and my Francis . . . well, he's been waiting for the ice to thicken up for weeks. Like a kid he was, to see the fresh snow this morning." The singsong quality returned to her voice, and she hummed shakily to herself.

"Mum . . ." Jacs kept her voice level, ignoring the flash of panic in her heart, and hurriedly gestured for the attendant to remain where she was by the door.

"Where is he? Where is my Francis?"

"Mum, Dad's gone."

Maria's grin remained frozen on her face as she turned her eyes slowly toward Jacs. Her gaze lacked warmth and for a moment she did not appear to recognize who she was talking to. In the corners of her eyes, tears gathered and fell onto flushed cheeks. Jacs felt a needle of fear pierce through her.

"I've baked them a cake for when they return. Would you like some?"

"I—"

"A cake? A cake!" Maria's voice rose with each word until it had become a shrill shriek, and she giggled. The high-pitched sound set Jacs's teeth on edge. "A cake I baked while Francis froze. Some wife I am. He sank while I sang into my mixing bowl. Drown your sorrows— well, he had none. But I'm full of them. Full of them!" She giggled again, squeezing a chess piece tightly in one fist and upturning the board with a wild thrash of the other. Blue and gold pieces clattered to the floor, and Jacs jumped up to clasp her mother's hands in hers.

"Mum, I'm here, you're safe."

"Who are you to keep me safe? Francis had my Plum and little good that did him."

"Mum—"

"He sank and drowned my heart with him."

"You don't know what you're saying."

"But who needs a heart? Who needs this useless thing?" Ripping her hands free from Jacs's with alarming strength, she angled the pointed tip of the queen chess piece and thrust it forcefully toward her heart, punctuating each word with a violent jab. Jacs was able to intercept it just before it struck her mother's fragile frame. "Who. Needs. A. Heart?" Jacs scrambled to protect her mother from herself as the attendant called for help and rushed to Maria's bedside.

"No!" Jacs cried as the attendant wrestled her mother's wrists into their restraints.

"Who needs one? Who needs one! Take mine out! TAKE IT OUT!"

A second attendant arrived and pulled Jacs from the room as the first forced a glass of milky liquid down her mother's throat.

"Best not to watch, Your Majesty," the second attendant said. Her grip was gentle but as solid as a rock and irrefutable.

"Let me help her," Jacs demanded, her mother's shrieks following her from the room.

"It's not safe just now."

"I can help."

"She's got all the help she needs at the minute, not to worry. Come back tomorrow, I'm sure she'll be right as rain after a good rest."

"But—"

"She'll be all right, Your Majesty; she just needs more time," the attendant said kindly with a firm grip on Jacs's wrist.

Hesitating as her mother's shrieks died to a disoriented mumble, Jacs finally conceded. "Let me know if anything changes."

Reaching behind her, the second attendant pulled her mother's door shut with a snap, muffling the garbled chattering from within. After a moment's hesitation, she released Jacs's wrist. "Of course. You have a good evening, Your Majesty."

Jacs, helpless, turned and retreated, feeling the attendant's eyes boring into her back as she walked down the long hallway. Away from the infirmary.

Back in her rooms, Jacs paced restlessly. Poor Adaine, attempting to dress her Queen down for the night but unable to catch her in one place long enough to remove any article of clothing effectively, finally said, "Your Majesty, please!"

"What?"

"Sit down."

Smothering a scowl, Jacs did as she was told. Ears still ringing with her mother's shrieks, she struggled to sit still. She needed to focus on the positives. Her mother had been lucid for much longer than yesterday. They'd even managed to have quite a pleasant chat before—Jacs forced the image of her mother struggling against her restraints from her mind.

Her mother would be fine. The attendant was right. Master Epione was right. She just needed more time.

Adaine handed her a gold-backed mirror without being asked and, as she was removing the pins from her auburn hair, Jacs said, "Cornelius Frean," into the mirror. With two words she replaced one worry with another.

The surface clouded over and, as it had since she'd lost him, the handle began buzzing in a sporadic pattern. Jacs tried to make out a rhythm she recognized, intrigued by the new idea that there could be a musical connection. The beats were a mixture of lengths, but nothing familiar. They had discovered that the buzzing continued until Connor's name was dispelled. If he wasn't on the other end at all, the mirror should simply cloud for an instant, then clear. So, did that mean he was near a crystal? Was the buzzing an attempt to message her? She listened for a moment longer; no, nothing that could be deemed a code either. That was an idea though: Was Connor trying to contact her through the scry crystals?

Unexpectedly, the buzzing stopped. Jacs spun to look at Adaine in alarm. "What do you think that means?" she said in a nervous whisper.

"I'm not sure, Your Majesty. Maybe the buzzing has gone to bed? It's well after sundown after all."

Jacs furrowed her brow. It was late. If it was Connor sending messages, then he would have gone to bed by now. But it just didn't make sense. Why wouldn't his face show up in the mirror? She set the clear looking glass beside her as a knock on the door interrupted her thoughts.

"Enter," she said, rising to her feet. Adaine straightened Jacs's half-dismantled hair and stepped back to stand next to the fireplace.

"Good evening, Your Majesty," Edith said. She strode across the threshold, books and papers under one arm, with a serving boy, Barlow. The latter balanced a full tea tray with tight-lipped, nervous determination. Jacs had assigned the boy to Phillip as his valet before the gala and ever since Phillip's disappearance, she hadn't seen him smile once. He'd thrown himself into his work with fierceness that made her think he'd taken the loss as a personal slight. Adaine hurried to help the boy set the tray on the table by the fire. Edith dismissed him with a wave of her hand. Once the door closed behind, she turned to face her Queen.

"I'm sorry for the hour, but this was urgent," Edith said. She was a small handful of years older than Jacs with a round face, deep dimples, and bright hazel eyes. Her hair was neatly tucked behind both ears and, Jacs noticed, she wore a thin band of black around the upper portion of her right arm. Not thick enough for it to be deemed a mourning band, it tended to represent remembrance.

Gaze lingering on the band, Jacs asked anxiously, "Have you heard anything? About Cornelius?" She gestured for Edith to take a seat, indicating to Adaine to do the same. The latter hesitated, took a step forward, then shook her head and remained at her post. She did, however, accept a lavender shortbread biscuit when Edith offered.

"Yes and no, Your Majesty," Edith said while pouring the tea. That done, she set the teapot down and turned her attention to the books and papers. Trying not to hurry her, Jacs teased her hand flinchingly against her slightly steaming mug, lightly withdrawing from and replacing her palm against the heat of the porcelain.

"And?" Jacs blurted out.

"We received a letter and books from the dowager King addressed to Cornelius that I thought you should see. The messenger also said that the dowager King will be postponing his visit. Apparently, the winter is best spent on the coast." It took a moment for Jacs to understand what she'd said, and another moment to disguise the disappointment on her face.

Edith handed over a letter and two notebooks. The letter was weighty, and Jacs hesitated, unsure if it was her place to open a private correspondence between Connor and his father. Setting that aside, she turned her attention to the books. They were both bound in navy-blue leather. Opening the cover of the first, she read:

The following is a summary of the late Queen Ariel's private journals spanning the five years prior to her death.

Flicking through, she saw the neat handwriting of a scribe filled the pages. Underlined headings denoted a week's date range, and key events and entries from that date range were listed below. The scribe had evidently been focused on maintaining objective accuracy rather than tone, and Jacs felt a twinge of regret at the loss of the Queen's voice. She would have loved some insight into who Queen Ariel was. She paused to read:

Queen's birthday celebrations. Champagne stores ran low within the castle. At midnight, Her Majesty, the King, Lord Claustrom, Genteel Claustrom, and two knights rode into Basileia. They visited five different taverns sampling the various champagnes each establishment offered. It was clear the palace was not aware the Queen had left her own party until she returned with a wagon filled with the small group's favorite bottles two hours later. Many tavern patrons accompanied their return. The celebration lasted well into the following days.

Jacs would have to read between the sterile lines to find the woman she had been. She picked up the second book expecting something similar only to flip from cover to cover in confusion. It was blank. Why would the dowager King include a blank notebook? Sighing, she set the second book down with the other items and took a sip from her mug. Edith perched on the edge of her seat like a bird ready to take flight. She opened her mouth as if to speak and then closed it, looking away. Jacs, still not used to her elevated status and how it affected those around her, was in no mood to dance around station propriety tonight.

"Edith, you look like you have something on your mind."

Edith bit the edge of her thumbnail and said, "I do. Only, I was wondering why you chose me to oversee Lordcouncilor Claustrom?"

"Ah, have you started with her yet?"

"Just this afternoon."

"And how did it go?"

"She was frosty but said nothing about her opinion of the arrangement. If anything, she had so much on her mind, I think she was grateful for the extra set of hands."

Jacs nodded thoughtfully. "I hope you don't mind the task."

"Well, that's where I'm confused. I have minimal experience as a scribe, or as an assistant . . . what, if you don't mind my asking, what role would you have me take with her lordship?"

"I need you to watch her. Oversee her actions as Councilor and keep me informed of any suspicious behavior. She is in a unique position where she has enough power to quickly take control, and I can't have that happen."

"Oh." Understanding washed over Edith's face.

"I just—honestly Edith, I'm trying to figure out the best way to keep my eye on her and you're someone I trust."

"I'm honored, Your Majesty."

"And once Cornelius returns, you will of course return to his service, but I also had the feeling you might like a task to occupy your mind in the meantime."

Edith colored around the ears and nodded. "For that I thank you, Your Majesty. The distraction is appreciated."

"How—" Jacs hesitated, not wanting to overstep. "How are you doing?"

"I'm fine," Edith said quickly. Jacs set her cup down.

"You know, in our letters, Cornelius always spoke so highly of you. You're very dear to him, and if as I suspect, he's as dear to you, I know this must be hard for you."

Edith swallowed and nodded curtly. "As it is for you?"

"Exactly," Jacs whispered. The two women shared a look of understanding.

"I pray for him every night."

"Is the band for him?" Jacs asked, pointing to the strip of black fabric.

Edith looked at it and nodded again. "Yes. His Grace is missing and I . . . I don't know how to help find him. I don't even know where to start. This is something I can do, and I can't wait to have reason to be rid of it."

"We'll find him."

"I know. I just wish I knew when. He's always made me worry, but never like this," Edith said softly. Her words hung in the air. The fire crackled, interrupting the silence. "You know, when he was younger, he used to play at being an adventurer and go wandering off into the woods for hours at a time. He always came home safely, but every so often he'd get lost. Usually, it would take the trackers no time to find him, but there was this one time when he was gone all night. He'd walked for miles upstream and the hounds lost his scent. Oh, we worried then." She shook her head. "He was about seven. The poor boy was shivering enough to shake a house when they finally found him in the early hours of the morning. He'd found a little island in the middle of the river and made camp, but of course had no shelter. His clothes were soaked through, the wood was too wet for a fire, and he'd eaten all his food." Jacs laughed in shaky disbelief as Edith smiled and rolled her eyes fondly at the memory. "For most it would have been the trip of nightmares, but I heard him recount the whole and I've never seen a smile so wide."

"Smile?"

Edith nodded. "He loved every minute of it. Said he felt like the heroine from one of his favorite stories. So, I hope that whenever we find him, it'll be with a smile on his face and a story to tell."

Jacs's heart ached. "I hope so too."

"It's just hard feeling so helpless in the meantime. Watching over Lord Claustrom really will be a needed occupation for my mind." Focus suddenly returned to Edith's eyes and she regarded Jacs carefully. "Lord Claustrom did say something of note this afternoon."

"Oh?"

"She mentioned you intend to marry Lordson Theo." There was no accusation in her tone, but Jacs felt the comment like a blow to the chest. She looked away and frowned.

"She speaks rashly."

"I see."

"But if I can't find a way to achieve what this marriage promises any other way, it may be my only option. For the Queendom."

Edith nodded slowly. "The Queendom must come first."

Jacs shifted uncomfortably in her seat and hugged her elbows.

"I'm sure Lordson Theo would be an appropriate match, Your Majesty," Edith remarked.

"So I've heard," Jacs said, suddenly wishing they were talking about anything else.

Edith regarded her steadily. "It's not my place to say—"

"No, it's not—"

"But he will understand."

"What?"

"Cornelius."

"He . . . but . . . ." Jacs reeled, trying to form the question that had been plaguing her heart ever since she'd shaken Hera's hand on the matter. "But would he be able to forgive me?" Each word passing through Jacs's lips was barbed with guilt's poison.

Edith set her cup down. "He will learn to," she said simply. "He more than anyone knows what it means to live a life devoted to the realms. But speaking as his friend, I must tell you it would break his heart."

Jacs swallowed around the lump in her throat. "Well, let's hope I can find an alternative."

"His Grace always said he loved you for your brains," Edith said lightly with a reassuring wink.

"He—"

"Although, once he finally told me who you were, the list got longer and longer. I couldn't get him to stop talking about you."

"Sorry about that." Jacs laughed.

"If there's any way that I can help, please let me know."

"Thank you, Edith. He's lucky to have a friend like you in his life."

Edith shrugged. "I would give the world for him."

It wasn't long after that Edith gathered the tray and bid Jacs good night. Adaine quietly finished dressing her down and Jacs fell into the welcome embrace of her blankets. She tried not to worry about Connor, but there was no helping it. She felt lost, ungrounded, viciously and irrevocably tethered to him. Somewhere along the way she had coupled her heart to his, and now that he was missing, she knew her heart and mind would be restless and uneasy until she knew he was safe. Her anxious thoughts gave way to uneasy dreams.

7

AN EDUCATION

"I don't like it," Masterchiv Rathbone muttered as she paced the perimeter of their secluded clearing. The Lower Realm's extended dusk had just forced them to make camp in a wooded clearing out of sight of the main road's traffic.

Dryft helped Connor from their horse and set about hitching their steed and Masterchiv Rathbone's to a tree at the edge of the clearing.

Connor stood in the middle, unsure what to do with his hands as the women worked around him.

"They're probably just merchants," Dryft said.

"Dryft, how frequently do wagons pass by the battlements?"

Dryft appeared to think for a moment before replying. "This does seem to be excessive."

"Exactly. All covered wagons, all very similar, traveling in groups of twos and threes. The riders are always cloaked, and the day was warm. I don't like it."

Connor was shattered. His joints ached, his head pounded, and he had the added humiliation of finding out mid-journey that he'd talked all through his fevered state in the caves and battlements. He didn't remember what he'd said, and the guards were kind enough to omit the details, but all the same, Masterchiv Rathbone had been much warmer toward him ever since. He could just be imagining it though. Stiff and limping, he hobbled over to a large tree opposite the horses and lowered himself to sit among the roots.

"At least they're not purple cloaks though," Connor said, not looking up as he searched his pockets. He retrieved a small paring knife, plucked a stick from near his knee, and began carving a spoon. Or at the very least a long fish with a wonky head. His fingers worked at half strength, and it was laborious just trying to strip the bark from the stick.

"True. Let's just keep our eye out for them. Something doesn't feel right."

"Understood."

"What are we looking for?" Connor asked.

"You, Your Grace, are just focusing on recovering. We'll watch for anything suspicious," Masterchiv Rathbone said.

Connor raised his eyebrow and peeled another strip of bark off with a flick of his knife. "Three sets of eyes are better than two, Masterchiv. I'll keep mine open just the same."

"Of course, Your Grace."

"If they're not merchants, who do you imagine they'd be?" he pressed.

"Highwaywomen, thieves, charlatans, smugglers . . . the Lower Realm is filled with undesirables."

Connor frowned. "No more than the Upper Realm though?"

Dryft shrugged. "Poverty breeds the worst kind of person. There's more poverty in the Lower Realm, so there're more criminals down here." A twig snapped beyond their circle of trees and Masterchiv Rathbone spun toward the sound. After a few seconds of attentive assessment, her shoulders relaxed, and she continued her inspection of the area.

Connor, distracted by her reaction, returned his attention to his stick. Their statements made him uneasy. "But . . ." he hesitated, trying to put his discontent into words. He thought of his conversations with Jacs all those years ago, about the hard winters and the high taxes. "The poverty isn't their fault. Surely most people just do their best to get by. If anything, it's a fault of us in power, isn't it? If we allow conditions to—"

"Keep your voice down a moment, Your Grace," Masterchiv Rathbone said softly. She had paused again and squinted into the wooded gloom. All three within the clearing appeared to hold their breath. Dryft sank into a defensive stance and moved to sync with her captain. Connor got shakily to his feet and tried to peer into the shadows of the trees. The forest was very still.

With a muffled thump, one of the horses snorted and stamped its hoof. In a flurry of fur, a squirrel erupted from the undergrowth. Chittering angrily, it darted up the tree Connor had been sitting against just a moment before. He allowed himself a relieved smile that neither guard nor knight echoed.

"The sooner we're out of this pit, the better," Masterchiv Rathbone muttered. Dryft raised an eyebrow and resumed unloading their saddlebags.

A shadow shifted off to Connor's left and he turned, taking a few steps toward it. Nearing the edge of their clearing, he placed a hand on the trunk of the tree separating light from shadowed wood and leaned around it to better see into the gloom. Nothing. Just a trick of the light.

"I can start gathering firewood," he called over his shoulder.

"Your Grace, rest. Please," Masterchiv Rathbone said without hiding her exasperation.

"I'll carry small piles, don't worry."

"I'd feel much more comfortable if you remained close."

Irritation flared in Connor's chest, and he stepped into the dim light beyond the clearing. He was not some child who needed minding, and he'd stay close to camp. The stubborn desire to do something of consequence consumed him, and he grabbed fallen branches and twigs from the mossy undergrowth. Following the trail of sticks a little farther from the clearing, he straightened, with his arms now half full, to return the way he'd come.

He froze as cold steel kissed his throat.

"Release him," Masterchiv Rathbone demanded, materializing beside him with one hand outstretched in a calming gesture, the other hovering low near her hip. Dryft appeared to her left.

"One move and the boy's blood's on your hands," a male voice rasped near his ear. Connor dropped the sticks and lowered his hands. He located the paring knife in his pocket, and attempted to conceal it in his closed fist. The man roughly seized his wrist and squeezed hard, forcing him to drop the blade with a yelp. So much for that plan.

"You have no idea who you're dealing with, release him now and leave in peace."

"I know he's a fancy boy. Heard you call him 'Your Grace.' You ain't gonna risk ruffling his pretty feathers."

"What do you want?"

"Your horses."

Connor's heart thrummed in his ears, and he felt every millimeter of skin pressed against the man's blade. Masterchiv Rathbone looked calm, and Dryft had edged toward Connor.

"Take them," Masterchiv Rathbone said softly. Connor noted the challenge in her tone.

The man laughed and forced Connor to walk backward with him toward where the horses had been tied and hobbled. "Once we're away, you can have your fancy boy back. One move I don't like, and I'll slit his throat. Benji, get them free." He barked the last as an order over his shoulder. Connor saw a shadow detach from a nearby tree and approach the horses. How many more were concealed in the darkness? Masterchiv Rathbone appeared to have the same thought as her eyes began scanning the woods.

Everyone stood rooted in place while Benji worked to release the horses, but Connor noted the subtle flurry of hand movements of first Masterchiv Rathbone, then Dryft. With the exchange concealed below their hips and behind their thighs, Connor would have been surprised if his captor had noticed anything.

"Where are you headed, traveler?" Dryft drawled. She shifted her weight subtly between front and back foot in a way Connor was sure masked slight forward movement.

"What's it to you? Facts are I'll be there well before you make it out of these woods."

"Likely so, but see, my partner and I are trackers. No matter where you end up, we'll find you. Is a lifetime of looking over your shoulder worth two horses?" She shifted her weight and took a few steps closer.

"You're a guard and she's a knight, you think I don't know how to tell you lot apart? Ain't neither of you trackers," the man sneered.

"A woman can be many things," Masterchiv Rathbone commented, drawing the man's attention. Connor watched Dryft take a few more steps closer.

"So can a man," the stranger rebuked almost reflexively. Connor watched a half smile flare on Masterchiv Rathbone's face. In his peripheral vision, Dryft edged closer still.

"I have no doubt, why even now you are a traveler, a horse thief, and a fool. You're likely many more things, but there is one thing you are not," Masterchiv Rathbone said.

"And what's that?" the man scoffed.

"Prepared," she whispered. In a flash, Dryft lunged forward, wrenching the man's knife-wielding arm and sweeping his legs out from beneath him. Connor felt a sharp sting flare along his throat as he narrowly avoided the knife's eager bite. Snatching the leather strap from her belt, Dryft wasted no time restraining the would-be thief. A swift blow to the neck and the man crumpled in a heap on the forest floor. Before Connor could think, she had forced him behind her protectively, and began scanning the woods for any more attackers. Masterchiv Rathbone dove for Benji, disappearing into the gloom. Connor heard a scream, a series of groans, then silence.

Muscles still achy, head light from fever, and adrenaline cooling in his veins, Connor fought a wave of dizziness. He stumbled and, to his horror, saw the ground rush up to meet him. Before his body hit the earth, Dryft spun and caught him awkwardly in her arms. With a muffled grunt, she lowered him gently to the ground. His vision flickered.

"Your Grace? Can you hear me?" Dryft's voice drifted toward him as if from far away. He blinked the darkness back and attempted to sit up. A strong hand pressed his chest down. "Take a minute, Your Grace. You've had a shock," she said kindly, then louder, "He's fine, coming to now. Bring the wine."

Dryft helped him sit up slowly.

"Thanks," he muttered. "I'm all right, just give me a moment."

"Take your time," Dryft said.

"That was—"

"Must have been terrifying."

"No! That was incredible!" Connor said with shaky enthusiasm. "What?"

"We were just ambushed by bandits in the woods! That is, you were, and Masterchiv Rathbone just, I mean, look, my hands are still shaking!" He laughed in wonder. He looked down at the little paring knife he'd dropped and frowned. "And I just stood there! I had a knife

I didn't know what to do with and you just felled him with your fists. You must teach me some moves for next time."

"Next time?" Dryft asked.

"Yes, I want to be ready. I don't want to play the prince in peril, I want to be able to help."

"This . . . Your Grace, this isn't a game. You could have been hurt."

Connor waved his hand dismissively. "But I wasn't, and next time I want to be useful."

"You're still mending."

"Then teach me slowly."

"Found something!" Masterchiv Rathbone called from the darkness. Dryft helped Connor to his feet, offering an arm for support, which he gladly took. Hesitating a moment, she looked him over thoughtfully, shook her head, and walked him toward Masterchiv Rathbone's voice.

"Are you all right, Your Grace?" Masterchiv Rathbone asked as she came to meet them. "You're white as a sheet."

"I'm fine."

"He wants to learn our ways," Dryft said mildly.

"Oh?"

"Just a few defensive maneuvers. It can't hurt . . . What did you find?" Connor hastened to ask.

"See for yourself," she said and led them back toward the road.

There, pulled off a short way from the main road, was one of the covered wagons they had seen earlier that day. A black horse stood, stamping in the moonlight, hitched to the front. Connor exchanged a look of confusion with the knight. "So . . . they have a horse?"

"From what I can tell, the horse threw a shoe, and they came to us for a replacement," Masterchiv Rathbone said, indicating its right foreleg.

"High-risk move for sure, they must have been transporting something important," said Dryft, moving toward the back of the wagon to investigate.

The back of Connor's neck prickled and he checked over his shoulder; the bandit had snuck up behind him so easily. There was a slight *oof* from Dryft as she pulled a large blanket out of the back.

"It gets weirder," Dryft said, voice muffled slightly behind the wagon.

Connor joined her with Masterchiv Rathbone. "What is that?" he asked.

"A picture frame?"

"No, it's reflective," Connor said, waving his hand over the glass and seeing its twin wave back. In the bottom of the wagon was a large mirror, its silvered glass pitch black in the dark interior. Its thick golden frame twisted around the glass like ropes, and trumpeting flowers dotted the rim. Each flower was also gold-wrought and about the size of Connor's fist.

"What would two brutes be doing with a massive mirror?" Dryft asked.

"Maybe they're selling it?" Connor suggested.

"Maybe . . ." Masterchiv Rathbone said. "But they were desperate enough to try and steal our horses—all to transport a mirror?"

"We should ask them when they come to," Connor suggested.

His guardpair nodded, and Masterchiv Rathbone jerked her head in the direction of their camp. "Let's go see if they're feeling up for a chat."

They were not.

"I'll tell you nothing," the man spat. After almost an hour, they had no more answers than when they started. All they'd been able to glean was his name: Tarion, and he had once referred to the flowered mirror as "the transmitter."

But what that meant was anyone's guess. Connor thought back to the mirrors and basins his subjects had used to watch the Contest of Queens all those months ago. They had been transmitters of a sort. But with all the scry crystals rounded up both within the Upper and

Lower Realms, what could anyone hope to transmit? And why on such a large mirror?

Ironically, the fact that neither Tarion nor Benji could be persuaded to explain their mysterious package was more incriminating than if they had just admitted to stealing it. They were tied back-to-back around a beech tree on the edge of their camp's clearing.

"Give it a rest, Dryft, he's giving me a headache. Let's try again in the morning," Masterchiv Rathbone said, finally calling a halt to their line of questioning. Connor had been dozing, propped up against a tree, and he scrambled to his feet.

"You should rest too, Your Grace. We have a long day tomorrow."

"Show me how you tied their restraints first," he said. Dryft looked at him sharply. "I wasn't kidding when I said I want to learn. This seems like a safe place to start."

With a glance toward her commanding officer for confirmation, Dryft beckoned Connor over. "Hold out your wrists," she said and slowly talked him through how to bind them together. Testing the restraint's hold, Connor tried to pry his wrists apart, but found them tied tight.

"Okay," he said happily, "now untie me and I'll give it a go."

After a few failed attempts, Connor was able to successfully bind Dryft's wrists behind her back. The bandits watched from the sidelines. They'd been gagged shortly after Benji made a rude comment about Connor's first attempt and now muttered muffled curses into the fabric wads shoved into their mouths.

Much later, while curled up on his bedroll beside the campfire, Dryft's sleeping form barely visible across the flames and Masterchiv Rathbone taking first watch, Connor smiled. The air was still, the woods were silent save for the creaking of trees and the rustling of critters in the underbrush, and the fire cast a comforting glow around the small, unorthodox group.

Despite his aching muscles and his lungs, which still couldn't seem to pull in enough air, he felt invigorated. He was on his way to find Jacs, and he was learning from the most esteemed knight in the two realms how to protect himself. He had never felt more alive.

8

BREAKTHROUGH

"We've made no further headway, Your Majesty," Cyrus explained. With only days before the Alethian invasion, Jacs was running out of distractions to keep her from pacing a trench in her chamber's floor. Rather than wait for her hourly update from the scryers, Jacs had decided on an early-morning visit to the palace scryer's crystalarium, a three-tiered workshop comprising circular caves cut into the base of Court's Mountain. Each cave served a different purpose. The first was bright, spacious, and contained a variety of different-sized scry crystals on workbenches: the refinery, where all crystals were hewn and cut. This room also contained two antechambers: one filled with different-sized mirrors, and the other empty save for a giant purple scry crystal, a chair, and desk. Both rooms were used to receive and transmit information, and it was in the latter that the amanuensis had broadcast the task results to the Lower Realm during the Contest of Queens.

A short flight of stairs led to the second cave: the laboratory. Lit by lamplight, this room carried a certain hush about its walls, and it was here that all the experiments were conducted.

Finally, a tight and winding track sparsely dotted with glowing blue crystals led up and away from the second cave. The purple scry crystals, Jacs knew, emitted no light, seeming to absorb the light around them instead, so it was a surprise to see these blue ones shining so brightly in the gloom. They must be a different variety of crystal, and Jacs hoped they weren't ones that could watch those who passed near them.

The tunnel was silent. Her footsteps made not a sound on the earthen floor and Jacs was sure even her breaths were muted. It took her ten minutes to walk along the pathway into the final chamber: the mine. The eerie blue light gave way to a cavernous cave system filled with spiraling towers of uncut scry crystals and piles of discarded crystals recently collected from the Lower Realm.

Since Jacs had halted crystal production, the mine now stood empty of workers, save for Cyrus, who had led Jacs there, and two men tasked with unloading the many wagons of confiscated crystals. Jacs's conversation with the scryer was punctuated with the clank of crystal on crystal as the men added those from the wagons to the piles.

"And there's been no other instance of a name causing buzzing rather than showing a person's image?" she asked.

"Not in recorded history, Your Majesty," Cyrus answered regretfully. Jacs let her eyes wander around the stone room. The towers of uncut crystals made her think of the crystals she had seen in the Undercourt's chamber. She suppressed a shudder.

"And those blue crystals that lit the tunnels, are they also scrying crystals?" she asked suddenly.

"No, they don't absorb light at all; on the contrary, they emit it. It makes them very useful in confined spaces as torches tend to eat up all the oxygen down here, which causes a problem for our miners."

"Where are they found?"

"Farther down in the mine. They're much rarer—which is why we haven't distributed them as light sources to the public. We stumbled across them years ago when scry-crystal research started to gain traction and the miners began digging deeper into the mountain. The symmetry of their uses is just so poetic, don't you think? One absorbs light, one emits it. In many ways the blue are identical to their purple counterparts. It's almost a shame that they don't have scrying potential," Cyrus said with a little laugh. He rose on the balls of his feet, hugging his elbows.

"Have you found any other crystals in the mines?"

"No, just the purple and the blue."

"And do the blue crystals have any other properties?"

"Not that we've been able to discover, although you may have noticed they have a dampening effect on sound. That tunnel is the quietest place in the crystalarium, and we think it's just the way their shapes work with the acoustics of the tunnel."

Jacs wound a strand of hair around her finger absent-mindedly. "Wait, do they dampen sound or *absorb* sound?" she asked suddenly, a thought hitting her. "Have you investigated that difference?"

"Absorbed? No . . . we just assumed—"

"We need to test this theory, now. If they can absorb sound the way the purple ones absorb light, then they may have transmitting properties we don't know about." Her heart leaped to pound in her throat. "Come on!" she barked at a bewildered Cyrus and charged back down the tunnel.

Sound travels in vibrations, she thought. *What if . . .* "I need an amplifier! Someone get me an amplifier!" she called as her jog became a sprint.

If the buzzing isn't music . . .

Barreling into the refinery, she encountered two pop-eyed apprentices. "Do we have an amplifier, something that can transmit sound?" she asked in earnest.

"N-no, Your Majesty," one spluttered.

"Then anything of a conical shape?" she demanded, "a cone or a–a bowl?"

"We have a bowl!"

"Will that work?" Jacs demanded.

"W-work for what, Your Majesty?" the second stammered.

"If a blue crystal is absorbing sound the way the purple crystals absorb light, can we tap into its ability to transmit sound?" she asked. The apprentice's eyes widened further. Cyrus, who had fallen behind, burst into the room, slightly out of breath.

"Yesmina, fetch a bowl. Fill the bottom with water," Cyrus ordered. He then turned to Jacs and added, "We rarely use water basins for scrying anymore as we've moved mostly to mirrors. The image is much clearer, you understand. But if you're right, this might be the best way to test your theory until we can locate something better."

Yesmina, a small bowl in her hands, hurried over, careful not to spill a drop. Thrums of electricity passed between everyone in the room, denoting the excitement of discovery. The apprentice placed the bowl on a counter and everyone edged closer.

"Cornelius Frean," Jacs said. The room held its breath as the seconds ticked by. The surface of the water fogged over briefly and cleared, but otherwise nothing happened. Jacs frowned and picked up the bowl. It wasn't even buzzing. *But only the handheld mirrors had buzzed,* she thought.

Cupping the bowl in her palms, Jacs brought it close to her lips and said, "Cornelius Frean." The surface of the water clouded over again. This time, however, as it cleared, the smooth surface became distorted. Tiny pulses, starting at the center of the bowl, sent a pattern of concentric ripples to its rim. Her ears straining, Jacs heard a very water-logged mumbling rising from its depths.

"How do we translate it?" Yesmina whispered.

Impatiently, Jacs tipped the water onto the floor. With trembling hands, she cupped the bowl in her palms again, brought it close to her lips as if blowing on hot tea, and repeated, "Cornelius Frean."

". . . so, we're just going to hope someone with good intentions finds the poor men and releases them? Isn't it more likely whoever finds them takes off with their wagon and fancy mirror? Or worse?" a voice that was unmistakably Connor's echoed hollowly from the bowl's center.

Jacs cried out in relief, a shaking hand flying to cover her mouth, the other gripping Cyrus's forearm for support.

"It's him!" she said. *He's alive*, her heart sang.

The reply to Connor's question was either too quiet to hear or not captured at all because after a moment he said, "I'm not saying it's not our best option, I'm just saying it feels wrong."

"Who's he talking to?" Cyrus asked.

"Not sure, maybe Masterchiv Rathbone if they didn't get separated. This is incredible, it's him! We can hear him!"

"The implications of this breakthrough, Your Majesty, can you imagine! Transmitting your voice from across the Queendom. Between realms! You wouldn't have to wait days or weeks for a messenger, it would be instant!" Cyrus said, positively fizzing.

Jacs's heart froze in her chest, and she looked at him sharply. The memories of how the purple crystals had been used against her people rose in her mind like bile in her throat and she shook her head. "Cyrus, this breakthrough has larger implications than we can predict. All of you must promise to keep this information contained. If news got out, and these crystals were weaponized, there would be no safe conversation left in the Queendom. No, this stays quiet. We will continue to study these, but I want every decision and step in the upcoming research to pass by me first. Nothing moves forward without my okay, is that clear?"

The blood had drained from Cyrus's face, and he swallowed. "Crystal clear, Your Majesty, you'll pardon the pun."

"And I want tighter security on both entrances to the mine."

"Yes, Your Majesty."

"Excellent. I must return to the castle; I'll be taking this basin with me."

Her attention returned to the basin for a moment as Connor's voice said, "It's a long way from here to Bridgeport, what if no one finds them?" There was another pause as his conversation partner replied.

"He's in the Lower Realm," Jacs whispered. "He's in the Lower Realm!" The realization burst from her like a firework. He was alive, he was in the Lower Realm, and he was coming home.

"Fine, no, you're right. But we're leaving them some water," Connor said.

"I-is there anything else you need, Your Majesty?" Cyrus asked, hesitant to interrupt the phantom voice.

An idea began to form in her mind, and she said, "Yes, fetch me one of the blue crystals."

9

BATTLE CRIES

Hands clasped behind her back and gaze purposefully averted, Amber listened to the conversation behind her only to determine that its nature was benign. As prison cells went, this one wasn't the worst she'd seen by far. That made sense; the Queen wasn't a monster, and these women were old. Achy joints did not fare well on stone floors. The former members of the Council of Four now resided in an inn's converted wing in a poorer part of Basileia. The Blushing Bard venue had never had such patronage before, and in exchange for a handsome fee, its innkeeper was doing all she could to meet the Queen's requirements.

The beauty of the arrangement was that none of the Council's former supporters would ever think to grace the threshold of this particular establishment, and the innkeeper's past conflict with the Council and their tax laws meant she was only too eager to ensure justice was served. Amber knew after two minutes of speaking with her that she would be the last to betray the Queen's confidence. With a constant rotation of guards, the old bats now found themselves beginning the rest of their days with simple comforts. Three meals a day, weekly baths, heavily guarded walks around a short track in the moonlight, and pre-approved reading material. Jacqueline had extended them a kindness that, in Amber's eyes, was undeserved.

"How could you do this, Bea?" Flent said. "To the Queen? To our family? You . . . you were Councilor, overseer of the egg count. Such honors were bestowed upon you, and you threw it all away for what? You risked dragging our family's name through the coals for what?"

"You won't understand, child," Beatrice said softly.

"Try me."

"I would have brought you with me. To the top. I would have brought you all with me. I thought to name you as my heir, you know?"

This was getting close to treason. Amber cleared her throat meaningfully from the doorway.

"None of that matters now," Flent replied hurriedly. "You have shamed us all, and I'm just lucky our rightful Queen has seen fit to separate your actions from the future prospects of our whole family."

"We were shaping the future of the Queendom."

"You were rotting it at its core."

"Did you come just to berate me?" Beatrice snapped. "Does it please you to kick a woman when she's down?"

"No," Flent said meekly.

"Have you come to release me? Does your new role grant you that power?"

"No."

Amber stole a glance to see the former Councilor rise from her chair, thick waves of brown hair cascading around her shoulders in unwashed disarray. Her high cheekbones were flushed in agitation, and something of a challenge lingered around her eyes. Without warning, she seized Flent's hands in hers.

Amber decided they were finished. "Enough. Flent, let's wrap it up."

Flent pulled away with clenched fists. Drawing herself up, she glared down her nose at her aunt. Softly, she said, "I came to say goodbye."

"Goodbye, niece," Beatrice sneered.

"And good luck."

With that, she spun on her heel and marched out the door. She never once looked back.

Amber followed a moment later, signaled to the guard on duty to relock the cell, and took her time walking down the stairs to the main landing.

Flent had already walked out onto the street, so Amber thanked the innkeeper, Rita, a woman shorter even than Amber with a twice-broken nose, gnarled, arthritic fingers, and a tidy gray braid extending down her back to her waist.

Amber lingered at the bar a moment, her gaze traveling over the assortment of chipped teapots, tarnished silverware, and peeling paintings to land on a particularly fine statue of an Alessi—a winged woman of legend—with her wings extended overhead and fine golden wire shaping the rays of light surrounding her. "That one's beautiful," she said.

"Aye, that one I nicked from my late wife's cousin's shop."

"You . . . Rita, you understand I'm a knight of the Queensguard, right? You can't just go around admitting to theft," Amber said incredulously.

"Well, it wasn't theft now, was it? I nicked it, sure, but her cousin was a right plip and stole my cat first. Fed Buttons the good cuts when she knew I only had scraps. So the way I see it, we're even. Call that an equivalent exchange."

Amber suppressed a laugh. "Let's chalk that up to poor word choice then, shall we?"

"Aye, I've been known to muddle my words sure enough," Rita agreed solemnly, a picture of humility. The effect was spoiled slightly when she added a wink.

"Well, you let us know if you need anything else in the way of prisoner comfort and security. They'll be out of your hair soon enough, I imagine."

"Tell our dear Queen they can stay as long as she pleases, I've not had this much fun with guests in a dog's age. Treated proper sweet they are, mind you. Not a hair out of place that you'll find. But I do like our chats. I've had a few decades' worth of talkings-to pent up, so you tell Her Majesty that they're safe with me. I'm even teaching them a few lessons, I am. Thems free of charge too."

Amber shook her hand and promised to pass along the message.

Flent was waiting outside when Amber finally joined her a few minutes later, arms folded, face dark.

"You all right?" Amber asked.

"Yeah."

"You sure?"

"What do you think?" Flent snapped.

They walked past the Blushing Bard's No Vacancy sign and down the cobbled lane toward where their coach was waiting for them on the main road.

Amber took a breath before replying, "It's why I'm asking."

"Yeah, well. That didn't . . ." Flent gestured uselessly.

"Go as expected?" Amber supplied.

"Something like that."

They walked in silence for a time. Amber fought the urge to ply her with empty platitudes, not sure what to say to comfort her.

"Thanks, by the way," Flent said finally. "For coming with me. It was never going to be the most fun of excursions, so . . . thanks."

"Happy to," Amber said. "If you're to continue working closely with the Queen, there needs to be zero reasons to doubt your loyalty. You did well in there."

At her praise, Flent seemed to inflate, and a satisfied grin flickered across her face. They arrived at the coach and Amber held the door open for Flent to climb in first. She shared a nod with the driver before disappearing inside and the coach lurched into motion. It felt nice not being on horseback for a change; they'd decided two military women riding through cheapside on palace horses would be too conspicuous. The area was full of people desperate to grasp the glittering gold that an Upperite life promised but did not always provide. The coach, borrowed from one of the palace delivery women, was of an understated make. Its paint flaked off in places, its door did not hang straight and it shuddered with each rotation of an ill-fitted wheel. The driver had been careful to park a few streets away from the Blushing Bard. Amber doubted they'd been followed.

Sitting knee to knee with Flent, Amber felt suddenly nervous. Flent broke the silence. "I never asked, how is training going with the troupe?"

"It's going well, actually. From day one, the boys all showed up early and seem eager to prove themselves. I haven't had that dedicated a group in a while," Amber admitted reluctantly.

"You don't sound too happy about that."

"No, no it's not that . . . It just feels like I'm doing something wrong. We've never had men in the military before, and . . . I mean, I've been temporary head of the Queensguard for less than a month and already I'm turning everything upside down. It's a risk. It's a risk to my career, my reputation, and to countless women's lives if it doesn't work out."

"And how likely is it that it won't work out?"

"Well, it's only been a week, so time will tell, I suppose. And that's the kicker: if I had more time, I'm sure it'd be fine . . . but these boys are eager to fight against Alethia. They won't be ready by tomorrow and have not been cleared to join our ranks, but what if they disobey orders and decide to fight anyway? There are so many dangerous variables when boys get involved. They're just so unpredictable."

"Do you trust them enough to follow orders?"

"Well, how far can you really trust a man, you know?" Amber replied sardonically.

Flent looked thoughtful for a moment and said, "They may surprise you. I think you sticking your neck out for them like this gives them ample motivation to earn your trust and respect. But . . . if you don't mind me saying, if you go around saying things like that, you might create a self-fulfilling prophecy."

"What do you mean?"

"Well, if the troupe finds out you don't think men are trustworthy, and they do all they can to prove they are and yet you keep prattling that belief off, then they may resign themselves to dishonesty. It's sometimes easier to play the part people expect you to play than to waste your energy trying to change their minds."

"So, you're saying I should be more trusting?"

"Or at least pretend," Flent said with a smile. "Have a little faith. If they give you a reason to doubt their honor, fine, but until then, have faith."

The corners of Amber's mouth quirked, and she looked at her hands.

"And as for your reputation, I doubt a troupe of dancers have the power to erase your years of service, your victories, and all of your medals and honors."

"I don't know, have you seen their backflips?" Amber said.

Flent laughed and tucked a curl up into her headband. "It will be a sight, won't it? Fighting alongside men." She nibbled the corner of her lip and brightened as a thought struck her. "Have you considered the flip side?"

Amber cocked her head. "The flip side? Like, training with flips?"

Flent scrunched her nose playfully. "No! The other side of the coin to this dilemma of yours."

"No?"

"If it does work, if you are able to successfully incorporate men into the military, you will change the face of Frean warfare forever. You'll go down in history. Your name will echo through the halls of time. Young women *and* young men will grow up thinking, 'One day I want to be just like Chivilra Everstar.' You'll inspire generations to come," Flent said excitedly.

Amber felt a blush creep up her neck and cleared her throat. "Well, let's not get too far ahead of ourselves," she said gruffly, but already her mind was buzzing with what Flent had said.

"You're already an inspiration. Think of the lives you'll touch," Flent added in a reverential undertone. Amber looked up sharply to see Flent's eyes on her; their usual green gray appeared almost silver in the dim light of the coach.

Flent rested her hand on Amber's thigh, sending a wave of pin-prick electricity up her leg.

"Flent, I—"

"Dyna, please, at least when it's just the two of us. Flent sounds too formal," Flent said softly.

In the tight confines of the coach, she shifted forward on the bench, parting her knees to fit Amber's between. They were such small movements: a hand lightly resting on her thigh, knees barely brushing hers, but Amber felt each point of contact like a brand.

"You know, you never told me," Flent said.

"Told you what?" Amber's brain struggled to keep up as her gaze flicked to Flent's lips and then hurried away, anywhere else. No, not her eyes.

"If you were ready to break that rule of yours?" Her hand slid an inch further up Amber's leg. "Or maybe even just bend it a little?"

Amber felt the moment speed up. Her heart beat a panicked rhythm in her chest. Flent leaned forward and Amber felt her body respond in kind. Both on the edge of their seats, her legs now brushing Flent's inner thighs, Amber's hands itching to hold her, to catch her waist, to cup her cheek, to draw her close, to . . . "No, Flent," she heard herself say.

Flent raised an eyebrow in disbelief. "No?"

"No." The word rang around the coach like the slamming of a cell door. Amber shifted back in her seat and folded her arms, the heat quickly cooling as she detached herself from Flent's touch. They sat in silence for a time. Amber oscillated, not wanting to say anything that would lead Flent to hope, but not wanting to spell out a complete death to whatever was passing between them.

Flent fidgeted with her headband. "So, Chiv. Everstar, are you hungry? Should we make a quick stop for pastries before heading back?" she said with forced cheer.

As if on cue, Amber's stomach growled loudly. It was almost ten, and as she'd done every day this week, she'd broken her fast earlier than usual to accommodate her training session with the troupe. "I could eat," she admitted. "But I really don't have time. I'm meeting with Chiv. Turner before our attack-force briefing."

Flent frowned. "It'll take five minutes. You need to eat. Hang on." Reaching above Amber's head, Flent slid open the small window to speak to the driver. "Can you make a stop at the Whistling Whisk?"

With the length of Flent's torso now inches from her face, Amber averted her gaze and counted the brass studs keeping the curtain in place above the side window. The smell of jasmine engulfed her and made her head spin. Flent closed the window with a snap. A jolt. The coach lurched as it hit a bumpy patch of road, and Flent tumbled into Amber's lap.

Both froze.

Amber forgot to breathe.

Flent, arms still raised to the small window, lowered them slowly and brushed her fingers along Amber's clavicle. "Whoops," she whispered.

Amber, face aflame, pushed her from her lap. "I mean it, Flent. You can't . . . You need to stop."

Straightening her tunic and sitting back on her side of the coach, Flent glared at her. "Why?" she demanded. "Don't tell me you don't feel something too."

"Of course, I feel something!" Amber exploded. "You've been driving me mad ever since I first laid eyes on you! But I can't! Too much is at stake—I can't risk my career. It's unprofessional, this, what I feel for you. I'm your superior, I can't . . ." With a mind unable to form a complete thought and words unable to shape her meaning, she gestured vaguely and saw her hands were shaking. Quickly she clasped them behind her neck and squeezed her forearms together in front of her heart.

"What's the big deal? No one's around, no one would know. I wouldn't tell anybody."

Taken aback, Amber floundered for a response. "I don't court in secret," she said as she slowly lowered her arms, keeping them crossed in front of her like a shield.

Shock, confusion, hurt, then irritation flashed across Flent's face in rapid succession. "Oh, Everstar," she scoffed, "I'm not asking for love."

Amber narrowed her eyes. "I wouldn't offer you less, Flent," she said softly. The proud sneer that flared on Flent's face vanished as quickly as it had come. "I'm afraid I mistook your intentions, but it's clear now that we want different things," Amber said, suddenly cold.

"Apparently."

"Right. From here on out, I think it best our relationship remains strictly professional."

"Fine."

The coach stopped in front of the Whistling Whisk. Amber slid the window behind her head open and barked, "Ride on."

"I feel like such an idiot," Amber said as she walked with Andromeda in the gardens. On her better days, Andromeda stood over a head taller than her partner, with dark eyes and long ash-blonde hair. Pain and injury had transformed her. Hunched and hobbling, she limped beside Amber. The lines around her eyes were drawn tight, and her hair hung limply over her wounded shoulder.

Andromeda was healing slowly. Her leg still couldn't support much weight and her punctured lung was heavily bandaged. Not surprisingly, their walk consisted of many breaks. Master Epione had gently recommended against their excursion, but Andromeda was determined, so here they were, walking along the stone pathway in front of the infirmary. In one hand, Amber carried a stool for Andromeda to sit on whenever she needed a rest, while Andromeda held tight to Amber's other arm.

"You weren't to know," Andromeda said. Her replies came slower than usual, and she paused to breathe every few words.

"But you did. You knew right away she was trouble. I should have listened to you, save myself this whole embarrassment."

Andromeda chuckled. "Listen to me? Come on, Everstar, things haven't changed that much since I got shot. Besides, you like the chase. She was a challenge. I'm just glad it didn't get out of hand."

Amber set the stool down and helped Andromeda onto it so she could catch her breath. The yard was bright with an autumnal sunshine that offered little warmth. "I just wish this had blown up after we stormed Alethia—sorry—after I *wait to hear how it goes* as my troops storm Alethia. This is the last thing I need on my mind right now."

"Don't tell me you're bitter about sitting this one out?"

"Fine, I won't tell you."

"But you are."

"Just a little."

"You're unbelievable," Andromeda said, not unkindly.

"And I don't bemoan one moment of having the honor of guarding the Queen. It's just, I know she'll be sitting safely behind these palace walls while many risk their lives for her underground. I know I can be helpful down there . . . I wish I could be in two places at once. I'm not going to sleep a minute knowing our women are in those catacombs."

"How's morale?"

"Could be higher. We're trying not to make mountains out of molehills, but it's a fine line to walk. On the one hand, we want to be honest about what the tunnels do to the mind, and on the other, we're now mitigating the spreading superstitions and attercoppe lore. Once they latch onto the imagination—" Amber let out a low whistle. "But it can't be helped. All we can do is prepare them the best we can."

Andromeda nodded, appearing deep in thought. "I wouldn't go back down there," she said softly. "Not if I didn't have to."

Amber shot her a look, remembering the horrors they witnessed in the Alethian prison. She shook her head and attempted humor: "I mean, two arrow wounds seems a bit of an extreme measure to get out of going back there, but no one will say you're not dedicated."

Andromeda managed a tight smile and with Amber's help rose to her feet. "But you have a briefing to get to, and I take an age to walk anywhere."

"Right, let's get you back to bed."

An hour later, Amber was standing before a sea of guards and knights. Her vantage point on the barrack's walls allowed her to see every corner of the courtyard. A glowing pride filled her, from fingertips to toes, to see all these women ready to defend their Queendom. Each face was familiar, each heart was true, each fighter represented a sister.

"You've all been briefed on our mission," she said, her voice ringing out across the yard. "You all know the dangers. Remember, we fight to liberate, not to harm. These men and the Undercourt Griffins are not our enemies. The enemies you will face within the catacombs will be the ones your minds are forced to create. Do not let the darkness in. Do not succumb to shadows. Our mission is noble and true, it is blessed by the Court of Griffins. We will prevail, and in doing so, we will liberate the Griffins and men enslaved in the darkness. Tomorrow, we fight for freedom!"

"For freedom!" Hundreds of voices echoed Amber's call. The sound washed over her and made every particle of her being vibrate. Her gaze swept the sea of determined faces before her, and for a moment, her eyes met Flent's. She felt a jolt of panic somewhere around her navel. Flent shouldn't be down there; she was remaining behind with the rest of the Queensguard. Why was she with the troops headed for Alethia? Had she decided to go after all? Regardless of Amber's opinion on the matter, regardless of their tiff earlier, as the second half of Amber's pair, Flent should have told her. The last cry died, and the troops waited for Amber's next order.

Tearing her eyes from Flent's, she proclaimed, "We leave for Alethia at dawn. May the Alti and Sotera guide our actions." Her hands formed fists and she tapped her crossed upturned wrists twice in salute. The women below all followed suit.

"For freedom! For Queendom! For honor!" she bellowed, punching the air.

"For Frea!" the sea roared back.

10

WINGBEATS, WATERFALLS, AND WOOING

Wind swept coarse fingers through Jacs's plaited hair as Altus Hermes banked to the left and she felt her world tip beneath her. Gripping tightly with her thighs, she whooped to the skies, head thrown back, arms outstretched for a moment before quickly returning to clutch at the feathered neck of the Griffin. Altus Hermes roared, the sound crashing around the plains like thunder, and far below, the army spurred their mounts on with added zeal. *This* was how a Queen led her troops into battle.

The pounding of hooves and the occasional shout met Jacs's ears when Altus Hermes swooped low over the formation. Jacs could see commands spreading through the ranks via hand gestures held high overhead. From above, the women appeared to be working parts of a greater whole. Hoofbeats synchronized, movements fluid, the battalion moved as a cohesive unit. Wagons trailed slightly farther behind, carrying a modest fleet of small, lightweight boats.

Altus Thenya and Riesa soared on either side of Jacs, dipping in and out of her peripheral vision and adding their roars to Altus Hermes's. The plains, covered in the racing mounts of guards and knights alike, were sliced in half by a cerulean river before being swallowed by the dark woods that concealed the Catacombs of Lethe and Alethia. Golden autumn dawn lit the realms, and Jacs knew that if she turned to look behind her, she would see the long shadows of the Lower Realm. Her home. Seated high on the back of Altus Hermes, she felt an ache grip her. She was so far from it, so far from Connor.

The front lines had reached the edge of the woods, their pace slowed as the trees rushed to meet them. Jacs knew those woods, knew they were filled with low-hanging branches and hidden roots. The army would be forced to slow down to pick through the trees, but should arrive at the entrance of Lethe in under an hour.

Miera Jaenheir, Faline Cervah, and Dyna Flent, all guards who had accompanied Jacs into Alethia over two weeks ago, had volunteered to lead the troops through the catacombs and into the underground city. Flent had been the only one who had also been to the Undercourt's chambers, so she was the perfect candidate to head the rescue mission. It had been brave of her to volunteer her services. They all knew the mission was dangerous, and Flent knew better than anyone the perils that lay in wait for the minds that ventured too close to the Griffins.

She was also the perfect candidate to entrust with the crystals. Despite Jacs's misgivings, she had decided this mission was too important not to monitor. So, strapped to Flent's belt beside her dagger and restraining strap were two crystals. A purple and a blue. The blue was wrapped in a dark cloth to shield its light. Flent had registered her name into the crystal, and now Jacs had a way to check in on the mission.

Yes, Flent's offer to volunteer had been invaluable, and the knights of the Queensguard saluted her. To Jacs's surprise, Amber's reaction had been muted, if Jacs was being generous—cold if she was being honest. There had been a hurt in Amber's demeanor that made Jacs think Flent hadn't discussed her departure with her partner first. Odd for a guard's pair to be the last to know of a move like that. Amber had readjusted the remaining Queensguard's pairings to accommodate the loss bitterly. However, it could just be that the knight was worried for Flent's safety. Another reason why arming her with the scry crystals was a good idea.

Wheeling in midair, Altus Hermes stopped at the edge of the forest. Great wings beating the air down, forcing the ground away, it loosed another roar into the dawn. The sound reverberated off Court's Mountain and echoed through the valleys and hills of the Upper Realm. It was the sound of the ancients, of the forces that shaped the world. It was the sound of mountains rising and oceans expanding. The sound of new dawns. She hoped that if Celos could hear it, it stilled the blood in his veins.

In no time at all, the Queen's forces had disappeared into the forest. Jacs directed Altus Hermes to fly slow, sweeping loops above the treetops. How she wished she were joining them. But her mother's advice rang in her ears, and with one last look at the viridian acres beneath her, she gave the command to return. Altus Hermes whirled around and spurred upward, climbing to the clouds' mantle. The other Griffins followed closely behind. Jacs felt as though she could reach up into the cloud layer above her head and drag her hand through the white swirling plumes, leaving a trail like a finger swiped through icing. Her heart lifted. So often these days she found herself teetering on the edge of joy and sorrow. She seized this moment of joy and held fast to its warmth.

All too soon they returned to the palace. Slowing to maneuver around the pillared tower and dropping through the belvedere's oculus, the large circular hole in its ceiling, they touched down in the throne room as the sun rose above the far-reaching mountains. Light spilled through the long narrow windows lining the walls and ceiling of the hall, coating everything in liquid gold.

Jacs dismounted, thanked Altus Hermes, and watched it take off. She knew members of the Court would be circling the entrance to the catacombs in shifts, ready to swoop in and support the outpouring of their Undercourt sisters.

She turned to the tableau awaiting her arrival: Hera, Edith, Adaine, and her guardpair, Amber and Chiv. Michelle Ryder. Hera looked exhausted, Edith looked satisfied, and Amber and Chiv. Ryder looked alert. Adaine took a shy step forward and handed Jacs a single yellow lily. Jacs accepted it gladly and tucked the bloom into the tail of her windswept plait.

"Good morning, all," Jacs said briskly. "The battalion has made it to the forest and will have entered the catacombs by now. We can all send our thoughts and prayers their way and wish them quick success and a hasty return."

"Your Majesty, if I may request a moment of your time?" Hera bustled, her usual calm demeanor shattered, and Jacs noticed dark rings under her eyes. Surprisingly, the sight didn't bring Jacs any pleasure, and she felt the beginnings of guilt burrow its way into her chest.

"Of course, Lord Claustrom. What is it?" she asked respectfully.

"With Edith's help, I've been finalizing the lists of duties of each Councilor and request an audience with the former Councilors to get more information."

"With the former Council of Four?"

"Exactly. I think it would make much more sense to talk to them directly about how they managed to support this Queendom for so many years."

Jacs thought for a moment. She was hesitant to allow Hera alone time with the Four. Who knew what strings they could still pull with the Lord of Hesperida, the Queendom's most affluent county? "You will compile the list of questions you wish to ask, and I will send a trusted scribe to gather a report."

Hera pursed her lips and said slowly, "With all due respect, I believe it will be much more efficient if I simply ask them myself."

"And yet you will work within the limitations I've just given you," Jacs said firmly. "How are you finding your additional duties?"

"There are a lot more of them than I anticipated, Your Majesty."

"Then I am happy to take this interview off your plate."

"Thank you," Hera said through gritted teeth. "When will you appoint more Councilors?"

"Courtierdame Glowra will be elevated to Councilor once she is well. I have told her not to take on too much work while she heals, but I'm sure you would be welcome to meet with her before that"—Jacs stressed her next words—"*if she feels well enough to receive you.*"

Minute relief passed over Hera's features. "Thank you, it will be nice to have another set of hands to help. And the other two?"

"I've not yet decided who I trust enough to fill those roles." She wasn't going to tell Hera yet that she was considering having a citizen from the Lower Realm sit on the Council. A change like that required more planning and deeper contemplation. Instead, she added, "I do recommend you compile a list of individuals you would nominate for the position."

Hera's face fell a fraction before she smoothed her mask in place. "Of course, Your Majesty."

"Any news of your brother?" Jacs asked and was rewarded with a smile.

"Yes, he is on his way, and will be arriving this evening. He is excited to meet you."

Jacs's heart sank. This evening. "Excellent. Anything else to report, Lord Claustrom?"

"No, that's all."

"Wonderful," Jacs said, dismissing the Lord. Nerves ignited in her stomach. She was still not sure how far she could push Hera. A cat will only allow its tail to be pulled so many times before it decides to swipe. Hera splayed her skirts in a shallow bow and departed. Edith shared a wink with Jacs behind her back before obediently following in her wake.

As her footsteps echoed down the corridor, Jacs allowed herself to breathe easier and turned to her guards.

"I have Cyrus watching the scry crystals for Flent so we will receive updates on the mission as they come. Flent also expects us to be checking in every hour so we will be giving reports at the designated times."

Amber and Chiv. Ryder nodded their understanding.

Next, Jacs turned to Adaine, who stood with her hands behind her back. "Did you bring it?" she asked, excitement coloring her words.

"Yes, Your Majesty, and the horses are saddled, per your request," Adaine said softly. From behind her back, she presented a velvet pouch about the size of a large book, with a lumpy shape inside.

"Excellent. We have a mission of our own today, Chivilras. Let's go."

"Where are we going?" Amber asked, momentarily shaking off her somber mood.

"You'll see! Surprises are much more fun."

They followed her at a trot as Jacs's feet hardly touched the floor, and soon all four of them were mounted and spurring their horses out of the stable yard. Peggy, Jacs's horse, had searched her pockets for treats and, finding an apple there, finally allowed her Queen to settle into her saddle. The difference between Griffin and horse was jarring, but Jacs still enjoyed the bumping, jolting feeling of horseback. Somehow it felt more real, whereas every time she rode with the Griffins, it felt like a dream.

The horses could only take them across the expansive lawns of the palace grounds to the edge of the woods. The overgrown forest, with its gnarled roots, patchy brush, and low-hanging branches was much easier to manage on foot. They dismounted near the banks of the river, and followed it away to the right, walking toward the Cliff. Adaine offered to stay behind with the horses, and Jacs could hear her talking to the animals in a low voice as they left.

Amber and Chiv. Ryder refrained from asking more questions and focused on escorting their Queen through the woods. For that Jacs was thankful, as she knew her excitement would make her words come out in a jumbled mess. Far better for them to see it. This had to work.

As they approached the edge of the Cliff, the trees began to thin, and the river widened as it hurtled toward nothingness before tumbling into the void and crashing into the Lower Realm leagues below. A large oak tree clung to the precarious cliff face, gnarled roots stretching away from its trunk and burrowing deep into the earth. Its limbs stretched out into the empty sky as if determined to test the limits of the strength of its hold.

Stopping several meters from the edge, Jacs reverentially opened the velvet bag. Inside was a green wooden boat. She handed the bag to Chiv. Ryder, who accepted it without comment and retreated to guard the perimeter.

"Jacqueline, have you lost your mind?" Amber said finally, when Chiv. Ryder was out of earshot.

Jacs laughed. "No! No, I promise I haven't, or at least I don't think I have. If Cornelius is in the Lower Realm, which I am almost certain he is, he'll be heading to Bridgeport to come back up the Bridge. I just know that if he's heading to Bridgeport, he'll visit my house, he'll check my nets, he'll want to see where his boats ended up. So, I'm going to make sure there's a boat waiting for him."

"Why?" Amber asked hesitantly.

"So I can send him a message!" She turned the boat to show the rectangular wooden hatch set into its hull. Gently, she pried it open to expose the glass vial stoppered with wax containing a tightly curled letter.

A kind, crooked smile spread across Amber's features, and she shook her head.

"What?" Jacs asked.

"Nothing, that's just cute."

Jacs shrugged. "Cute can still command an army."

Standing on the edge of the river, the water disappearing over the dizzying heights off to their right, Jacs sent a silent wish for the little boat to find its maker. She took a breath and lowered it into the rapids. It disappeared for a moment under the water, then popped up and spun around a boulder before sailing to the edge of the waterfall and vanishing over the Cliff. Clasping her hands in front of her, Jacs bounced on the balls of her feet, then motioned for the knights to follow her back to the palace.

It took all of Jacs's newfound queenly restraint not to run and twirl as they crossed the palace grounds. It was all coming together. Sure, she would have to deal with Theo in a few hours, but besides that, they were going to rescue the boys, free the Undercourt, and Connor would return home. She would finally feel like a queen worthy of the crown.

11

CAT DUTY

"It really is beautiful down here," Connor said, looking off to the left of the road across the deep green marshland and shrubbery. His gaze followed the tendril of a vine that had tangled itself in with the delicate strands of a willow tree. "A different green. And everything seems damp."

"Yes, it's just peaches, Your Grace," Dryft teased in his ear; after a week of travel, they continued to share a horse as he still wasn't strong enough to ride long days alone. "Until you find yourself in wet socks for over a month because nothing will dry properly in the rainy seasons."

Connor suppressed a shudder. "You could buy more socks?"

"Then I'd just have more pairs of damp socks. It's not so bad though, the summers are beautiful, and the colors we get down here for autumn are worth the weeks of rain after."

"So, you enjoy living in the Lower Realm?"

"I suppose."

"I never asked, why did you decide to transfer? You used to guard my mother. How does a member of the Queensguard get transferred to a ruined outpost in the Lower Realm?" he asked innocently, but at his words, he felt the length of Dryft's body stiffen behind him.

To his right, Masterchiv Rathbone's eyes snapped to his and she shook her head.

"I apologize, Dryft, that was a personal question. You don't need to answer," he said quickly.

"No, it's all right," Dryft said finally. "I . . . I spoke out of turn. While guarding your mother in a meeting with the Council of Four, they recommended a policy that I didn't agree with, and I spoke out of turn. When I went back to their chambers to apologize, I overheard something I shouldn't have and the next day my papers had been approved for transfer, my things had been packed up, and I was escorted down the Cliff to continue my service in SouthGate."

"I didn't know that," Masterchiv Rathbone said incredulously. "I mean, I knew you were transferred for insolence, but I never knew the whole."

"Yes, well . . . it wasn't something they would have made public."

Connor whistled low. "I'm . . . I'm sorry. That's . . ."

"Not your problem, Your Grace. I've enjoyed my life here. Even if it is different from the life I had imagined for myself."

"What did you overhear?" Connor asked, his curiosity getting the better of his tact.

Dryft hesitated and cast a nervous glance at her commanding officer.

"Speak freely," Masterchiv Rathbone said. "Our allegiance is to the Crown, not the Council."

She huffed a sigh. "It seems so minuscule now. Their idea was to shift our major trade partners, they wanted to eliminate their need for the Lower Realm in favor of expanding trade with Nysa. I voiced my concerns about where that would leave the Lowrians . . . then when I went to apologize for my outburst, I overheard them discussing ways to sever the last Bridge. 'Cut them off entirely' were their words. Thankfully, nothing came of it . But it still cost me my position."

Connor shook his head. "I'm sorry that happened," he said quietly.

Masterchiv Rathbone ran her reins through her fingers in an agitated manner. "Dryft, would you consider returning to the Queensguard?"

"Absolutely," Dryft said without hesitation.

"Right. Well, once we return to the palace, I think that can be an option for you."

"Thank you, Masterchiv," Dryft said stoically, though her voice held a smile, and Connor noticed she remained in a charmingly good mood for the next two hours.

"Lights! I see lights!" Connor called. Dusk had officially settled in, and they had been riding through twilight for far longer than he had imagined possible.

"Excellent spotting, Your Grace," Masterchiv Rathbone said, perking up in her saddle. "We'll be in Bridgeport before night falls. No use starting up the Bridge in the dark, so we'll find somewhere to sleep and head up in the morning."

"I could use a stretch, an ale, and something covered in gravy," Dryft muttered low so only Connor could hear. Her grip tightened more securely around his waist, and she spurred the horse onward. Hooves pounded the dirt road sending clumps of earth spraying behind them. As the galloping rhythm kept pace with Connor's heartbeat, he felt a smile spread across his face. They were close. He would see Jacs soon.

As they approached the outer town wall, Masterchiv Rathbone pulled her horse up short and signaled for Dryft to do the same.

"What is it?" Connor asked, looking around warily.

"If you're wondering where the inn is, it's near the town square. The Stroppy Mule, I think it was called," Dryft said.

"We don't have coin," Masterchiv Rathbone replied.

"I'm the royal advisor. We can send them coin when I'm back at the castle."

Masterchiv Rathbone made a hushing motion with her hands. "It might not be safe. No, I don't like this. I've seen the reports from Bridgeport. I'm not sure they'll take kindly to us, and if they do, there will be a lot of fanfare. We're only here for a night. Let's not ruffle any feathers. I say we camp outside town and make our way up the Bridge at first light."

"Camp? Again? When an inn could offer us beds, warmth, and a hot meal . . . I'm just thinking of my condition. I don't think it would be wise if I were to spend another night in the cold," Connor said and allowed himself to sag wearily in the saddle. He didn't mind playing the patient if it meant a soft mattress.

"I don't like it," Masterchiv Rathbone said stubbornly. "We're camping."

As if to mock her decision, a light mist of rain started to dot their noses and sprinkle their shoulders. It was going to be a long night.

"I have a better idea," Connor said suddenly as a thought struck him. "Why don't we spend the night at Jacqueline's farm? It's a short distance away from town and dry. I'm not sure of the state it'll be in since she and her mother left, but it'll be better than sleeping on the ground."

"Brilliant, Your Grace," Masterchiv Rathbone said approvingly. "Do you know where it is?"

Connor thought for a moment. "Not exactly, but I know where she described it to be in her letters."

Masterchiv Rathbone barely concealed an exhausted sigh. "That's a start. Lead the way."

Connor chalked his quick discovery of Jacs's farm up to his expert navigation skills; however, he did have to acknowledge that there were very few roads to choose from when deciding where to go. He knew that her farm was close to the Cliff, and they really only saw one farm near it. But still, without his knowledge they would be sleeping in the rain, so he lowered himself from his horse's back and looked around the empty farmyard proudly.

"This is it!" he beamed. "Look, there's the apple tree with the stump chairs she told me about. Did you know her dad carved those? And over there is her barn. Apparently she used to milk her cow herself before they had to sell her. And oh! This must be Ranger. Hi, little guy. Look he's even got the crooked tail!" A snaggletoothed gray cat eyed the group warily from just inside the barn door, its cloudy eyes two pinpricks of yellow in the dying light of the day. Connor crouched down, feeling a pop in his knee, and coaxed the cat over. "Here, puss."

Dryft landed lightly behind him and walked over to accept Masterchiv Rathbone's reins. "I'll take care of the horses," she said.

"I'll check out the house," Masterchiv Rathbone said.

"What can I do?" Connor asked, straightening quickly, and stumbling upright as a wave of dizziness swept over him. The two women looked at each other. "See if that cat needs any medical attention," Masterchiv Rathbone said.

Connor folded his arms. "You need to stop babying me. I can help."

Masterchiv Rathbone had the decency to look apologetic. "I know, Your Grace. But you're still recovering and I'm really not comfortable putting a member of the royal family to work. So, you can accept a fake job, or I can find you a place to sit and rest."

"Fine," Connor said. "I'll check on the cat."

"Excellent, that's a great help."

Scratching the back of his neck, he walked to the barn. As he approached, Ranger turned tail and loped farther inside. The gloom made it almost impossible to make out anything more than vague shapes, but Connor spied a lantern hanging on a hook near the door. Locating the nearby flint, he made quick work of lighting it. The flame spluttered to life after his third attempt. Holding the lantern high, he entered the barn.

At least, on the outside it looked like a barn, but the interior had been completely refurbished into a workshop. A long workbench lined one wall, which was decorated with dozens of empty pins and the ripped and torn remains of diagrams and schematics. Fragments of the latter lay strewn about the room and an empty notebook lay open on the workbench.

Sifting through the papers, Connor recognized some of the drawings. It was Jacs's hot-air balloon. But these were not designs for the small letter-carrier balloons he had received for years, these were for a balloon large enough to carry a person. This was where Jacs had built the balloon that had allowed her to visit the Upper Realm. He looked around in wonder.

He had seen the workshops in the castle. Heph's goldsmithing studio was three times this size and he also had areas for woodworking and non-gold metalworking. Jacs had created her hot-air balloon in such a humble space with far fewer resources while evading detection by the authorities.

Connor jumped as something warm and fluffy brushed his leg. Ranger. He bent and picked up the old cat, cradling the purring bundle in his arms as he walked around the room.

"What's all this?" Dryft's voice called from the doorway. She looked around her with eyes that didn't understand, didn't appreciate, her lip curled in distaste.

"Where Queens are forged," Connor said softly. Ranger still purring in his arms, he made his way toward the house.

It was in an even worse state than the barn. Signs of a fight were imprinted in the packed earth floor of the kitchen, and Jacs's room had been pillaged and most definitely slept in by someone else. Her mother's room had been picked through, but with much less purpose. He hesitated in the doorway of Jacs's room before stepping over the threshold. This space felt sacred, as though he needed approval or an invitation before entering.

"So, this is where our Queen grew up?" Dryft said, following him into the room. Connor nodded. "It's not much, is it?" she added, flicking a book over with the toe of her boot. The pages were warped with water damage and the title *Rise of the Fallen* had the words "Upper Dog" scribbled across it in a childish hand.

"It was enough, I guess," Connor mused. "I had such a rosy little picture in my head of this place. From her letters it always sounded quaint and peaceful. But it's still life, isn't it? This was her life. No life is roses all the time."

"And this life looks like it contained cold, wet winter mornings," Dryft said, pointing at the ill-fitting shutters on Jacs's windows.

Connor smiled as he moved closer to inspect them. "Not necessarily," he said, fingering the heavy curtains hanging on either side and crouching to examine the row of metal domes running along the bottom of the window frame and their counterparts spanning the curtain's hem. When snapped in place, the insulated curtains likely did a decent job at keeping the worst of the chill at bay. "She's always been resourceful."

Masterchiv Rathbone's voice cut across his reverie. "House and grounds are clear. Two beds for two sleepers. Dryft, you and I will rotate watch." Connor opened his mouth to protest, but Masterchiv Rathbone pressed on and said firmly, "No, Your Grace. Royalty or not, you're still recovering and need rest if you're going to have strength enough for the Bridge tomorrow."

"Fine."

"How's the cat?" she asked, nodding toward the bundle cozied up in his arms.

"Fit as a fiddle." He grinned.

"Excellent work." She hesitated, wiping the sides of her mouth as she considered her next words. "I've been thinking. Dryft has done an excellent job this past week teaching you the basics in restraining, deflecting, and blocking. Given our current situation, I think it's probably wise you know a few defensive moves should an assailant come for you again."

Connor's grin broadened.

"That's not to say I'm going to lay down all the secrets of being a knight at your feet, but it definitely can't hurt to teach you some of the basics," she hurried to clarify.

"Of course. Thank you, Masterchiv Rathbone."

"Well, no use fluffing about, let's go." With a curt nod, she beckoned for him to follow.

"Now?"

"Of course now."

"Right." He let Ranger drop from his arms onto the bed, caught the wink Dryft threw his way, and hurried after the knight.

"Wider stance, hands here. Good." Masterchiv Rathbone circled him with a critical eye and made minor adjustments where needed.

They were standing in the yard, the darkness and the misting rain falling about their shoulders.

"Now, if an assailant comes from behind like the man in the woods, you have a few options. Your instinct will be to either stay completely still—this is natural, a person with a knife to your throat commands stillness, so that's what you give them. Or to reach up for the knife— also natural, your survival instinct is thinking of nothing more than to get the knife away from your throat. But your assailant will likely be anticipating these moves. Here's what you're going to do. React immediately. Keep your hands nice and close to your body. You want your attacker to have as little warning of your moves as possible, and keeping your hands close means they won't see what you're about to do."

As she spoke, she motioned for Dryft to demonstrate. Dryft, who had been leaning against the house, pushed herself off the wall and obediently stepped behind her commanding officer, wrapping one arm around her neck and aiming a short stick at her throat. Connor watched with rapt attention.

"See, I draw my hands up the midline of my body, but Dryft can't see. So right now, she thinks she's in control of the situation."

Connor nodded.

"Next, a few things need to happen at once, I'm going to reach up with both hands, grab Dryft's knife arm and pull it diagonally down and away from my throat, we don't want to pull it down across my neck because that'll do her work for her, and I'll likely slit my own throat. While this is happening, I also want to pop this shoulder up, keeping her forearm close to my shoulder. Now I have a split second where the knife is away from anything vital. I have control of her forearm, and most important, I have control of her wrist. If you have the wrist, you have the knife. Now watch carefully, because this is the point where she's going to realize she's losing control and will likely start struggling. I'm keeping tight hold of her arm and making sure it stays connected to my shoulder. I'll duck under her arm; this will twist it slightly. And remember, I still have her wrist, still have the knife. And now I can fight back. I have her wrist, her arm is aligned with my shoulder, now I can either squeeze this tendon here which will make her drop the knife, or I can direct her wrist toward her ribs and effectively make her stab herself with her own blade."

She made three short sharp motions with Dryft's wrist, stopping the stick just short of her ribs each time, before releasing the guard with a nod of thanks.

"Amazing," Connor breathed.

"Okay, your turn," Masterchiv Rathbone said, taking the stick-blade from Dryft and coming to stand behind Connor. He had a moment for his mind to catch up with her words before she grappled him from behind.

Hours later, and sporting a few new bruises, Connor lay awake and buzzing in Jacs's bed, Ranger purring under his chin. Despite his aches and his lingering fever fatigue, he felt alive. He felt strong. He couldn't wait for his next lesson.

An hour after first watch had started, he was still tossing and turning before deciding a change of scenery might be more useful. Leaving the cozy cat behind, he slipped his feet into his boots and gathered his blankets around him. After a moment's fumbling, he untangled the blue crystal from his cloak. Using its eerie blue light, he tiptoed his way through the debris of the house. The door creaked slightly as he edged his way outside.

It was a clear night. A gentle breeze played with the hair at the nape of his neck and attempted half-heartedly to lift the hem of his heavy blanket. He padded across the lawn on less than silent feet, scrunching across stones and snapping twigs as he went. Without realizing he'd made up his mind to do so, he made a beeline for Jacs's apple tree. Lowering himself carefully into one of Jacs's father's chairs, he covered the light with his blankets and let the darkness envelop him.

As his eyes adjusted, more and more stars dotted the night's sky. He had expected them to feel farther away than they did from the Upper Realm, but they looked just as distant. There were fewer of them though. The black stripe of the Cliff cut out half of the sky from where he sat. He could just make out Pegasus, the winged horse. The constellation always made him smile. Four bright stars arranged in a wonky rectangle was, of course, the perfect representation of a flying horse. Whoever had penned that one must have had an active imagination.

A flying horse would come in handy now though. He strained his eyes to make out the Bridge in the darkness. While he was excited to go home, excited to see Jacs, he did not relish the idea of climbing it tomorrow.

The last time he had scaled that Cliff his head and heart had been in very different places. The former had been filled with vicious visions of his mother's murder, and the latter had been broken by the knowledge that Jacs's people were to blame. He'd surfaced from the Lower Realm a different man.

With a sigh, he leaned back in the chair and drew the blankets around his shoulders.

"May I join you, Your Grace?" a voice floated on the breeze toward him.

Connor turned to see Dryft approaching from the open kitchen door.

"Of course," he said, gesturing to the nearby chair. The breeze died away, and in the sudden silence he only just heard the soft scrunch of her boots on the gravel of the farmyard. She took the proffered seat gladly and rested her forearms on her knees, clasping her hands in front of her. For a moment she studied her thumbs.

After a week on the road and only the odd bath in the springs and creeks they had encountered along the way, they had arrived at Jacs's farm tired, worn, and grubby. Her home had been a welcome respite, and each of them had been allowed the small luxury of a warm bath. With the dirt stripped from Dryft's face and wet hair combed neatly behind her ears, she looked years younger.

He thought back to the Iliana Dryft he had known as a boy, the smiling and confidant woman with whom he'd been infatuated. A wariness hung around the corners of her eyes now. He wasn't surprised. She'd been exiled from her Queen and family to live in a crumbling ruin within a foreign realm. All for trying to do the right thing. He couldn't imagine how that must have felt.

As if sensing his thoughts, she looked up and met his gaze. In her eyes, amusement danced a shaky waltz with concern.

"How are you feeling?" she asked softly.

12

A NEW BEAU AND AN OLD FLAME

The evening air hung heavily around her. Compressed, as though the night had paused at the height of its inhale and strained to contain it. Jacs stood, palms resting on the balcony, searching the night sky as if the stars held answers in the riddles of their constellations. She rubbed absently at her ear. To say she was nervous would be an understatement. Until now, Theo had been two syllables on the edge of her mind. A sigh of a name, it lingered in her thoughts but never consumed them. Now the name would become a man, a person, someone she was supposed to promise her heart to while knowing it already belonged to another. Someone she was, even now, figuring out a way to evade.

She paced the few steps of the balcony and rubbed her arms though she wasn't cold. Adaine hovered in her periphery, ready to provide anything she might need. But what she needed was a way out. That, Adaine could not provide. Her Queendom had to come first, but her mother was right. A love like Connor's was a rare gift, and one that should be protected, fought for. She continued to pace the cobbles.

A serving boy approached Adaine and whispered in her ear. She nodded once and stepped forward tentatively. "Your Majesty?" she said. "He's here."

Jacs drew herself up and took in a shaky breath. "Okay. Show him to his quarters and let him freshen up. I will meet him in the . . ." She paused; a wise woman optimized her battlefield. "I will meet him in the conservatory. Light the candles and set out a table and chairs. Wine, two glasses. He will be tired after his journey. Lord Claustrom's presence is not required, if she protests, say that I insisted on an evening alone with her brother."

The serving boy bowed and scurried to obey his Queen. She bit the inside of her cheek. "Adaine," she said, "I'll need my crown, the smaller one with the sapphires."

"Yes, Your Majesty."

Theo was already waiting for her when she swept into the conservatory. The room was dotted with small candles that flickered prettily through the leaves and petals of the surrounding plants. A gentle trickling from the water feature on the north wall caressed her ears as the sweet scent of the flowers tickled her nose.

Her first impression was that he was a boy, about her age, made up of angles. Elbows and knees jointed long limbs that he did not seem to know what to do with. His eyes didn't lift from the floor for very long, but when they did, Jacs saw they were kind. Where Hera was a force of golden curls and spite, Theo was an apologetic wisp. His unusually white-blond hair fell into his pale, almost gray eyes, and his short thin nose was dotted with freckles. As she entered, he hurried to rise, dislodged his wineglass, and fumbled to catch it just before it toppled over.

"Good evening, Lordson Claustrom," Jacs said sweetly, purposefully ignoring his clumsiness and inclining her head toward him as he bowed respectfully.

"Good evening, Your Majesty," he replied. His voice was gentle. She beckoned him to sit, and Adaine smoothly pulled a chair out for her to join him.

"You made good time; I trust your journey went smoothly?"

"It did, thank you."

"And how are your quarters?"

"Excellent."

"Wonderful." She beamed.

He managed a weak smile in reply and took a sip of his wine. Jacs noticed his hands shook slightly and recognized a familiar pattern of calluses on his fingertips.

"Do you play the fiddle?" she asked suddenly, breaking the silence that threatened to form a crust on their evening.

Theo looked up quickly. "Y-yes, well, the violin," he stammered. "How did you know that?"

"Your fingers, those calluses are a violinist's badge of honor. How long have you been playing?"

"Since I was seven."

Jacs held her tongue and waited for him to continue. He fidgeted with a ring on his finger. Jacs's ring. A gold band studded with sapphires. A token that represented her promise to him, and a symbol of the deal she'd made with Hera. A knot formed in her stomach. Her eyes flicked back to his when he finally added, "I've always loved the way it sounds like it's singing. It's got a voice; it just needs someone's help to use it."

"It's a beautiful instrument," Jacs said.

"Do you play?"

"I do, though not well. I don't hold a candle to my father—he played as though it were breathing—but I used to perform in the village fair and no one plugged their ears." She laughed. "It's been a while since I've played though." She held up her hand to show a few smooth, and a couple peeling, fingertips. "I'll have to earn mine back."

Theo reached across the chasm between them and held her fingers lightly in his hand, passing a thumb across their tips. "They'll come back quicker than you think. With practice," he said, then his eyes widened as though he had just realized what he'd done, and he dropped her hand, pulling his away sharply.

His cheeks flushed red, and he ducked his head. "You mentioned your father plays," he said quickly. "Do you two ever play duets?"

Jacs considered her words, not wanting to torture the poor boy unnecessarily. "We did. I started learning when I was five. My fingers were so small on the strings, but he took such care showing me where to place them and how to tune it. Dad always used to tease me and say I'd tune it a half tone higher than his ear liked. Said we were on different frequencies." She smiled fondly at the memory, then the upturn of her lips wavered. "He passed away when I was eight."

"Oh . . . oh, I'm sorry, I should have known."

"It's okay. I was lucky enough to have eight years of his melodies. Do you have a duet partner?"

"No. No one in my family plays. My father tried, he thought it would be something we could bond over . . . but he is not a patient man, and he ended up throwing the violin in the fire in frustration. Luckily, he had his own. It was still sad to see such a beautiful instrument destroyed though." He added the last part as though to himself.

"Well," Jacs said kindly, "we'll have to play a duet together sometime."

"I would like that, Your Majesty."

They each sipped their wine. Jacs studied him thoughtfully over the rim of her glass. He was so unlike his sister. "What else is it you like to do?"

As though prepared for this question, Theo launched into a businesslike recitation of his accomplishments and hobbies. Jacs had the vague feeling that she was interviewing him for a prospective job.

". . . and above all I love to read. I have a lot of time for it and the library in the Claustrom estate is enormous. I prefer reading to learn new things and tend to move through topics as my interest finds them. I know it may sound dull, but at the moment I'm learning about county law, and you would be surprised the discrepancies and loopholes that exist between individual counties and the capital. In fact, there is a particular oversight that I think you would be interested in, as it is costing the Crown a significant amount every year but"—he paused to draw breath—"that may be a conversation for another time, as it is quite dry. My studies have taken me down the rabbit hole all the way to when the first laws were established from the treaty between Court and Crown. I don't know why, but I always considered that document more of a myth or legend than a tangible thing. But you can still read it. Obviously, I've only read a copy of the original. Did you know two treaties were drawn up? It's true. One copy is preserved within Court's Mountain. The other one is somewhere in the Royal Archives, which would be an absolute dream to see.

"I feel like I've been nattering on too much. May I ask you a question?" he blurted out, bringing his rapid speech to a close with sudden apprehension.

"Of course."

"What am I doing here?" Jacs raised her eyebrows in surprise, and he hurried to add, "Not that I'm not grateful for the invitation, or–or humbled to be here. I just wondered. Hera mentioned you invited me explicitly, and I'm even wearing your ring." His gaze darted to the sapphires dotting his finger and he frowned. "But given what I know about your relationship with your royal advisor, I just wondered what it is I'm doing here."

Jacs felt a seed of hope bury itself in her chest. "Well," she said, considering her words carefully. "While I have an amicable relationship with my royal advisor, the time is fast approaching for me to choose someone to rule by my side. Someone who knows the Upperite ways, someone I can trust to be the voice for the Upperite people in the same way I am able to be a voice for the Lowrians." She paused delicately, and swept his hand into hers. The movement caused candlelight to dance across the surface of the ring and ignite the facets of the gems. "Your sister has expressed an interest that we get to know one another."

Theo flashed her a knowing look. "I see."

"And I *would* be interested in getting to know you better."

"A-as would I."

"You must know of my intention," she said carefully, indicating his ring, "and I feel it's important to get to know one another before I make you any lasting promises. Could I interest you in a walk in the gardens tomorrow morning, Lordson Claustrom? Among many things, I would like to hear more about this loophole you mentioned."

"I would be honored."

"Then I will meet you by the herb garden after you've broken your fast." She stood and he hurried to do the same. "Good night."

"Good night, Your Majesty," he said softly.

There, she thought as she walked briskly back to her rooms, *Hera can't be disappointed with that.* Although Jacs couldn't deny that she had enjoyed their somewhat stilted conversation more than she thought she would. To see him light up talking about treaties was endearing.

He's just not Connor, a voice whispered from her heart.

With Connor on her mind, she hurried to sit before the small basin set up below the mirror on her vanity. She checked the clock on her mantel: she was late to hear Flent's scheduled report. Before allowing herself to call Connor's voice forth, she cupped her hands around the bowl and said Flent's name into the mirror and basin. The mirror fogged over, and a mess of purple outlines filled its frame. From the looks of things, the army was slowly picking its way through the labyrinth of the catacombs.

Flent's whispers crept from the basin and Jacs was able to hear the second half of her report. ". . . slow progress, not yet at the lake. The boats we've brought with us are difficult to maneuver through some areas, and we've decided to break them down and rebuild them on the banks. It's taken much longer than anticipated, but without another way across the lake, Command agreed it was the best way. Will check in again in an hour."

Labored breathing replaced her report, and Jacs watched a moment longer as the outlines of women contorted themselves around the rocks and crags of their surroundings.

A delay, but an understandable one. Jacs tried not to worry as she made a quick note relaying Flent's message on a sheet of parchment and handed it to Adaine. "Send this to Chiv. Everstar," she said. It was unlikely Amber missed the report, but they had agreed to send transcripts of any updates they received. If Amber had seen it, Jacs expected to receive her own copy momentarily. Hopefully it would include the information she had missed.

She heard Adaine close the door behind her and took a breath to steady herself. She knew it was late, knew he was likely already asleep, but she had to hear him.

"Cornelius Frean," she said into the mirror. Its surface fogged over and remained opaque, but the basin began to leak his voice.

"I'm feeling much better, just couldn't sleep." Jacs's heart fluttered in her chest. It was him. He was okay. She was saved from wondering whether she would be able to hear the voices of those around him again when she heard a much quieter woman's voice say, "You did well today. It's nice to see some color in your cheeks too."

"Thank you for all your help, and for being my minder this past week. If it weren't for your support, I'd have fallen off that horse leagues ago."

"It was my pleasure." Jacs couldn't place her voice. It wasn't Masterchiv Rathbone, so who was he talking to?

"I still can't believe what happened. With the transfer. That wasn't right, and I'm glad that Masterchiv Rathbone seems to be of the same mind enough to get you reinstated when we return."

"If I can keep you safe until then," the woman chuckled.

Connor returned the laugh. "I promise I'll make it easy for you."

"Off to a great start, sneaking out at night to sit under an old tree. It's just lucky you have the footfalls of a bear, or I wouldn't have noticed."

"Maybe that could be our next lesson, how to walk stealthily. You'd be a good teacher for that, I didn't even hear you coming," he said, and Jacs was relieved to hear he sounded happy, his voice light and playful.

"It seems you have a lot you want to learn."

"I always wanted to be a knight. Since you two are willing, it would be a wasted opportunity to not learn what I can while I have the chance."

"You always wanted to be a knight?"

"I know it sounds silly. It's not a job for men, but who knows? Jacqueline is already making changes to what we consider normal. It might not be so far-fetched a notion in the future."

"She certainly knows how to rock the boat. She reminds me a lot of your mother. Queen Ariel had a mind for change. She was always butting heads with the Council over it. Those meetings were often as intense as an hour on the battlefield."

"Really? What kinds of things did they disagree on?"

There was a pause. "I think the major one was the Bridges. Queen Ariel wanted to rebuild the other four and encourage travel between the realms. The Council had every excuse under the sun why it wouldn't work, and sometimes the Queen would leave in a rage or in tears. The meetings were hard to watch but your mother was tough, she stood her ground. I had so much respect for her. Still do." Her words faded into thoughtful silence.

A flurry of questions assaulted Jacs's mind. She hadn't known Queen Ariel wanted to rebuild the Bridges, hadn't known she had been trying to unite the realms. Was this why the Council got rid of her? Connor still didn't know the Council had been behind her murder. How would he react when he found out? Was it better that he didn't know?

She spun around at the sound of her door opening. Adaine slipped into the room, a letter—likely from Amber—in her hands. Seeing Jacs was listening intently, she placed it quietly on a side table and ducked back out.

When Connor next spoke, his voice was thick with emotion. "She . . ." He cleared his throat and tried again. "She was one of the best of us. Those hooded brutes will pay . . ."

"I wish I had been there to help, to protect her, or to at least try," the woman said.

"I was. I couldn't save her. I should have done something."

"It wasn't your fault."

"But I was right there, two paces behind her at most. I saw the hoods halt the parade. If I had known—"

"There's no way you could have known, Your Grace. That kind of thinking is only going to lead to more pain. Your mother wouldn't have wanted that. She loved you so much."

Connor said shakily, "I just . . . I miss her." Those three words sent an ache through Jacs's heart. She wished he wasn't so far away.

"She would be proud of you."

"Thank you, Dryft. It means a lot, especially coming from you," he said softly, and Jacs felt a pang of recognition at the name. Dryft.

Iliana Dryft? Connor had written about her in his early letters. She'd been part of the Queensguard for a while, and he had been enamored with her. A sticky uneasiness settled in her chest, and she suddenly felt dirty, like a voyeur. He didn't know she was listening in on his private conversation. It was wrong. It felt all wrong. She hesitated about breaking the connection, torn between a desire to hear his voice, curiosity about the direction of their conversation, and her newfound discomfort.

"From me, Your Grace?"

"Of course. I admired you so much growing up. I could barely string two words together around you." He laughed awkwardly, and Jacs could almost picture him scratching the back of his neck.

"I remember," Dryft said kindly. "You were a cute kid. Wore your emotions for the world to see, and I don't think I ever looked at you without your face turning brick red." Connor groaned and Dryft hurried to add, "It was sweet! I was flattered. And it's lovely to see you haven't changed."

"What do you mean?"

"You still wear your emotions for the world to see. The way you light up talking about our new Queen . . . she must be some kind of special."

"She really is," Connor said. All embarrassment had vanished from his voice.

Despite Jacs's desire to keep listening, this conversation was not intended for her ears, and she reluctantly broke the connection. Silence settled around her room once more. He had sounded so close. If she'd closed her eyes, she could have imagined he was beside her. What she would give just to sit with him again. Instead, she'd spent the evening sitting with Theo, promising him a courtship. Planning a silly little walk in the gardens. Saying things like *I would be interested in getting to know you better* and acting like she meant it.

What was worse: she might have meant it.

Meanwhile, the man who had her heart was apparently risking his health riding across the Lower Realm to reach her, singing her praises all the while, as if she were some kind of saint. Shame's mantle hung heavily from her shoulders, and she buried her face in her hands.

Spirits low, she rose from her table, changed, and climbed into bed. She'd placed her candle at her bedside, unwilling to plunge the room into total darkness. It was going to be okay. Once he knew the situation, he would understand. She had to hope he got her message, had to hope she could speak with him tomorrow morning before he returned. That she could speak with him before he heard it from someone else. She would explain everything. Theo was a means to an end until she could figure out a better ending, but Connor needed to hear it from her.

Outside, the stars glittered atop night's dark canopy. Jacs's little candle flickered in hopeful imitation. All was quiet, all was still, but her racing heart and flurried thoughts kept slumber's soft embrace at bay. Morning was slow to come.

13

A SMALL WORD OR THREE

The predawn darkness lingered in the Lower Realm as it had the last several days. Connor, accustomed as he was to waking up with the early sunrises of the Upper Realm, still couldn't get used to how the shadows lingered over the Lower Realm mornings. It was still very early, but his excitement prodded him awake and he hurried to pull his boots on.

Thinking about his conversation last night with Dryft, he endeavored to walk more quietly through the farmhouse, but he hadn't made it more than three steps before Dryft's face appeared around the kitchen door from where she'd been sitting on last watch. She arched one eyebrow and waited for an explanation.

"I want to see the waterfall before we go," he said simply.

"I'll come with you, let me tell Masterchiv Rathbone fir—"

"Tell me what?" Masterchiv Rathbone said crisply from the doorway of Jacs's mother's room. From the looks of her, she had been up and alert for hours.

"I want to see the waterfall before we go," Connor repeated.

The knight exchanged a look with Dryft and nodded.

"Lead the way."

Dew stained the bottoms of their boots, and a light mist hung low along the ground as the small group walked toward the waterfall. The sound of roaring grew louder and louder and matched the excitement building in Connor's chest. He hoped Jacs's nets and traps were still there. After all these years, he would finally get to see where his boats ended up. Where it all began.

As they neared the Cliff, Connor noticed the narrow chimney-like groove traveling its face three quarters of the way up before it petered out. That was probably where she launched her balloons. She'd mentioned how the little natural chimney had increased the balloons' success rates. Craning his neck, he saw the edge of the giant oak at the top, its roots reaching out into the void. That would be where they got caught. So many things had to go right for their setup to work, it was a wonder he'd received any letters at all.

In no time they had arrived at the waterfall. Dryft shielded her eyes as she looked it up and down, releasing a low whistle.

"Cliff looks taller here than at SouthGate," she marveled.

Connor hurried to the shoreline and began searching the banks of the river.

"What are you looking for?" Masterchiv Rathbone called.

"A net!" he replied, eyes scanning the various outcroppings of rocks. He saw where Jacs had built up the river rocks to span half the distance between the banks, not damming the river but restricting its course. Just below the surface of the water in between the Jacs-made wall and the bank was a strand of woven flax. That must be it. He stood with his hands on his hips, a proud grin splitting his face. He felt as though he had completed a pilgrimage.

"What's that?" Dryft's voice came from behind him.

"A net. Jacs built it to catch the boats I'd send down. She must have built the wall so that she didn't have to make as big of a net—"

"No, not that—*that*," she interrupted, pointing. Connor followed her finger to where a glinting green object bobbed in an eddy on the far side of the river. He squinted but couldn't make it out.

"Not sure. Bit of driftwood?"

"But it's green."

"Mossy driftwood?"

"We should get moving if we want to make it up the Bridge before noon." Masterchiv Rathbone cut across their inquiries. Connor nodded, his gaze returning to the wall and the net Jacs had crafted, lingering a moment longer. The driftwood rolled and caught his eye. Its rounded base disappeared to reveal a more detailed top.

A mast, he thought. Then almost shouted, "It's a boat! Wait, we have to get it." He made a dive for the river, but a strong arm caught him roughly around the middle.

"I swear on my sword, traveling with a fever, training every evening, wandering off on your own, jumping in rivers when you're still not well. You must have a death wish. Dryft, go get the boat," Masterchiv Rathbone chided.

The short time it took Dryft to walk up to the waterfall, squeeze her way behind it, walk down the opposite bank, and retrieve the vessel stretched out like an eternity. Connor did his best to keep from fidgeting, and he noticed Masterchiv Rathbone observing him from the corner of her eye and suppressing a smile more than once. Finally, it was in his hands.

"Is it one of yours?"

"Yes, I sent one down just before the Contest, though I swear that one was red." He turned the boat over in his hands and pried open the little hatch. Both knight and guard peered over his shoulder, curiosity getting the better of them.

A glass vial with a letter inside fell into his palm. He handed the boat to Masterchiv Rathbone, broke the wax seal, and unfurled the note. His heart leaped into his throat to see Jacs's writing covering the page.

"I don't believe it," he breathed.

"What?" asked Dryft.

"It's from her, it's from Jacqueline."

"From the Queen?"

"How did she know you would be here?" Masterchiv Rathbone added.

Connor's eyes flew across the page as he read:

Dear Connor,

I am hoping against hope you find this letter and that it does not fall into the wrong hands. You told me once that your mother made the most wonderful treasure maps. We must speak.

I am forever,
Yours.

The rest of the page was blank. Connor turned the letter over, hunting for more. It was the most cryptic letter he'd received from her, but he knew immediately how to decipher it. He looked from Masterchiv Rathbone to Dryft.

"I need to get back to the house."

"What for?"

"You'll see," he replied, already quickening his pace toward the little farm. He cursed his still-weary muscles, his weakened lungs, and felt them burn as he urged himself onward. Bursting through the kitchen door, fingers fumbling with excited urgency, he lit a lantern.

"Your Grace ￼" Dryft began, but he waved a silencing hand at her.

Carefully, almost afraid that he was wrong, he held the parchment near the flickering flame. For a moment, nothing happened. Then, as the tiny fire's warmth reached its hesitant fingers toward the paper, words blossomed across its surface like ink dropped into water. Connor could have laughed with relief. The rest of the letter read:

This information is extremely sensitive. Tell no one, as the implications are monstrous. There are different types of scry crystals, all seem to operate within the same connection, but the blue ones absorb sound. You must have a blue crystal because when I say your name into an empty bowl, I can hear your voice! You can't imagine how relieved I was to hear you were okay, and I can't wait to see you again. You will be able to hear mine too, use the name Jacs Frean and say it while holding an empty bowl. Have a mirror nearby and you will be able to see me. It will be like I'm in the room with you. We must speak, I will be checking in every hour on the hour and as often as I can on the half hours.

Yours always,
Jacs

Connor's gaze darted around the room, hunting for a clock. "Does anyone know the time?" he demanded to the bewildered women hovering in the doorway.

He spotted an overturned bowl under the kitchen table and grabbed it, then disappeared into Jacs's bedroom as Dryft called behind him, "Just past seven o'clock."

He swiped the handheld looking glass from Jacs's bench, dug the blue crystal out of the folds of his cloak, and now clutching his odd assortment of items, he arranged himself on her bed and took a breath. "Jacs Frean," he said into the bowl. His fingers pressed into its edges tightly. Stiff knuckles popped out white and were tinged blue in the light of the glowing crystal. His eyes were fixed on his own reflection in the small mirror.

The surface of the mirror fogged over, his reflection swallowed by the eerie smoke, and was replaced with—

"Jacs!" he cried as her worried features came into focus. She looked well but exhausted. Dark rings stained shadows beneath her eyes, and a strand of hair hung limply in front of her left ear from where she had been twisting it.

"Connor?" she breathed. "Connor, is that you? Can you hear me?" In Connor's mirror, her reflection sat, hunched in a chair, with eyes fixed on a small bowl held between her palms.

"Yes! Yes, I can hear you."

Relief washed over her face, making her glow. A sparkle returned to her green eyes, and Connor reflexively reached forward to cup her cheek in his palm.

To see her. To see her safe. It was all he had needed.

"By the Goddess, you are beautiful," he said, making her laugh.

"I wish I could see you!"

"No, you don't, I haven't had a proper wash in weeks, and I've been on horseback and sleeping in forests. I'm just glad there isn't a green crystal that sends smells."

She wrinkled her nose playfully and asked, "Are you well? Are you safe? What happened in the catacombs?"

He wasted very little time sharing with her his adventures, and even though he downplayed the severity of his fever, he couldn't prevent her brow from furrowing with worry. He hurried to change the subject, "But enough of me—I'll be up the Bridge by this afternoon. How are you?"

Jacs bit her lip, and he felt his smile slip.

"Jacs, what is it?" he asked.

"Connor, so much has happened since we were separated. I need you here. The Council of Four admitted to treason and are locked away. I've sent a rescue battalion into Alethia to liberate the boys and the Undercourt and we're still waiting to hear how they've fared. Last I checked, they had managed to make it to the lake. They're constructing boats on the shore, so it shouldn't be long now. But . . ." Here she hesitated, and Connor saw something that looked like shame seep into her expression. She took a breath and Connor realized he had been holding his. "Connor, I don't want you to be caught unaware when you arrive, but Lordson Theo Claustrom is here too."

"Hera's brother?" Connor asked, bewildered. Jacs had sped through her accomplishments so quickly, and he took a moment to process what she'd said. "The Council of Four were found guilty of treason? They're locked away?"

Jacs nodded, "I can explain more when I see you, but they confessed to working with the hoods and were behind the ambush at the gala." Here Jacs appeared to hesitate. She opened her mouth as if to say more but closed it again with a snap.

Connor reeled. These women had helped raise him. They were the pillars of the Queendom. To think they'd been behind the ambush, that they'd work with the hoods to eliminate Jacs. Unbidden, the image of a hooded figure at the base of a clocktower rose in his mind. The sound of a bowstring being drawn and released filled his ears.

"Hera's brother is here." Jacs said firmly. Interrupting his line of thought, she pulled him back to the present. With the *creak, twang, thud* still ringing in his ears, he ignored the tightness in his chest and followed her lead. "Theo? Sweet kid. I've met him several times. What's he there for?"

Jacs's lips disappeared into a thin line and a twisted coil of confusion and dread wrapped itself around Connor's middle.

"Jacs, what is it?"

"In exchange for Hera's support and allegiance, in order to gain the power I needed to overthrow the Council of Four, I've promised to make Theo King."

A new sound entered his mind: the deafening roar of a waterfall. Its discordant rushing, crashing, numbing thunder swept away his thoughts.

"Connor?"

"Jacs . . . I . . ."

"But I won't let it happen. I can't let it happen."

"Why are you telling me this?"

"Because I need you to understand. When you return there are any number of people who may speak with you first. I don't want you to find out from any gossip flying around the palace before I see you. I need you to know I'm working on finding an alternative. I did what I had to do to dethrone the Council."

"That's considerate."

"Obviously Theo means nothing to me. You—"

He cleared his throat. "Theo Claustrom is a good man." His insides had grown cold. He had only been gone a few weeks.

"It wouldn't matter if he were the best man."

"Jacs, I don't know what you want from me."

"I want you to understand. I didn't have a choice."

"The Queendom comes first. I understand that," he said. His voice was alarmingly calm. He needed it to remain calm. The roaring of the waterfall in his mind grew louder, threatening to consume him. She had replaced him so easily. "I just . . . this—" How do you shape a heart with words? She was there, in front of him, and so far away. "I thought we . . ." But he couldn't say it. As her royal advisor, he couldn't deny she had acted with the Queendom's well-being in the forefront of her mind. His feelings belonged to Connor, not Cornelius. He needed to be Cornelius for her, for the realms. He knew all this, but something else lurked in his heart.

"Connor, I won't let it happen. It's not even an issue, I just didn't want you to hear about it and think that it was."

Jealousy's gnarled fingers wrapped around his throat and seized his voice. "I just need a . . . I mean, for weeks I've thought of nothing but getting back to you. I didn't imagine that in the meantime you'd be making arrangements to move on," he heard himself say.

He hated the words as soon as they left his lips. Hated the anguish they ignited in Jacs's face.

Hated himself for creating them.

"Connor, don't," she said softly, pleadingly.

"It's fine, Your Majesty. I'm fine. It's like you said, you did what you had to do."

Anger and hurt flared in her eyes. "I get it. It's not ideal. But I will find an alternative."

"What does this mean when I return? I expect he's staying at the palace?"

"Yes."

"Are you two courting?"

"N-No!"

"Not yet, then?"

"Connor, stop it. I told you; I won't let it happen."

"But it might."

"It won't. And if it does, it'll be a facade, nothing more, until I can figure something else out. If you think otherwise, then you have zero faith in my ability to think my way out. Aren't I the Queen your tasks chose? Someone who could keep calm and work her way through any problem, no matter the situation? You sent us into those caves to prove it! I'll prove it again. This is a more complicated problem, yes, but I have a crown on my head that says I will find a solution." She finished her speech with cheeks flushed and a fire flashing in her eyes. Shame crept up Connor's spine and uncurled jealousy's fingers from his throat, banishing the horrid beast.

"You're right," Connor said softly. "It's just a lot to take in."

"I know, which is why I couldn't bear if you heard the wrong thing from someone else."

"Jacs, I don't want to lose you."

"You won't."

"Especially to Theo Claustrom," Connor muttered. "We've had a lot worse things separating us in the past, I can't lose you to a Lordson."

"I promise. I'm yours, Connor. Always have been," she said simply, a sad smile lingering around her lips.

"And I'm yours, Jacs. Regardless of what that looks like." A vision flashed in his mind's eye of Jacs placing a golden crown on the white-blond head of Theo, and he hurried to shove it aside.

They were both quiet for a time. Jacs stared into the depths of the small bowl, fingers white where they gripped its edges. Deep worry lines creased her forehead, and Connor was struck again with how worn she looked. He longed to hold her.

"Jacs," he began, tentative now.

"Connor, I love you," she said softly. Despite her worry, a small smile lifted the corner of her mouth. "I *love* you," she said, louder, firmer. "I was so scared to say it before, but I do. I love you." Like a ripple from a stone cast into a still pond, her smile spread across her face and passed through the space between them to alight on Connor's. "I love you!" she laughed. "I love you, and I miss you, so hurry up and be here with me. We'll figure this all out together. Connor?"

"I love you too." The words burst from his heart like a firework, like an—

The sound of an explosion ripped through the little bowl at the same time a deafening *Crack!* echoed through the basin of the Lower Realm. The earth shook violently beneath him, and Connor saw Jacs disappear from view as someone threw themself at her, forcing her down as a bookshelf crashed around her.

"JACS!" he roared.

"Take cover!" Masterchiv Rathbone said as she burst into the room and dragged him bodily from the bed, shoving him beneath it as objects were thrown from shelves and tabletops. Dust and thatch showered down on her shoulders, and she lay with her arms over her head, using the side of the bed for cover.

"What's happening?" he asked. The small mirror had flown from his hands and lay just beyond reach, reflecting the trembling ceiling.

"Earthquake," Masterchiv Rathbone growled. "Stay down, Your Grace."

He remained beneath the bed for what felt like an eternity; every fiber of his being screamed at him to run, every muscle tensed. An earthquake that had rocked the Upper Realm too? He heard another explosion and a series of deep, echoing crashes in the distance. They fell like blows upon the earth and Connor felt each vibrate violently along the length of his body as they rocked the Lower Realm. The distant hollow booms set his teeth on edge and smothered everything, drowning out the small din coming from the house as pots and plates fell from shelves, dancing to the rhythm of the ricochet. He clenched his fists, feeling the grit compress as he squeezed handfuls of the earthen floor into his palms.

A third explosion and a distant crash sent another shockwave through the earth. As suddenly as they started, they stopped. A silence fell around his ears that scared him more than the explosions.

"Is everyone all right?" Masterchiv Rathbone asked.

"Fine!" Dryft called from the next room. "Ankle's bruised, but nothing broken."

"Your Grace?" Masterchiv Rathbone said softly, searching his eyes.

"Fine," he replied, crawling out from under the bed and retrieving the mirror. "Jacs Frean," he said desperately. The mirror's surface fogged over.

14

AFTERSHOCK

"J ACS!" Connor's scream echoed in Jacs's ears as the bowl clattered to the floor, knocked out of her hands by the force of her quick-thinking knight. Where she had been sitting a moment before was now a mess of books and splintered wood. Amber lay across Jacs, arms shielding her head as her study dissolved into entropy around them. So many beautiful possessions transformed into a precious broken mess.

An earthquake—it must have been, the world shaken out violently like line-drying linen in a gale.

Then silence. The falling jagged snowflakes of dust and debris settled over them and Jacs allowed the world to take a breath before venturing to look around.

"Are you all right?" Amber asked as Jacs shifted beneath her.

"Fine, I think." She drew in a sharp breath as movement sparked a flash of pain down her side.

"What is it?"

"My ribs." Jacs pushed herself to sitting and tentatively touched the sore spot on her left side. It was tender but didn't feel bad enough to be broken. "I'm fine."

Amber cast a worried look over her and wordlessly instructed Jacs to lift her arms, confirming that her side was not badly bruised and checking her over for any other wounds.

"Sure you are," she said sarcastically. "No, sit *still*," Amber scolded as Jacs made to retrieve the bowl. "Stay there, I'll get it." She rose with a groan. "I'm fine, just fell awkwardly on my elbow," Amber assured her.

As Jacs accepted the bowl, she noticed a missing presence. "Adaine?" Jacs called, gaze searching the room. Before the blast, her valet had been standing on the far side of the study near the window, likely in an attempt to give Jacs the semblance of privacy while she spoke with Connor. But the window was now a gaping, splintered hole. Jacs set the bowl down. "Amber, where's Adaine?"

"Adaine?" Amber called. No one answered.

Amber sifted through the rubble with more and more urgency. Books, fragments of shelving, and broken sculptures littered the room.

"Adaine!" she repeated, desperation cracking her voice. Jacs scrambled to her feet and, clutching her ribs, looked around wildly for her valet. "Adaine, please!" she cried.

It was as though her cry broke a barrier and suddenly, she became aware of the screaming. Her palace, full of people, full of lives, full of screams.

"ADAINE!" she pleaded with the room, fingers ripping into the fallen wood and stone.

A sound like a mewing kitten came from near the windows.

"Over here!" Amber called.

Jacs stumbled toward where the knight was clawing through the remnants of a mosaiced sculpture and fallen crossbeam.

"No," Jacs whispered. Blonde hair streaked through with white dust and a rust-colored wetness lay limply amongst the rubble. A hand, perfectly curled at rest, poked through. With every stone Amber flung from her, she revealed more of Adaine's broken and bleeding form. "No, Adaine, say something, please," Jacs begged, frozen in place.

"It's . . . I just . . . can't feel my—" Adaine said, breaking off with a weak cough. Her eyes fluttered closed.

"Jacqueline, stay back," Amber said. Adaine's finger twitched, dislodging a small stone.

The door burst open, and four knights flooded the room. "Thank Sotera you're okay, Your Majesty," Chivilra Fayworth said upon seeing her standing. The thick smattering of freckles that normally covered her nose and cheeks were obscured by streaks of soot. "It's chaos in the palace, many people injured, and if I were to make a guess, a few dea—"

"I need a stretcher for Adaine. Immediately," Jacs snapped, terror and confusion sharpening anger's blade. "Organize the guards. Check the infirmary, rally Master Epione and her apprentices, all beds within the palace are to be given over to the injured. I need a report on my mother's well-being. Guardpairs are to be deployed in search parties immediately. Sift through the rubble. Find everyone."

"Understood," the knights said together and dispersed to obey.

Jacs edged closer to where Amber was muttering, "You're okay. We're here."

With a shuddering breath, she allowed her gaze to find Adaine's face. The valet's eyes fluttered open again, unfocused and searching, then blinked closed. Covered in broken glass and dust, she lay very still. Amber had cleared away the larger pieces of debris but continued to dig her body out of the rubble's embrace. The more she exposed, the worse the reality of the situation became.

Adaine's arms were streaked with blood, and one leg lay at an unnatural angle.

"Jacqueline, she's breathing. It's faint but there. Definite internal bleeding, open fracture of the leg, no obvious signs of head trauma, you can see h . . . never mind." Amber had caught sight of the look on Jacs's face and broke off, shifting to check Adaine's pulse. "Weak pulse, likely going into shock," she muttered, more to herself now. She seemed hesitant to move or jostle her.

Jacs fell to her knees. Her scratched and bleeding fingers met Adaine's wrist, replacing Amber's. Was that her own pulse or Adaine's? No, there it was. It was very faint, a trembling glimmer of life. But it was there.

It was there.

Adaine's face was so still that—breathing or not—Jacs couldn't taste relief yet. Not until she opened her eyes, moved, something.

"Adaine, please," Jacs whispered.

"Your Majesty!" Cyrus burst into the room, a large cut spanning from ear to chin and bleeding freely. His eyes were wild, and he didn't seem to notice the blood dripping onto his collar. "It's the catacombs. They've collapsed. We lost sight of Flent shortly after the explosion." Beside Jacs, Amber stiffened.

"Explosion?" Jacs asked, dimly aware that Amber had seized the bowl and commanded, "Dyna Flent."

The bowl remained silent.

Cyrus said, "Yes, Your Majesty. We have reason to believe the blast was not natural. What we saw in the scry glasses was a woman-made, or in this case man-made, explosion."

"What do you mean *man*-made?"

"Hoods were spotted just before the blast. It's suspected they are responsible for the collapse."

A guardpair had followed Cyrus into the room with a stretcher and Jacs watched helplessly as they lifted Adaine's limp form onto it.

"Be careful with her," Jacs said uselessly. Amber watched with a distant look in her eyes as the valet was carried from the room.

Jacs's thoughts reeled. Too much had happened. She took a breath. One step at a time.

"Okay, Cyrus, I want someone checking in until we get sight or sound back from Flent, the rest of the palace scryers I want deployed to search and rescue within the palace. The palace was hit hard, but we need to make sure any survivors within the catacombs are rescued while we still have time. Speak with Chiv. Fayworth, override my last order as a priority for the guards and send as many able-bodied women as possible to the catacombs. Alert the Griffins, light the beacon. I will speak with them. They likely saw the blast, and their strength can be utilized to clear the tunnels. Celos has destroyed his catacombs, but a blast that big would surely fell Alethia. Why would he . . ." She paused, imagining the giant stalactite city blasted free and plunging into the black abyss below. It didn't make sense. "Is there any reason to suspect the blast in the catacombs was not responsible for our damage here?" If Celos was behind it, had he intended to doom his own city?

"Cyrus, let me know the *moment* you hear anything from Flent," Amber said, her voice rough. Cyrus bowed and left the room.

Jacs watched her friend teeter on the edge of crumbling and pull herself together before her eyes. Brow cleared, lip stiffened, back straightened, shoulders set.

"You're right. The catacombs are too far away," Amber said evenly. "Why did we feel it?"

"Unless it was a massive explosion," Jacs said.

"Celos would have sent that pointy city of his straight into the Lower Realm if so," Amber said.

"Exactly," Jacs replied, rising to her feet. Still clutching her side, she took the bowl from Amber and picked her way through the rubble to retrieve the glowing blue crystal. She couldn't find the purple crystal anywhere. "Cornelius Frean," she said into the bowl's shallow base. Her heart beat a panicked flurry of blows within her rib cage, and she feared for a moment it might break free. A confusion of sound erupted from the bowl, and she struggled to separate words from the cacophony.

"What are we going to do? We have to get back!" Connor said, his voice strained and thin.

"Obviously we have to get back, but how are we going to do that now?" a woman, possibly Dryft, said.

"Try again," Masterchiv Rathbone ordered.

"Jacs Frean," Connor complied.

"Connor!" Jacs said, worry sparking in her chest. "What's happened?"

"Jacs!" Connor's voice cracked with relief. "Explosions, or an earthquake. Maybe both."

"How is everyone?"

"Few bruises, but everyone's fine. Is everyone okay on your end?" Connor's voice cut through Jacs's building anxiety.

"We're still assessing damages in the palace. I'm fine, so is Amber, but Adaine—"

Her next words caught in her throat, but Connor had begun talking as soon as she'd confirmed she was okay. "The Bridge, someone blew up the Bridge."

Jacs shared a look of panic with Amber.

"The Bridge, the palace, and the catacombs," Amber confirmed. "This was a planned assault."

"Do we know if any other locations were targeted?" Masterchiv Rathbone asked.

"No, but we'll keep you informed," Amber reported.

Jacs swore. "Connor, we think Celos was the one who collapsed the catacombs. We've lost contact with the army."

Masterchiv Rathbone's voice cut across Connor's next comment. "Your Majesty, are you safe? Who's with you?"

"I am. Chiv. Everstar," Amber said. "Acting Head of the Queens-guard per your contingency plan. Masterchiv Rathbone, and may I just say how relieved I am to hear your voice?"

"Glad to hear you've got the reins up there, Chiv. Everstar," Masterchiv Rathbone said, and Jacs noticed Amber sit up straighter at the comment.

"What do we do now?" Connor asked.

"Damage control," Masterchiv Rathbone replied.

"Masterchiv, I've taken these first steps already," Jacs said quickly and relayed the few orders she'd already given.

"Excellent. Our priority will be to check in with Bridgeport, make sure the town is all right and that they know this was not an act of an Upper-Realm war. Then we will find a way up the Cliff. With the Bridge destroyed and the catacombs collapsed, we may need to enlist the help of the Griffins. It's a long shot as none of us have been deemed worthy to fly with them, but they may be willing to make an exception. What is our status with them?"

"I'm deploying the Griffins to the catacombs; their priority is unearthing those trapped within, since I know their hearts are focused on the Undercourt . . . I will try to send a message to—"

"We might not need the Griffins," Connor's voice cut across Jacs's.

"What do you mean?" Dryft asked.

"We never received it at the palace, which means it's likely still down here," Connor said, barking a laugh that felt jarring given all that had happened. "How do you two feel about heights?"

"Connor, what are you thinking?" Jacs asked impatiently.

"I'm thinking we need to have a chat with General Hawkins. She might have our ticket out of here."

"Your ticket being . . ."

"Your balloon."

Silence followed his words and spanned both realms.

"I thought she'd burned it," Masterchiv Rathbone said.

"She may have, but so much happened so quickly, and I know the Council of Four took particular interest in the design. I bet they kept it to study, just like they kept Master Leschi for questioning."

"Even if it still exists, that . . . would be incredibly dangerous," Jacs said with concern.

"It will work. You did it just fine."

"But it was just me, and I was desperate," Jacs said.

"So are we. We can't ask the Griffins to be our delivery service," Connor said firmly. "Our relations with them and their opinion of us can't be in the best shape at the moment, and we don't want to do anything that damages either. They're better equipped to unearth the army, and it aligns with their priorities. Having them take time to rescue three very safe people in the midst of so much rubble is a request that lacks tact at the very least."

"Last resort only," Masterchiv Rathbone said in a small voice. "Let's start on our first objective. Your Majesty, we will carry our crystal with us and relate an update every hour. Make sure you do the same so we know you're getting our messages and vice versa. Use the names Jacs Frean and Cornelius Frean to check in, because neither my nor Chiv. Everstar's names are in the crystal's memory bank."

"Mine is," said Amber quickly. "Left over from the Contest. I'll carry a crystal with me too and relate a report at ten minutes past each hour if it differs from Her Majesty's."

"Okay, be safe. We'll reconvene on the hour," Jacs replied. Ignoring the ringing in her ears, the aching in her heart, the vision of Adaine's too-still body, she broke the crystal's connection and took a breath.

"Are you all right, Jacqueline?" Amber asked, eyes hard.

Jacs barked a laugh. "No, are you?"

"Nope."

"Well, let's get on with it," Jacs said, sharing a nod with the knight. Both women winced as they got to their feet and headed for the door, leaving the destruction of the study behind them.

15

WAITING FOR THE DUST TO SETTLE

Coughing in the wake of the maelstrom, Lena covered her mouth with her sleeve to avoid inhaling too much dust. The air was thick with it.

"Anya?" she called through the gloom, trying to recall where she had been standing before their world had inverted.

They were in an antechamber just off the Falstaff corridor. Following the earthquake, the lamps had spluttered out, the only light now coming from the shattered, dust-coated window. Had Anya been by the window? No. She had led Lena into this room to find her a seat. Somewhere quiet to catch her breath. They'd been on their way back to the infirmary and Lena had felt faint. So where was she now?

"Anya?" Lena called again. The dust was beginning to settle, and the edges of the room slowly revealed themselves to her.

"Over here," Anya coughed from a corner. Relief washed over her as Lena saw her silhouette outlined against the clouds of debris. "Lee, are you all right?"

"I'm fine, are you all right?" They staggered toward each other, and Anya gathered her into a careful embrace.

"What was that?"

"No idea, earthquake?"

"And you're okay?"

"I'm fine."

"How're your stitches?" Anya pulled back and hurriedly reached to inspect Lena's side. Unbidden panic spasmed through Lena as it had that day in the infirmary and she flinched as though scalded before Anya could touch her.

Anya froze. "Sorry," she said gruffly, dropping her hands and stepping away.

"No, it's fine."

"I'm just going to see if anyone's in the corridor. Here, sit down a second." Anya busied herself righting a chair and gestured for Lena to take a seat, then moved toward the door. She didn't quite meet Lena's eye.

Lena sat down slowly and heard Anya rattle the door handle, pause, then thud her shoulder into it.

"It's stuck," she said by way of diagnosis. "Something must be blocking it on the other side."

"I hope everyone's okay out there."

Anya tried the door again. "Maybe we can fit out that window?" she mused and crossed the room to peer out the jagged hole, careful to avoid the glass scattered on the floor. "If we were kittens, we could get through easily, but I don't think my shoulders will fit."

"Anya, come sit down, I'm sure someone will find us."

Tearing her gaze from the circle of sky beyond the kitten-sized hole in the wall, Anya picked her way back across the room to join

Lena. She dragged a chair of her own with her and set it a short distance away, dropping her forearms to her knees and running her fingers through her hair. Dust and debris shook itself free and fell to the floor under her fingertips. It almost looked like snow.

Lena scooched her chair closer so that they were sitting side by side and interlaced her fingers with Anya's, resting her head on her shoulder.

"Thank you."

"For what?"

"For checking my stitches. I know it didn't seem like I appreciated it, but I did. I do."

"Oh. You're welcome."

In the silence, Lena could hear people shouting on the other side of the wall. "We should call for help, make sure they know we're in here."

"Yeah," Anya said, rubbing the pad of her thumb across Lena's forefinger.

Neither of them moved.

"Lee?" Anya hesitated. She seemed to be steeling her resolve, working herself up to say something. "About before—"

"I know, I promise it's nothing—"

"No, it's not nothing—"

"It is, I'm fine—"

"Stop saying you're fine when I can see—"

"I don't know where that came from—"

"—you're not. It's not the first time—"

"I just wasn't expecting . . . and my side's still tender, but it wasn't anything you did."

"Lee, please. Stop for a minute." Anya swept her chair around so they were knee to knee and caught her hands. "Just listen, please. I'm not oblivious. There are a few things in this life I know very well, and your heart is one of them. I know you. I've never known how to ask you before, but since the caves it's gotten worse, and I can't just sit back and watch you face whatever it is alone."

"Please, you don't know what you're asking," Lena whispered.

"I know you're strong, and I know that whatever those catacombs force you to see must be unimaginable to bring you down the way it does. I know you came back that summer when we were girls, and you were . . . different. You never wanted to talk about it, and I never pushed, but I also know you never attended anything to do with Queen Diana's ruling after that." The last escaped her as a whisper. "I'm not demanding an explanation. I will never need an explanation. But I am offering to help. I can listen, I can give you support or advice. *Depths*," she swore, "I can even dole out some vengeance, if that's what you need from me." Lena laughed shakily, a tear slipping down her cheek to be caught by Anya's thumb and wiped clear. "I need you to know that you're not alone, in whatever it is. I'll be here by your side no matter what. There's nothing you can say that will change that. You can't get rid of me, sweet pea."

Lena's vision blurred. Her breathing hitched and she managed a smile before Anya slid forward, gathered her in her arms, and held her tight.

"Thank you," Lena whispered. "I just . . . I don't know how to start." Anya shifted and for a moment Lena worried she would pull away, but instead, she gently kissed her hair and rested her cheek on the top of her head.

"We have time," she murmured.

Lena was silent for a long while, gaze turned inward. She was barely aware of the sounds coming from the palace, safe as she was in Anya's embrace. Closing her eyes, she reached for the walls within her mind. She knew what lay beyond. Knew the exact topography of the toxic garden she'd left to flourish there. The garden that required constant attention lest it overgrow its borders. The weeds that threatened to choke her. The vines ready to bind her. The seeds he'd left behind.

Brick by brick, she broke down the walls she'd spent so many years fortifying. Memories made of gnarled roots plunged deep through her core. Barbed branches rose to ensnare her until all she could see was the poisonous green of his tunic and the oily black of his hair. The cloying scent of his stale breath caught hers in her throat. But in the little room with the kitten-sized window, Anya held her tight, and she did not let go.

Taking a shuddering breath, Lena squeezed her eyes shut and invited Anya, tentatively, into the garden. In bursts and starts, the words tumbled free; with each broken sentence, she brought the memory's twisted thorns into the light, each detail a noxious bloom in an ugly bouquet.

"—when mother found out, she threatened to kill him. Fought against the knights' oaths to protect life with a ferocity that was beyond anything I'd ever seen. Snipped. . . *him* and kept him locked and gagged in Queen Diana's stocks for a month. In the end, probably just to shut my mother up, the knights put his fate in my hands. But I couldn't—to have his blood on my conscience? No. It was almost worse having to defend him afterward. I just wanted him gone. I wanted it all to disappear. So we sent him away and I tried to forget. We both know how well that went," she finished.

"I'm so sorry," Anya said finally. "I didn't understand. And you've held this with you all this time?"

"I couldn't share it. It wasn't your burden. And I worried you m-might not . . ." Lena cut off in a shuddered gasp.

"Not what?"

"That you couldn't love somebody so broken."

"Oh, Lena," Anya said, resting her forehead against hers, tears falling onto her cheeks.

"You deserve someone whole," she whispered.

"My love, my light, my Lena. You're not broken. Even if you were, I would love you no matter how many pieces you crumbled into. I would travel the realms searching for every last fragment of your broken heart and kiss each stitch as we sewed it back together."

"And if I'm never whole?" Lena said, finally putting the tear she'd held tight for so many years into words almost too soft to hear.

"Then I'll adore each and every facet of you. I don't love you because you're some unblemished doll. I love you. No matter how many scars you bear, to me you are perfect. And this, what he did, it doesn't define you. I can't imagine what it's been like living with this weight all by yourself." Anya took a shaky breath of her own and kissed Lena's knuckles. "But I'm so glad you told me. I'm only sorry I couldn't have helped you lift it sooner."

Lena felt the shame, the pain that had so long been hers to bear alone, begin to retreat. It was still there—one does not uproot such a garden overnight. But Anya was there too, and who better than a florist to cull the weeds and help new flowers bloom?

"I love you."

"I love you too."

"Somebody help me with this door!" a voice barked from outside.

16

DATURA

"It's going to be fine," Connor muttered. All eyes turned in their direction as their two horses clattered into the town's main square and stopped near the fountain. Connor, sitting behind Dryft, had one arm loosely looping her waist, and the other braced against his thigh. The place sent a cold ripple of déjà vu through his core. He took in the still-dark streets and remembered them bright and filled with cheering and adoring subjects. Where a glorious clock tower had stood, there was nothing more than its ruined and empty shell. The fountain that had been covered in townsfolk vying for a better view and careless of the rushing water was now a much sorrier sight surrounded by handwringers.

A lot had changed since his last visit. The square was already filled with people, all muttering in confusion or worse, all stealing glances toward where the Bridge used to stripe the Cliff in the distance as if in a blink the illusion would fade and the Bridge would return to where it had always been.

"Our goal is to keep the peace and reduce panic," Masterchiv Rathbone said in a low voice.

Dryft turned their horse in a circle. "Where is the mayor?" she asked the crowd.

The citizens remained silent, and a patrolling guardpair stepped forward. Studying their travel-stained attire and ragged cloaks, one sneered, "Who's asking?"

"Masterchiv Cassida Rathbone of the Queensguard, and this is guard Iliana Dryft. We travel with the Queen's royal advisor and have news concerning this recent act of treason." She gestured toward the Bridge. "Dryft asked you a question. Where is the mayor?"

The guard paled and tapped her wrists together, fists tight, palms up, hurriedly.

"I'm the mayor of Bridgeport, you have news?" A short, hook-nosed woman with thick graying hair stepped forward from where she had been speaking with a small group of people near the fountain's edge. "Odette Linheir," she said by way of introduction. "And I think we'd all benefit from an explanation." Multiple heads nodded their agreement.

Looking around the crowd, Masterchiv Rathbone let her voice carry to the outer reaches of the square. "Fair Lowrians! The Bridge was *not* destroyed by our Queen. The Bridge was destroyed by a group of radicals who do not represent Her Majesty nor her wishes for the realms. The Queen is working hard to find those responsible and bring them to justice, and will no doubt be planning to unite the realms again as quickly as possible."

"I knew she wouldn't do this to us! Didn't I tell you, Merope?" an older man said from near the clock tower. Relieved murmuring fluttered through the square, but Connor noted several faces appeared unconvinced.

Mayor Linheir nodded slowly, then addressed the crowd, "You see? Queen Jacqueline loves her people, especially her kin in Bridge-port! Why else would she send the head of her Queensguard and her royal advisor to tell us this in person!"

"Goddess save the Queen!" a few townsfolk cried in response.

"How did they get here so fast?" a man's voice called above the rabble.

"Yeah, what if she planted them here before blowing the Bridge so that they would be first on the scene to feed us lies?" another deep voice supplied.

Connor felt his gut clench and shouted, "We were here on other business."

"On business for realm relations and were caught just as unawares as you all by this explosion," Masterchiv Rathbone finished. The crowd looked unsure, and Connor saw a few people turn to whisper to their neighbors. "Mayor Linheir, I think it best we speak in private," Masterchiv Rathbone said. "Is there somewhere we can go to discuss next steps?"

"Of course, we will figure this out together. The Upper Realm is and always will be our ally," Mayor Linheir said, addressing the last part to the crowd. With a swift gesture, she pointed the way and walked to the edge of the square. The two horses followed slowly behind, Connor's ears prickling with words muttered in dissent.

"What do we do?" he whispered close to Dryft's ear.

"We speak with the mayor, we show our support for the Lower Realm, and we don't feed the suspicions," Dryft said softly. "Then we get that balloon and get out of here."

"They don't seem convinced."

"And providing excuses that don't reveal the true reason why you were down here will likely weaken our message and shift focus to where it shouldn't be. Let's hope Masterchiv Rathbone has a better plan."

"I didn't realize the Lower Realm would still be so hostile, after all Jacs has done for them."

"Taking away the scry crystals? For some it's a case of too little too late. Changes take time, even with her work on recruiting Lowrian guards into the military, it all happens too slowly for people who wanted solutions yesterday."

Connor sighed and cast a worried look behind him at the retreating square. Rather than take them to a town hall or private abode, the mayor led them to the local tavern. Its wooden sign was worn, and the paint was flaking off the carving of a donkey heartily kicking a buffoonish man who had his hands clasped over his rear in pain as he leaped into the air behind the beast.

The sign read, "The Stroppy Mule."

Quickly dismounting, the group handed their horses to a waiting worker and crossed the threshold.

The tavern was empty save for a lone woman behind the bar, all the patrons likely still in the square. She turned at the sound of the door opening and at a curt word from the mayor, led them through to a private room behind the bar.

"Round of gin? Whiskey maybe?" she asked. "Seems a day for it."

"Just a round of ciders for us, please, Kitty," the mayor said.

"Okay, but I'll be having gin." Kitty muttered. "Bloody Bridge comes tumbling down and it's supposed to be business as usual? This calls for something stronger. What are we supposed to call ourselves? Bridgeport needs a bridge to port. So, what are we now? Cliffbottom?"

"We're going to figure this all out, but for now just the ciders."

"Hungry? I've just put the soup on. It's good."

"Just the ciders."

"Right," Kitty said with a nod and disappeared. The door swung shut behind her. Connor looked around the room. It wasn't much. A few cushioned stools were arranged around a low table. The one window was high and narrow, so most of the room's light came from gas lamps housed in acorn-shaped sconces. To Connor's eye, this might have been a storeroom once upon a time. The walls were thick stone, and the air was cool. He pulled his cloak around his shoulders and took a seat. The three women did the same and Masterchiv Rathbone immediately took the lead.

"Mayor Linheir, as I said before, the severing of the last Bridge was not an act of Upper-Realm violence. It was done without the Queen's knowledge. While your citizens may not believe this, we need to do what we can to reduce panic and contain any possible acts of retaliation. This cannot be the spark that ignites another feud between realms."

"I agree."

"What do you suggest?"

Mayor Linheir thought for a moment. "We'll send messengers to the surrounding towns and cities at once. They need to know it was not an act of war immediately."

"Agreed. How quickly can you get proclamations drawn up? We can sign whatever you need."

"A half hour, tops. I have two scribes," she said with a touch of pride. "As for Bridgeport, I'll hold a town meeting this afternoon. I'll gather as many of the conspiracy theories as I can in the meantime and try to quash them before they spin out of control. I didn't see who spoke out against you earlier, nor did I recognize their voices, but I can see where their suspicion comes from. It is convenient that you were all here at the right time. How do you explain that?"

Connor looked at his guardpair and saw their hesitation. How could they admit they were here because they had escaped a secret organization in a secret city within the Cliff and in doing so discovered a secret stairwell between the realms? It sounded far-fetched, even to him. "They're here as my guard," he said. "I was sent by the Queen to travel through the Lower Realm undercover to get a sense of public opinion toward the Crown as well as to ensure the scry crystals had all been collected and sent to the palace."

Masterchiv Rathbone nodded in agreement and Dryft added, "We were set to return up the Bridge today, and this happened."

The door opened and Kitty returned, delivered their drinks, and departed. Connor accepted his and took a sip while Mayor Linheir ran a finger around the rim of her glass and chewed her lip. "Let's simplify it. We'll tell them you were here to check on the scry crystals."

"Sounds good, keep it simple," Dryft said.

"And that will remind the Lowrians that Queen Jacqueline is fighting for their rights and making good on her promises," the mayor added.

"Exactly," Masterchiv Rathbone agreed.

"We also have a request," Connor said.

"Oh?"

"We need the balloon General Hawkins confiscated. Where would we find that?"

If the mayor was surprised by the request, she hid it well. "It's still in custody. In the storehouse beside the prison."

Hope surged in Connor's chest but was quickly stunted as the door burst open again.

"Ms. Mayor, you should get back to the square," Kitty said. All prior swagger had evaporated.

"What's happened?" Mayor Linheir demanded, rising from her seat, her untouched cider wobbling violently on the table.

"Shyna Wetler just came in, said there's a bunch of men riling up the crowd. They're out for blood, she said. Apparently, there's going to be a demonstration of sorts. I'm gonna close up shop to be safe. Last thing a mob needs is liquor."

"Good idea."

"You go, Mayor Linheir, we'll follow at a distance and assess. If there's something we can do to help, we will, but we don't want our presence to trigger a riot," Masterchiv Rathbone said. The two leaders shared a look of understanding, then the mayor dashed from the room.

"This day keeps getting worse," Dryft muttered as they all rose to follow.

Hugging the shadows of the side streets, Connor and his guardpair hurried on foot toward the square. Careful to stay out of sight, they hung back, following the rising sound of the crowd. As if moving through scenes in a dream, Connor ran through the cobbled lanes, keeping Masterchiv Rathbone in his sights, with the sound of Dryft's steady breathing following close behind him. His head spun.

Half a block from the square, Masterchiv Rathbone held up a hand and they slowed to a walk. Pressed against the wall, she gestured for him to remain behind while she scouted the area ahead. He doubled over, hands on his knees, and attempted to catch his breath. Never again would he take a healthy body for granted. The sound from the square beyond was louder now.

Over his disjointed inhales, he heard a man's voice boom, "Your Queen has abandoned you."

Connor's heart sank and he started forward without realizing what he was doing until Dryft grabbed his elbow roughly to pull him back into the safety of the shadows.

"You deserve the truth!" a different man cried. The crowd roared its agreement.

Despite Dryft's grip, Connor edged toward the sound, desperate to see what was happening. As he poked his head around the building, the square came into view and his jaw dropped. Standing beside the fountain, on the same raised platform where he and his father had stood after the massacre, were two men in purple cloaks, a large ornate mirror between them.

It was a twin to the one they had seen in the wagon: oval face surrounded by a thick gold frame festooned in golden ornate trumpeting flowers. It reflected the enraged faces of the crowd. Each man had placed a palm almost reverentially on the golden rim of the mirror and one held up his other hand for silence. Connor held his breath. As a single unit, the two men holding the mirror and half a dozen men from within the crowd in identical purple cloaks cried, "FATHER CELOS."

The mirror's surface clouded over. The foggy vortex swirled and twisted. Its sinister sinuous smoke captivated the crowd.

A man's face, larger than life, filled the mirror. Pale, pointed features with angles cut as if from stone loomed over the townspeople of Bridgeport. His pale gray eyes stared out across the square from beneath white eyebrows and slicked-back white-blond hair.

"Your Queen has abandoned you," he said, repeating the words of his Sons. His shifting gossamer voice echoed from the gaping maws of each trumpeting flower that surrounded the mirror.

A jolt of familiarity passed through Connor as he recognized a much more elegant version of the little mirror and bowl combination he had used to see and hear Jacs.

"She has abandoned you and left you to rot. She does not see your strength, does not see your worth. Celos does. I see you. You are not the rotten core of this Queendom, but its salvation." The deep resonance of the voice echoed inside Connor's chest, while its feathery touch wormed its way into his mind.

"We need to destroy that mirror," Connor growled. Masterchiv Rathbone pulled him back to stand with Dryft out of the mirror's view.

"We need to get out of here," she said, regret etched into the lines around her mouth.

"What? He's spewing poison," Connor spluttered.

"And we're outnumbered."

"But you're the best there is."

"Think, Your Grace. We're two—"

"Three—"

"Two," Masterchiv Rathbone pressed firmly, "against at least eight plus the ever-increasing number of townsfolk who now hear their own fears parroted back to them out of those baselow flowers. A good warrior fights for what's right; a great warrior knows when to fight another day. We need to get out of here. Now. While they're distracted."

Connor passed a clenched fist across his brow in frustration. "I can't stand here and do nothing!" he hissed.

"If you want to see Jacqueline again, you will. We can win this, just not here. Not today."

Connor swore. With a final look back at the square, he slammed his fist into the stone wall of the building beside him. "Fine." As he turned his back on the crowd, Celos's spell continued to weave venom around his ears.

"—and like the phoenix, we will rise from the ashes she has condemned us to," Celos's voice crooned. "How foolish our false Queen is. She thought to abandon us here, thought that would strangle our towns, thought we would perish without the Upper Realm's support. Who fills their larders?"

"We do!" the townsfolk cried.

"Who fills their grain stores?"

"We do!

"Who will strike back?"

"We will!"

"Let's get to the prison," Masterchiv Rathbone said. With a face now devoid of color, she scratched at her temples and led the way.

17

WIELDING A SHIELD

Casualties were a reality every knight was trained to face. Amber knew this. Amber *knew* this. But her heart was a stubborn mistress and kept insisting on its painful stutter within her rib cage.

Useless thing. She balled her shaking hands into fists and lengthened her stride.

She needed more information.

Her gaze took in the wreckage of the palace as she sped through it. Where had the blast come from?

"Perkins!" she snapped as she approached the end of the hallway, stopping a trusted serving boy in his tracks. "I need palace blueprints and the guest list from the gala."

"Of course, Chiv." He hurried to bow and take his leave.

"And a mirror, get me a handheld."

"Right away." He was gone before she had finished rounding the corner.

The farther away from the Queen's rooms she walked, the lesser the damage. So, it must have been localized in that wing of the palace.

Oh, Everstar, Flent's voice echoed in her mind. *I'm not asking for love.*

"Idiot," she muttered.

A different serving boy at the end of the hall spotted her and made a beeline in her direction, hand outstretched, holding a small looking glass. She accepted it with a nod of thanks and quickened her pace.

"Dyna Flent," she said into the mirror. The surface fogged over and after a few moments cleared to reveal Amber's frown. "Idiot," she hissed again and lowered the glass.

"Chivilra Everstar!" a familiar voice called from behind her. She pulled up short and allowed Yves to catch up. His hair flounced perfectly in place as he came to a halt, a devilish grin on his face.

"What are you smiling about, Yves?" she snapped, not in the mood.

"Oh, the world is tumbling around us, yet there is always a reason to smile. Your presence has brought this one on, dear Chivilra," he almost sang with a smug little bow.

"People are dead—"

"People die, this is not new," he said flippantly.

Amber crossed her arms and glared at him.

"Poor taste, I apologize. Sometimes perspective helps lessen the weight of a situation, sometimes all it does is piss one off. I fear I've done the latter."

"What do you want?"

"To offer help. The palace is a wreck and word from the walls is the catacombs have collapsed. If ever you needed the capable brawn of the Sons of Yves—working title—it is now."

"We don't—" She sighed and caught herself. "Actually, Yves, that is exactly what we need."

"Here to assist. Where are we most needed?"

Amber thought for a moment, pinching the bridge of her nose.

Unfortunately, her thoughts weren't quick enough for Yves, and he added, "While anywhere is fine, I do think going back to the catacombs would be the men's least favorite option. Now, I understand that in war we don't get to choose, but even if we were to send them beneath the palace rather than the catacombs next to Ale—"

"What?" Amber said sharply.

"You can understand, it's not the *underground* aspect they dislike so much as it's the proximity to Alethia that—"

"No, Yves, focus. Are there tunnels beneath the palace?"

Yves faltered and looked at her curiously. "Well, of course. How do you think my brothers snuck in during the gala? My troupe could walk through the front gates, but did you think those hooded brutes were capable of sneaking into the palace undetected otherwise? You give them too much credit."

Amber was at a loss for words.

Seizing his opportunity, Yves prattled on: "If we are to be joining your forces, I have a thought for you to consider. Don't need an answer now, of course, but I was thinking about our chat before, about the knight slogan you so proudly preach. *You have to make life to take life.* Well, maybe that's the idea, it's not a man's place to take life, but it is our place to protect it . . . now how do we make that into a catchy rhyme?" He tapped his chin thoughtfully.

"The explosion came from beneath the palace," Amber said quietly to herself.

"Oh! We could call ourselves the Queendom's SHIELD, Strong, Handsome, Intelligent, Elite Lads Defend . . . no, no—Life Defenders."

"Yves, shut up for a second."

"You're right, it needs work, I'll think on it."

"Yves, I want you to send four of your boys to the tunnels beneath the palace. Find out what happened, and if the culprits are still there, bring them in alive."

"Understood," Yves said with a winning smile. "We'll defend, not end! And the rest of my *men*?"

Amber pursed her lips. "The rest I'll have on search and rescue within the palace walls, that gives us more women to send to the catacombs. Also"—she sighed—"I need two with me to help guard the Queen."

Yves's smile broadened and he bounced on the balls of his feet. "The Queendom's SHIELD is at your service."

"I'm not agreeing to that name, Yves, but . . . thank you."

"It is an honor, Chiv. Everstar. Any men in particular you want for the Queen?"

Amber thought back to her last two weeks of training. "The tall blond one with the scruff of a beard and the one built like a bull, with the hairy forearms," she specified.

Yves raised an eyebrow and said pointedly, "Druine and Thomas?"

"Sure."

He shook his head but appeared in the mood to let it slide. "I'll relay your orders immediately."

"Thank you, Yves," Amber said, and seeing the barely concealed glee on his face, could have almost smiled. Almost.

18

A QUEEN'S PRIDE

After a morning and early afternoon spent setting her wheels in motion, Jacs now paced beside the rosemary hedges restlessly. Each twist in her torso, every breath drawn too deeply sent a splinter of pain through her ribs. She had come out into the gardens when the whirling in her mind became too much and her frenzy left her of little use to anyone, but the chilly breeze and nodding sprigs did nothing to calm her thoughts.

Chivilras Ryder and Fayworth stood at one entrance to the herb garden while a guardpair consisting of the two men from Yves's troupe, Druine and Thomas, stood proudly at the other entrance. The knights kept shooting wary looks at the male guards, but so far there had been no comments made about them. Jacs chose to ignore the flurry of hand gestures discreetly shared between the knights below hip level.

Taking a breath, she ran a wavering hand through her hair, flinched as the action tugged at her still-sore ribs, and rested it on her hip instead. A jagged cobble snagged her split skirts, and she ripped it free. Reaching the end of the hedge, she turned on her heel and charged back the way she'd come. She needed to steady herself. So much had happened.

How had Queen Ariel managed? She wished she could talk to her. Wished she could talk to someone who knew what it felt like to have your head and heart pulled in so many different directions. The former Queen had her secrets, of that there was no doubt. Jacs pulled the small blue leather-bound book from a pocket within her bodice. Absently, she passed her thumb over the cover to reveal the word *Missing*. Yes, the former Queen had had her secrets and her own mysteries to solve, but how had she managed? Jacs's mind flew to the image of the journals she'd received from the King. The filled one held very little applicable advice from which a successor could draw wisdom. The blank one simply mocked her. Her hand froze midway to slipping the little book back into her bodice.

Blank one? What if . . .

Spinning on her heel at the other end of the hedges, she almost bowled someone over on her way back down the path.

"Sorry!" Theo squawked, hopping out of the way, and almost landing in the herbs. Jacs reached out instinctively and caught his elbow before he toppled over. Her side screamed and she gritted her teeth against the reflexive curt remark that almost escaped her lips. Blinking away the pain and her train of thought, tucking the little book into her bodice, she set him to rights and looked at him expectantly.

"Hello," he said.

"Good afternoon, Lordson Claustrom. What brings you out into the garden?"

He fidgeted with his doublet and replied, "Well, obviously because of the explosion our garden walk this morning was postponed, but when I heard you had come out this afternoon, I figured I'd check if you wanted company."

Jacs's face softened.

"Did you want company?" he asked.

"That would be lovely, Lordson. Thank you," she said gently, offering her arm for him to take. He tucked his fingers into the crook of her elbow nervously and fell into step beside her.

"I was glad to hear you were all right, Your Majesty. Is there any news on the nature of the blast?" he asked.

Jacs sighed. "All we know is that it originated beneath my chambers, and it was a targeted explosion. We are almost certain the culprits were connected with . . ." She caught herself, shooting him a look. He seemed interested but not suspiciously so. He grew up in the Claustrom household; did he know about the Sons of Celos? ". . . a rebel organization we've been tracking."

"Rebels?"

"Yes, it's likely they're behind all three attacks."

"Well, I hope you bring them to justice."

"Thank you, we're trying."

Jacs noticed a messenger hurriedly share a few words with Chivilra Ryder, who nodded curtly and dismissed the boy. Catching Jacs's eye, she shook her head twice. Jacs felt a breath punch its way from her lungs.

"Is everything all right, Your Majesty?"

"No, it's not," she said quietly. "But no news from the scryers is better than bad news at this point, so we just have to keep waiting."

Regardless of whether Theo understood what she was talking about, he nodded compassionately. "Waiting can sometimes be the hardest part."

"It really can."

"I feel like life as a Lordson prepares one well for waiting."

"Does it?" Jacs asked, intrigued and happy for the distraction.

"Oh, indeed," he said feelingly. "Firstborn Lordsons have it worst; they spend their childhoods waiting for their parents to produce or select an heir. We already had Hera by the time I was born, so I've just had to wait for my parents to decide on a match. Then I have to wait for my intended match to approve of me, and if she doesn't, I start the cycle again and I must wait for the next eligible Dame of favorable connections to decide she wants a husband."

Jacs considered this. "That must be unsettling, going through life at the whim of other peoples' decisions."

"It's not all bad," Theo said with a shrug. "You end up meeting some lovely people. And you're pretty much left alone in between these meetings, so you pick up some hobbies."

"How do you pass the time?"

"I play my violin, I read, I draw, and have walked the paths of our estate's gardens till I could map them from memory."

"And how do you cope with the waiting?"

Theo was silent a moment, gray eyes hidden by his mop of white-blond hair. "I find it helps to write out the best-case scenario. My . . ." he sucked in a breath, "my mind has a nasty habit of spinning webs of all the things that may go wrong. If I write out what I hope will happen, it feels more concrete. Like a plan rather than a wish."

"I can see how that would be useful," Jacs conceded.

"So, what would be your best-case scenario?" he asked. Jacs was struck with how much calmer she felt in his presence.

"Best-case scenario? There are so many factors."

"Start small. Close your eyes and start with something manageable."

Jacs closed her eyes. The mess in the Upper Realm felt too tangled to unravel right now, and her mind leaped to the Lower Realm. "Okay, well, best-case scenario is Cornelius returns. Cornelius returns safely."

"That seems easy enough. He's at least in very capable hands. What else?"

"The relations with the Lower Realm are positive and we can rebuild the Bridge."

"A matter of time and hard work. You have the advantage of being one of them, so you will be able to sway favor more readily than any Upperite. What else?"

Her mind's eye shifted up the Bridge and focused on the palace. "Best-case scenario . . . is we have zero casualties within the palace, and we're able to rebuild."

"If not zero casualties, we can hope for minimal injuries and few deaths. Rebuilding provides vocation. What else?"

Her thoughts traveled the path to the Catacombs of Lethe. "The catacombs, best-case scenario is that all my women return home safely. The Griffins and reinforcements got there in time and pulled everyone free." Her mind's eye watched the Court of Griffins soaring in the sky, and a vision of the chained and bloodied Undercourt intruded on the happy image. "We free the Undercourt of Griffins, and the Sons are happy to be liberated. Celos falls," Jacs said quietly. Her eyes snapped open, and she pulled up short, looking at Theo in horror.

Watching his feet, still deep in thought, he replied: "Easy to do if you know how to sneak into Aleth . . ." He looked up and caught her expression. "Or . . . After all, anything is simple if you . . ."

Jacs's shock at her own slip of the tongue was replaced by her shock at his. "Lordson, do you know about Alethia?"

"N-no."

"About Celos? The Undercourt?"

"No!"

"Yes, you do, what do you know?" She rounded on him, his fingers now pinned in the crook of her arm, her opposite palm resting firmly on his shoulder.

"Nothing! I know nothing. No one tells me anything," he said earnestly.

Jacs studied his face, unconvinced.

"Any and all information about Alethia is only going to secure our prosperity and save lives. I trust that you understand this, and would share anything—useful or no."

"O-of course," Theo said, unable to meet Jacs's eyes. A shadow flickered across the sun and Jacs looked up reflexively. Scanning the skies, she noticed a dark spot contrasted against the bright white of the clouds.

Excellent, she thought. The Griffins got her message. She looked at Theo again, and a thought struck her. "I must meet with the Court in the throne room. Have you ever met a member of the Court before?" she asked.

"No, I've only seen them in portraits and tapestries."

"Well, then I insist you accompany me. It's a rare privilege I'd like to share with you. Especially if"—and here she paused as a knot formed in her stomach—"you are to rule by my side one day."

With a nervous, mystified look on his face, Theo allowed Jacs to lead him toward the throne room. Meanwhile, Jacs's mind spun out theories faster than she had time to process them. Theo grew up on Lord Claustrom's estate. Lord Claustrom had a direct connection to Alethia. It had been her that the Council of Four would contact when they needed the hoods to take on one of their tasks. There was more to this, and Theo might be the key.

What had he just said? *No one tells me anything?* But Jacs had a feeling it did not stop him from listening. What had he heard in the great Lord's manor? What had he seen?

They marched toward the throne room, sandwiched between her front and rear guardpairs. The palace halls were less frenzied than they had been that morning as all the injured had been moved to the infirmary. The most recent report indicated only one death. The word *only* twisted like a poisoned barb in her mind. Only one life, but that was an entire life. Someone's whole past, present, and future snuffed out by a falling crossbeam. His name had been Barlow, a serving boy within the palace. There was no meaning in it. And Adaine was still in critical condition.

The four fireplaces were freshly stoked, and flames flickered brightly within each when she entered the throne room. The warmth was welcome against the day's chill, and Jacs was relieved to see this room had suffered minimal damage in the blast. With a few words she pointed out where Theo could stand; then she took her position in the center of the hall, facing her own golden throne at the base of the dais.

She didn't have to wait long for the Griffin to soar through the oculus above and land without a sound on the raised platform. It was Altus Hermes. Jacs sank into a deep bow and in her peripheral vision saw Theo and her guards do the same. Altus Hermes leaped forward, wingbeats whipping the wind within the hall, and landed before Jacs. She felt its beak run through her hair, preening as it had done so many times before. Its touch was gentle. Satisfied, it returned to its perch on the dais and waited.

"Your Altus, thank you for coming at such short notice. You no doubt witnessed the explosion in the catacombs firsthand and have likely seen the destruction of my wing in the palace on your flight in." Altus Hermes inclined its head, gold-dusted gray feathers gleaming in the afternoon light. Jacs continued, "The Bridge between realms has also been destroyed. Cornelius and Masterchiv Rathbone are now stranded in the Lower Realm without a way up, and I—" Jacs's explanation died on her lips as Altus Hermes approached her again and gently placed its beak against her forehead. She felt its pressure span from her hairline to the tip of her nose and instinctively inhaled. The Griffin's scent tickled her nose: sun-warmed oak entwined with a sharp crispness of fresh mountain air. There was a moment's pressure against Jacs's mental defenses, and she lowered her mind's walls to let the Griffin in.

In a flash, all her thoughts were quickly conveyed to the Griffin via their mind link, including Connor's idea about flying her hot-air balloon to the palace. In response, Altus Hermes sent her the impression that it agreed with Connor, seemingly satisfied that he could find his own way up the Cliff.

However, as her recent suspicions that Theo possessed important information about the Undercourt passed into the Griffin's mind, it pulled back from her sharply and screeched. Piercing eyes snapped toward where Theo stood, now trembling, beneath a marble pillar. She hadn't meant to share that information, but seeing Altus Hermes's reaction she suspected she was about to get some answers.

"What happened?" the boy asked, panic staining his words. He backed up hurriedly, pressing himself into the pillar when he reached it as if wishing to disappear within. Altus Hermes walked slowly toward him.

"Altus Hermes believes, like I do, that you have information about Alethia, about the Undercourt, that you are hiding from us," Jacs said quietly.

"I–I promise I don't know anything!" he stuttered, eyes widening as the Griffin continued its approach. "Just things I'd overhear. M-mother never really noticed if I was in the room or not, so I heard things. But nothing of importance. Just about tunnels." Altus Hermes stopped to loom in front of the boy. It waited, staring down at Theo with an intensity that made Jacs's insides shrivel. She hadn't ever been at the receiving end of a Griffin's ire and did not envy Theo.

"What else, Lordson?" she asked softly. "We're talking about the well-being of this world's most divine creatures. If you know anything, you would do well to tell us now. Altus Hermes does have the ability to rip it from your mind if you don't comply."

"Call it off!" Theo cried.

"Griffins answer to no woman. Queen or no. Their actions are their own."

"Okay, okay! I promise, I don't know much. Mother was always disappearing into her study and locking the door. Every once in a while I'd get curious and hide in the room to listen. It was all normal! She talked about gold store deposits, mostly, and moving a group she called the Sons of Celos. The Sons, you know, that dancing group? She—she was their primary patron. But once or twice she mentioned the 'other Court' and that's when she talked about tunnels. Tunnels beneath the Upper Realm. Tunnels beneath Hesperida. Tunnels to a place called Alethia. I didn't know if she was digging them or transporting things through them. Most of what she'd say was like a code. It didn't make sense. She never told Father about any of it. I promise that's all I know."

Jacs considered his words, saw the terror on his face, and felt something ugly twist within her heart. "Altus Hermes. I believe he's telling the truth," she said. The Griffin continued to approach. Without looking at Jacs, and never breaking its eye contact with Theo, it lowered its beak toward Theo's chest.

"What's happening?" Theo whimpered.

"Altus Hermes, stop! The boy is telling the truth!" she said, panicking now. She knew what it would mean for the Griffin to draw the truth from his heart and was desperate to save him from that pain. "Stop!" she commanded, rushing forward. When she was halfway to Theo, the Griffin's beak connected with his sternum. A pause, a breath, then Theo screamed and fell forward.

Jacs froze, hand outstretched, and watched in horror as Altus Hermes ripped the truth from Theo's shaking form. Solid and steady, the Griffin pressed the dorsal portion of its beak into the boy's chest. It was almost a gentle gesture. The steady pressure of someone holding a drowning woman beneath the water. Theo trembled on the stone floor, each muscle taut and racked with shudders.

"Stop!" Jacs commanded. Shaking herself out of her paralysis, she threw her shoulder into the Griffin.

The creature didn't even flinch. Jacs's knights started forward from their posts.

"Enough!" Jacs cried and placed the flat of her palm against Altus Hermes's beak, shoving the creature back and attempting to push Theo clear with the other hand. The moment her hand connected with its beak, she felt the nerves from fingertip to shoulder seize and burst into flame. She gritted her teeth against the pain and held fast to the Griffin, Theo's shaking form beneath her other palm still writhing with the aftershock.

The Griffin, two heartbeats slow, broke its connection. It staggered back and the pain stopped just as quickly as it had started. Snorting, it shook its head clear and rounded on Jacs. Terrified at what she had just witnessed, terrified at what she had just done, but determined, Jacs stood her ground.

"No," she asserted, clutching her arm to her chest, forcing the emotion from her voice and ignoring the echo of Theo's screams that would not escape her mind. "You risk breaching our treaty, Altus Hermes. You cannot interrogate one of my subjects this way. Not in my throne room. Not without my consent."

Altus Hermes, with its unreadable face, leveled its ancient gaze at her. She took a step back, body still positioned between Theo and the Griffin, and lowered herself to one knee.

"Your Altus, you will always have my unwavering respect and loyalty. But I cannot condone this act of violence. Especially if performed by a member of the Court. You hold me to a high standard as Queen of the two realms, and I must hold you to one as well."

Their eyes locked for what felt like an eternity.

Finally, Altus Hermes bowed in return, sinking low over a taloned foreleg. Jacs inclined her head and felt the Griffin's beak run through her hair. She lifted her chin and allowed it to press its beak against her forehead. There was a hesitation as it waited for Jacs to let it in, then an image of Altus Hermes filled her mind, its wings bound, and beak muzzled: a feeling. This image was swiftly replaced with one of the Court redoubling their efforts in freeing the trapped army: a promise.

The next were a series of images and impressions that were shrouded in fog. These belonged to Theo. Snippets of memories moved in flux as certainty blended with estimation. Looking through eyes that were not her own, she saw a sketchpad with a half-drawn horse on its surface, felt the weight of a charcoal pencil between her fingers and the pressure of the floor along her stomach. Her lips buzzed with the soft humming coming from her throat, and the heat from a nearby fire warmed her toes. A muffled conversation echoed through this half-forgotten memory from a different time. It came from within the walls. Panic, scrambling to gather the pad and pencil. Foreign eyes flashed around the unfamiliar study and settled on a cupboard next to a large tapestry, its subject warped into oblivion. A flurry of movement, then sudden quiet. Her thin arms clutched knees tightly to her chest as she hid, pulling the cupboard door almost all the way closed.

Shallow, careful breaths. Through the crack in the door, a single sliver of light came from the room beyond, and she saw the tapestry ripple as two figures emerged from the wall behind it. Both disappeared past her field of vision as they moved to stand before the fire. The body she inhabited froze, ears pricked, gaze turned inward.

A stern woman's voice evoked an unsettling flutter in Jacs's chest: Theo's mother, now-Lady, then-Lord Claustrom. "My love, you risk too much coming here. We agreed to only speak via crystal. He already suspects."

"He is a jealous fool," a low voice purred.

"But he is not an idiot. If he discovers us, we are ruined. If he doesn't air our affair, he will most definitely collapse the tunnels. They are my only connection to you; they must be protected."

"Forget the cuckhold. All I ask is to see *him*, if I can't meet him— just one look. Allow me that honor. It is my right."

"You have Sons aplenty in your city."

"It's not the same and you know it. Allow me a glimpse of him. Please."

"No."

Jacs felt young Theo's dawning realization and horror bloom in her own chest as his muddied memories faded, and the sharp focus of Altus Hermes's thoughts filled her mind again. A pluraled image of Jacs standing atop Court's Mountain, the sky below thick with Griffins, all bowing low in support. A golden light shone from behind Jacs, casting her in silhouette. She stood tall and proud, but the image had a dual quality, as though Jacs were turning a two-sided coin over in her fingers. In an instant, the mountain beneath her feet flickered. Solid stone became brilliant gold-dusted bones. The skyborne Griffins disappeared, the air was empty, cold, and Jacs's golden halo vanished. The only light came from the shine of millions of Griffin bones piled high beneath her feet. Far, far below, iron-spiked armies cloaked in purple gazed upon their Queen. In the next heartbeat, the Griffins returned, the stone was solid underfoot once more, and Jacs felt warmth between her shoulder blades. Bright light radiated from her spine, along her arms, beyond her fingertips: a prophecy.

Jacs exhaled shakily and nodded as their connection ended.

"I understand," she said, wishing that saying it made it true.

In a few swift movements, Altus Hermes straightened and launched itself up and out of the throne room. Only as the Griffin's last wingbeat died from her ears did Jacs allow herself a sigh of relief, and she turned to check on Theo.

He was curled in a ball on the throne-room floor, shaking.

"Theo?" Jacs asked tentatively, resting her hand lightly on his shoulder. She signaled for the knights to return to their positions by the door. "I need you to say something."

He squeezed his eyes shut and curled tighter. She hesitated, unsure. She needed to pull Theo out from where the Griffin had sent him. Lowering herself to the ground, she gathered him gently in her arms and helped him sit upright.

"Theo, what instrument do you like to play?" she asked softly.

"T-the violin," he whispered.

"Good, and what is your favorite piece?"

"'Pearls in the Mist,' by Percival Bairden."

"I can't wait to hear that one." She kept her voice low. "Now, what's your favorite food?"

"Candied ginger." His responses came stronger, but still held a hitch in their timbre. Jacs snapped her fingers toward Chivilra Ryder and requested some to be brought immediately with a flagon of wine. The knight bowed, poked her head outside to relay the message, and moved back to her post.

Jacs returned her attention to the boy sprawled in her arms. She knew only a few years separated their ages, but in this moment, hurt and scared, he looked so young. "Theo, I'm so sorry. I didn't know that would happen. Are you okay?"

He blinked his eyes open and hesitated a moment as focus stole into their depths. He stared at his palms. "No."

"Take it slow, it will take a while for the aftereffects to wear off."

"Why did you . . ." his words had a dreamy quality to them.

"I swear I didn't know that would happen."

"A Griffin just attacked me."

"It was out of line and angry. You're safe now."

"You set a Griffin on me?"

"I didn't anticipate—"

"You set a Griffin on me for information and ask if I'm okay? Of course I'm not okay, what in the name of brutes was that?"

"I had no idea Altus Hermes would—"

"Obviously," he snapped. All whisper was gone from his tone, replaced with something hard, something hurt.

Jacs frowned. "It shouldn't have ever gone that far. I should have reacted sooner. I just never imagined . . . and if I hadn't been able to throw it off—" She suppressed a shudder at the thought and interlocked her fingers with his, giving his hand a reassuring squeeze.

Theo glanced at their clasped hands and appeared to finally register where he was. His gaze shifted to Jacs's face and she watched his hurt slowly dissipate.

Relief surged in its place. He appeared to struggle with his reply for a moment. As though forcing a muzzle on an obstinate dog, he collected himself.

"A Griffin attacked me . . . but you saved me."

"Wh—" Jacs began, taken aback.

"You attacked it back. You threw it off. You took my place. You risked breaching the treaty."

"Yes, but so did Altus Hermes."

"But our side has more to lose in a falling out."

"Altus Hermes was in the wrong." She sighed. "We both were. I was wrong to think I could control a Griffin's actions, but it should have never approached you. It should have never laid its beak on you."

"You saved me."

"Theo, you shouldn't have needed saving. It was my poor judgment that put you in danger in the first place."

He attempted a grin, but it wavered at its corners. "You know," he said with a shaking bravado, "if I knew that was in my cards, I probably should have just told you what I knew."

Jacs cocked her head and noticed the furtive look that flashed across his face. "Why didn't you?" she asked.

Shrugging, he pushed himself upright into a more comfortable seat, careful to retain her hand. "It didn't seem important. Just scraps of conversation gleaned from doorways."

"Well," Jacs said evenly, "I'm just glad you're all right."

The wine and ginger arrived, and he accepted a goblet in a daze. "What did it do to me?"

"Griffins can pull thoughts from the depths of your mind; that's what I thought it was going to do when it approached you. However, they can also pull truths from the heart. A much more painful experience, as you discovered. I suspect Altus Hermes was impatient to know the full truth."

"It found a lot more than that," Theo said quietly, face still ghostly white. He took a sip of wine, and Jacs was relieved to see two spots of color bloom and fade on his cheeks.

"Theo, I promise I never imagined Altus Hermes would be so ruthless. I underestimated its ferocity, and you paid the price. I'm sorry."

Theo studied her over the rim of his goblet. "You fought a Griffin for me. The Queen fought a Griffin to keep me safe. That's something from a fairy tale."

"I wouldn't go that far."

"It certainly makes for an interesting beginning to our courtship. Far more exhilarating than a walk about the gardens."

"Nothing if not memorable," Jacs agreed softly. In her mind's eye she saw a little wooden boat concealing a tightly rolled letter, felt Connor's gaze on her as he pulled her from the river in the palace woods, failing to hide his smile at her fumbled attempt at decorum. Theirs had been a memorable beginning too. Unaware of her sudden reverie, Theo placed his goblet carefully off to one side, selected a piece of ginger, and nibbled on the corner.

With considerable effort, she pushed the memories away. She'd made a deal, and she'd yet to find a way around it. In the meantime, thoughts like that would only make it harder to uphold her end. Returning her attention to Theo, Jacs gently extracted her hand from his, picked a piece of ginger off the plate, and took a bite. She coughed as an unexpected heat seized her throat.

"*This* is your favorite food?" she asked.

Theo grinned.

19

BREAKING AND ENTERING

Heads low and steps light, keeping to the shadows and side streets, they ran through Bridgeport. Clutching a stitch in his side, Connor let his anger fuel his strides. He hated the feeling that they were running away. Hated that a man like Celos was spreading lies about Jacs to her own people and hated that people were humoring them.

"We should at least destroy that mirror," he hissed.

"And they'll say we're silencing the truth, and it will solidify their cause. No, history will prove him wrong. We need to focus on what we *can* do that will succeed," Masterchiv Rathbone replied, taking a sharp left and forcing him to skid around the corner.

As they approached the prison, they slowed to a walk. "She said it was in the storehouse beside the . . . Do you think that's it?" Dryft asked, pointing at a windowless barn beside what was unmistakably the town's prison.

"It better be, I want us clear of this town before that brute finishes his spiel," Masterchiv Rathbone said, striding up to a small door to the left of the large warehouse doors and wrenching on the handle. It shifted in its frame but didn't open. She cursed and inspected the lock. "Likely the owner's with the others," she muttered to herself. "But we can't wait for her to come back."

She walked back a couple of steps, then produced a well-aimed kick. The door flew inward on its hinges, and a crash of splintering wood spoke to the fate of its former lock.

"Hurry, we don't have much time," she said, waving Connor and Dryft inside.

"That was incredible," Connor remarked as he passed her.

The room was dimly lit, and dust motes peppered the strips of light coming in from the open door.

"Where do you think it'll . . . oh." Connor stopped as his eyes adjusted and he saw a wagon in the middle of the storehouse with the fabric of a giant hot-air balloon piled inside.

"We need a horse," Masterchiv Rathbone said, looking at Dryft.

"On it," she replied and dashed out the door.

"And firewood," Connor said, remembering what Jacs had told him about her voyage up the Cliff. "We can pick some up from Jacs's farm on the way to the Cliff. I saw a pile by the barn."

"Good eye, Your Grace. Let's see if we can open these doors so we can get the wagon out."

Together they approached the storehouse's large barn doors. It was locked with a heavy chain and padlocked from the inside. "There's got to be a key somewhere in here," Masterchiv Rathbone said. "Have a look in those drawers over there, and I'll check this desk."

"You mean these keys?" a creaky voice from the shadows asked. Both Connor and Masterchiv Rathbone spun around to see a tall woman with arms as thick as birch trees leaning against the door frame. In her hand, silhouetted against the light, she held a ring of keys. "You owe me a new lock," she added mildly. "Where do I send the invoice?"

Masterchiv Rathbone gestured for Connor to stay behind her.

"We have orders to retrieve this balloon."

"Whose orders?"

"And permission from Mayor Odette Linheir."

"That's nice. Do you know how questions work, Knight? I ask, you answer, I don't want an unrelated fun fact. Who are you and why do you want the balloon?"

Masterchiv Rathbone glowered at the figure in the doorway.

"I'll hazard a guess. You're the Upperites from the square sent by our very own Jacqueline, aren't you?"

"Yes."

"The man in the mirror didn't have very nice things to say about your kind, you know. Or her, for that matter."

"I can imagine."

"The nerve of him. Trust a man to be full of muck."

"So . . . you don't agree with him?" Connor asked.

"Of course not. Left early, didn't I? Don't have time for hogwash."

Masterchiv Rathbone lowered her shoulders.

"And the rest of the town?" Connor asked.

The woman considered for a moment, then shrugged, pushing herself away from the door frame to approach them. "Some people will believe anything. I'd say a lot of them were willing to believe this flavor of attercoppe story. I have enough dealings with prisoners to know evil when I see it, and Jacqueline has never once struck me as flying even close to his painting of her. So, let me try again: Who exactly are you, and what do you want with her balloon?"

"I'm Masterchiv Cassida Rathbone, Captain of the Queensguard. We need to get to the Queen and tell her what's happened here today. The balloon is our only way to do that."

The woman chortled heartily. "You're mad."

"And running out of patience."

"Okay, okay, hold your horses, let me just open this door for you. Captain of the Queensguard—well, that is a treat. I wonder if you have a moment to sign my guestbook. I've had a few important women come through here and have quite a collection of autographs," the woman said sincerely.

"Fine," Masterchiv Rathbone grumbled, but Connor caught the quirk of her lip.

"I'm Cadence, by the way, Cadence Fentree."

"Thank you for your help, Ms. Fentree," Connor said, stepping around Masterchiv Rathbone. "If you could keep our visit here to yourself, I promise the Crown will pay you handsomely for your silence and reimburse you for damages to your door." At his words, her face lit up.

"That would be much appreciated. There we are," she said as the lock fell into her awaiting hand. With a hearty tug, she pulled the chain free of the doors and began to slide them open. Her muscles rippled from the strain, and slowly but surely, the door scraped open. Masterchiv Rathbone threw her weight into the other one and the two doors eased open.

Connor saw Dryft leading their horses toward the storehouse and waved her over. In a matter of minutes, they had hitched the horses to the wagon, thanked Cadence heartily, and lurched into motion. The cobbles clattered as Masterchiv Rathbone spurred the horses out of town.

"We'll lay low at Jacqueline's farm for the rest of the day, then get ready to fly before dawn tomorrow," Masterchiv Rathbone said.

"Why not now?" Dryft asked.

"The balloon is too obvious. If we launch it during the day, it'll draw those men to us, and we can't know they won't shoot us down."

"Plus, it's better to fly the balloon before the heat of the day. Warm air makes it harder to obtain lift," Connor added, drawing looks of interest and amusement from his companions. "What? I'm the reason Jacqueline needed to make hot-air balloons. She's been sending me letters with them for years; you think I never asked how they work?"

20

LOVE, SUBTERFUGE, AND INVENTION: EVERYTHING A YOUNG QUEEN REQUIRES

The horror of the last few hours thrummed through Jacs's veins, and Theo's kindness only made her feel worse. What was she thinking, bringing the boy to face a member of the Court? How did she not foresee the Griffin's wrath? It was just as she'd said to Theo; the Griffins answer to no woman. She had been a fool to think she'd had any form of control over that situation. Releasing a shaky breath, she turned her attention to the Lordson walking quietly beside her. He was still a little pale, but at least the shadows had faded from beneath his eyes. For that she was thankful.

"Your Majesty," Cyrus panted from behind her. She stopped and waited for him to catch up, Theo hovering nearby. Amber, Chiv. Ryder, and the two male guards halted as well. "News from the catacombs. The Griffins have broken through and a half dozen women have been pulled from a section of the labyrinth. Injured but alive. The Court have doubled their efforts. The way the tunnels collapsed left pockets untouched, so-called safe zones. The hope is that we will continue to find groups of survivors. So far, however, four bodies have also been pulled from the wreckage. Not all of them ours."

Jacs's heart sank as she exhaled and thanked him for the update.

"Also, we caught a fragment of Flent as she ran away from a crystal."

"Ran away? What do you mean?"

"Well, that's what's concerning. From the looks of things, she buried her crystals in the rubble. We can't make out why she would try to bury her lines of communication."

Jacs frowned. "That's odd. Do we have eyes on any of our other knights?"

"No, Your Majesty."

Amber stepped forward. "And you're sure she deliberately buried her crystals?"

"Almost certain."

"That doesn't make sense," Amber whispered.

"Thank you, Cyrus, keep sending updates," Jacs said, dismissing the scryer before turning to Amber. "What are the chances she's turned on us?"

"Flent? She wouldn't."

"She might. What if she led our troops right into an ambush?"

"She's loyal to the Crown."

"Her aunt may have had more influence over her than we thought."

"But I oversaw their interaction at the Bard. There was nothing that indicated treason." Amber shook her head, crossing her arms.

Jacs studied her face and saw doubt flicker behind her eyes. "It could have been a ruse," she said softly. "But it doesn't matter now, the facts remain the same: we need to extract our troops and hope

Flent has been seized by a momentary madness. We all know what the catacombs do to the mind."

"Yeah . . . that could be it," Amber said softly.

"Your Majesty," Druine interrupted, "five minutes."

"Thank you," she said, pulling her attention from Amber and propelling the small group down the halls to the library. Her study was out of the question as it was still in ruins, but fortunately the library had only suffered a minor jostling. The librarian, Master Nicola Eyren, greeted Jacs's entourage curtly as they entered and resumed her task of replacing several fallen books on the shelves.

"Master Eyren, I trust you're well?" Jacs asked.

"Hardly, Your Majesty. But it's been a good excuse for a dusting, and I did find a tome that had been incorrectly shelved months ago, so I suppose every earthquake has an upside," she said, then pointed across the room. "I've set you up in the corner as you requested."

"Thank you," Jacs said and made a beeline for the table decorated with both colors of scry crystal and a bowl. Theo followed a half pace behind, and her four guards took up their posts without a word. On her way to the small table, Jacs glanced over to where Theo had pulled up short, eye caught by a title on one of the shelves. His hand shook as he removed a leather-bound volume. Pausing, she said, "Druine, can you take Theo to get some refreshments? This might take a while. Theo, why don't you take it easy this afternoon? Maybe spend some time in the pools? If there's anything you need, don't hesitate to ask."

"Many thanks, Your Highness." He returned the book to its place and paused, looking suddenly apprehensive, "There's just one thing before I go. With all that happened this morning, I never had the chance to present you with my token." From deep within his doublet, he withdrew a small golden box. "It is customary that when a token of promise is given, one reciprocates. While we are courting, I honor your intention by wearing your ring. In return, I hope you will honor mine by wearing a treasured symbol of my family."

Jacs felt the blood drain from her face and she quickly ducked her head in a way that she hoped conveyed coy pleasure rather than alarm. She could do nothing but watch as Theo closed the distance between them and offered her the box. Somewhere behind her, Amber cleared her throat, and as if by ordered command, Jacs drew a smile on her face.

"You are far too generous, thank you," she managed to say before he flicked the clasp open and revealed the box's contents. Sitting on the cream velvet pillow within, a small gold brooch in the shape of fanned peacock feathers glistened. She thanked the stars it wasn't a ring.

"May I?" he asked, only pinning it to her tunic once she'd nodded her consent.

"I'll wear this proudly," she said, wishing it were true and floating a forefinger to rest on the cold metal. The Lordson bowed, a grateful smile passing his lips, and allowed Druine to whisk him from the room.

She shot a look of apprehension to Amber, refused to meet the eye of anyone else, dropped her hand from the brooch, and took a breath.

Collecting herself, she flicked her hair to cover the pin and sat in front of the bowl. "Cornelius Frean," she said quietly and felt her heart leap to hear his voice a few seconds later.

"Can you hear me?"

"Yes! Connor I can hear you. Is everyone okay on your end?"

"Just fine, we have the balloon and are waiting out the day before we set it up. I can't wait to see you."

"I can't wait to see you either."

Connor's next words were hesitant and laced with forced enthusiasm. "I couldn't quite see but I . . . heard . . . What was . . . what is Theo's token?"

Jacs felt her stomach drop and she looked at the purple and blue crystals, then at the clock, which showed she had been three minutes late to their agreed check-in time. Connor wouldn't have been late. Connor would have checked in on time. From the purple crystal's angle, he might not have seen much, but the blue crystal shone smugly next to it. He would have heard everything.

She brushed her hair aside and showed the peacock pin to the purple crystal. Silence emanated from the bowl. She tried not to look as guilty as she felt.

"It's pretty," he said.

"It doesn't mean—"

"So you two are officially courting."

She couldn't say it. Couldn't form the word, so she just nodded. She wished, not for the first time, that she could see him. It was torture, hearing the hurt in his voice and guessing his reactions. She pulled her hair back over her shoulder and covered the pin again.

"I'll figure this out," she said.

"Yeah. Just . . . just keep me updated on its progress. I won't be made the fool."

"Of course! I will, of course I will. Connor, I promise—"

Clearing his throat, Connor cut her off and firmly changed the subject. "How is everyone up there?"

Jacs followed his lead. "Not the best. Adaine is still unresponsive, a handful of people were injured, they're pulling four bodies from the catacombs, and . . . we lost Barlow."

"Barlow? No . . . have you contacted his family? I think they live in Bregend?"

"Yes, I sent a messenger this morning."

Connor was quiet for a moment. "He was so young."

"I know." Jacs cleared her throat. "How did the meeting with Mayor Linheir go? How's Bridgeport?"

The silence that radiated from the bowl was so long and so loud, Jacs almost said Connor's name into it again. Finally, he replied, "Jacs . . . I think it best I tell you in person."

"What is it?"

"It's . . ."

Masterchiv Rathbone's voice cut across Connor's, "Your Majesty, Celos has got to the minds and hearts of the people. He's been planning this long before we even knew of his existence. To retaliate now would be foolish. We need to take a step back and plan our next move."

"What has he done?" Jacs asked.

"It's a matter that we can address when we see you. You have enough on your plate for the moment, and there's nothing you can do to help the situation as it stands. Suffice it to say Lowrian faith in the Crown has been forced into the ground."

"Do they know I didn't cut the Bridge?"

"Some do, but many aren't convinced."

Jacs sat back in her chair and closed her eyes. "Okay, you're right, we can work on that once you're back. I'll focus on getting our troops out of the catacombs and finding another way into Alethia. I've discovered that there might be tunnels connecting it to the Claustrom manor."

Amber stepped forward. "Did you say tunnels?"

Jacs spun around and regarded her. "Yes, what have you heard?"

Frowning slightly, Amber said, "Yves claimed the Sons of Celos used tunnels to sneak into the palace during the gala. I was waiting for my scouts to confirm his story before telling you, but if it's true, the explosion in your wing likely came from tunnels beneath the palace. And if there's more, if there's a network of tunnels beneath the Upper Realm connecting Alethia to key locations . . . Yves might know where they are. He might know how to get in from the Claustrom manor."

"You think?"

"I can ask."

Jacs's heart fluttered. "Amber, that changes everything. That gives us a way in! Okay, let's work on that."

"And we'll work on flying your balloon," Connor said.

Switching tracks, Jacs returned her gaze to the bowl. "Right. Okay, let me walk you through the setup. I checked in with the Griffins, and they"—she paused as the image of Theo writhing on the throne-room floor filled her mind. Hurriedly she pushed it away—"are occupied with digging out the tunnels, so will not be able to help you. Here's what you need to do."

She spent the next few minutes outlining the correct way to lay the balloon out, how to attach the basket, what rigging should be in place, and how to control the lift. The more she talked, the more she worried.

"Are you sure you're comfortable trying this?" she asked suddenly after suggesting they find an anchor or grappling hook for when they make it to the Upper Realm. "You can always lay low until we can find another way to get you."

"That's no longer an option, Your Majesty," Masterchiv Rathbone said curtly.

"We'll be fine," Connor said, although Jacs could hear Masterchiv Rathbone and Dryft muttering to each other in the background. "We're flying in a Jacs-made hot-air balloon. I can't think of anything I would trust more."

"Okay, but if it's too windy tomorrow morning, or if the balloon doesn't inflate, or if the basket doesn't feel sturdy, please just stay where you are. I'm sure I can build favor enough with the Griffins soon to convince them to help. Or I could create something to bridge the realms and . . ."

"Jacs. Stop worrying. We'll be fine. This is the fastest way to get to you, it will work."

"Okay. Just please be careful."

"Your Majesty?" Masterchiv Rathbone's voice cut in again. "Permission to speak with Chiv. Everstar. I have a few updates to relate to her."

"Of course," she said, beckoning Amber over and switching places. While the knights discussed tactics, Jacs wandered over to stand in front of the large windows overlooking the rose garden. Back home, rosebushes were planted at the end of every row of crop. They were a more sensitive flower, susceptible to disease, so if the row was in danger of catching something, the rose would suffer first. That gave her and her mother enough time to do what they could to save the rest of the crop. Its sensitivity was its greatest asset. Without fair warning, whole crops might perish. Here in the Upper Realm, roses were used just for enjoyment. Any sick bush was quickly removed to save the other pretty blooms.

She massaged her temples with her fingertips, willing her mind to settle. They hadn't had any warning before Celos had attacked. No rosebush omen had foretold his assault. There were no clues to hint at what he might do next. She needed to stop him. Soon. Cut him out before his poison took root in the hearts of the people. She needed another way into Alethia.

"I simply must speak with her!" Hera's shrill cadence made Jacs turn around in time to see the Lord sweep into the library with a face like a thundercloud. Jacs heard Masterchiv Rathbone sign off, and Amber broke their connection before approaching to stand nearer to her Queen.

"Good afternoon, Lord Claustrom," Jacs said mildly. "To what do I owe the pleasure?"

"You're stalling."

"Excuse me?"

"You're stalling. My brother has been here two days and he's just informed me you've made no offer of marriage to him yet. Where is the proposal?" she seethed, fists balled in her gown.

Jacs blinked. "Lord Claustrom, I'll encourage you to watch your tone," she said, turning her back on the window. "We are in a library, after all."

"We had a deal."

"There's been an *explosion*."

"It takes four words at most, two if you disregard grammar; I find it hard to believe you haven't found the time."

Jacs narrowed her eyes and stood her ground. "Hera, be reasonable. I'm not going to rush something as important as this."

"This isn't some airy-fairy romance, Your Majesty. This is a transaction, and you are *not* upholding your end of the deal," Hera snapped.

"There's a proper way these things are done."

"That doesn't give you leave to drag your feet every step of the way. We made that deal weeks ago."

"He's wearing my ring, I'm wearing his brooch, progress is being made, but I refuse to rush something as important as this," Jacs said firmly. She pushed her hair over her shoulder to reveal the pin, and Hera's face softened when her gaze fell on the golden feathers. Jacs glanced down as a thought struck her. "But you're right," she said quietly. "I guess I just can't shake my romantic fancies. I want to do right by your family and right by your brother, Hera. He deserves that. The truth is," she paused, as the idea took root and bloomed in her mind, "the truth is, it doesn't feel right without a proper blessing."

Hera faltered. "A proper blessing? I gave it!"

"While I respect the blessing of his Lord, and accept it gratefully, I just can't justify making a proposal of marriage without receiving a blessing from his mother."

"Mother?"

"Of course. It's the appropriate course of action, if we are to join our two families, I must ask your mother's blessing. In fact," she added brightly, "why don't I visit your mother in Hesperida? Theo's childhood home would be the perfect setting for a proposal as well! Oh, that's a fantastic idea, don't you agree, Lord Claustrom?"

Caught on the back foot, Hera said, "Yes of course. That's very thoughtful of you, Your Majesty. I feared . . . but no, of course you're right. It is only proper."

"I understand I've put a lot of weight on your shoulders, and that no doubt has led to you feeling overwhelmed, so I will excuse your . . . outburst. Would you be so good as to contact your mother and prepare her for my visit? Since you are eager, we can aim to leave by the end of the month. I admit it will be a happy distraction from what's happened here."

"Yes! That is wonderful news, I'll write a message to her immediately. Thank you, Your Majesty." Hera dipped her knee into just shy of a bow and disappeared.

In the silence that followed, Amber cleared her throat. "You're going to spend your life humoring that plip."

Jacs sighed, making sure the library door was closed before replying, "I hope not . . . for now she's simply our ticket to Alethia. Besides, my absence will give the palace builders an opportunity to repair my chambers without me hovering around." Throwing a glance out the window at the setting sun, she twisted a strand of hair around her finger. Turning to one of Yves's men, Thomas, she said, "But first, I need the late Queen's journals, both. They were in my study, so whoever is sent to fetch them must be careful, as that room is still in shambles. Oh! And I need some paper and writing utensils." The dancer bowed and left to follow her command.

The room was now empty save for Jacs, Amber, Chiv. Ryder, and Master Eyren, who was on the third floor muttering about shelf stability.

"Amber, I need you to speak with Yves and find out if he knows how to get into the tunnels at the Claustrom manor. He's about to take the role of guide once again. If he needs a little more incentive, do what you must without going overboard. You know how he is—last time we spoke he honestly asked me about jewel-studded collars for his peahens. Apparently, he feels bad that they're so drab when compared with their male counterparts. I didn't even know I was funding peahens!"

Amber nodded slowly. "Peahens aside . . . There are a lot of what-ifs in this plan."

"There always are, but we have a bit of time to smooth out most of them. What we need to make sure of is that we're able to bring enough military support with us to take on Celos, but not so much that we raise suspicions when we arrive."

"It's only proper that the Queen travel with appropriate security. I'm sure we can figure something out," Chiv. Ryder said.

Amber looked thoughtful.

"And if a dozen of them didn't look like military, then we'd get an extra dozen fighters accompanying us, and no one would be the wiser."

"Also true. What are you thinking? Disguising knights and guards as serving staff?" Jacs asked.

"Yes . . ." Amber hesitated and sighed. It looked like her next words physically hurt her to say. "We could also consider . . . I mean, male dance troupes are all the rage at the moment. The Sons of Celos belonged to Lady Claustrom, but they aren't the only male troupe in the Queendom. I'm sure with new livery, and a different leader . . . Without Yves as their face it's unlikely that she would suspect . . ." She sighed. "The truth is, Yves's men are shaping up to be capable soldiers. We could have a troupe of ready warriors with us that we could pass off as a gift of entertainment for her ladyship."

Jacs gaped at her.

"Not that I'm saying we change the whole structure of the military as we know it!" Amber hurried to add. "It's just one troupe of already highly skilled men. All currently trained under my supervision, might I add. I know that they more than anyone would be eager for the opportunity to help bring Celos down."

"Very wise, Chiv. Everstar," Jacs said with a smile. "I'll leave you to sort out the details with Yves, and I'll call Master Moira in to design their livery. We'll have to give them a new name as well."

"Oh, I'm sure Yves can be counted on for that," Amber replied with a lopsided grin of her own. A serving boy came in with his arms filled with papers and writing instruments, which he set at a desk near the window at Jacs's instruction.

"We're still trying to locate the journals, Your Majesty," he said apologetically.

"That's understandable," Jacs said. "Have them brought to me as soon as they're found. I especially want the empty journal. They were on a table beneath the mosaic of the Azulon Sea."

"I'll let them know," the boy said before taking his leave.

"Okay then, we all have work to do. Amber, go find Yves, I'm sure I'll be fine in the library for an hour or so with only Chiv. Ryder as my guard."

Amber shook her head. "I'll send someone to cover for me. Let me know if you need anything."

Jacs thought for a moment. "Just an update on Adaine's condition."

"Of course, I'll also have the kitchens send up some snacks."

Jacs smiled. "Thanks, Amber."

The sun had long since slipped below the horizon, and candles now burned brightly around Jacs's table near the window. Refreshments arrived frequently, and every hour she would move to her crystals and bowl and check in with Connor. It seemed like they were both caught in an evening of waiting. It was so wonderful to hear his voice each time, even if it brought additional anxiety about how the balloon ride would fare the next morning.

The papers that littered her worktable were filled with different designs and plans. She had compiled a list of guards and knights she wanted at her side when they snuck into Alethia, as well as instructions for Lena and her mother while she was away from the palace. Her to-do list had become so overwhelming that she had put it all in a pile, pushed it to the side, and allowed herself to work on something different.

The late evening now found her hunched over a design that was the descendant of a small pile of scrunched paper to her left. Despite the disappointment each tossed idea brought, she was beaming. To be faced with a problem like this, to have a tangible problem in need of solving, was a relief. She only wished Master Leschi were with her to help her find a solution. Sitting back, she stretched the kink in her neck and felt a small pop between her shoulder blades. On the paper before her was her next project. One she could tackle once Celos was defeated.

But don't think about that just yet.

She would use a controlled fire and the same principles that lifted her hot-air balloon, while not forgetting the need for a counterbalance—well, that would simply add the opportunity for multiple carriages . . . but it was there, spread out before her. The beginnings of a new bridge system between realms.

"Your Majesty?" A voice cut across her musings, and she spun around.

"Yes?"

"We found them; we found the journals."

21

SOMETHING NEW

"You surprise me, Chivilra, and I'm not easily surprised."

"Didn't mean to keep you guessing, Yves. I'm only thinking about what's best for the Queendom."

"Of course," Yves said with a shallow bow. His eyes held a smile.

After Amber received confirmation from Master Moira—who had remained in the palace since the gala—that she would be able to meet with Amber the following afternoon, she'd sought out the dancer. Expecting to find him in the pools or pestering the serving staff at this time of night, she had been surprised to hear that he was training in the ring. Alone.

She had watched him shift through several sequences from the sidelines before interrupting his movements and hadn't quite known what to do with the look he gave her when he realized she'd been watching him. Rather than decipher its meaning, she quickly got to the point.

"You mentioned tunnels beneath the palace, tunnels that helped the Sons sneak in while you and your troupe used the front door."

"That I did. Excellent memory, Chiv."

"How much do you know about the tunnels?"

Yves raised a brow suggestively. "Most women ply me with wine for such delicate information." He tucked his grin away at Amber's stony expression and amended, "How much would you like to know?"

"Do you know about the tunnels connecting the Claustrom manor to Alethia?"

"Yes."

"Could you locate their entrance?"

"Naturally. I bet I could do it blindfolded. In fact, I believe I have."

Amber exhaled sharply and quickly caught him up to speed with the Queen's plans for him and his troupe. When she was done, she leaned against the railing while he ran a towel across the back of his neck, deep in thought.

"So, I can't lead my men?"

"Not if you think Lady Claustrom would recognize you. We can't risk her knowing that the dancers we bring into her manor are also her very own Sons of Celos. It would also be wise to identify any other boys you think she'd be able to point out."

"Men," Yves said reflexively. He shook his head. "The troupe hardly interacted with her face-to-face. Any assignment was shared with us by messenger, and we were rarely invited into her manor . . . especially after I embarrassed her genteel at a palace performance for Queen Ariel, and that was years ago." Yves bounced on the balls of his feet at the memory and looked a very long way from sorry about whatever had happened to cause him to fall out of favor with Genteel Brovnen.

Amber considered this. "Do you think there is a chance she would recognize you?"

At the question, Yves's smile broadened, and he winked. "Oh I should expect so, Chiv. Everstar. Regardless of how few face-to-face meetings we've had, I assure you, I made a lasting impression."

Amber wrinkled her nose.

"Let's just say Genteel Brovnen has every reason to be suspicious of his lady's fidelity."

"I get it, Yves," Amber said, causing him to chuckle.

"But I would be happy to suggest a substitute leader and could always take on a disguise as part of the entourage so that I'm at hand when the time comes to lead my Queen to Alethia. Not to mention, I'd love a chance to see my men put your training to use in the battle that follows."

Amber blinked. "You would stay and fight?"

"Of course."

"Don't you have a cottage to furnish?"

"Yes. Fret not, I've already spoken with the palace scryers about refurbishing some of those unused crystals into a chandelier, but I would be a spineless leader indeed if I abandoned my men before the biggest performance of their lives."

"Well, you surprise me, Yves," Amber said.

"I assure you, Chiv. Everstar, it is my every intention to keep you guessing."

22

WAITING

"This is madness," Iliana Dryft muttered for the umpteenth time. Connor decided to ignore her. Jacs had said once that madness and genius tended to dance side by side, so he just had to believe they were waltzing on the side of genius.

The night was still and calm, and though the moon was near full, the thick cloud cover obscured most of its light. Every dip and rise in the road caused the wagon wheels to creak and groan. If Jacs's home had been any closer to town, Connor was sure the ruckus would have drawn a crowd. Instead, their only follower was Ranger, and he disappeared without a meow of goodbye after the first ten minutes of their journey.

The trio spoke very little as the farm shrank into the distance. Connor's mind was too full of balloon-flying instructions for him to want to make small talk. Like holding water in his cupped hands, he was afraid they'd all trickle away. Of course he had faith in Jacs's balloon, but he also knew that she'd flown it solo, and they would now have the weight of two extra people in the basket. But Jacs had given strict instructions as to how to make the necessary adaptations to account for the extra weight. They had followed her instructions to a T. No, it would be fine. It had to be fine. He needed to return to the Upper Realm.

"This is as good a spot as any," Masterchiv Rathbone announced when the farm was no longer visible, and the town lights were far enough away to appear as pinpricks of gold behind them. Pulling the horses up, Dryft jumped from the wagon and helped Connor down to the ground. Masterchiv Rathbone stepped over the driver's bench and into the wagon bed. Between the three of them, they lifted the basket and balloon out of the wagon and dragged it into the clearing. It took several minutes to spread the canvas out, and several minutes more to set the basket to rights and fill its base with firewood. Connor ignored the little voice that kept reminding him that he was going to be standing beneath a flame on a pile of firewood inside a flammable wicker basket.

"People don't fly," Dryft muttered to his right. "This is Alessi territory, and none of us are Alessi. Well, maybe you are, Masterchiv." She shot a sidelong look at Connor, the ghost of a smile quirking her lips. "Any tips for us mortals?"

"Learn how to hide the feathers," Masterchiv Rathbone said lightly as she placed another piece of wood in the basket.

"You two are hilarious," Connor said. Scanning the balloon, he checked the rigging the way Jacs had instructed. It would work. It was time to light the fire.

"Jacs Frean," Connor said into the bowl he'd taken from her farm.

"I can hear you, Connor, can you hear me?" her voice came as a whisper as if she were frightened to speak across realms.

"I can hear you. We've just set the balloon up, and Masterchiv Rathbone's lighting the fire. How long does it usually take to inflate?"

"About half an hour? Maybe longer, depending," Jacs said. "Connor, are you sure about this?"

"Definitely," Connor replied. "We'll be fine. I'll be seeing you before dawn's light."

"Okay. Please be careful. I'll be on the edge with a few guards so we can help pull you in if needed. Did you remember a rope and hook?"

"Check and check. We have a rope attached to a grappling hook we found in your barn. Why did you have so many different grappling hooks, by the way? There were about four to choose from."

Jacs's laugh emerged from the bowl. "Master Leschi was experimenting with designs. She ended up favoring one with a bit of a barb on the end to increase the chances of it catching on to something. It looked like a giant fishhook."

Connor picked up the one he had chosen, turning it this way and that. "I have one with three inverted prongs."

"Excellent choice," Jacs said, her voice carrying a smile.

"Your Grace, we need your hands," Dryft said.

"Okay, Jacs, I have to go help with inflation, but I'll check in soon." His superstitions got the better of him and he dared not say anything that sounded like a goodbye. "Yours," he said instead.

"Yours, always." Jacs's whisper emboldened him, and he slipped the bowl into his pack.

Connor let his gaze shift back to the balloon. It was beginning to fill steadily with air; the only sound was the crackle and hiss of the fire and the occasional creak of the canvas and rigging. He had to keep reminding himself to breathe. This was happening.

23

QUEEN ARIEL'S JOURNAL

Jacs held Queen Ariel's journal in her hands reverentially before placing it in front of her on the desk. Suddenly nervous, she rubbed her hands together, creating friction and heat, then pressed her warm palms into the leather cover. Pulling her hands away, she saw *Cornelius* appear for an instant before disappearing. Just like her book of missing boys, Queen Ariel had used invisible ink to protect the journal's contents. An equal measure of excitement and apprehension jolted through her. Eyeing the candles on her desk, she drew a short stout one nearer.

Taking a shuddering breath, Jacs opened the journal and held the first page above, but not touching, the little dancing flame. A date appeared in the top right-hand corner. Jacs realized with a start that this was a letter dated the week before Queen Ariel was murdered. It was a letter addressed to Connor. The words unfurled themselves across the page as the heat from the flame lovingly revealed each letter. She read:

My darling son,

If you are reading this, I am no longer with you. I only hope you have found peace, that your father is well, and that you remember every day that I love you. I love you, and I am so proud of the man you are becoming. You will do incredible things for this Queendom, and if you have found this journal, it is because things are about to get worse before they get better.

I have spent years searching for an ever-increasing list of missing boys and have finally discovered their whereabouts. Lord Sybil Claustrom visited me late last night in a frenzy. She asked me to share the burden of her secret. I, not knowing what this secret was but eager to honor our decades of friendship, accepted. I fear that, in sharing this knowledge with me, she has put my life in danger. She asked for a compliance I was unable to provide. Our inability to see eye to eye may be my downfall, but if I can best her first, I may have a chance to right the years of wrongs she has inflicted upon our Queendom.

But I am talking in riddles. Here are the facts. Unfortunately, the missing boys are leaving their homes willingly to join a secret organization deep beneath the Upper Realm. The organization is called the Sons of Celos, and they live in a city named Alethia. It lies past the Catacombs of Lethe. You may recognize the name of the organization as the name of a popular dancing troupe that has visited our palace once before. This troupe is a front for Celos. It is how they find their victims. They target disillusioned, isolated, and jaded men, twist their minds against the Crown, and offer them the promise of a better life.

Celos is their leader, their "father." He is the head of the snake that must be severed. His story may help you understand how to beat him. As a young man, he fell in love with Lord Claustrom, and from the look on her face when she told me, it is likely she loved him too, once. But as she was the heir to the most powerful county in the Upper Realm, she married for power, not love. Celos, once rejected, disappeared for five years. Sybil thought he had vanished forever, until the day she received a letter from him. In the letter, he reiterated his vow of love and offered her the services of Alethia. He offered her gold, and he offered her an army of shadows. In exchange, he begged to see her, to be with her, but for his existence to remain their secret.

Sybil accepted, and began her affair, her deception, her treason. It was not long after the deal had been made that Sybil offered Celos's services to the Council of Four, and his resources have been utilized by her and by the Council ever since. With the Diversary celebration fast approaching and our upcoming meeting with the Queen of Nysa, I fear she hoped to win me over to the Council's idea of severing ties with the Lower Realm. She told me all. I refused.

I must fight to free these boys. I must fight to end Celos's hold on my Queendom. If I am unable, it will be up to you to finish what I started. You are strong enough. You are brave enough. You are kind enough, and you are exactly what this Queendom needs. Do not let fear guide our realms to ruin. We must prevail.

I love you with all my heart,
Your mother

Jacs finished reading the letter and sat back, stunned. She had known. She had known not only about the Sons, but also that her life was in danger. Put there by a close friend. And if it was this knowledge that had doomed her, then she had been unable to share it with anyone she loved. What a terrible burden.

Flicking through the remaining pages, she held each up to the candle's heat to be sure she hadn't missed anything. There were a few subsequent letters of a more personal nature. Letters reminiscing about happier times shared between Ariel and Connor. The writings of a woman who knew she did not have much time left to her beloved son. Not for the first time that day, Jacs wished Connor were with her.

After the letters were lists of instructions. With a pang, Jacs saw how many of them were discovered too late. There was a note about where to find the little book with the names of missing boys, the same book Jacs now had hidden in her bodice, and pages upon pages of ideas, descriptions, and diagrams of various tasks Connor could use to help create the Contest of Queens. The contest that, without this journal, Connor had ended up having to design on his own. A few lines jumped out at Jacs, revealed by the heat of the flame:

> *The Council is too powerful. Our next Queen will need support. Ensure the candidate is politically well connected with the lesser Lords. There is strength in numbers.*
>
> *With regards to task locations, there are a few places you would do well to avoid:*
>
> *Wrenstrom: Its citizens hold little love for the Crown, and the people's patience will not endure the ceremony of a royal visit.*
>
> *The Catacombs of Lethe: this will put you on Alethia's doorstep and may leave you vulnerable to interference from Celos and his Sons.*
>
> *Remember our discussions, consider what makes a queen. Strength without compassion becomes brutality when given power.*

Reaching the end, Jacs closed the book, deep in thought.

She read over the first letter again. One thing was for certain; Lady Sybil Claustrom held the key to Alethia.

24

ESCAPING THE LOWER REALM

Connor had never felt more alive. His every particle was on edge, his nerves wound tight and ready to snap. Bridgeport had suddenly become enemy territory, and it was his mission to sneak a giant balloon out of town without raising suspicions or alerting the townspeople. He felt like a character in a book, and he finally felt like one of the important ones. Dare he dream to be the main character? A dashing heroine like Amelia the Daring? No, he needed a few victories under his belt before he could claim that, but it felt good to finally be useful.

Working closely with Masterchiv Rathbone and ensuring the balloon was inflating without issue, he shared a look with Dryft.

She took in his broad grin and frowned. "Your Grace, remember, this isn't a game."

"I know, I know," he whispered impatiently. *Killjoy.* Of course he knew this was serious. It didn't mean he couldn't enjoy himself.

It was happening.

The balloon was almost ready for its second flight. Connor felt the excitement thrum through him as he pushed another log into the fire.

"What's that?" Dryft said suddenly, pointing in the direction of the town. Both Connor and Masterchiv Rathbone spun around. A distant drumming of hoofbeats floated toward them over the meadows.

"Lights," Masterchiv Rathbone said.

"Torches," Connor added.

"I doubt they've come to cheer us on," Dryft said with a curse. The balloon was just over halfway filled.

"We might be up and away before they reach us," Masterchiv Rathbone said with an appraising glance at the balloon. "They're still a long way off."

"Okay, then we need to be ready to go as soon as we can," Connor said.

"Agreed," said Dryft.

Masterchiv Rathbone's gaze darted to each variable, and she said briskly, "Your Grace, get in now. Dryft and I will be the ones to cut the tethers and jump in after. No arguing, we've got the dexterity. You're still functioning at reduced capacity. The last thing we need is you getting stuck on the wrong side of that basket. Besides, you know more about how the balloon works, so we need you by the burner."

"Understood," Connor said and hoisted himself up and over the lip. The handful of minutes that followed were the most harrowing of Connor's life.

He sat on a small pile of firewood, every muscle tensed for action. The two soldiers looked just as tightly wound. Dryft kept flexing her fingers around her rope, and Masterchiv Rathbone had unconsciously assumed a defensive stance.

As each second trickled by, the lights came steadily closer. Golden specks became flecks, then dots, then orbs that illuminated the faces of a dozen men on horseback.

Men? Connor thought with a start.

"Those are *men*, right?" he hissed over the edge of the basket.

"Yes. We'll be facing the Sons, it seems," Masterchiv Rathbone said, rolling her shoulders. Walking the short distance to the wagon they had used to transport the balloon, she picked up a length of rope from the back. With a few deft motions she tied a short log to one end and hung it from her belt. That done, she motioned to Dryft, and together they pulled the wagon directly between the horde and the balloon.

Connor felt a spark of fear ignite somewhere around his navel. The rope tethers lay slack along the earth, basket still grounded.

We're going to make it, Connor thought. *We just need more time.*

"Halt!" one of the Sons roared. His cry spurred the horses into a gallop and the group began to quickly close the distance between them. Connor forced more wood into the burner, willing the balloon to fill faster.

"Your Grace," Masterchiv Rathbone said calmly. "You are to get yourself up to the Upper Realm no matter who gets left behind. Is that clear?"

Connor balked. "What? No. We go together."

"Dryft, be ready to lift the no-kill order on my command. It may not come to that, so let's try to avoid casualties at all costs. Our priority is Cornelius."

"Understood."

"Masterchiv——" Connor began.

Eyes never leaving the approaching horde, she shook her head. "Promise me, Your Grace. Whatever happens, you need to make it up the Cliff."

"Don't make me leave you behind."

"Stoke the fire," she hissed. "Your duty is to the Queen. We'll hold them off as long as we can."

"No! Promise me you'll both climb in before we cut the tethers. I won't leave you!"

"You'll follow orders," Masterchiv Rathbone snapped.

The men were close enough now that Connor could make out their twisted facial expressions as torchlight writhed against their shadows. They thundered toward the balloon with the inevitability of the tide, some with swords drawn, others holding spears or maces. He glanced up at the balloon and his heart sank. It wasn't ready, and they were out of time.

"Dryft?"

"Ready."

"No!" Connor yelled.

"NOW!"

The two soldiers charged at the horde. Hoofbeats tattooed scars into the earth and the horses were upon the guardpair.

"Don't let them escape!" a deep voice barked.

With practiced grace, Masterchiv Rathbone launched herself over the wagon and side-stepped as a spear hurtled toward her. It missed her by inches, and she quickly ripped it from the earth, balancing it in her palm. A breath, a grunt, and she'd launched it back at the oncoming riders. This time, the pointed tip found its mark. Connor watched in horrified awe as a horse screamed, a rider fell, and the horse behind him reared to avoid landing on its comrade. She dashed forward, using the fallen horse as cover, and loomed over the rider now pinned beneath his mount. Tearing the sword from the prostrated Son's hand, with a cry of warning, she threw it to Dryft, who caught its hilt deftly and faced the remaining men. Masterchiv Rathbone's eyes snapped to her next opponent.

Retrieving the handmade rope weapon from her belt, she wrapped one end loosely around her elbow and shoulder. Bouncing the weighted end lightly in her palm, she spun it in a lazy circle at her side before launching the piece of wood toward the next mounted Son. It struck with a solid thunk. The man groaned, keeling over and falling from his horse before the steed could realize it had lost its rider. Four strides and a bound, and she'd floated into the saddle of the horse and spun it around. One hand on the reins, the other now whipping her makeshift meteor hammer in an arc above her head, she let it fly, striking another man.

Dryft swerved beyond the reach of another horse and with a running leap, threw herself up and onto the back of the stallion. Three swift blows, a shove, and a grunt pitched the rider unconscious to the ground. Dryft seized the reins and turned the horse about. She shared a look and a nod with Masterchiv Rathbone.

"Hyah!" she cried and spurred her mount back toward its own herd.

Connor fed two more logs into the furnace and watched the fire flare. The basket lifted feebly off the ground and touched back down. Gaze drawn to the clash of steel, he saw a hooded rider charge toward Dryft, who was now engaged with two others. A spear embedded itself into the earth beside him, thrown by an unknown assailant. He shoved another log into the flames and made a decision. He had time. He could help. Launching himself over the rim of the basket, he staggered a few steps as he landed, careful to keep the wagon between him and the oncoming hoods. He ripped the spear from the ground and tossed it at the nearby rider still making a beeline toward Dryft.

Missing his target, the spear glanced off the saddle and the rider snapped his attention to where Connor stood between the wagon and the balloon, unarmed and without a horse. With a cry, the rider pulled at the reins and changed course, thundering straight for Connor.

A different rider swerved and darted across the attacker's path, causing him to pull up short on his reins, his horse screaming as it reared against the tight bite of the bit. Momentum now lost, the attacker struggled to regain control of his mount before resuming his advance toward Connor.

Hope flared in Connor's breast and he faced the oncoming rider. He may still be new to combat, but he knew horses. He'd ridden them all his life. His attacker, judging by his awkward seat, lifted heels, and clumsy grip on the reins, was no equestrian. Connor licked his lips. He might just pull this off.

The oncoming rider shifted from a walk to a trot, and Connor climbed on top of the wagon. His breath came short already and not for the first time he cursed whatever illness had seized his lungs.

Stance wide, a slight bend in his knees, he bounced a little on the balls of his feet, balancing on the edge of the wagon. To his left, Masterchiv Rathbone struck another man off his horse, slamming the butt of her weapon into his temple as she rode past. Dryft was now being forced back by two more hoods. She needed help, and her partner was busy.

Connor's attacker charged toward him, mace sweeping low. Calm stole through Connor's mind, and he saw the next few actions fall into place like a sequence of chess moves. With the horse almost upon him, he placed his right foot on the edge of the wagon and jumped. Clumsy and heavy, he flew through the air like a brick and launched himself at the rider. Colliding with his shoulder, he flung his arms around the man roughly. In the confusion of limbs and curses, the mace struck Connor a smarting blow to the knee and fell to the earth.

With a muffled cry, the rider attempted to throw him off, but Connor trapped the man's arms and torso and used gravity's help to wrestle him from his mount. The horse sidestepped its fallen rider and usurper as they crashed to the ground.

Struggling to his feet and breathing hard, Connor straightened, limping a little, and gave the sprawled man a hearty kick in the gut for good measure before retrieving his mace, seizing his horse's reins, and swinging himself up into the saddle.

He wheezed and tried to sit up straight, but a newfound pain in his ribs caused him to double over as he kicked the horse into motion. He'd always assumed in battle you'd get stabbed once and that was it, the toughest knights able to withstand maybe two or three fatal wounds. Who knew it involved so many smaller bumps and scrapes? He was speckled with a constellation of painful points. Each one burned or twinged, demanding his attention. But he had to focus. Wheeling the creature around, he sought Dryft and Masterchiv Rathbone in the fray. There, to his left. Dryft attacked three, no four, circling hoods. Masterchiv Rathbone fought to reach her.

"Hyah!" Connor spurred his mount toward Dryft, mace raised high. The jolting rhythm of the horse's hoofbeats traveled up his spine and entwined with his own beating heart. With another cry, he raced toward the group and watched the hoods scatter as he bore down on them.

Dryft loosed a laugh of triumph to the skies and charged after one of her retreating attackers while Connor swung his mace at a hood of his own and heard the sickening crack of bone as the Son's forearm snapped beneath his blow. The man's sword fell from his now useless fingers and he howled in agony. The sound, more than the impact, shocked Connor into releasing his grip on the mace and it clattered away behind him. His stomach rolled and he fought a desire to flee. As if he could escape the screaming and newfound knowledge of what a snapping bone sounded like, felt like beneath his mace, if he ran fast enough.

Curving his course, Connor looped around and headed toward Masterchiv Rathbone, back toward the balloon. For a brief moment, he cleared the clustered chaos, riding along the perimeter of the torch-light, the night breeze whipping through his hair. Masterchiv Rathbone turned from another felled opponent and caught his eye, then widened hers and barked a warning. Too late. A low whistling sounded to his right.

Like it had collided with a stone wall, Connor's horse suddenly screamed and toppled over forelegs no longer able to support its weight. From somewhere in the dark, a volley of arrows flew and protruded from the horse's shoulder, leg, and neck. Connor felt a searing pain cut across his shin moments before his world inverted and he fell with his tumbling steed. Flinging his arms above his head, he crashed to the earth. The smell of dirt and blood filled his nostrils and he rolled instinctively to one side as he skidded to a halt. His ears filled with the horse's screams.

"Your Grace!" Masterchiv Rathbone cried. Ears ringing, he squinted through the gloom and crawled toward the cover of the balloon, away from the thrashing horse.

Reaching the wagon first, he pulled himself upright, leg throbbing, ribs burning, and looked around for a weapon. Before he could take stock, a pair of arms grabbed him from behind and angled a blade at his throat.

"Don't move. Don't scream. You're mine, balloon boy," the voice growled. A plume of foul breath curled around Connor's ear to his nose, and he fought a gag. The man's grip tightened, and Connor felt the skin of his throat part beneath the blade under the weight of his attacker's shaking fist. With a feeling of grim satisfaction, Connor let his training take over.

Sliding his hands up his midline, he seized his assailant's wrist and forced the dagger away, ducked under his shoulder while keeping control of the man's arm, and thrust the dagger into its owner's ribs. The moment he felt the dagger catch in the man's flesh, Connor cried out. Shock and revulsion rippled through him. Unwilling to force the blade deeper, he ripped it free and staggered backward with it. He clutched it in his palm as he ran for the balloon.

Like a dog too-long chained, the balloon pulled against its tethers. It was ready. A flash of light caught Connor's eye and he ducked just in time to see a torch spin toward him, thrown from one of the Sons.

It landed in the basket. He scrambled up the ropes and over the side, wheezing and gasping for air. His muscles screamed in protest.

Burning tar dripped from the torch and spread onto the stack of firewood. Connor swore, his stolen dagger dropping to the basket floor. Gripping the torch, he peered across the battle, took aim, and launched it at a cluster of riders. A cry of pain was his reward. He turned his attention back to the small fire now burning in all the wrong places. Ripping the cloak from around his shoulders, he frantically smothered the flames.

"Go! We're out of time!" Masterchiv Rathbone's order charged at Connor as she did.

With a series of slashes from a borrowed blade, she cut the four tethers that held the basket to the ground.

The balloon began to rise.

"Grab the ropes! Pull yourself up!" Connor yelled, but Masterchiv Rathbone now sat on her horse with her back to him, guarding his ascent. Dryft was locked in combat with two sword-wielding Sons on horseback and did not turn around. Masterchiv Rathbone knocked one man from his horse with the hilt of his own spear and rounded on a second.

A third rode for the tethers, launching himself from his horse to grasp the trailing cord. The basket dipped wildly to one side as it accommodated the extra weight. Connor stumbled and quickly scrambled to his feet, peering over the basket to the man now dangling in midair beneath it. Retrieving the blood-soaked dagger from the bottom of the basket, he began to saw at the rope as, hand over hand, the man hoisted himself toward Connor.

Locked in combat below, Masterchiv Rathbone cried, "Dryft! Fall back!" and struggled to disengage from her opponent. Dryft shifted her course for the balloon.

With a roar, Masterchiv Rathbone reared her mount. Its hooves sliced through the air and forced her attacker backward. Her gaze snapped skyward and then locked on to Dryft's. With her free hand, she clenched her fist and drew a thumb across her throat. Dryft nodded grimly, disengaged from her quarry with a neat sword thrust through the man's chest, and sped toward Connor's unwanted passenger. Standing in her stirrups, steering around the wagon below, she swung her stolen shortsword and struck the man down in a scream of pain and a shower of blood. He fell from the rope as the life left him. The balloon rocked violently and began climbing faster.

Blood-splattered and grim-faced, Dryft glanced up at Connor with a curt nod before charging at a cluster of three hoods.

Connor averted his gaze but could not escape the sounds of steel striking flesh and bone. The screams of men and horses filled the air with added desperation as Dryft unleashed a bladed hell upon her foes. No longer restrained, she ended each of her opponents quickly.

Scrambling for something to use, Connor weighed a piece of firewood in his hands, eyes scanning the battlefield. Hoisting it high above his head, he threw it at a hood on horseback, mid charge on his way to Masterchiv Rathbone. The log hit home with a satisfying thud, and the man crumpled, rolling off his horse. Connor punched the air in triumph.

"The ropes!" Connor yelled again. For the moment, it appeared they had the upper hand, but he didn't know how long that would last. Connor hesitated to put more wood in the fire, unwilling to speed his ascent, as soon he would be out of their reach.

Now poised just below the tethers, Masterchiv Rathbone waited for Dryft to join her behind the meager barrier of the wagon. Connor shut off the fire to slow the balloon's progress.

"Come on!" he yelled.

Dryft, now intercepted, was locked in combat with two hoods and unable to break through their barrage, their two horses forcing hers back, farther from the balloon. Masterchiv Rathbone's horse danced in place, as though sensing the hesitation of its rider. With a cry, Masterchiv Rathbone spurred her horse back into the fray, galloping toward Dryft. The two horses corralling the guard scattered as the knight's thundering hoofbeats approached. Again, she swung her roped weapon and a horseman fell. Connor inspected the flame, careful not to extinguish it as the balloon continued to hover.

From below, Masterchiv Rathbone screamed. Connor shot toward the basket's edge and searched the battlefield. Despite his efforts, the scene was getting smaller and smaller as the balloon rose, and the flickering torchlight illuminated the action erratically. He saw Dryft, still mounted, fall back toward her captain, Masterchiv Rathbone hunched protectively over her right side. Her fingers clutched at her ribs. She swayed dangerously on her horse and as if from nowhere, two more hoods emerged from the gloom, slashing at the straps of her saddle. The horse reared in panic, the saddle broke, and Masterchiv Rathbone tumbled to the ground. She was barely able to roll out of the way as her horse's hooves came down inches from where her head had been moments before.

A spear flew toward Connor but fell short and plummeted to the earth. Another glanced off the bottom of the basket and disappeared below. More men continued to step into the torchlight, appearing from the cover of surrounding darkness like shadows made flesh.

The men circled the women. Some on horseback, some on foot.

"There's too many of them!" Dryft roared, her short dark hair clinging to her face, damp with sweat and blood. She positioned her horse to shield her captain but couldn't cover all fronts as the men closed ranks around them.

"You dare defy our Father!" a man bellowed, rage staining his words.

Dryft circled to face all of them at once, sword raised. Masterchiv Rathbone, the felled horse and two moaning men beside her, reset her stance and dropped her hand from her ribs, reaching across her body instead as the roped weapon fell from her fingertips. With the cold hiss of steel on steel, she unsheathed her sword for the third time in all her years of battle.

Crouching low, she roared and leaped forward. With a slash, she severed the first horse's saddle, and the man crashed to the ground cursing. Not breaking her momentum, Masterchiv Rathbone twisted to the side, ready for the next. Another keen slice struck flesh. The steed's tortured whinny ripped through the night and echoed in Connor's mind. Its foreleg buckled and it crashed to the dirt. Its rider rolled too late and screamed as his horse crushed his leg beneath its bleeding, twitching mass.

Spinning her sword in a continuous motion, never once breaking its flow, Masterchiv Rathbone dashed at the next oncomer, slashing up and through the rider's stirrup and wrenching the blade clear through rider's bone. The horse screamed in terror and bolted. Its rider crouched, winded and moaning, at Masterchiv Rathbone's feet. He stared up in horror as the knight stepped above him, sword tip silencing his cries.

"Behind you!" Dryft cried, too late. Masterchiv Rathbone's body lurched off course as a spear materialized from the gloom and embedded itself in her thigh. She dropped to one knee and Dryft repositioned her horse to cover her.

"Get up," Connor urged from what seemed like half a realm away.

The remaining riders tightened their formation. Dryft wheeled around frantically and screamed in pain, a dagger's hilt now protruding from her shoulder blade. Connor hadn't seen who'd thrown it. It had all happened so quickly. Not knowing what else to do, he picked up another log from his pile and hurled it at an approaching rider. It glanced off the horse's flank and the steed danced to the left but was quickly brought back in line.

"Get up!" he yelled, helpless horror all but choking him.

Masterchiv Rathbone ripped the spear from her leg with a scream of pain and threw it through the sword arm of a Son. His screams mingled with the echoes of hers, and his sword clattered to the earth. She rose shakily to her feet.

"Enough," she growled, sword lowered in surrender. "No more bloodshed. We yield. Take us to Celos."

Connor fought to catch the reply. His ears strained in the darkness. Finally, the Sons spoke; three different voices with a single message.

"Father was clear."

"We'll take no Upperite prisoners."

"Your kind is beyond saving."

Masterchiv Rathbone looked up at the balloon; her eyes found Connor's and she gave her last command: "GO!"

"No," Connor croaked. He watched as Masterchiv Rathbone, as if in slow motion, braced herself against the tide of assailants. Dryft bellowed a war cry, her horse diving into the fray. Steel crashed against steel, the clear notes ringing out among the screams. Thick, solid thuds summoned roars of pain. With swords flashing, the women fought with the fury of the damned.

Still the balloon rose. Away from the screams. Away from the battle. Away. Connor fed the fire and kept a promise he'd never made to a knight he'd never thanked. The serene grace and linear flight of the balloon mocked the wild mess of zigzagging violence below.

But it was the sudden silence that broke him.

His legs gave way first.

"I'm so sorry."

It was all his fault.

For the next eternity, he huddled in the basket, feeding the fire with a measured regularity, refusing to think. Refusing to look beyond the basket's rim. The fire needed tending; he could do that. As if coming from a different world, he finally heard a triumphant shout. Its vibrancy pierced his mind like a rusted stake.

"There he is! Quick, grab one of the ropes! Connor! Thank the stars you're okay! Connor! Toss us your hook! We'll pull you in!"

He took a breath.

Scrubbed his eyes.

And stood up.

25

THE ULTIMATE PRICE

Amber had not been prepared for this outcome. Watching that logic-defying balloon rise over the lip of the Upper Realm had been a thing of wonder. Finding out why *only* Cornelius rode within had been a horror. They'd heard the muffled cacophony of the chaos below as it emerged from the depths of Jacqueline's bowl. Cornelius's pocketed blue crystal had fed them a confusion of sounds that they'd struggled to understand from a realm away. The reality was far worse than she could have imagined.

"Their sacrifices will not be in vain. We need to retrieve their bodies from the Lower Realm and give them the honors they both deserve," Amber said bluntly.

Of course, she should have anticipated this. Of course. Masterchiv Rathbone herself had given contingencies the day before for Amber to follow if she did not make it. But that was standard procedure. Amber had never dreamed that she wouldn't successfully breach the Upper Realm. If there were to be a failure in their plan, it would have been due to delay, not death.

"They can't be allowed to get away with this," Cornelius growled, the first coherent sentence he had spoken in a while. After they'd safely planted his feet on Upperite soil, he had conveyed the gist of what had happened, though words had failed him several times and much of the details had been left up to the imagination. Jacqueline sat with her arm around him now, and Edith hovered nearby. She seemed eager to be of assistance, but unsure how best to help. No one really knew what to say, and the poor boy was still in shock.

"I couldn't help. I just kept floating away while they fought," he all but whispered.

"They knew what they were doing. You did all you could," Jacqueline assured him in a low voice. Edith draped a spare cloak around his shoulders and received a grateful nod from the Queen. Cornelius did not seem to notice the weight settle around him but glanced at Edith with a vacant look in his eyes and caught her hand in his.

Amber chimed in. "She's right, Your Grace. Though the loss is great, the price is one any good soldier would have paid. Your safety was their number-one priority. The fact that you are safe, the fact that you are here, only means that those two women were the best of the best. Two soldiers on foot against an army on horseback? It's a wonder they were able to hold them off long enough to give you time to escape." Amber felt the words rush out of her as duty surpassed emotion. She couldn't grieve yet. "Let's get you back to the palace. A bath and a meal will set you to rights."

Jacqueline and Edith helped Cornelius to his feet, each taking up an arm.

"I'm fine," he said.

"It's okay if you're not," Edith replied gently.

With a nod at Chiv. Fayworth and a curt instruction to two male dancers, Remy and Dax, who had accompanied their small welcoming party, they created a formation around the royal couple and slowly began making their way back to the palace. The balloon remained on the edge of the Cliff, air still leaking from its now deflated form. The way the canvas had collapsed in on itself reminded Amber of a crinkled autumn leaf. She would send someone to collect it once they were back at the palace.

Their group was a somber one as they trudged through the woods. Jacqueline shot Amber worried glances over her shoulder from time to time, and Cornelius remained silent for most of the walk despite Jacqueline's prompting.

Amber could only imagine what he had witnessed and knew it would take much more than a bath to wash those memories away. The brutality of it. Those men had no right extinguishing the life of such a decorated knight. Celos obviously disregarded much of what her soldiers were trained to hold sacred. His soldiers were all the more dangerous because of it. Unbidden, her training sessions with Yves's men rose in her mind—SHIELD. She grimaced at how the name appeared to be sticking. Those boys were an example of how soldiers should act, how men should fight. It seemed Celos had no qualms with dishonorable combat. They'd had orders to take no prisoners. Now the lights of two women's potentials were forever snuffed out.

With Masterchiv Rathbone gone, that means—she stumbled on a protruding root and tentatively continued the thought—*I'm likely to become the head of the Queensguard.* She frowned. She'd dreamed of one day holding this title. But to obtain it this way? What kind of a cruel joke was that?

The memory of smoke filled her nostrils, and the ghost of ashes filled her mouth. Suddenly she was transported to the blood-soaked fields of Wrenstrom: her first major failure, and the battle from which she'd earned her Soterian Medal. She'd received one of the highest honors in the Queendom for initiating their strategic retreat after her commanding officer fell. Their retreat had saved the battalion and led to their later victory. A woman she respected and revered had paid the ultimate price, and Amber won the awards.

Was her success always to be built on the bones of better women?

After Cornelius had been handed over to Master Epione, after Jacqueline had delivered an address to the remaining women within the Queensguard, after Amber had found herself with a spare hour and at a loss for what to do with it, Yves came to find her. She stood in the empty battle room, hand resting lightly on the map of the Upper Realm, eyes distant.

"I heard what happened," he said gently, leaving all swagger and sparkle at the door.

"Yeah," Amber replied, her voice thick with the tears she would not shed.

"I'm very sorry for your loss."

"Thanks, Yves."

He stood beside her and covered her fingers with his, giving them a comforting squeeze.

"Is there anything I can do?"

Amber met his gaze. His eyes held no jest, just concern. In the span of a couple of days, Amber had lost so many women. Nothing a dancer could do could change that. But there was something about his presence now that was a comfort. Turning to face him, she said, "A hug wouldn't be the worst thing."

He smiled a sad, knowing smile and gently gathered her in his arms.

With her cheek on his chest, enveloped in the warmth of his embrace, she closed her eyes and counted his heartbeats until hers slowed to match. The faint smell of cedar and geranium tickled her nose, and the leather of his doublet was smooth against her cheek. A five-pointed warmth spread from where his hand was splayed on her mid back, his other arm wrapped around her shoulders.

Finally, she pulled back and wiped her eyes. "Thank you, Yves. That's enough. You can go."

He bowed and tapped his wrists together in a perfect guard salute. "Yes, Chiv."

An obedient subordinate would have left immediately, but Yves paused at the door and said, "If you're in need of distraction, Chiv. Everstar, I believe Master Moira is due to measure my men this afternoon. I'm sure, if nothing more, it will be an hour or so of levity."

Amber was surprised at the ghost of a smile that tickled the corners of her mouth.

"I may just take you up on that," she said.

"Oh my word, I do love a good subterfuge. Creating sheep's clothing for a pack of he-wolves, that's what we're doing. Now, of course Her Majesty knows I am an absolute vault when it comes to secrets, isn't that right, Juliana? Didn't she say just that when she set me up in the east wing? She knows she can count on me, and I even remember saying, indeed I said distinctly, 'Why, I wouldn't be surprised if I were to be called upon again to outfit another secret mission.' And here we are!"

"Yes, Master Moira, here we are. And I thank you from the bottom of my heart for tending to my men with such care," Yves said gaily with a half bow.

Amber stood to the side, leaning against a pillar with arms folded, watching the pantomime unfold with a hint of her crooked grin. Yves stood at Master Moira's elbow, offering advice about each of his men as the master worked her way down the row. Her swarm of assistants hovered like bees around a particularly enticing flower and hurried to scribble down each measurement as it was called out and each suggestion as it was accepted.

To Amber, it looked like Moira and Yves were trying to out-flourish one another, like two peacocks attempting to boast a more luxurious tail feather in a room full of chickens: the prize nothing more than vanity. Master Moira appeared to have the upper hand, as her outfit alone was a coruscating kaleidoscope of fabric that seemed to emit actual light as she moved. With dark gray panels half-heartedly obscuring lustrous stripes, the effect was dazzling. Standing over a foot taller than her assistants, she floated about the room among Yves's men with a grace not expected for her size. Juliana, apparently one of her favorite assistants, or at least the one whose name she liked best, was a willowy woman and appeared all elbows and knees by comparison.

Yves, not to be outdone, oscillated between admirer and critic. The constant shift appeared to keep Master Moira half caught on a back foot and intrigued enough by his presence to give him her ear.

"A thick cuff, I think, yes, at seven and a half inches around," she said.

"For Bertrum I'd recommend a looser cuff as he tends to roll his sleeve back. Ladies and men alike are always bewitched by his forearms," he said of a now beet-red Bertrum. "Lad, roll them back and show the master your assets."

Obediently Bertrum exposed his forearms and Amber smothered a grin to see Master Moira lift a trembling hand to her throat. "My word, but the forearms! You are quite right, Yves. Yasna, scratch my last, we'll be sure to include a button closure so the man can unleash his gift upon his audience should he so desire."

"Your wisdom is paramount, Master Moira," Yves said with a half bow.

While their banter continued, the quiet opening of the door drew Amber's attention. Holding tightly to Anya's arm was Lena. Grin widening, Amber stood up and walked over to greet them. "Lena, it's so good to see you on your feet, and Anya, it's been a while. How are you?"

The women's answers were cut off by a shriek. Amber spun around, automatically placing herself in front of her friends and assuming a defensive stance. She jumped aside at the last second to avoid colliding with Master Moira as the latter flew across the room and swept Lena into a careful embrace.

"Oh Lena, my dear child! What a vision you are, what a sight for these weary eyes of mine! To see you up and about, to see the color in your cheeks, and to see this dish of a fiancée on your arm, why it is an absolute treat!"

"It's lovely to see you too, Master Moira," Lena said softly.

"You know I always knew that Councilor Perda had a core of rot and offal. She never wore the appropriate neckline for her figure, dear. You can tell a woman is hiding something by the state of her neckline. I just wish I had acted on my suspicions sooner! I would have saved you an entire ordeal had I only trusted my instincts."

"Oh, Master Moira, you weren't to know!"

"But I *did* know! Fashion trumps stars, cards, and tea leaves, darling, every master seamstress knows that! Yet I turned a blind eye. No matter. My heart has paid a heavy price for my hubris. You're safe now. My dear one, I am so relieved to see you well. A new gown! A new gown is in order! Yes, every recovery from near-fatal wounds must be followed by a new gown!" she announced with a clap of her hands.

"That's what I've always said," Yves said softly in Amber's ear. Amber fought a jump; she hadn't heard him approach.

"How often has that ditty been put into practice?" she asked.

Yves shrugged his shoulders. "It depends on what I define as near fatal, and how badly I need a new frock. A look may strike the heart, after all," he added with a wink. Amber raised an eyebrow, and he staggered backward, clutching his chest. "Alas, I am slain. Master Moira! Quick! A new garment at once!"

Upon hearing her name Master Moira's gaze snapped away from her reunion. Taking in the waiting troupe, she announced, "But Her Majesty's work beckons. Lena, my dear, I will call on you shortly, but I must finish up with these stallions." With a final squeeze of the hands, she walked back to the men and resumed her measurements and notes. "Come, Yves, your men need you."

Inclining his head to Lena and Anya and tapping crossed wrists at Amber with an unnecessary embellishing twist, he joined Master Moira's entourage. A bewildered silence followed in their wake.

After sharing the initial pleasantries, Amber asked, "So, to what do I owe the pleasure?"

Lena shared a look with Anya and said, "We just wanted to check you were all right. Andromeda has kept me up to date with what's been happening with the army and what happened in the Lower Realm. I just hope you know, if there's anything we can do, we're here for you."

Amber's smile faded, and she scratched the back of her neck. "Thanks. It's definitely been a hard first month on the job." Hearing the banality of her words, she scrunched up her nose. "We'll get through."

Lena nodded. "Of course we will. I've started looking over previous enlistment strategies, and I have some ideas I'd love to share with you. Since many of our soldiers were sent to recruit in the Lower Realm, I know we're hurting in numbers. I've already drawn up some ideas for Lowrian training programs to optimize our limited number of knights and reduce the strain on our resources. Councilor Dilmont used to be the woman on top of that area along with others so, bear with me because I'm still healing, but I'll be assuming her responsibilities once I'm back to normal."

"Excellent," Amber said. "And I should say congratulations, Councilor Glowra."

Lena nodded her thanks.

"I'm trying to make sure she doesn't take on too much too quickly, but she's never been one to sit still," Anya said fondly.

Catching the concerned downturn of her mouth, Amber suggested, "Why don't we sit? I've been on my feet all day and could use a rest."

Lena allowed Anya to lead her over to a bench at the edge of the conservatory while Amber followed closely behind, shooting a glance over her shoulder to see Yves demonstrating where a certain waistline should fall.

"Once I'm more mobile, I'd also love a tour of the barracks and battle room. If I'm to oversee our Queendom's defense, I want to make sure I have all the facts," said Lena.

"Great, and I'll have to fill you in on our new . . . er . . . SHIELD. We're—I'm—trialing an all-male attack force that Yves has had the creative freedom to name. Please don't ask me what the acronym stands for. Jacqueline approves, but I'm sure as the program evolves and she has more ideas, it will begin to change aspects within the Queendom's defense, so we'll keep you in the loop."

"But there's no rush. You still need to heal," Anya insisted.

Lena nodded and patted her hand affectionately. Directing her question to Amber, she asked, "How's Jacqueline?"

Amber exhaled forcefully. "Definitely been better."

"And Cornelius?"

"Couldn't be worse."

Master Moira's boisterous cadence wafted toward their somber group. "Positively dashing, darlings. Lady Claustrom won't know what hit her. Indeed, she'll likely thank you for the pleasure of your betrayal."

26

UNREST

He just needed time—that's what Master Epione had said. Time would fill the hole in his chest. Time would silence the echoes of screams, clashing steel, and cracking bones. Time would make his hands forget how it had felt to slip a blade through another man's flesh, and how easily ribs could cave beneath a kick. Time would fix him.

Two days after he'd returned, Jacs knocked gently on his chamber door and let herself into his room. He sat by the window in a tall-backed armchair, looking out over the grounds.

"Hey," she said softly. He didn't turn around, so she approached his chair and crouched before him, gently lifting his hands into hers.

His gaze shifted from the window to focus on their interlocked fingers.

"I brought you something," she said, and presented him with a letter and a blank journal. His fingers traveled over his father's handwriting to rest on the cover of the journal. "It's from your mother," Jacs said. Delicate veins and bones stood out briefly as he pressed down on the cover with his hand. Beneath the heat of his withdrawn palm, *Cornelius* flared and vanished on its surface.

"Thank you," he said. He opened the journal, brushing his thumb pad over the top of the page to briefly reveal *My darling son*. His breath caught and an ache threatened to split him in two. Conscious of Jacs's eyes on him and desperate not to worry her any more than he had already, he scrunched up his nose against the emotion and looked out the window. "I think I'll read these later."

"Okay, whenever you're ready," she said.

He knew it would be a long while yet, so after Jacs left, he placed the journal carefully in a locked cabinet that contained a few treasures and the box of Jacs's letters. His father's letter had been easier to read as it contained many words and little substance.

The dowager King was enjoying the seaside and planned to visit soon. The only line of encouragement read, *Keep your chin up, boy.* Connor shook his head as he placed the letter next to his mother's journal. A level chin made little difference when the weight was on one's heart.

Two weeks passed, and a dreary morning saw Connor and Jacs sitting on opposite sides of a small table by the window in the conservatory, breaking their fast together. Master Epione had recommended Connor be around nature as much as possible to help him heal. She'd also suggested a frequent change of scenery. Since these prescriptions, he'd found himself dining in a different location with different plants each morning.

The conservatory air was thick and sticky and coated Connor's tongue with a damp, earthy taste that did not pair with his meal in the slightest.

The humidity was typical of the greenhouse. It wouldn't normally be an issue. Today it was. Everything felt bunchy, like he'd put his clothes on backward. Or maybe he was the wrong way around. He slathered jam on a scone he had no intention of eating. It seemed to make Jacs more comfortable if he at least had something on his plate.

Eyes turned inward, he'd missed Jacs's last two attempts at conversation but tuned back in to hear her ask, "Would you like to accompany Theo and I for a walk in the gardens after this? The fresh air might do you some good."

Theo now, he noted, not Lordson Claustrom. Replacing his butter knife on his plate he stood up suddenly, taking himself by surprise.

"Sorry," he said to Jacs's widened eyes. "I've just remembered some paperwork I need to get to. Enjoy your walk though, I'll see you at lunch."

"Oh! Of course, I'll see you at lunch."

Connor strode away from Jacs. The desire to be far from her consumed him and he couldn't remember if he had said goodbye. He had just needed some air. To be in motion. To be alone.

The feeling was becoming a familiar one. Something had taken root in his bones that now lay in wait, biding its time. A panic. A compulsion. Like an itch he needed to scratch, it would emerge sometimes mid conversation and demand he leave lest he crumble. As the Queen's advisor, far better for others to think him rude than weak, so he'd leave. But the thing within his bones had a brother. A fear. The fear of being left alone. No sooner from escaping the smothering presence of others would he feel the crushing threat of isolation and crave company.

Each step that took him away from Jacs simultaneously brought him relief and anxiety. It was enough to drive him mad.

He strode down the corridor, past paintings and tapestries. The pictures blurred in his peripheral vision as he sped past them. Colors blended and melded as subjects were lost in the mess of threads and fabrics. Ahead, just entering the corridor, Hera beamed as she caught sight of him heading toward her. She wore a blue velvet gown with a high collar and deep neckline.

"Your Grace," she said by way of greeting, and he slowed his pace to stand before her as their paths met. His flush and frazzle from earlier had vanished.

"Good morning, Lord Claustrom."

"I wonder, given Her Majesty and her beau will be walking in the gardens this morning, if you'd accompany me to the lily pond?"

"Thank you, but unfortunately I have business I must attend to this morning."

"I see. I so miss our walks," she said coyly.

"Another time perhaps. I'm sure the Queen and your brother would welcome the company. If my memory serves, Lordson Theo has a wealth of knowledge when it comes to shrubbery."

Hera pursed her lips. "Yes, he certainly has a lot to share." She closed the distance between them with a sway of her hips and rested a heavily ringed hand on his arm. "He will certainly make a fine King, don't you agree, Your Grace?"

"Indeed," he replied, lips barely moving around the word.

"And when he assumes his role at the Queen's side, I'm sure he will put his wealth of knowledge to good use. Assisting her where he can." She paused delicately before adding, "Advising her where he can. Just as your father advised his Queen. I imagine dear Theo will be able to take a few duties off your plate once he accepts Jacqueline's proposal."

Hera's eyes glittered in the lamplight. With the tip of her fore-finger, she traced a small circle on Connor's sleeve. "You know," she continued, "if that's the case, you may find yourself with time on your hands. Time I'm happy to help you fill. Hands I'm happy to help you occupy."

Connor caught her fingers in his and gently removed them from his sleeve. "Thank you for the offer, Lord Claustrom. But if you'll excuse me." Brushing her knuckles with his lips he made to extricate himself from her confines. While she didn't stop him from taking his leave, she did call after him once he was halfway down the corridor.

"She'll never be yours, you know."

He spun to face her.

"Oh dear, it seems I've struck a nerve," she said with hands clasped prettily on top of her skirts, eyes wide with innocence. "Cornelius, I've known you for many years. I consider us friends at the very least. I only want to protect you, even if it is from your own delusions."

Heat flared in his chest. "Delu— I'm under no delusions, Hera."

With an infuriatingly indulgent calm, Hera simply nodded. "Of course, Your Grace. In any case, I await your invitation should you change your mind." Hiding mirth behind lowered lashes, she sank into a deep bow before gathering her skirts and departing.

It was with a curse that he entered his chambers and a kick that he slammed the door shut behind him. He crossed the room in eight long strides to the curtained window and shoved the fabric roughly aside. The steel rings slid across the curtain rod with a metallic snicker akin to the unsheathing of a sword and he froze, heart pounding.

It was several minutes before the cold sweat beading his forehead warmed, and his heart rate returned to normal. His gaze fell short of the view beyond the window and he held tight to the curtain.

All he needed was time.

The door behind him opened, and Edith's voice snapped him from his reverie. "I've brought your green doublet, Your Grace. Neglect does terrible things to a wardrobe, and these wrinkles were a different breed of stubborn entirely. Never fear, I've set it to rights. Are you well?" Her tone changed as she looked at him properly.

"Quite well, Edith. Just thinking."

"Well I advise you to take a break, or you'll need more than a hot iron to smooth out those wrinkles above your brows."

Despite his mood, he cracked a smile and turned his back on the window. "I'll try."

Edith studied him for a moment longer, a slight crease appearing above her own brows. She said briskly, "Right, I'll fetch the tea."

"Edith, I'm fine. Honestly."

"Fine or not, a cup of tea never hurt anybody. Try this on in the meantime and see I haven't shrunk it by mistake."

They both knew that was not a possibility, but with a dry laugh, he accepted both the doublet and defeat. Shortly after he had pulled the garment over his head and buttoned the final button under his chin, Edith returned with a tea tray set with two mugs, milk swirling at the bottom of each.

"Would you like to talk about it?" she ventured once they'd perched in the chairs by the fire and she'd poured.

Connor shook his head. He wouldn't even know where to start. Instead he said, "We leave for Hesperida at the end of the month."

Edith nodded, blowing a little on her tea.

"And we've discussed what the trip will entail. I just want to be sure you're comfortable accompanying me. You'd be more than welcome to remain in the palace and to oversee the reconstruction if not."

"My place is with you, Your Grace," she said simply.

"It will be dangerous. I'd understand if you preferred to remain here, where it's safe."

Edith shook her head. "If it's all the same, I'd prefer to be where I know I'll be useful. Someone has to tell the Claustrom's staff how you like your tea."

Connor smiled and looked away. "Your sisters live in Hesperida, don't they?"

Dimples deepening, Edith nodded.

"One does, Jane. Annalise is in Bregend with my mothers."

"That's right, Annalise just had a baby?"

"Her second. He's got her lungs, that's for sure. Hasn't drawn a breath without screaming, apparently."

"Good lad. Not afraid to use his voice; that'll serve him well."

Edith chuckled, "In this world when he's older maybe, but right now for his mother it does not. However"—and here a mischievous glint stole across her features—"Annalise used to torment Jane and I to no end with her awful singing when we were girls, so I say it's justice well served."

"It all works out in the end," Connor said, mirroring her grin and raising his still steaming mug. Their cups clinked and the fire crackled in the hearth. All was well, but a shadow lingered on the edges of his vision. A weight hung within his heart. Connor felt a sense of foreboding follow his hopeful claim and he set down his cup to hide a tremor. There was no certainty it would all work out. No certainty they would be safe, that Edith would be safe.

Trailing his palm around the back of his neck, he stood and walked to his bedside cabinet. He shifted papers aside and dug to the back, retrieving a small velvet pouch.

"Edith," he said softly, returning to the fireside with the pouch cupped in his hands. "I have no idea how the events will unfold in Hesperida, but I need you to promise me something."

"Of course, Your Grace." She placed her cup on the table.

"Promise me, if it all falls apart, if we fail, promise me you'll get out." Dropping to his knees in front of her, he pressed the pouch into her palms. With an expression caught between curiosity and alarm, Edith upended the pouch, dropping an object into her hand, and gasped. It was an egg—a small solid-gold egg about the size of a chicken's. An entire Griffins egg's worth of gold melted down into a solid lump. "It's enough to get you set up anywhere. Spent wisely, it's enough for a lifetime. Get your sisters, get your mothers, and head for

Nysa. Cross the sea if you must. We don't know what Celos is capable of, but if he's successful, his reach will only grow. Get out before it spreads. Before it's too late."

She shoved the golden egg back into his chest and glared at him as her eyes reddened around their edges. "I can't accept this. You will be fine, Your Grace."

"We don't know that. I'll be going back to Alethia, back into that joyless labyrinth, and the one thought that will bring me light is that I did what I could to make sure you're safe. I need to know that, if I don't resurface, you will be taken care of." Gently, he folded her fingers around the egg. "Please let me do this."

Blinking furiously, she slipped the egg back into its pouch and tucked it away in her apron. Her eyes lingered on the new lump in her pocket and she scowled. Lifting her gaze back to his, she said, "I'll hold on to it until you return. But"—and she punctuated her next points with painful prods to his chest—"don't let it come to that. Come back safe. Come back sound. Come back in one piece."

"Ow! Okay, okay, at ease, soldier, I promise," he said, catching her finger before it hit home for the fourth time. Unable to put what their years of friendship meant to him into words, he tripped awkwardly through. "Edith . . . what would I do without you?"

They stood. Edith dropped her hand and allowed Connor to pull her into a much less aggressive embrace. With her cheek resting on his chest, he heard her reply, "The world for you, you know this."

"Thank you," he whispered.

"Well," she said briskly, struggling to keep her voice level. "I'm just glad to see the doublet fits after all that ironing." As though she were seeing him off before his morning ride, she brushed his shoulder clear of lint with a business-like sweep, collected the tea tray, and departed. Connor watched her go, rubbing absently at the spot to the left of his sternum.

27

THE LADY OF HESPERIDA

Finally, after weeks of planning, Jacs's entourage was ready to visit Hesperida. Hera was convinced the recent attacks had prompted Jacs to choose power over love, and if she was surprised with Connor's compliance, it had been a fleeting thought swept clear by the thrill of the proposal preparations.

Theo seemed shyly excited by the trip and, following his encounter with Altus Hermes, looked at Jacs now with a gratitude and awe that only increased her feelings of guilt. Every morning leading up to their departure, she made sure to pin his brooch to her bodice, and she and Theo walked the gardens as a matter of routine after she broke her fast with Connor. Connor never said anything about her walks with Theo, and he never joined her, but she saw the muscles around his eyes tense as she bid him farewell each time.

It would be easier if she could say she didn't enjoy these walks. If she could say with sincerity she found Theo to be a bore, or worse. But the truth was, he was lovely. Kind and intelligent and able to calm the storm of her anxieties without judgment. Try as she might, she couldn't hate him for that.

As for Connor, it had been a month full of change, most of it positive. After they'd pulled him from the balloon, it had taken a few days before his eyes would focus properly on Jacs when she spoke with him. Master Epione had done all she could for the illness that had infected his lungs and weakened his body in the Lower Realm but had no cure for the memories plaguing his mind. In an effort to distract him, Jacs had filled him in on all he had missed since he'd been away and shared her upcoming plans to infiltrate Alethia. He listened intently and provided suggestions and insight. However, despite Jacs's prompting, he refused to talk about what had happened to him and had adopted the habit of disappearing mid-conversation. She could glean no more information about that day in the Lower Realm than he'd given already.

Jacs sat with him now in their private carriage as they trundled through Basileia toward Hesperida. Theo rode with Hera at Hera's request, so Jacs was awarded some time alone with Connor.

Given she was not usually without her guardpairs, this was a rarity. Even their morning meals were had in the presence of a handful of others.

The inside of the carriage was laden with furs and thick woolen blankets to stave off the chill that hung in the air. Jacs wore her winter cloak and was thankful for the scarf she had wrapped around her neck.

They rode in near silence. Any attempt at conversation from Jacs was reciprocated politely and dropped at the earliest opportunity. Whatever was on Connor's mind appeared to be winning the battle for his attention. She watched him gaze out the window as the city slipped past them and reach with his right hand to worry at the slightly worn patch of embroidered fabric to the left of his sternum. Jacs removed her gloves and caught his hand in hers before it reached its destination.

"How are you holding up?" she asked.

He nodded reassuringly. "Fine."

"It'll all be over soon."

"But not soon enough. While we've been planning, Celos has been broadcasting his poison to every town in the Lower Realm."

Jacs sat back. "I know, but we needed time to prepare. He may have had a few weeks of messages, but that gave us time to make sure our plan is foolproof. I couldn't send us back there without a plan. Not again."

Connor shook his head. "Masterchiv R—" He swallowed. "—said history will prove him wrong. We just need to make sure he becomes history. We need to finish this. End him. Destroy the Sons. Soon."

"Destroy the Sons . . . Connor, they're just as much his prisoners as the Undercourt of Griffins. We can't just destroy them. Their minds have been warped, but Celos is the source. *Celos* is our enemy."

Connor glared at her. "They're worse than brutes, Jacs. You didn't see them, you weren't there."

"I know. But I also know that Phillip was taken in by them, and I know his heart. He's not an evil man. We at least need to give these men a fair trial. A chance to atone. If we go in wanting to wipe them all out, we're just as bad as Celos."

Connor's lip curled. "They're monsters."

"They're people. Misled, misguided, misused people, but people. Our people."

"Jacs—"

"Please, Connor. Don't let your grief blind you to that."

"Blind . . . you don't know what you're talking about," he said, his voice hard.

"I know you're angry."

Connor scoffed.

"Don't let anger take your heart," she said gently.

"You have no idea," he snapped. She saw it then—saw it lurking behind his once-clear blue eyes. The fire that had burned in Phillip when she'd last seen him. The anger that had haunted Mal all those months ago on the banks of the river.

Jacs kept her voice steady. "I watched my friends and townsfolk die at the hands of guards looking for phantoms the Upper Realm created. I watched your father burn my clock tower to the ground, deny us the right to a proper memorial, and act like it was a mercy. I saw what the Sons did to my mother. I know what you're feeling. I know that anger."

She slowly took both his hands in hers. Holding them tightly, she waited for him to finally meet her eyes.

"And you have every right to be angry. But Connor, that anger will warp your mind and poison your heart without Celos's help. You are so much more than who it'll force you to become. You are stronger, you are kinder, and you need to let it die before it destroys you."

"What do you expect me to do?"

"Love."

"What?"

"Choose love." Still holding his hands in hers, she kissed his knuckles. "My father once told me that everything we do comes from either a place of fear or a place of love."

"Fear? I'm not scared."

"Anger is fear's disguise. To act in anger is to act from a place of fear. Nothing worth having is gained when you act from fear. Everything precious in this world is gained through love. We will beat Celos, we will free his men, and we will hold those who have done wrong accountable for their actions. But we will not stoop to their level. We can't take fear's path."

Connor's grip tightened within hers and he took a moment to collect himself before speaking again. "How can you find even a scrap of kindness for brutes like them?"

"Honestly? After what they did to my women in the Catacombs, to the people in the palace, to Masterchiv Rathbone . . . to my mother? . . . I don't know. But we have to try. Master Leschi taught me no woman thinks of herself as the villain. We're all just doing the best we can with what we have. If we think about the Sons like that, just a group of broken boys trying to do the best they can in their brainwashed state of mind, maybe we can at least find their humanity."

"It's a start," Connor said softly.

"It's a start."

He pulled her hands toward him, shifting her weight forward on the seat, and kissed her cheek. "I love you."

Theo's pin hung heavily over her heart and she couldn't meet Connor's gaze. Theo deserved a whole heart. Connor deserved a whole heart. Both men deserved better. But she was given these moments with Connor so rarely, and no one was around to see.

Wrapping her hand around the back of his neck, she drew Connor's lips to hers briefly, then rested her forehead against his. "I love you too."

"And I'll try."

"That's all I ask, Connor. I don't want to lose you."

"You won't."

"And I couldn't bear if you lost your heart."

He smiled. "Well I gave that to you years ago, so you've only yourself to blame if you misplace it."

Jacs felt heat rush to her cheeks, and she looked away. "You know, Celos's mirror invention may be our saving grace," she added suddenly.

"What do you mean?"

"Well, once we've beaten him, all we need to do is get someone to say my name into that mirror and I can broadcast a message to the Lower Realm. We can explain everything, or the parts the realm needs to know, and hopefully begin to mend what's been broken."

"Use his tools to serve our purpose. I like that," Connor said, and Jacs was relieved to see a glimmer of his old self in his gaze.

It was a start.

After hours of traveling, the road beneath the wheels changed from compact dirt to carefully laid cobbles. A jolt of the carriage marked the border.

"Welcome to Hesperida, Your Majesty!" Edith called from where she sat with the driver at the front. Jacs drew back the blinds and looked out the window. She had been here shortly after her coronation as part of her Upper-Realm tour, and it took her breath away now just as it had then—although this time the streets were not festooned with bunting and strewn with flowers. It felt more like a city people lived in, rather than one kept behind glass for display.

Bordering where the river left the Court Mountain range, the city spiraled within the foothills at its base. Sudden dips and rises in the topography encouraged imaginative city planning, and the roads zigzagged and wound their way between buildings in a style that was dizzying to observe from afar. Close up, however, Jacs was fascinated to see there was a method to the madness. Each incline remained below a certain pitch to allow even the most laden wagons to trundle up without trouble. If this meant the inclusion of an elevator, or a series of switchbacks, then the surrounding stores simply accommodated the need. With a pang, Jacs imagined Master Leschi's wonder at the sight. One day, when this was all over, she would bring her mentor here so they could marvel at the wedge-shaped buildings and roadside lifts together.

She watched a group of men perspiring and cursing to wind a crank that lifted a particularly stiff elevator. There was definitely a fault in the design if it took three grown men to move the thing. Master Leschi's voice rang in her ear and made her smile. *Efficiency over effort, Jacqueline! Why work harder when you can just work smarter?* With any luck, Jacs would be seeing her mentor soon.

She took a shuddering breath in and felt Connor still her jittering knee with his palm.

"Your plan will work, Jacs," he said softly.

"What if Yves was mistaken about the tunnels? What if they've collapsed them or blocked them off?"

"Then we've paid a long overdue visit to a very influential county."

"We could be helping with the Lower Realm."

"We are."

"But if this turns out to be fruitless, I've wasted valuable time the Lower Realm doesn't have."

"You can't do everything at once. You can't be everywhere at once. What was it you always said in your letters? Let's take this one step at a time." Connor's thumb brushed across her knee and Jacs forced herself to take a breath.

"Okay."

The journey through the city took less time than expected, but then it was Jacs's experience that time was always eager to introduce you to the thing you were dreading. With a clatter and a jolt, the carriage stopped in the expansive, terraced receiving grounds of Lady Claustrom's manor. Although no longer Lord, she still lived in the Claustrom estate and now stood in front of its grand front doors draped in a peacock-blue coat and gown studded with sapphires and amethysts. Her bright blonde hair was streaked through with white, and a deep purple stone hung in the hollow of her throat from a strip of the same silver velvet that lined her coat.

A surly man stood two steps behind her, deep creases carved into his forehead and around his lips. His hair, likely jet black in his youth, was now streaked with gray to match his salt-and-pepper beard trimmed with fine-combed precision. He too was lavishly dressed, and while he echoed Lady Claustrom's manner of welcome, the warmth was far from reaching his eyes. This must be Genteel Brovnen.

Jacs allowed Edith to help her down from the carriage. Connor followed close behind. At the edge of her vision, she saw her Queens-guard take up their formation, saw Hera and Theo emerge from their carriage, and saw her SHIELD dressed in their bright purple-and-yellow dancer's livery emerge from their carriages and sink to one knee, facing Jacs.

"Her Royal Majesty, Queen Jacqueline!" a woman's voice announced. Lady Claustrom sunk into a reverential bow, arms open in greeting. "Welcome, Your Highness," she said as she descended the stairs magnanimously. "And welcome home, my children!"

"Thank you for your hospitality," Jacs said solemnly, "and for the comfort your daughter and son's company have been these past weeks."

"It is a mother's sorrow to be parted from her children, but one I was happy to endure for the pleasure of my Queen. Come, you must be travel weary, I have baths drawn and rooms prepared."

Jacs felt like an actor in a play, each line of script preplanned and rehearsed but delivered as if freshly formed. She had Lena's etiquette training to thank for that, and so the next hour passed in a floating blur as she paid her host all due courtesies and made sure she and her household settled into their rooms. All the formalities ate away most of the afternoon and left her anxious to get to the purpose of her visit. She hoped that any outward display of impatience would be chalked up to preproposal nerves.

Walking down one of the many hallways of the manor, Jacs thanked her lucky stars that Yves knew where the tunnel's entrance was. Without his knowledge, the endeavor would have surely failed. She'd seen the tunnel to Alethia in Theo's memory and knew it was hidden behind a tapestry. In most homes, that would at least narrow down where to look, but this manor was a maze of woven and embroidered cloth. Every inch of the windowless walls was draped with an elaborately woven tapestry.

Step by step, Jacs passed threaded depictions of women hunting, Griffin ceremonies, mountainscapes, a group of finned folk pulling a sailor from the depths of stormy seas as her ship sunk far below, maps of cities, the Goddess cradling a golden egg in her palm, a winged woman soaring through the skies with a Griffin, a giant bouquet of flowers, and dozens more.

"You have quite the collection of tapestries," Jacs said to her host. They spoke as if they were alone, yet Hera hovered near her mother's elbow, Genteel Brovnen strode beside Connor and slightly in front of Theo, Jacs's Queensguard covered their flank, and her SHIELD wandered a fair distance behind them all. Lady Claustrom had appeared delighted to hear that Jacs had brought a dancing troupe for their entertainment that evening and had eagerly eyed each well-built member, insisting they accompany her through the manor. One of the more handsome members, Druine, now had his fingers secured in the crook of Lady Claustrom's arm with little hope of getting them back, a willing accessory for the noblewoman. Jacs could feel the cold fury radiating from the genteel behind her but didn't know how to extricate her man from the arms of the Lady, so Genteel Brovnen was left to fume in silence.

"I have always held a deep respect for the woven arts. It takes a true master's mind to know where each thread must go and where each thread is at any given moment. Only a select few people have the ability to weave together a larger image from dozens of unrelated colored threads," said the Lady.

"Well said. I would love a tour of your collection."

"Of course, Your Majesty."

And so it was that forty-five minutes later, Jacs found herself walking down yet another corridor plastered with floor-to-ceiling tapestries.

"That door leads to my bedchambers, and the one adjacent is for my private study. Of course, Brovnen has his own wing, but that's on the other side of the estate, isn't it, darling?" She laughed shrilly and cast a dismissive glance behind her at her genteel, shifting her attention quickly back to Druine and playfully tracing the embroidery of his lapel.

"And here you'll find a piece that is likely to pique your interest, Your Majesty," Lady Claustrom said, stopping short in front of yet another tapestry, this one depicting the uprising of the Lower Realm. From a deep muck-brown pit, Lowrian women with twisted, snarling features, dressed in scraps of cloth and soiled garments brandished sharpened sticks and reached claw-like hands desperately toward their lofty, well-dressed, straight-backed Upperite counterparts. The women of the Upper Realm cast looks of pitying disdain at the Lowrians below and lifted the hems of their elaborate gold-edged gowns away from the lip of the Cliff, out of reach of the filth below. Their delicately slippered feet were cradled in the soft green grass of the meadow.

"It appears your artists take many liberties with their subjects," Jacs mused mildly, eyes scanning the tapestries on either side of Lady Claustrom's study and committing them to memory.

"Of course, art can be a brutal yet beautiful thing," Lady Claustrom said calmly, apparently unconcerned with the insult this tapestry represented.

"I trust it does not reflect the sentiments of your household?"

"By Alti no, it merely keeps us humble."

"In what way?"

"Well, to blind ourselves to the prejudices that exist within our realm only perpetuates their existence. This tapestry reminds us that these horrid views exist. With this reminder, we are able to more consciously counteract them."

Jacs took in the twisted features of the Lowrians and the beautiful figures of the Upperites. "I see. Where is your tapestry depicting the prejudices against Upperites?"

"My what?"

"Well, here you have the Lowrians depicted as their worst possible stereotypes. Where is the one depicting the Upperites as theirs?"

"Well . . . I . . . my collection is not yet complete, and that particular perspective has yet to be included in my displays."

Jacs leveled a gaze at her host. "As a Lower-born citizen, I would gladly sit with your weavers and share the vile depictions my realm holds of yours. If it would help keep your household humble, and . . . what was it you said? Counteract these beliefs more consciously? I myself have never found an emphasis on the negative nor an exaggeration of differences to be the most effective way of uniting a people, however."

Lady Claustrom studied Jacs with barely veiled intrigue before her gaze shifted back to the tapestry. "It seems you are as wise as my son says. Perhaps you are right. The tapestry shall be removed and replaced with an image of unity as soon as I can have one commissioned."

"That sounds like a marvelous addition to your collection," Jacs remarked. Positioned as she was, she saw from the corner of her eye a couple of Yves's men lifting the edges of the tapestry they passed. One stifled a yawn. Her gaze drifting, she caught Theo's eye. The Lordson smiled sweetly at her, a blush stealing across his cheeks, before he quickly looked away. Jacs felt a twinge of something cold seize her heart. Was it guilt? Shame? Or was it just detached resignation?

Not much longer now, she reminded herself.

Lady Claustrom had pulled up short. Distracted, Jacs was too slow in realizing the Lady was now watching her closely, and with a start she rearranged her features into an easy smile. Lady Claustrom raised an eyebrow knowingly and, Druine's bicep now forgotten, she dropped the dancer's arm to sweep Jacs's hand into her own.

"The gardens next, I think. It's a lovely day after all, too lovely to be cooped up with the textiles."

Jacs, now trapped in a surprisingly polite vice grip, replied, "That sounds delightful."

They wove their way through the corridors and stepped out onto the terrace at the back of the estate. All the while, Jacs felt the moments meander past her like molasses. Was it a Hesperidan trick? Surely time didn't usually pass this slowly.

A cloud moved high overhead and sunlight lit the cobbled court-yard before them, illuminating the gardens beyond. Jacs's eyes widened in wonder.

"It's beautiful."

"Yes, we had the landscapers brought in from Nysa. You'll notice the raw terrain has been combined with deliberate cultivation so it is at once natural and woman-made. But where the seam between the two lies, I'll let you decide." Lady Claustrom gestured with a gracefully ex-tended finger, winking at Jacs as though to include her in a private jest. The terraced labyrinth of the city appeared reflected in this garden's design, steep, sweeping stone staircases cut into the natural rock. Each rise of the earth had been carefully sculpted into bizarre geometrical shapes. What at first glance appeared to be a mess of nature was, upon closer inspection, a careful taming of chaos.

Arm still firmly controlled by Lady Claustrom, Jacs allowed her-self to be led toward the tall hedges and jagged stone of the gardens.

"I have something I would like to show you, but it is not some-thing that requires a large audience. Perhaps the rest of your retinue could explore the various corners of the grounds at their leisure while you are occupied?" Lady Claustrom suggested. "Besides, it gives you and I some time to ourselves. I would so love an opportunity to speak with a woman as . . . interesting as yourself." She wove her words into a gentle caress and took on a tone better suited to hushed evenings and wine-stained voices.

"I . . . would be honored to accompany you, Lady Claustrom," Jacs replied.

"Please, I must insist, call me Sybil." Lady Claustrom's gaze flicked back and forth from Jacs to Theo, a self-satisfied smile lifting the corners of her lips. Connor, who had been studying a peculiar arrangement of succulents, snapped his attention to their exchange.

"Perhaps my party could excuse us for an hour, and we can reconvene at dinner?" Jacs suggested slowly before adding, "Chiv. Everstar, you may follow at a distance."

"An hour, maybe more," Lady Claustrom remarked.

"Your Majesty, don't you think—" Connor began with a hurried step forward.

"Your Grace, I'm sure my children have a few haunts of their own to show you," Lady Claustrom insisted.

"Of course, Mother. He will be in safe hands with us," Hera purred. Jacs fought to ignore the prickle of irritation that scuttled down her spine.

"I can accompany you, my lady," Genteel Brovnen suggested, but he seemed to anticipate a rejection as he spoke, for he shrunk back before Lady Claustrom responded.

"No. Tend to the troupe. Let them know my preferences." She turned to Jacs. "What did you say they were called?"

"The Heliotrope Canaries."

"Charming. I do look forward to their display."

Unsure why her heart had started beating an irregular rhythm in her chest, Jacs nodded in farewell to Connor and dismissed her party. The dancers dispersed quickly, but her Queensguard lingered for a moment longer, seeming reluctant to let her leave with just one knight as protection.

Lady Claustrom directed her along the cobbled path lined with dark green plants. Fat, jet-black berries hung from their stems and Jacs was careful not to brush against them as she followed her hostess up a steep set of steps to the top of a ridge. From the top, panting slightly, Jacs saw the grounds stretching away around them. A stone-and-hedge maze filled with gnarled and twisted trees and shrubs spread away from her. Jacs shivered despite the sunshine. To call the garden beautiful would be to corrupt the meaning. It was bewitching. Dangerous. She felt like they were three fat flies balancing on pretty strands of silk, blissfully unaware of the eyes glistening from the shadows. She couldn't imagine how anyone could feel at ease in a garden like this.

Lady Claustrom beckoned, and they walked down the other side of the ridge on stairs that, had the hillside been a fraction of a degree steeper, would have been described as a ladder.

"Not far now," she said over her shoulder. Once their feet touched flat earth, Lady Claustrom reclaimed Jacs's arm. Her grip was firm but tender, and she swayed into Jacs with an almost practiced deliberation. Amber's presence was a welcome comfort in Jacs's peripheral vision.

Lady Claustrom steered her in the direction of a greenhouse. Its domed glass roof reminded Jacs of the conservatory in the palace, but these walls and doors were a dark charcoal gray. The door squealed on its hinges and swung inward. As they stepped over the threshold, a wall of damp warmth clamped itself over her mouth and nose and stuck in her throat. She blinked in the gloom while her eyes adjusted.

"Come," Lady Claustrom said and led her past waxy palm fronds and drooping lilies to a door at the back of the greenhouse. This door swung open silently, and with a fluttering feeling in her stomach, Jacs allowed Lady Claustrom to pull her into the dimly lit antechamber beyond. Tall candles wavered as the air shifted to accommodate their presence. The room contained a wide daybed strewn with black satin cushions, a low table, and glass cabinets filled with exquisitely wrought golden flowers and feathers. Each could be worn as a brooch or pendant, but all looked as though they had not been removed from their velvet pillows in years.

"It appears you are a collector of many beautiful things. Your manor is truly breathtaking," Jacs said conversationally, finally managing to detach herself from Lady Claustrom's grip and moving closer to the cabinets to study the brooches. She idly fingered Theo's brooch on her bodice and noticed a break in the dust within one of the cabinets about the same size and shape.

"It is nothing compared to the beauty of the palace."

"You will have to visit; I would be interested in your opinion on some of the pieces in Queen Ariel's collection."

"I trust my children have been providing you with sufficient entertainment," Lady Claustrom said mildly, and Jacs felt her eyes on her as she bent to study a rose brooch more closely. The candlelight danced along the petals and caught on the sharp point of a thorn. The contrast between sweeping curve and pointed tip was jarring in this place of quiet.

"They have." Jacs paused delicately. "You must be proud of them both. They do you credit."

"Of course." Sybil paused, the room filling with the weight of it. "Although while a bud may hold the promise of splendor, it is nothing to the brilliance of a rose in bloom." Jacs straightened and turned to meet Lady Claustrom's gaze, struggling to mask her confusion as she continued: "Green buds are hardly worthy of a queen's bouquet."

Amber cleared her throat from where she stood in a corner of the room, and Lady Claustrom's eyes flicked away from Jacs momentarily. She couldn't describe why she was thankful for the interruption until Sybil set her gaze on her again.

"A queen's bouquet accommodates beauty in all forms. Although the buds may be green, the promise within is a treasure worth cherishing," Jacs replied, hoping she had followed the metaphor correctly.

Sybil considered her reply with the leisure of a spider watching a fly tangle itself more tightly in her web. The thrill of the hunt lurked within her eyes, and from the prickling on the back of Jacs's neck, she had the sinking suspicion she knew who the fly was.

"It seems an eye for beauty is something we have in common."

"So it is. How long have you been collecting brooches?"

"It is my understanding you've come to unite our families," Lady Claustrom said, seizing the reins of the conversation.

"Yes."

"How are you hoping to do that?"

"I hoped to wait to speak with you more formally tomorrow evening," Jacs answered evasively. She had hoped to stall for as long as possible, convinced the situation with Theo would resolve itself if given enough time. To be forced into it mere hours before they moved on Alethia was something she had not accounted for.

"I see. And your reason for waiting until tomorrow evening?"

"I would hate to rush an important conversation. Good things take time."

"A wise observation. I have a few suggestions of my own."

"A . . . a few?" Jacs asked. Her bewilderment brought a slow smile to the Lady's face.

"Yes."

"Well, I'm always willing to hear suggestions from influential women such as yourself. And you have a union of many years to boast your success in joining families. How long have you and Genteel Brovnen been together?"

Lip curling, Lady Claustrom said dismissively, "Of that, I've lost count. Over two decades."

"You . . . you seem happy together."

"He pleases me some of the time."

"I see."

"And for the rest, I find enjoyment elsewhere."

"I . . . see."

"As a powerful woman, you will soon learn that many doors remain open to you. You are Queen. I imagine your count is far higher than my own. My door, for example, barely opens for Brovnen, but I think *you'll* find it accessible regardless of the hour—"

"I—"

"—should you have any questions, needs . . . desires"—she lingered a moment on the *s*—"that I'm able to accommodate." Lady Claustrom let the words slip from her lips like a secret.

"You . . ." Jacs scrambled, her mind playing catch-up with the implications. "You are a very gracious host," she finished lamely.

"Gracious, and . . . discreet. After all, I was a favorite of your predecessor in all ways but the one I desired most. I could be even more of a comfort to you." Lady Claustrom fingered the stone at her throat as she took a half step closer, the fabric of her gown rustling against Jacs's split skirts. Her gaze traveled over Jacs as though she were appraising a particularly precious brooch for her collection.

"I—"

"You intrigue me, Your Majesty. And I am not often intrigued."

"Oh?" Jacs said, reeling. The scent of the Lady's perfume lingered around her, making her head spin.

"It is clear you are not necessarily as interested in my son as my daughter's letter led me to believe. So I ask myself, if the purpose of your visit is to unite our families, and you have no particular romantic fancies for dear, sweet Theodosius, why saddle you with a burden for the rest of your days when the union can be secured through more . . . entertaining means? For a woman with backbone enough to confront me in my own home is well worth the effort to get on her back."

A crash came from Amber's corner, and Jacs turned to see the knight standing beside a glittering wreckage. The pieces of a gilded glass vase and a handful of dried flowers sprawled on the floor at her feet.

"Whoops," she said, tilting her chin up in challenge as her eyes bored into Lady Claustrom's.

Jacs took a couple of hurried steps backward and reclaimed her composure. "Lady Claustrom, while I am flattered, I worry you have the wrong impression."

"So, you do have feelings for my son?"

"I . . . your son is . . . I fear we've deprived the rest of my retinue of our company for long enough, and if I'm to feel like a human before dinner, I must have time to change."

Lady Claustrom's gaze darted between Amber and Jacs, a knowing smile curling the corners of her mouth. "Of course."

"I can show you back to your chambers, Your Majesty," Amber said, eyes still fixed on the Lady.

"Yes," Jacs replied in a daze. "Yes, Lady Claustrom, I'm sure you have a number of tasks I've kept you from. I will see you at dinner."

"As you wish," Lady Claustrom purred.

"Sorry about the vase," Amber said by way of farewell.

Jacs and Amber walked at a brisk pace back to her chambers and it wasn't until the door was firmly closed behind them that Amber rounded on her. "Where in Sotera's name did she get such bold skirts? Honestly! *That's* how she speaks to her Queen?"

Jacs sank into a chair and shook her head. "I know, I was expecting a lot of things, but definitely not that."

"No kidding. No wonder Brovnen looked so out of sorts when she whisked you aw—" The door opened and cut Amber off. It was Connor.

"I saw you return. What happened?"

"Lady Claustrom was making Jacqueline feel right at home," Amber scoffed, and Jacs threw her a withering look.

Connor looked from Jacs to Amber and closed the door quietly behind him. "I'm missing something. What's wrong?"

Jacs sighed. "She may have sensed that I was not romantically interested in her son and decided to offer herself as a substitute paramour."

"What!"

"I'm just so glad Amber was there and was quicker on her feet than I."

Amber performed a little bow and said humbly, "Not the first admirer I've had to deter. You were so sweet about it too. A regular bunny in the fox's den. You should have heard the Lady, talking about getting you on your back. Where's the poetry? Where's the romance? Does she think she's above the subtle art of courting?"

"Shut it," Jacs groaned, good-naturedly tossing a tiny pillow at the knight. Amber caught it deftly and passed it between her palms.

Connor scrubbed his face, pulled Jacs to her feet, and embraced her. "You're all right?"

"I'm fine," she said softly.

"Good. I knew Lady Claustrom had a reputation; I just didn't think she would be that bold."

"Neither did I. This family has a seriously skewed sense of loyalty."

Connor studied her a moment, and Jacs could almost see the thoughts chasing one another through his mind. Finally he said, "I suppose that's the whole Claustrom clan you'll have to deal with in one way or another when all this is over. From the sounds of things, they'll all be expecting something from you. Hera will expect to call you sister, Theo will expect to call you wife, Sybil will expect to call you . . ."

"Lover?" Amber suggested.

"Thank you for *that*," Jacs retorted over Connor's shoulder. Amber merely shrugged.

"And Brovnen is always in a mood, so he'll have a number of names for you," Connor finished, without looking at Amber.

Eager to change the subject, Jacs asked, "Have we heard from Yves? Is the troupe ready for tonight? They'll have to put on a show after dinner and we should let them and the Queensguard know the plan so we're all ready to go at midnight."

There was a knock, and the door flew open. Hera swept into the room with a face of thunder. "What are you playing at? What did my mother say to you?"

Connor quickly let her go and Jacs took a half step back. "Excuse me?"

"My mother, what did she say to you?"

"She just . . . showed me her brooch collection."

"Squirrelling you away, and you're here to ask her blessing. What did she say? Did you ask?"

Jacs held up her hands for calm. "Lord Claustrom, you forget yourself. I didn't have a chance to ask for her blessing, and somehow asking while still travelworn and barely arrived didn't feel right. I assure you I have everything under control and plan to speak to her before the end of our visit."

Hera frowned and tucked a curl behind her ear. "And she said nothing? Nothing . . . indecent?" she whispered the last word.

Jacs saw Amber turn her head to hide a sudden laugh inside a cough.

"Indecent? Your mother was nothing more than a gracious host. She was kind enough to show me her private collections and seemed eager for our . . . conversation later this weekend."

Hera dropped her shoulders and said in a much calmer tone, "Oh, good. I mean, of course that is to be expected. I'm sorry, I've been so busy lately, my mind is all over the place. I shouldn't have stormed in like this; that was beneath me. I do apologize."

"No need, Lord Claustrom." Jacs said and took a beat to actually see Hera. She looked much more exhausted than Jacs remembered from their last encounter. Her hair, usually a bright, shining mass of curls, was now limp and dull, wound tight at the nape of her neck. Her eyes were murky, pink staining the whites, with dark shadows hanging beneath. Sincerely, she said, "I worry that I've put too much on your shoulders, Lord Claustrom."

"I am managing just fine, Your Majesty."

"But you are still doing the work of more than three women on top of your own duties as lord. When we return to the palace, would you be interested in renegotiating your role?"

Hera looked at her shrewdly, then let her shoulders fall. "Yes. Yes, I think I would like that very much."

"Very well. Then, I'll see you at dinner?"

With a lingering look, Hera bowed in farewell and left. The door snapped shut behind her. Jacs looked at Connor and Amber, who both struggled with grins. "It's not funny," Jacs said.

"Of course not," Connor said quickly.

"Imagine having to keep tabs on your mother's affairs," Amber mused, sticking her thumbs in her belt and rocking on the balls of her feet.

Jacs shook her head. "Right, well we need to regroup. And I need help dressing." With a pang she thought of her valet Adaine, still healing in the infirmary. "The quicker we can get into Alethia and stop Celos, the better."

Stop Celos. If only it were as easy as those two words were to string together. After weeks spent planning, she was beyond eager to dive in but was painfully aware of the last time she went sprinting into Alethia. She wouldn't be unprepared again.

This time they would be ready.

"Agreed. I'll speak with the Queensguard. Yves is still playing the role of stable hand, so I'll send a message to him and rally the Canaries in the meantime," Amber said.

"It might look odd if the head of the Queensguard is seen talking with stable hands and dancers. I can go speak with the Canaries, and I'm sure Edith won't mind popping out to the stables to speak with Yves," Connor suggested.

"Good idea. You just focus on getting through this evening, Jacqueline, and we'll be ready to move for midnight," Amber concluded.

"Excellent."

Amber bowed and left. Jacs heard her bark orders for the two guards outside before the door closed behind her. Connor moved to follow, but Jacs held him back. Somehow the thought of him disappearing too was unbearable in that moment. He looked at her questioningly and returned to her side.

After the flurry of the afternoon, the room felt too quiet. Lady Claustrom's perfume clung in her nose, and she remembered the look she had given her. Holding fast to Connor's gaze, she searched his eyes. "Tell me we're doing the right thing," she whispered.

"Oh, Jacs," he said softly, holding her hands in his and pulling her close. Catching her chin with a bent forefinger, he tilted her head so she couldn't look away. "We're doing the best we can. That's all we can do. But if we don't try, Celos wins."

A clock chimed on the mantel, and she pulled back. "It's time."

He sucked in a breath. Drawing her over to the looking glass at her vanity, he helped her into the chair and set up the bowl she used to receive reports. Instinctively, she wrapped her fingers around it. They each drew a breath and he said into the mirror, "Father Celos."

The surface clouded over, and a man's angled features filled the frame. His voice leaked from the depths of the bowl as though emerging from Jacs's cupped palms.

"Your Queen has abandoned you, but I would never. Join me, Lowrians. Join me as we fight for a new order. Join me in the light. The hour draws near, and we will prevail! Look to the East as we bring the dawning of a new era in our wake. Tonight marks the last night you need fear the darkness." Jacs reached behind her and held fast to Connor's hand where it perched on her shoulder. Quickly he cut the connection and the image faded. Jacs dropped the bowl and the voice died.

"He's building up to something," she breathed, her mounting suspicion all but confirmed. Ever since Connor told her about the mirrors, she had made sure they listened to Celos's messages. All of them. They came out at the same time every day, and while the words varied, the message was consistent. The only major variation had been their building urgency. Something was coming.

"We'll stop him first."

Jacs nodded and, standing, turned her back on the empty mirror to face Connor. "We have to."

"He'll pay for his crimes," Connor said, almost to himself. There it was again, that flicker of something twisted lurking behind his eyes.

"Connor . . . I want more than anything for you to fight alongside me in this, but . . . if it's going to be too painful . . . you don't have to come. No one will think any less of you, and everyone will understand if you remain behind."

"What's that supposed to mean?"

"You've been through so much recently. You know what the Undercourt does to the mind. I know you want to come, and it's not that I don't want you there. I'm just . . . I'm worried about you."

"Jacs, I'm fine. I'll be fine. I have to . . . There's no way I could live with myself . . . I couldn't bear it if something happened and I wasn't there. I need to be there. I can't lose you. I won't."

He caught her cheek in his palm and she closed her eyes, opening them to see his gaze flick downward to the peacock feathers pinned to her bodice. A crease formed between his brows briefly. She longed to draw his lips to hers, longed to lose herself in his embrace, but guilt rooted her to the spot. He deserved all of her, not furtive kisses stolen between her promenades with Theo and advances from Lady Claustrom.

Instead, she drew him into an embrace, claiming this moment for her heart, the fractal memory suspended in a dewdrop of time.

"Whatever happens," she murmured close to his ear, "know that I am always and forever yours."

She felt his smile against her neck. "And I'm yours."

"But Connor?"

"Yes."

"I've been thinking." She drew away and held him loosely by the forearms. "Maybe it's better. Or maybe it's less confusing. If, until we're done with Alethia, until I've figured out what to do with Theo . . . if we don't . . . I mean if physically we keep . . . we keep things . . . neutral." She gestured between them.

Connor frowned, taking a step back and wiping a thumb down the side of his mouth. With a slow nod, he said, "You're right."

"It's not that I don't—"

"I know."

"It's just that—"

"Of course. I will remain your faithful advisor until such time as pleases Her Majesty." Jacs's heart sank, and he scratched the back of his neck, adding, "I didn't mean for that to come out so cold. I understand, really." Clearing his throat, he attempted a smile. "Now, we both need to get ready for dinner, and I think I need a bath. Shall I meet you in front of your chambers in an hour, and we can go down together?" Not quite meeting her eye, he took a handful of steps toward the door. The back of his neck was red, but otherwise his tone was light.

"Okay. And Connor?"

He turned.

"Thank you. I'll figure it out, I just need time."

He nodded once and departed. Jacs watched the door click closed behind him and tried to ignore the chill that trickled down her spine.

She just needed time.

28

TORCHLIGHT

"**L**ady Claustrom, Genteel Brovnen, it is my greatest pride and deepest pleasure to introduce the Heliotrope Canaries!" Druine's voice sang above enthusiastic applause. A small army of servants had promptly whisked the remnants of dinner away and shifted the tables to the edges of the room. The banquet hall was thick with the scent of roasted meat and mulling spices. Tall, thin tarrow candles lined the diamond-shaped hall and dotted a spiraling chandelier. Amber had wondered idly what contraption had been needed to light the candles at the very top of the chandelier, as it was far beyond the reach of any ladder she had seen.

The small audience sat on chairs in a horseshoe before a grand fireplace. Jacqueline sat in the center, Cornelius to her right, and Lordson Theo to her left. Amber noted that Theo had claimed the

Queen's hand in his as soon as they had sat down, and ever since then, Cornelius had refused to look their way.

Amber and the rest of the Queensguard stood two paces behind them, casting flickering shadows on the stone floors. Amber felt the heat of the fire at her back and shifted uncomfortably, sweat beading her forehead. Unfortunately, right in front of the fire was the best vantage point to both watch Jacqueline and to communicate with her fellow knights.

Druine was a natural leader. While not quite as charismatic as Yves, he held himself with the easy confidence of one accustomed to capturing the attention of others. He quickly had the room in the palm of his hand, and with a lit torch held aloft, motioned for his troupe to start. The men stepped forward, circling Druine, and held their slightly shorter unlit torches to his. In moments, all torches were aflame, and the men shifted into a staggered, spiraling formation around their leader. Amber's gaze darted around the room, and she noticed buckets filled with liquid dotted at evenly spaced intervals along the room's perimeter. Whether these were filled with water or something else, she was not sure, but she eyed the torches warily all the same. Cornelius shifted in his seat, and Amber saw his eyes narrow as a muscle worked along his jaw. She snapped her fingers once and sent a flurry of hand gestures down the line. In response, two guards shifted formation to better keep an eye on the royal advisor.

The men began stamping their feet and twirling their torches. Dots of flame became circles, circles merged into sweeping rivers of gold, and suddenly the burning wings of—what was that? A Griffin? No, Griffins had four legs, this creature had two. The flames wove a story as a heartbeat rhythm filled the room and the chests of the audience. Amber pulled her eyes from the display and blinked away the afterimage seared into her retinas. She needed to remain vigilant.

Her gaze swept across the profiles of Jacqueline and Cornelius. The light and shadow danced across each face. While Jacqueline's features were alight with wonder at the display, Cornelius's face was twisted in something akin to fear. A dancer twirled his torch in a sweeping arc in front of him and Cornelius flinched, his hands forming fists on his lap.

Amber narrowed her eyes and sent her decision to the guards in another quick succession of hand gestures. In a few short strides, she approached the back of his chair, clocking the speed with which the other guards and knights reformed their ranks behind her with a jolt of satisfaction.

Bringing her lips beside his ear, she said in a low voice, "Your Grace, may I request a word?"

He nodded and rose, giving Jacqueline's shoulder a reassuring squeeze as he stepped between their chairs and left the circle. Amber felt his presence two paces behind her as she led him from the room. Once out in the corridor, she turned to face him.

"Are you okay, Your Grace?" she asked matter-of-factly. In the light of the candles dotting the hallway, she noticed his face held very little color, despite the heat of the room they had just left.

"What? Yes, I'm fine," he said too quickly. She leveled her gaze at him and waited. Scratching the back of his neck, he looked away. "Why do you ask?"

"Just a hunch," she said kindly.

"No, I'm fine. I just . . . I wasn't expecting torches. I didn't think they'd be a problem. Turns out they are. I confess, I forgot where I was for a moment. Suddenly I was back there."

"Back where?"

He pressed his knuckles into the space to the left of his sternum as if working out a knot. "Back in that basket," he said so softly Amber almost missed it.

"Ah."

"But I'm fine. I just needed some air apparently; I thank you for that."

Amber brushed her thumb along the side of her mouth. "Did you want to talk about it?" His eyes met hers, and before he could reject her offer, she added, "If you're willing, I know I could use an excuse to talk about her."

After a moment's hesitation, he acquiesced and allowed Amber to lead him to an alcove window seat. The distant sound of stamping tickled the edges of her hearing, but otherwise the corridor was silent. Cornelius braced his palms against his knees and wouldn't meet her eye.

Amber watched as he appeared to work himself up to saying something once, twice, then closed his mouth again each time and rocked backward in his seat. He pressed against his knees as if to push himself away from whatever was trying to surface, then shook his head and said abruptly, "No. I'm sorry. I don't know if I can talk about it yet." With a snap, he slapped his hands against his thighs and made to stand.

Not one to sweeten her tea, she said bluntly, "There was nothing you could have done, you know. Nothing could have changed what happened."

He froze and lowered himself back down. "You don't know that."

"Sure I do."

He scoffed. "How?"

"Because it could have only happened one way, and that was the way you lived it. We can't change the past, and it's a waste of energy thinking about the ways you could have done things differently."

He was silent for a time, but she had waited longer for less. Finally, he said, "I tried . . . I couldn't help them."

Clasping and unclasping his hands, forearms resting on his thighs, he studied his thumbs. Amber watched the emotions at war in his expression and had a moment of realization. To be unable to defend, to be ill-equipped to fight, to be untrained and unprepared does not mean you'll never encounter a situation where your life is on the line. It just leaves you at a disadvantage when you do. If Cornelius had been trained, would it have made the difference? Would it have saved those two lives? Maybe, maybe not, but the reality is that he never had the choice. He was set up to fail, and there can be no comfort in that. If Cornelius had been given the basic tools of defense, he could have at least entered a more level battlefield instead of one pitched against him.

He was forever at the mercy of others. She couldn't imagine how that felt. Maybe her time with the dancing troupe was changing her after all, but somehow the idea that the highest-ranking man in the Queendom was so vulnerable was deplorable. No one should walk through this life helpless.

"Your Grace, may I speak freely?"

"Go ahead."

"That line of thinking will drive you mad. Especially with our next destination in mind, you can't entertain it, or I will be forced to leave you behind."

His head shot up and he said furiously, "No, I will be going to Al—"

She held up a hand and cut him off. "Let me finish. You need to understand. The past is the only thing in this life untouched by change. We can't revisit it, we can't improve it, we can't alter it. It is what it is . . . or . . . what it was. It's the stepping-stone that will propel us forward, so don't let yourself get stranded on it."

"What if I can't seem to move forward?"

"What you saw, I can only imagine. Take it from someone who has lived the horrors of battle, I understand. It makes no sense, who's chosen for Death's journey and who's left behind. I don't have the perfect answer for you. All I know is what'll serve you, and what won't, and dwelling on the things you can't change will not serve you." She took a breath and placed a heavy hand on his knee. "The past can't hurt you unless you give it the power to."

"What . . ."—he gestured to his chest angrily—"what do I do, then?"

"Use it for its intended purpose."

"And what's that?"

"Learn from it. It's a lesson, so use what you learned in the next battle. Your past, when used properly, becomes armor, it becomes weapons forged specifically for you. It becomes your best defense in the battles to come. Used *improperly*, those weapons turn against you."

"Why are you telling me all this?" he asked softly, finally meeting her gaze.

Amber took a beat before answering. "It's something every soldier needs to hear, something I end up having to tell all my recruits at one point or another in their career."

"Every soldier? I am no—"

"In title, no, but in heart? In deed? If your actions are any indication, Frean, you are well on your way to ranking yourself among my guards. It seems only fair I subject you to one of their lectures."

A ghost of a smile lifted the corners of his mouth, and he sat up straighter.

"Healing will take time we don't have, but can I rely on you not to lose your head down there?"

Cornelius nodded and his next words seemed to catch in his throat. Scrunching up his nose, he slowly exhaled. "You talk like her, you know?"

"Like whom?"

"Masterchiv Rathbone. You have the same . . . the same intensity. And she was wise too. Brutally honest, but wise."

Amber, momentarily lost for words, gave his knee a squeeze and shifted back on her seat. "That . . . is an honor of a compliment. Thank you."

A cheer erupted from the banquet hall.

"So?" Amber prompted.

Cornelius met her eye. "I can try."

Amber nodded. The steady thumping from the next room stopped and the sound of applause followed. "It sounds like they're winding down. Are you ready?"

Cornelius rose to his feet, jaw set. "Yes."

Studying his face carefully, Amber stood. "I meant what I said, Your Grace. Your safety is a top priority, if I get an inkling that you are going to lose yourself down there, I will send you topside, is that understood? I won't let Masterchiv Rathbone's sacrifice, nor Dryft's, be in vain."

"Understood."

She nodded and gestured for him to lead the way out of the alcove. He stepped forward, hand resting on the stone column, then hesitated and half turned back. "And Everstar . . . thank you. For what you said. You've given me a lot to think about. Maybe once this is all over . . . I'd like to talk about them. Masterchiv Rathbone and . . . and Dryft. I owe them . . . everything."

"Of course. It would be an honor."

29

CROWNING GLORY

T ime no longer held the same meaning in Alethia. Here, it was a fickle thing. It waxed and waned. Sometimes it stretched thin like a long, drawn-out sigh. Sometimes it slipped by rapidly, water spilled from a goblet. Phillip often prayed for the latter, but it was rare that time granted him the mercy of haste.

Phillip had grown up in a household full of clocks and things that ticked and whirred. A house full of regular intervals and metronomic rhythms. Wait. Had he? Those felt like memories borrowed from another, brighter time. Maybe he had simply heard about a house of clocks through the walls and created a memory around it. That seemed like something he would do. He could be an imaginative Son. Full of lies and deceit.

But he was trying. Father knew he was trying.

The pain still came for him. Never the same. Sometimes sharp and wicked. Sometimes soft, something to savor. Its regularity was a comfort. However, he had been in Alethia long enough that he should have found bliss by now. He was careful to hide this from his brothers, careful to adopt the expression of bliss whenever he lowered his hood. Was he defective? Broken? He didn't know why the pain still came for him, didn't know why Father couldn't grant him bliss and be done with it for good. He just knew that the pain, in a backward way, kept him sane. It reminded him that he used to wake in a room filled with sunlight spilling from wide-open windows. He could almost say he welcomed it. Almost.

He walked silently through the cold stone halls of a labyrinth he now knew better than he knew himself. Mallard followed silently behind him. They entered a tunnel that Phillip knew had poor acoustics. Something about the wall's angles stopped sound in its tracks, and he seized his opportunity.

"Mal," he hissed.

"What?"

"Have you found Gad yet?"

"No."

Phillip cursed. "Do you know why we've been summoned?"

"No. But it is an honor."

"Yes. Praise be." Phillip closed his mouth with a snap of his jaw as the tunnel changed again and his window closed. It wasn't long before they found themselves in front of the rift chamber. Phillip had never stepped inside before, and he hesitated at the doorway before knocking once and stepping to the side.

The door swung inward on mute hinges and Phillip shielded his eyes against the sudden brightness that radiated from the room beyond. A brother he recognized as Gentry beckoned for them to enter. Arranging his features and sliding his hood back, Phillip stepped inside.

His jaw dropped. He was in the belly of a cavernous room, but to call it a room was to call the sun a candle. It was enormous. He felt as though he had stepped into the hollowed-out core of a mountain. Craning his neck, he tried to locate the ceiling and was surprised to see a circular hole impossibly far away, speckled with stars. Bright white light, from a phosphorescent source smeared across three walls, lit the room. The far wall, Phillip noticed, was devoid of any light, and it took him a moment to realize that it was because it was open to the abyss below and above. He shuddered to think of the fall awaiting any who stepped too close to the edge.

His gaze returning to its center, he saw, suspended from thick chains hammered deep into the stone walls, a giant oval hot-air balloon. This was nothing like the little ones Jacqueline had made all those years ago. It looked deadly, cruel. Sleet-gray canvas wrapped in tar-black rigging. An elongated, horizontal balloon with a mean-looking point and a series of fins that reminded Phillip of a drawing he had seen of a large sea-swimming fish with impossibly sharp teeth. The basket was not free-dangling from the balloon, but mounted to the underbelly of the beast. What looked like a furnace with a chimney was perched in the middle of the mounted open-air platform, and a railing enclosed the space. The balloon's pointed bow had a rose-gold circle embedded in it, a giant version of the one Celos wore. Phillip shuddered to think the kind of pain that ring would bring.

"What . . ." he cut the question off and prayed no one had heard it.

"Isn't it beautiful?" Gentry whispered, following Phillip's gaze.

There were a great many words Phillip could use to describe that monstrosity, but beautiful was not one of them.

His gaze lowered to the long worktables meticulously placed at intervals around the base of the airship. There were at least two dozen tables, and each was topped with a mutilated, stone-hewn horse head and neck draped with a crude and cruel-looking set of chains that resembled an archaic sort of bridle. The horse heads looked as though they had been ripped from existing statues, as many of the bases were uneven and jagged, causing them to tilt precariously at odd angles. The noses had been hacked off. Bare and ragged stone edges exposed halfway down each nose allowed room for the mean-looking, barbed bit to hang loose in the air. The bridles were wrought from iron, and Phillip noticed a thick rose-gold ring suspended by chains at the center of each forehead. The ring was the same shape and color as the giant one embedded in the front of the balloon, as the one on Celos's finger. More pain bringers.

"Welcome," Celos said. He stood beneath the airship with several Sons scattered around him. Master Leschi stood with her head bowed two steps behind, hands clasped before her.

"Say hello to our guests, Bruna," he said with unearned familiarity.

Phillip gritted his teeth as Bruna lifted her unfocused gaze to settle beyond Phillip and squeezed her lips together.

Celos sighed. "Just once I wish you'd make this easy for yourself. Thus far the only gratitude I've received for protecting that precious mind of yours has been delays, excuses, and defiance. Thankfully, not even your stalling could halt our inevitable triumph. However, disobedience must be punished," he said and pointed his ring lazily toward Phillip. Master Leschi looked for a moment as if she expected to suffer the pain, and the instant before Phillip's knees buckled, her eyes widened as she recognized who had entered the room.

"Celos, you brute, stop! Hello! I said Hello!" she cried, and the pain left Phillip doubled over and panting.

"Good."

"Why is he here?" she whispered.

"I have a matter to discuss with him and Mallard. How fortunate that it has also created an opportunity for you to showcase your work. You must be commended, for it is with this fleet that I will finally be able to spread my love throughout the Upper and Lower Realms,"

Celos replied evenly, his keen eyes watching for every flicker of emotion that passed across Master Leschi's face.

"Please, let him go home."

"He is home, Bruna. Aren't you, my Son?"

Phillip, unprepared to be pulled into their exchange so quickly, hurried to stand to attention. Without allowing his gaze to lift higher than Celos's clavicle, he nodded, two short sharp ducks of his chin that caused Bruna to wince and his Father to regard him with something just shy of approval and leagues short of pride.

"You see?"

"You're more of a rusted-out manky old cog than I thought," she growled. "What need do you have of Phillip? Let him go. You have hundreds of ready and willing Sons. Release him. You can keep me for as long as you need, just let him g—" She cut off and seemed to fold in on herself as Celos pointed his ringed forefinger at her.

"No," he said. After a breathless eternity, he turned his attention away from the woman and released her from the pain.

"Besides, I thought you deserved an audience to admire your little creation."

"My shame," Master Leschi muttered.

"The airship, of course is to be celebrated, but you had already been working on similar designs for years, and despite this, found ways to delay at every juncture, so it was not necessarily a triumph, no. I made the true breakthrough. My collection of rings, all linked, all ready to obey, and it only required . . . what? A dozen Griffin eggs and the life blood of three fledglings? I doubt they missed their feathers once we drained them." Master Leschi scrubbed her fists in her skirts as if to wipe them clear of blood. "No, I don't recall you loving that task, but creation is often dirty business."

Angry tears filled her eyes and she dashed them away furiously. "It wasn't the task that bothered me, you brute, but the victims. I would have relished squeezing the sludge from your cold, dying heart."

Something about her pain, her defiance, stirred something in Phillip's chest. Celos curled his lip in disdain at Master Leschi's words and after a moment's apparent contemplation where his fingers flexed threateningly at his side, he turned away from her and focused instead on Phillip.

"Phillip. It is my understanding you are no further along the journey to bliss than when you first arrived here. Why do you reject it?"

"I–I don't, Father. I try my best, but I can't seem to find it."

"Mallard here is almost there, and he knows that once he achieves complete bliss, he will be ready to see his brother. Has this incentive been helpful for you, Mallard?"

"Yes, Father. Thank you, Father," Mal said quickly, head bowed.

Celos's attention returned to Phillip. "I wonder if you lack the proper incentive," he mused.

"No, Father. I promise I've been—" His words died as the pain settled its cloak around his shoulders and he dropped to one knee, shuddering.

"That wasn't a question."

Lips pressed tightly together, he nodded and waited for Celos to release him. Once the pain vanished, he could breathe again, and rose shakily to his feet.

"It is clear to me that this woman is impeding your progress. I have seen your mind. You cling to an imagined life elsewhere. A life far inferior to the life I offer you. You need to renounce this life, Phillip. Forget this fantasy. Accept that this woman is a stranger, nothing more. Will you do this for your Father?"

Eager for another look of approval, desperate to avoid another visit from the pain, Phillip hesitated only a moment before he nodded vigorously. The woman's face fell, and a coldness engulfed him. In a flash, a memory like sunlight refracted through a prism caressed his mind. He had received a beating, and two women hovered over him. One dabbed at his cuts with a damp cloth, the other cursed at the perpetrators. He felt terror seize his chest as the second woman's eyes filled with fury.

Something told him she would fight the culprits herself if he didn't do something, say something, admit the thing he hated most within himself. *I can't protect you.* The words fell from him. Shame smothered him. But the look in her eyes had been love, not disgust. Understanding, not disdain.

So different from the look in his Father's eyes now. It felt wrong—the memory remained lodged in the back of his mind—but no, Father was right. He needed to forget the fantasies that were keeping him from bliss. He couldn't protect her. This woman was a stranger to him. He needed to accept the truth.

"Monster," Bruna forced the word through gritted teeth. "Parading my son in front of me with your rot in his mind and your fingers on his strings. He is my son, Celos. Not yours. Nothing will change that. Waste your life torturing the answers you want from people, but that does not make them true. It just makes you delusional."

Phillip wished he could say he felt nothing for this woman, who now staggered and clutched her head. Jaw clenched and eyes furious, she braced herself against Celos's will, against the pain emanating from his ring. He shouldn't care. He needed for her to be nothing to him. But a ringing filled his ears, he clenched his fists and roared, launching himself at Celos.

He was halfway to throttling the man before he felt thick arms around his waist, and he fell as the force of a bull threw him off course and sent him sprawling. Landing painfully on the jagged stone floor, he looked up to see Mal towering over him, a blank look in his eye and lips spread in an unsettling grin.

"Interesting," Celos said quietly. "It seems in an instant I have been severely disappointed by one Son, and his punishment has brought me the greatest pride in another. Excellent work, Mallard."

"Thank you, Father," Mal replied, his voice eerily calm.

"The era of your usefulness is rapidly reaching its end, Bruna, and your insolence has long since lost its appeal. Phillip, I will give you a chance to redeem yourself. Mallard, help him to his feet."

Propped on his elbow, Phillip glared at Mal and refused to take his offered hand. Still with that steady calm, Mal moved to stand behind Phillip, hooked his hands under his arms, and hoisted him to his feet. He even had the decency to brush the grit from his back.

Celos looked up at his airship and sighed. "I had hoped to share the brilliance of tomorrow's new dawn with you, Bruna. Despite our differing visions, I confess I've grown somewhat fond of our banter. It's not often the wits I match are worthwhile. More's the pity." As if from nowhere, he produced a black dagger. He offered it, hilt first, to Phillip. "Kill her."

"What?" The question summoned the pain to nip at his mind like an eager dog. Celos waited for him to right himself again.

"Kill her and redeem yourself."

"You're mad."

Celos studied him carefully, his ringed finger tapping against his chin. "Then let's experiment. Eric, restrain her. Gentry, bring me my crown."

Phillip watched the color drain from Gentry's face as he hurried to obey his Father. Eric materialized from the room's shadows and waved cheerily to Phillip before holding fast to Bruna's arms. She did not attempt to struggle, instead her gaze flew around the room, and Phillip could almost see the gears in her mind spinning. Their eyes met and she looked pointedly at him, at Celos, then off to Phillip's left in the direction of the door. Phillip didn't know what she meant; his mind was filled with the sight of the twisted black dagger.

"And my brother . . . Gad?" Mal asked while they waited.

"Of course. You've earned the truth. I suspect his body was burned with the clock tower in Bridgeport."

"His—"

"Loss is inevitable. Seek comfort in the arms of your new brothers. You may go."

"But . . . but you said—" Mal broke off with a grimace under Celos's pointed finger. Again, his eyes adopted that same blankness and his face cleared. He bowed low before disappearing from the chamber.

Gentry returned, holding a heavy metal box before him. Placing the box on a nearby table, he opened it and withdrew a black iron crown. It was comprised of evenly spaced twisted black spears encircled by a band of red gold rings. With loving care, Celos removed the ring from his finger and slotted it into a groove at the front of the crown. Lifting it high, he placed it on his head.

"You are fortunate enough to be the first subject under my rule," Celos said quietly, shifting his head slightly to accommodate the weight of the crown. Closing his eyes, he took a deep breath.

Immediately, Phillip's mind was seized from all corners. Every segment, every engram, now thrummed with the awareness of another. Smells warped, colors wavered, his perspective oscillated between his own and a foreign force's. As though compelled to trade places with his shadow, he became insubstantial within himself. A reflection in a mirror, an echo in a cave. No longer the flame, but the calefaction.

"What are you—" he managed through lips that were and were not his own.

"Kill her," Celos repeated.

The sound of screaming filled his mind.

Phillip reached for the dagger.

30

SET IN MOTION

After dinner, after dancing, and after the good nights were said, Jacs was able to retreat. Lady Claustrom had appeared disappointed at her request to end the evening's festivities and had insisted upon two additional encores before she was willing to let the troupe retire. Eyes drooping, the lady appeared to fight fatigue until the last possible moment before giving in. Her fingers lingered around Jacs's wrist before she left the room with her retinue.

Theo offered to escort Jacs to her chambers, and she accepted his arm graciously, earning a satisfied nod from a yawning Hera. Theo walked her the long way back to her chambers.

"May I show you something?" he asked as they passed a tapestry of a winged woman wreathed in golden light.

"Of course, Lordson," she said softly.

Amber and Thomas followed at a modest distance. Ducking his head to hide a smile, Theo led her through the maze of tapestries to a small room in the west wing. No larger than her bedroom had been back in Bridgeport, it had a tall, skinny window on the wall opposite the door and a cast-iron stove in one corner for warmth. A bookshelf with a collection of thin folders stacked side by side stretched along one wall, and a music stand stood near the window. It took a moment for her eyes to adjust to the dim light coming from the little stove and the candles dotted about the room. When they did, she saw two violins set up on stands, their bows hung ready.

"After father threw his violin in the fire, I moved my music room here. It's small, but the stove is harder to force an instrument into," he said with a nervous laugh.

"It's cozy," she replied.

"I wondered if you would indulge me in a duet?" he asked shyly, inviting her into the room and gesturing to one of the violins.

"Oh, I couldn't possibly . . ." Jacs blustered, but felt Amber's firm hand push her gently between the shoulder blades to follow him across the threshold. "It . . . it would be a delight," she corrected. Theo beamed. As Jacs stepped into the room, Amber gently closed the door behind her.

Accepting the proffered violin, Jacs joined Theo and they spent a few minutes tuning their respective instruments and tightening their bows. Theo's cheeks were flushed, and Jacs doubted it was due to the little stove's heat. After a few cursory notes, Theo played a fragment of a melody Jacs recognized.

Lowering her bow in shock, she asked, "How do you know that song?"

Theo let the last note ring out and replied, "I heard you humming it one morning in the garden. I guessed it was one you liked and sought to learn it. I hope that wasn't too presumptuous."

"No, no it's fine, I just didn't expect to hear it again."

"No? If you don't mind my asking, what is the song's signifi-cance?" Theo asked with a curious tilt of the head.

"It . . . it was my father's favorite."

Theo's eyes widened. "Oh, I apologize, we don't have to play that one . . . Is there another duet you would like to try?"

Jacs drew her bow along the strings of her own violin and played the echo of Theo's few bars. "No, it's an excellent choice, and one I actually know, so I won't embarrass myself with errors."

Theo hesitated, and Jacs, with an encouraging nod, began the melody again. Wedging his own instrument beneath his chin once more, Theo joined in with the accompaniment. The two melodies danced joyfully with one another about the room. It had been years since Jacs had heard the twin parts played together, and she felt the music lift her heart to the rafters. Tears formed in the corners of her eyes and one spilled down her cheek, but she didn't stop playing until the last twinned notes died in the air.

Lowering his bow, Theo bowed. "Thank you."

Jacs replaced her violin on its stand to give herself time to regain composure and mirrored his bow. "I'm the one who should be thank-ing you, Lordson. I didn't think I would hear that song performed properly again. You can't know the joy that was to hear." With the back of her hand, she wiped at a rogue tear that had slipped free of her lashes. Theo, without saying a word, pulled a kerchief from his doublet and passed it to her kindly.

Their hands touched. Instinctively, she curled her fingers in his. He took a hesitant step closer and, the kerchief still clasped between them, brushed a tear from her cheek with the curve of his forefinger. His touch left a warmth in its wake.

"You play beautifully," he murmured, voice soft.

The candlelight danced along the walls. A log in the little stove shifted. Their eyes met, his a gentle gray of misty mornings, dusty silverware, and the fur of an old cat with a kink in its tail. Gray, not blue. She caught his hand in hers, lowered it to meet his other, and gave both a gentle squeeze. A small part of her was reluctant to let them go.

"I think it best I retire to my chambers."

"Of course." His gaze searched hers for a moment, then he pressed the kerchief into her hands and busied himself with loosening his bow, wiping a cloth over his strings, and placing his violin in its case. With his back to her, she had a chance to compose herself. The duet had brought forth an alarming cocktail of emotions she hadn't expected. By the time he snapped the case clasp closed, her expression had cleared and she handed his kerchief back to him with a nod of thanks.

Outside her chamber door, a chaste kiss passed from Theo's lips to her hand, and he wished her a pleasant sleep before departing. She breathed a sigh of relief. Amber and Thomas stood halfway down the hallway, and as Theo's footsteps retreated, Amber approached.

Jacs placed the flat of her palm on the door. "Thomas, you may go and ready the Canaries," she ordered. He bowed and departed.

Once she and Amber were alone in the hallway, Amber said, "That was sweet."

"I know."

"He seems kind."

"He is." Hand shifting to hover on the doorknob a moment, she settled her heart before entering her rooms.

Connor was sprawled in a chair beside the fireplace reading a book. At the sound of the door opening, he looked up, bookmarked his page, and rose.

"Is everything okay?" he asked.

Jacs nodded and watched his shoulders slump in relief.

"You were gone a while."

"We played some music together, nothing more. It was a nice distraction."

Connor raised his eyebrows and Amber said bluntly, "Violin, Your Grace. They both play." Directing her next comment to Jacs, Amber said, "I'll stand guard outside. Call if you need anything."

"Thank you, Amber," Jacs said and watched her leave and close the door. The fire crackled merrily in the grate behind her, and she sighed, returning her gaze to Connor's.

"What were you reading?" she asked, gesturing to the book he'd discarded on the side table. He moved to retrieve it and flicked through the pages.

"A book of myths and legends from Frea, Nysa, and Auster. A lot of the Frean ones have to do with Queens." He tapped his thumb against the spine and added, "Who knows, maybe they'll write one about you one day."

Jacs grinned and they both sat on the cushioned sofa. It was warm and cozy by the fire and she curled into his shoulder as he showed her the cover. Embossed across three crowns arranged in a pyramid, one gold, one obsidian, one wrought from pearls, were the words *Myths and Legends of the Treble Crowns.*

"We'd never have been allowed a book like that in the Lower Realm. All our books were about life in the basin, or the dangers of breaching the Upper. Lessons and warnings with no room for imagination, let alone other Queendoms. What kinds of stories are in there?"

"There's one about a secret love between the Frean Queen's daughter and the daughter of the Sea Queen. That one's a bit gruesome, actually, involving eye gouging and deep-sea diving."

"Yikes."

"Exactly. And there's the legend of the first Alessi. A human Queen forged by Griffins to rule the land and skies."

"Alessi? Impressive, I think I saw a tapestry in the hall of that one."

"I feel like there's a tapestry for everything in this manor."

Jacs laughed and snuggled more comfortably into Connor. He hesitated, then curled an arm around her shoulders. Tilting her chin up, she kissed beneath his ear. His gaze shifted from the book to her, and she lifted a hand to his cheek. The lightest pressure turned his head and she brought his lips to hers. So comfortable was the action that it took a moment before she realized what she'd done and froze. Connor broke away first, unlooping his arm from her shoulder. Jacs sat up straight. They began talking at the same time.

"Jacs, no, you can't just—"

"I didn't think," she said.

"You wanted *neutral.*"

"I know."

"*This* isn't neutral."

"I know! I know. It's not fair. It's not fair to you. Not while I'm here to potentially propose to someone else. Not to him, while I'm leading him to believe I will."

"I should go." He rose, and the book fell to the floor with a thud. He hurried to retrieve it and set it to rights on the side table.

"You don't have to. We could . . ." She looked around the room for inspiration. Her eyes fell on a nearby chess board, set to play. "We could play chess?"

Connor shook his head. "No. I have to get a few things from my chambers. Besides, it's late. It will raise more than eyebrows if I'm found in your rooms at this hour, and I doubt the Claustroms would believe chess at ten o'clock really is just chess." He scrubbed his face and sighed. "I'll be back in an hour."

She didn't want him to leave, but knew she couldn't ask him to stay. She'd set the rules. He was halfway to the door, and in three short strides, Jacs had closed the distance and clasped his hand, pressing it between her palms.

"I'm sorry."

He pulled away. "I'll see you soon."

The night folded in around the estate like the blooming of a flower in reverse. All things returned to stillness. Jacs paced the room, her eyes darting to the clock on the mantel as the hand ticked sluggishly around its face. She ran through the plan again, over and over, until it was tattooed behind her eyelids. Anything to silence the whispers of guilt lurking in the corners of her mind. Finally, as the eleventh chime died, she set to work.

Jacs changed swiftly, removing her skirts, stripping her sleeves, and placing her jewels safely upon velvet cushions on the vanity. She now stood in the center of her room in black leggings and tall leather boots. Daggers were strapped to her thigh, wrists, and tucked in her boots. Pulling a warm tunic over her torso, she settled the fabric over the top of her wrist daggers and wrapped a thick leather belt around her waist. Last, she tied four restraining straps to it and retrieved a folded purple cloak from one of her cases, tucking it under her arm. A thin gold band circled her temples, and she twisted her hair into a tight plait down her back.

A gentle knock broke her reverie, and Connor, Amber, Yves, and Edith tiptoed into her room.

"Where's the Queensguard? Where's the troupe?" Jacs whispered.

Amber replied grimly, "Druine may be a little detained as Lady Claustrom has requested a private performance. Don't know where she finds the stamina—she looked dead on her feet by the end of dinner. The rest were awaiting the eleventh bell in their quarters. It'd be too suspicious if suddenly your room became the new site of the evening's festivities. They all know to meet outside the study closer to midnight."

"We can only hope the Claustroms sleep quickly and soundly. That would be a fortunate aid to our plans," Jacs said.

"Fortune often favors forethought," Yves commented cryptically with a mischievous wink.

Connor raised an eyebrow at him. "What did you do?"

"Nothing!" he replied with mock indignation. "Only, I may have convinced the wine bearer to focus on certain members of our host's household, and I may have laced the wine in question with a wee dram of something to encourage slumber."

"You drugged them?" Jacs hissed.

"Not in a way they'd notice." Yves shrugged. "If anything, they'll chalk it up to the several goblets they quaffed in their excitement to entertain a new Queen. I must say, Lady Claustrom seemed quite taken with you this evening, Your Majesty. What did you say to her this afternoon? You know, she doesn't take just anyone on a tour of her private collection."

"Guard your tongue, Yves, last time you proved just as useful a guide gagged," Jacs snapped.

Amber hid her smile and said, "We need to move. Everyone ready?"

A chorus of yeses followed, and Yves performed a silent little bow with a side glance at Jacs as if to prove a point.

Jacs exhaled through pursed lips. "Remember why we're there. Free the Undercourt, free the boys. None of that can happen until we defeat Celos. Let's go."

As she led the way out of her chamber, she saw Edith pull Connor aside and say something softly in his ear. He nodded reassuringly and brought her knuckles to his lips. The swing of the door obscured the rest from Jacs's view.

31

CROSSING THE THRESHOLD

The corridors were still and silent, any scuffled footfall swallowed by the tapestry-covered walls. Their group moved like specters. It was eerie roaming these halls at night. Each woven face within the tapestries watched them pass by, stitched eyes following them down the corridors. Some looked so lifelike, Jacs had to remind herself that they were nothing more than fancy curtains.

Movement in the corner of her eye caused her to turn as Connor fell into step beside her.

"Is she okay?" Jacs whispered.

Connor nodded. "Worried."

"I can imagine. Let's get this done so she doesn't have to worry long." Edith had agreed to stay in Jacs's room while they infiltrated Alethia with the hopes she could cover for the Queen's absence if needed. Connor had been adamant she assume no larger role in their plan.

They came to a halt in front of Lady Claustrom's study. Jacs looked behind her to check they were all accounted for. Connor; Amber; the six members of the Queensguard, including Chivilras Fayworth, Pamheir, and Ryder, and three recent recruits; and guards Wendy Dustworn, Lily Breaheir, and Isabella Farthing stood awaiting orders. Jacs peered into the gloom and couldn't see any sign of Yves or the troupe.

"Where are they?" she whispered. Yves had been with them in her chambers, and she could have sworn he'd followed a half step behind as they left. Where had he gone?

Amber grimaced and made a soft, lilting birdcall with an apologetic look at Jacs. Bewildered, Jacs watched as the tapestries began to shift and flutter; then with a flourish, Yves and his troupe leaped from behind the folds of fabric and landed in the hallway on silent feet, bowing low. They were already dressed in their purple cloaks. The Queensguard hid smirks.

Yves rose first and winked at his Queen.

"Greetings," he said in a stage whisper.

Jacs's initial amusement was quickly swallowed by the sticky cold throat of dread as she remembered the last time she had encountered a group of purple-hooded men. No, this was different. They were on the same side. This would work.

With a brisk nod, she gripped the door handle and pushed her way into the room. In the distance, a grandmother clock began striking twelve. The room was dimly lit by a fire slowly dying in its grate. Snuffed-out candles lined the walls and framed a larger-than-life tapestry of a younger Lady Claustrom astride a pure white mare. Her blonde hair flared out behind her, merging with the rays of a rising sun. Jacs appraised it and commented almost to herself, "Her humility knows no bounds."

Movement from a wingback chair near the fire caused Jacs to jump and Amber to leap forward, seizing the perpetrator, hauling him to his feet, and twisting his arms behind his back. The rest of the Queensguard had readied their stances. It was Theo.

"What are you—" Amber clapped a hand over his mouth.

Mouth close to his ear, she whispered, "Shut it, keep it shut, and I'll let you go. Deal?"

He nodded, eyes wide. Keeping a firm grasp of his wrists, she withdrew her hand, watching him carefully all the while.

"Theo, what are you doing here?" Jacs asked, stepping forward. She saw his book had fallen to the floor in the commotion.

"What am I doing here? What are *you* doing here? What are any of you doing here?" he whispered angrily, one eye warily watching Amber for signs she was going to silence him again. Behind them, a flushed-faced and disheveled Druine slipped through the door to join their group.

"We . . ." Jacs didn't know what to say. It was midnight. Lady Claustrom's study was now full of people all dressed in or carrying purple cloaks, and she was clearly outfitted for battle. She decided on the truth. "We're going into Alethia. We're going to stop Celos."

"You're . . ."

His gaze darted to the tapestry of his mother on horseback as realization dawned on him.

"What are we going to do with the Lordson? We've got a long road ahead of us and can't waste time in discourse," Yves said.

"We could tie him up and leave him here," Amber suggested.

"No!" Theo and Connor said in unison. The two men looked at each other in surprise.

Connor explained, "If someone finds him, or if he gets free, we'll have the Claustrom household on our tails, or worse, they may have a quicker way to warn Celos and we'll arrive to an ambush."

Amber shot him a look of approval and nodded her agreement.

"We can't leave him behind, and we can't trust him not to say anything if we let him go."

"I didn't see anything . . . I swear," Theo said in earnest, but nobody was listening to him.

"Could we lock him up with Edith, have her watch him while we're gone?" Jacs suggested.

"With all due respect, I don't want to implicate her in a kidnapping if he's found under her watch," Connor said quickly.

"I promise I'll just go back to my chambers and stay there; I won't breathe a word about what I saw to anyone," Theo said.

"A Lordson's promise is about as binding as a sugar-spun bridle and not nearly as sweet," Yves said disdainfully, adding, "No offense."

Jacs bit her lip and suggested, "What if we locked him in one of the troupe's rooms?"

"That's true, we could lock him in and collect him when we return," Connor said.

"*If* we return," a purple-hooded man joked.

"You can't leave me locked up just to wait for someone to find me!" Theo said.

"Well, we can't leave you here," Jacs proclaimed.

"Then take me with you."

"What?" said Connor.

"No," said Jacs.

"Time is a fickle brute, and fortune favors no one without it," Yves said pointedly, arms crossed.

"Yes, take me with you, I can help. I owe you for saving my life, Your Majesty. Let me repay my debt."

Connor's gaze snapped to Jacs, demanding explanation.

"I didn't save your life, Theo, you owe me nothing."

"You did!"

"How did you save his life?" Connor asked.

"From a Griffin, it attacked me, and Her Majesty threw herself between it and me. She saved me. I owe my life to her. To you," he said solemnly, eyes now locked on Jacs.

"You don't know what you're signing up for," she said gently.

"I can be useful."

In two swift motions, Amber shook her head and said, "We can't risk him alerting Celos. We only have one shot to catch the basemutt unawares. Apologies, the *brute* unawares," she amended after Jacs shot her a look of disapproval. "If we let the boy go, we can't guarantee he'll keep his mouth shut long enough for us to benefit from the element of surprise. But if we take him with us, he might be more of a liability than he's worth and blow our cover anyway."

"He doesn't know what's down there, and we don't know how the Undercourt is going to affect him," Connor said quietly.

Sighing, Jacs said, "Theo, I'm sorry, but you can't come with us. Cornelius and Chiv. Everstar are right. We're too close to have an oversight trip us up now."

"Tick tock," Yves muttered.

"Right, Druine, you're on Theo watch," Jacs commanded. "You'll have to stay behind with him and make sure he doesn't give us away before we're back. It'll leave us a man down, but I don't see any other way around it. Keep him safe and make sure he stays quiet."

"A gag is an effective tool," Yves suggested.

"Gag—no, I'm—" Theo spluttered.

"Everyone ready?" Jacs said, signaling for Amber to release Theo's wrists while Druine reluctantly took up position to his left.

"Yes," chorused the others, all hosting looks of determination and some excitement. Druine, however, looked crestfallen, shooting Theo a look of bitter disappointment. All former spring in his step had vanished.

"Let's go."

With that, Jacs marched up to the giant tapestry and shoved it aside. Her mind still reeling from the unexpected turn of events, she scanned the door before realizing it would take the form of their second hiccup. Rather than a simple door with a lock as she had expected, she saw a heavy iron door handle next to a complicated iron grid filled with brightly colored gemstone spheres.

The grid was five by five and almost completely filled with gemstones; only a few spaces remained empty. Pushing a ruby with her index finger, she slid it to an empty cell. The ones above shifted to fill the gap left behind.

"What is this?" Jacs whispered.

"A puzzle lock. Mother keeps many secrets under some form of lock and key," Theo said softly, coming to stand next to Jacs, one hand rubbing the wrist of the other.

Jacs studied the color patterns and empty slots. She had no doubt she could crack the code, but it would take time they didn't have. "Do you know how to open it?" she asked Theo.

"Of course."

"Then make haste," she said, indicating the lock.

"No."

"You mutt, that was an order from your Queen," Amber snarled, stepping forward.

Theo shrugged, although Jacs noticed his face had lost some of its color. "I will open it, if you promise I get to join you to Alethia."

"He's wasting time! Bring the boy, and to the dogs with him if he gets himself in trouble down there," Yves growled.

Jacs studied the Lordson's face. "Why . . . why do you want to go so badly? You must know it's going to be dangerous."

Theo crossed his arms. "I told you before, this is my chance to pay back my debt. Besides, I'm sick of waiting. I want to be doing something for once. Let me help you. How am I to prove myself worthy to rule by your side if you don't give me a chance?"

A painful silence followed his words, and Jacs looked away, catching the stony expression on Connor's face before letting her gaze settle somewhere safe: Amber, who lifted her shoulders in a half-hearted shrug.

Theo set his lips in a thin line. Jacs glanced from him to the impatient faces of the others and relented. "Fine, but any sign of trouble, any indication that you're going to jeopardize the mission, and Druine will drag you back here if he has to. Got it?"

"Got it."

"Druine?"

"With pleasure," he said, face now alight with excitement.

"Fine. Open the door."

"Of course, Your Majesty," Theo said with a grin and a bow. Deftly, he swiped the gems back and forth within the grid, muttering as he went. "Citrine, emerald, lapis lazuli, opal, sapphire, and that should be . . . there."

With the five gems arranged in the iron grid, he gave the handle a hearty twist to the right and threw his weight into the door. A loud, hollow clunk echoed in the quiet room, causing Amber to wince and Jacs to hold her breath. Slowly, the door shifted inward, then with Theo's assistance, began sliding to the left into the hidden recess within the wall. A dry, stale breeze rushed to meet them from the tunnel and burst into the room, causing the fire in the grate to flicker.

Theo stood back looking pleased with himself. "After you," he said smugly.

"How did you know the code?" Amber asked suspiciously.

Theo's eyes widened and he hurried to explain. "I've never been in there. It's far too creepy. I figured it out years ago. I like puzzles."

Arching a brow with a look that was far from satisfied, Amber gestured pointedly to Druine, who hurried to assume his position as Theo's shadow. Jacs could see Theo holding tight to Druine's upper arm. Between him and his mother, it was a wonder the dancer had any feeling left in his fingers at all. With a nod, Jacs indicated for Amber and Yves to take the lead. Theo and Druine went next, then the

Canaries. Only after she was sure no backward glance from Theo would reach her did she claim Connor's hand. The Queensguard took up the rear.

Two by two, the pairs disappeared into the tunnel. Jacs hesitated on the threshold, Connor waiting patiently at her side.

"Here we go," she whispered.

Leading with her right foot, she stepped forward.

32

DISTURB NOT THE DARKNESS

A
mber's skin began to crawl the moment she stepped into the muffled quiet of the tunnel. Even Yves didn't seem to have a quip to lighten the mood. Not that this was the time or the place, but that had never stopped him before. Immediately to Amber's right as they entered, she spotted an alcove containing a shrine of sorts. A chest-high stone basin was carved into the rock beneath a polished silver looking glass. Golden trumpeting flowers adorned the mirror. Two purple crystals were embedded at eye level on either side of the mirror with a glowing blue crystal perched above. She shuddered and passed it quickly. Soon it was out of sight and mind.

Amber strode forward, stiff-backed with ears alert as her eyes adjusted to the gloom. The tunnel wasn't completely dark, which was eerie in and of itself. It was illuminated by the startling glow of a brilliant white phosphorescence, the same white stuff that had been smeared on the walls of Alethia.

Stopping at the head of the column, she drew the attention of the Canaries behind her and made a series of hand gestures. An arsenal of blank faces stared back at her. Just as she realized her mistake, Yves said softly in her ear, "Not fully fledged guards yet, Chivilra. I fear they don't share your language."

Waving him off, she said in a low whisper to one of the front-standing Canaries, Bertrum, "Watch out for any other crystals and stay quiet." Obediently, Bertrum nodded and passed the message along to those behind.

Swift and silent, the team made their way through the endless tunnel. Amber expected some deviation or forking in their path, but for the first hour it appeared Celos had only needed one route out this way. What she did notice was the gradient. From the moment they entered the tunnel, they began traveling downhill. Amber tried not to think about the increasing weight of the earth piled above their heads the farther they descended toward Alethia.

Finally they encountered their first fork: a circular room with four additional tunnels dotted around the circumference. Yves hesitated only a moment before selecting the second from the left and continuing onward.

"Where do the others lead?" Amber asked softly.

"Springbank, Newfrea, and Luxlow," he muttered, arm outstretched as he pointed them out, and they both fell silent again. The white light cast haggard shadows across their faces. The surrounding rock swallowed their words the moment they left their lips, leaving the tunnel feeling empty. Amber shook her head with something that hovered between disgust and admiration. To think, their whole realm was connected by secret tunnels beneath their feet. And what was worse, those tunnels were dominated by a force that wished harm to the Queen and all she stood for.

Another hour passed, or at least it felt like an hour. Really, Amber had no way of knowing beyond the increasing ache in her feet how long they had been down there. The sameness of the tunnel was enough to drive anyone mad. The Catacombs of Lethe had at least been interesting, with dripping walls, rocky terrain, and even an underground lake. This tunnel was infuriatingly uniform.

Yves stopped short with a signal to those behind to do the same. Sure, the Canaries understood *his* hand gestures. Peering farther down the passageway, Amber noticed that the phosphorescence ended. The tunnel beyond gaped open, wide, and . . . blue? Despite the excitement that any variability brought, she forced the column to approach it with caution. Yves ducked into the open chamber beyond to check that the coast was clear before waving everyone inside.

Beyond the narrow confines of the tunnel the passage opened to reveal a room full of glowing blue pools. Scanning her surroundings, Amber saw a shadow shift within the nearest pool's depths. She blinked and it was gone. Goose bumps prickled along her arms. Must have been a trick of the light. The pool's basins were lined with glowing blue crystals, the same ones that could listen and send your words across the realms. Long daggers of stone grew down from the ceiling. Not knowing what else to do, she signaled for silence; she wasn't sure if the crystals could hear underwater, but figured this wasn't the time to find out. The pools were separated by narrow paths of stone and were arranged in a spiraling circle around a copse of gnarled and knotted long-dead trees. Their age-bleached bark was tinged blue in the light from the pools. This copse of corpses looked to be woman-made rather than naturally grown and was mysteriously void of any of the moss or lichen that speckled the cave's walls and floor. Amber shuddered. She couldn't shake the thought that some of the branches closely resembled curled finger bones.

Yves brought the group to a halt and said in a carrying stage whisper, "We must move through this chamber quickly. Do not touch the trees. Do not disturb the pools. Follow me." He waved the group along the narrow rocky paths between the pools, cutting across the center of the room and skirting the small forest. Each step he took carefully, and Amber noticed a shiny green fuzz covering the stone. A tentative toe tap revealed it to be a kind of slippery moss that threatened to sweep her feet out from beneath her. If the situation were different, she might have called the place elegant, but the eerie dead trees stood watch and the steady *drip-drip-plunk* reminded her of her experience in the second task. She furrowed her brow and cast a glance around the group. All seemed okay for the moment, sane for the moment.

Jacqueline, who had been weaving her way up the line, came to walk beside her and Yves. Amber saw her eyeing the crystals warily. In a low voice, Jacqueline said, "Most of us aren't registered within the crystal bank, correct? The Canaries aren't, and none of the Queens-guard are."

Amber cursed. "Mine still is, from the Contest. I knew I should have wiped it."

Yves peered into one of the pools and shrugged. "I guess we have to hope Father isn't looking for you."

"Cornelius and I are registered too, but I'm under a coded name. I doubt Celos would know to look for you, Amber . . . I'm not sure if he'd think to look for Cornelius . . ." She worried her lip uneasily. "The other person I'm not sure about is"—she spun around—"Theo."

At the mention of his name, Theo's head shot up from where it had been bowed moments before, his eyes fixed intently on his feet as he picked his way across the moss. The sudden distraction caused him to slip, left foot splashing through the glassy surface of the water in the nearest pool.

Druine caught him by the elbow just before he fell in, and Theo's foot emerged dripping, sending ripples racing one another to the perimeter. Yves flinched and seemed to hold his breath, the moment frozen in time, waiting for a blow that didn't come.

"Theo, are you registered within the crystals' memory bank?" Jacqueline asked. Her question unfroze the party and they continued to pick their way across the room, skirting the dead trees.

"No? I don't think so . . ."

"What do you mean, you don't think so?" Cornelius whispered.

"Well, I can't remember if I have been. I doubt it though."

"Charmingly specific, isn't he?" Yves muttered beside Amber.

Amber ignored him, but her lips quirked minutely. "Okay, silence and stealth is still our key objective, so don't abandon either." A sea of faces nodded their understanding, and she turned to Yves. "How much farther do you predict we have until we reach the city?"

Yves cocked his head to the side as he thought. "At the jolly pace you've set for us? About half an hour . . . Maybe—" A splash interrupted his answer. His eyes darted over Amber's shoulder, widened, and he cried, "Run!" as something cold and wet grasped Amber's ankle.

Immediately, Amber struck the offender's bony knuckles and wrenched her foot free of its spindly grasp. With no time to take in the finned creature that had seized her, she focused on her main objective: getting Jacqueline to safety.

Her fingers encircled the Queen's wrist and they set off on a slipping run across the mossy path to the other end of the cavern. Pale, dripping arms broke the surface of the nearest pool, shooting out to impede their route, narrowly missing each footfall. Amber glanced down to see a cruel face twisted into a wicked grin staring up at her from beneath the pool's ripples.

Jacqueline cried out, her wrist almost wrenching free of Amber's grip, but Amber skidded to a halt and held fast. Long, pale fingers wrapped around Jacqueline's calf. The creature's deathly gray, scaly torso was briefly exposed above the rim of the pool. With a well-placed kick to a gaunt elbow, Jacqueline sent the creature hissing beneath the water, bubbles erupting from its clenched teeth. Several splashes sounded off behind them, but Amber fixed her eyes on Yves's back and hurried after him, Queen in tow. She realized with a curse that she'd left herself without the second half to her pair. Yves had been her walking partner, sure, but had not synced to fight alongside her. His retreating figure now darted away between the pools. She kicked out at another grasping hand and almost lost her balance on a slippery patch of moss.

Once they'd reached the far wall near the exit tunnel, Amber spun Jacqueline around to face her, quickly checking her over for injuries and registering that Jacqueline was not putting weight on her right foot.

"I'm fine, get the others," Jacqueline gasped, one hand propped against the cave wall, the other already tugging at her boot, likely to inspect the damage. Yves stood next to the cave exit, one eye on the pools, the other darting off to survey the next tunnel.

"Fleetfoot! Keep her safe," Amber barked, glaring at him with a frustration she knew he did not deserve; he didn't have her training. "Or I swear on my sword your fate will match hers."

She raced back into the fray, finally able to take in the nature of their foe. Amber's eyes widened. A swarm of nightmarish hybrid human-fish creatures attacked her troops. Thomas was now fighting three beasts to keep his head above the water of one of the pools. A few dancers stood on land, unable to get close enough to clasp his hand and unwilling to get any closer to the creatures for fear of going in themselves. The beasts clamored over Thomas, forcing his spluttering mouth beneath the waves. Their hair hung in oily black sheets, and each had a single bright coral-red pearl woven into the smooth strands, the only hue to grace their grayscale complexion. Beneath the ripples Amber spied scales and fins in place of legs and feet.

Amber scanned the bottlenecked group: all guards and knights were paired and fighting back. Cornelius burst past her, heading for the far wall, followed closely by two guards. Theo stood flinchingly to the left of Druine as the dancer warded off a creature's attempted slash at the Lordson's shin.

Amber called to the nearest dancer, "Bertrum, with me!" and fought her way closer to a drowning Thomas, Bertrum close behind. More and more guards and Canaries were now free of the pools and waiting on the far side with Jacqueline and Yves.

Amber raced over to the copse and ripped off a particularly pointy branch. Tossing it to Bertrum, she grabbed another for herself. Immediately, the creatures' eyes snapped toward her, and guttural growls escaped their waterlogged throats. Not stopping to think what that might mean, Amber hurtled toward Thomas and brought the stick down on the closest creature's head. As if she had slapped a Griffin in front of a priestess, the horde of monsters screamed in outrage. The screams tore through her. They released Thomas, giving him time to splash toward dry land, and suddenly a dozen or more glistening eyes fell on Amber and Bertrum.

"I don't think we should have touched their sticks," Bertrum muttered.

"Great observation," she replied, watching Thomas slip his way to safety. "Just chuck them and run." As one, they hurled their branches into two different pools, and the creatures dove after them with shrieks of fury. Dull, scaly fins cleared the surface, then disappeared below. It appeared the pools were interconnected beneath the surface, as they all raced toward the sinking sticks.

Seizing their chance, Amber and Bertrum made their escape, catching Thomas under his arms and helping him the rest of the way to the far wall.

"Everyone accounted for?" Amber asked to a chorus of yeses. Shrieks and splashes rang out behind her, and she watched the creatures for signs that they were resurfacing. It didn't appear that they could leave the pools.

"Right, Yves, did you know we'd have company?"

Yves shrugged. "Didn't seem important, and now you know why we don't touch the pools."

"You—" Amber, usually proficient in the realm of profanity, was at a loss for exactly what label to give the dancer. She changed tack, "You *knew* and didn't tell me?"

"You didn't ask."

Amber bit back a retort and said coldly, "In the future, assume all information pertaining to possible adversaries down here to be of top priority, Yves. Regardless of whether I ask or not, I expect you to keep me informed. Is that clear?"

"Yes, Chiv," Yves said, sinking into a smug little bow.

"What are those things?" Cornelius asked, his eyes still fixed on the writhing mass of soaking nightmares behind her. He was absent-mindedly massaging his wrist, and Amber saw an angry red mark peeking out from beneath his cuffed sleeve.

"Merrow, if I'm not mistaken," Theo said calmly. Everyone turned to look at him. Amber noticed a few of the Canaries and Chiv. Ryder nodding in agreement, Cornelius's eyes widened as if in recognition, but the rest looked about as clueless as she felt. Theo shrugged. "We have a tapestry of them in Mother's estate. She told me about them when I was a boy and I went through a bit of a phase, although in her descriptions they seemed a little more friendly, and while they're extremely rare, I definitely wouldn't have expected them in cave pools."

"Why not?" Amber asked.

"Because they live in the sea. There is a lot of discrepancy in the research surrounding their origin and true nature. What we do know is they're sea creatures that have the upper body of a human and the lower body, or tail, of a fish. They are reportedly hive-mind creatures that serve their Queen. That is, if you believe in the Merqueen. Interestingly, Hanna Anders, the esteemed nautical explorer whose research heavily influenced the Amelia Daring novel *Uncertain Tides*"—Cornelius said the title in unison with Theo—"Ah! Your Grace, you've read it? Incredible, I enjoyed that one myself as a boy. Anyway, she wrote that the red pearl in their hair, once removed, transforms them into a human, but it's unclear if this is accurate, as I was unable to find any more sources to back her theory. For them to live here though, that is interesting. I've never heard of them living anywhere but the sea. It would be worth investigating if they are here by choice or force, and what the nature is behind their aggression. As I mentioned before, most texts describe them as either friendly or apathetic toward humans. Their song is said to meddle with our emotions, although I heard no singing today. This opens up a——"

"Thank you, Lordson," Amber cut in quickly, sensing that the boy was quickly building momentum behind a lesson they didn't have time for. "Great, well, now we know. Swords, this place is brutal. Thomas, are you all right? Someone give him their cloak, he's shaking like a leaf. Right. Ready? Let's press on and hope that ruckus went unobserved. Jacqueline, Cornelius, you and your guardpairs will remain closer to me for this next part of the journey. Druine, fall in behind them with Theo."

With a quick reshuffling, the column set out once more down the tunnel, Amber and Yves resuming their positions at the head. The sound of the merrow's shrieks followed them out of the chamber. Amber noticed that this passageway was interrupted more regularly with alcoves and off-shooting tunnels, but Yves strode with purpose along a specific route. He walked with his usual swagger and had he been filling the silence with a cheerful whistle, it would not have felt out of place given the expression on his face.

Tugging on Yves's arm, Amber brought his ear closer to her mouth as she hissed, "You're playing a solo game, Yves, and that strategy is one I won't stand for. Can I trust you to have my back next time, or do you always run off alone when faced with danger?"

Yves looked at her in surprise, apparently not expecting the venom in her tone. "I . . . I didn't think——"

"No, you didn't, and your thoughtlessness would have saved your own hide at the expense of others. You and your boys want to fight so badly, what do you call yourselves, the something something *Life Defenders*? It doesn't count as heroics if the only life you defend is your own. Is that the kind of warrior you want to be?"

"N-no."

"Prove it."

"Yes, Chiv."

A clattering of footfalls came from ahead of them in the gloom. Immediately, Amber set her stance, ready. To her right, Yves did the same, albeit with a lot more unnecessary flourishes and wrist twists. At least he was synced with her this time. The column held their breath, poised for battle, when a face appeared from the shadows. A small light split the darkness, smaller than a candle's flame, then a figure emerged behind it, holding the lit object before them like a shield.

"Flent!" Amber exclaimed, forgetting herself the moment she recognized her face. Flent skidded to a halt and squinted into the darkness before sprinting toward Amber and embracing her roughly. Stepping back, Flent shoved a handheld looking glass, its surface reflecting Amber's worried profile and a small ball of light illuminating a point on its rim, into her belt, pressed a forefinger to her lips, and quickly used her hands to form the message, *I thought I'd never see you again. What are you doing down here?*

Amber signed back sharply with open palms facing up before twisting her pointed fingers downward. *What happened?*

Flent looked around her, seemingly at a loss of where to start.

A foul taste rose in Amber's mouth, and she signed, *You buried the crystals and ran. I thought you had betrayed us.* Her hands trembled as she formed the last sign in two disjointed parts: first she jabbed a forefinger painfully into the left side of her chest, *me*, then hesitated a fraction of a second before arcing a half circle across to jab the other side, *us*.

A pause, and Flent's eyes widened. *Never*, she signed, swiping downward with a flat hand.

Amber stepped back to appraise her and was horrified to see how gaunt she looked. Flent's face was strained, her eyes wide and wild. Scratch marks lined every inch of exposed flesh, and her fingernails were crusted with dried blood.

They're always watching, Flent gestured frantically. *They knew our every movement. Eyes in my pocket. Ears on my belt. They picked us off one by one. Made the earth fall down around us, and still they came. Shadows with eyes. Shadows with ears. Shadows with teeth.*

Amber looked at Yves in alarm, but of course he had no idea what they were saying. He instead looked at her impatiently and gestured ahead of them at the tunnel. Right, they still had work to do.

Flent, Amber replied, hands flying, *Where are the others?*

Gone, she signed, her left hand slipping through the fingers of her right.

Gone?

I lost them. There were too many shadows, then a light led me to you.

With a sinking feeling in the pit of her stomach, Amber realized Flent had somehow survived down here for almost a month. How she had managed it without losing her mind completely was a feat worthy of laurels. Amber, now wary of the frantic, faraway look in Flent's eyes, commanded, *You need to get out. We're going on—*

No! You can't! It's too dangerous—

Flent, go home.

I'll come with you.

No.

Amber clasped Flent's shaking hands in hers and held them tightly. They were coarse. There was so much more she wanted to say, but they simply did not have the time.

Follow this tunnel out. The pool chamber is full of beasts, but don't touch the water and you'll be fine. Leave the labyrinth. Find safety. She lingered on the last sign, holding crossed wrists together in front of her torso before breaking them apart.

Flent hesitated, expression lost and pleading, but Amber regarded her with the stoic eyes of a soldier. She reached momentarily within herself for an affection that, surprisingly, was no longer there, dismayed to find that somewhere between the Blushing Bard and Alethia, she'd lost it.

Flent lowered her gaze, stepped back, and saluted her commanding officer. "It doesn't matter. It's too late," she said, her voice dry and broken. Without another gesture, she hurried off down the tunnel. Amber watched her disappear through the rows of Canaries with that same alarming detachment, then beckoned the group onward.

"You loved her," Yves said in a voice only she could hear. No judgment, no question, just confirmation.

"I could have."

They pressed on, Amber turning Flent's parting words over in her mind.

33

WARM WELCOMES

As one foot perpetually followed the other, Jacs felt her doubts grow. She had seen on the map how far Hesperida was from where they judged Alethia to be, but each step she took brought it to sharp reality. She hoped the journey wasn't impacting morale; they hadn't begun feeling the effects of the Undercourt, but it was important they stay positive for as long as possible. She knew all too well that it was easier to sink when you were already low.

The tunnel continued to slope downward, the only light coming from a speckling of the white phosphorescence that dotted its walls. They must be getting close. Jacs jumped at the sound of a boot scuffing against stone.

Every shadow threatened to hide any number of scouts. She felt like a tightly coiled spring.

Connor bent close to her ear and asked, "How are you holding up?"

"Well . . . I definitely didn't anticipate my Queenly duties including fighting merrow and tracking down the leader of a secret organization of brainwashed boys, but I suppose every new occupation has its learning curve."

"Oh, did I not share those details when we placed the crown on your head? That was a complete oversight, sorry. It should have been listed in your daily considerations just before throne-room etiquette," Connor teased lightly.

"An oversight from my most trusted advisor! How dreadful!" Jacs replied, playing along with mock indignation.

"Indeed, *A merrow every morrow* is a well-known saying within the palace. I'm surprised you never heard it."

"*That's* what that was referring to? A merrow on the morrow and an Alethian Underlord biweekly, was it?"

"The very same."

"Oh dear, I thought they were dietary recommendations, I must have misunderstood."

Connor tsked and said solemnly, "You can't be blamed, must be the Bridgeport upbringing, not used to all our backward Basileian terminology."

Jacs swatted him playfully. "And unfortunately it seems I've had a lousy teacher."

"Hey! I was your most trusted advisor a moment ago."

"Moment's gone, I'm afraid."

"Alas, how swiftly one falls from fortune's favor. How will I ever redeem myself?"

Jacs shot him a look but was prevented from answering by a gentle throat clearing coming from behind her and a much more aggressive shushing from Amber up ahead.

Like chided schoolchildren, they fell silent. Connor softly jostled her shoulder with his, her grin echoed on his face.

The tunnels splintered more and more, the deeper they walked. What was once a single path soon became a maze of possible routes. Yves was able to guide their group at each junction, and Jacs had no reason at present to doubt his way-finding abilities.

She noticed he and Amber sharing occasional comments in low voices. Each time, Yves stooped low to hear the knight. One of his remarks even brought a smile to Amber's face, but it could have been a trick of the light.

What was important was that morale remained high. They still had a long way to go.

Something prickled inside her mind, a nagging tickle, as though a memory were fighting to resurface. She recognized the sensation a fraction too late.

Don't leave me, the ghostly pleading reverberated inside her mind. In a flash, she saw Phillip's wild eyes and outstretched hand.

It wasn't real.

Hello, Plum. The voice was soft, coming from a battered and beaten memory. The bright crimson of her mother's blood glistened in her mind's eye.

Her mother was safe in the palace.

Call it off! Theo's desperate cry drowned out the other voices, stopping her in her tracks as if someone had slapped her. She spun to look behind her and saw Theo trudging along beside Druine. He hadn't said anything. His face was pale, and he looked up from his feet with a glazed look in his eye.

She had made a mistake. It had been a mistake. Theo was fine. She was making amends. But the guilt grew from the hollow pit of her stomach and oozed its way upward. Weaving through her ribs, seeping around her heart. As if from far away, she felt Connor brush the back of her hand with his before swiftly pulling away. She caught his eye; his brow furrowed. This was it.

The column had stopped with her, and she turned to face them.

"We have entered the range of the Undercourt Griffins. It will only get harder from here. Remember, we're here to find Celos. Take him alive. He *will* face the consequences of his brutality."

In lieu of a cheer, she received a handful of solemn nods and grunts of agreement.

"Remember what's real."

It wasn't long before the tunnel gave way to their first view of Alethia. Just like the first time, it took Jacs's breath away and filled her with dread. They emerged into the open air, a deep, endless abyss dropping away just past the lip of the stone walkway skirting the ravine's walls. The void surrounded the enormous, inverted stone spike of a city like a moat.

It hung, suspended above the chasm. A wasp's nest. Layers of stone, chiseled walkways, and dark doorways peppered its slate-gray surface. Stone bridges extended across the void connecting it to the rest of the cavern. If Jacs squinted her eyes, she could make out purple-cloaked figures scurrying around their hive.

Yves ushered them all back into the covered safety of their tunnel. "There you have it, Your Majesty. I have kept my promise and upheld my duties as guide."

"Thank you, but we're not in yet, Yves."

"Of course, next stop, Celos's chambers. Now, I encourage everyone to don their hoods. Since this is a large group, I suspect we will draw attention if we cross the bridge all together, so I suggest we split up and space ourselves out along four or five adjacent bridges. Each group will be led by a pair of brothers, as they will be your best cover should anyone ask questions."

"I don't like the idea of us splitting up, Yves, and that wasn't in the original plan," Jacs said sharply. She looked to Amber for confirmation, but the knight appeared momentarily caught up in her own thoughts and hadn't heard.

Suddenly, Amber's eyes widened, and she gripped Jacs's arm painfully.

"What?"

"Flent. She used the mirror to find me, right? Just like we did in the second task . . . but how did the mirror know where I was, how did the light know where to point, if we were walking down a tunnel without crystals?"

"I don't . . ."

"There were blue crystals in the pool room, but she met us in the tunnel." Amber's next words rushed out of her as a horrified realization lit her features. "The light! The compass light, the one that helped us find Lena in the second task. It was on the rim of her mirror. How is that possible?"

Connor began feeling along the walls, fingers dancing along the stone. He swiped through a white patch and his fingers came away smeared with a glowing residue, but he kept searching for . . .

"Here," he said softly, shifting aside a thin veil of crumpled fabric to reveal a purple crystal lodged into a carved alcove within the wall. The fabric was almost perfectly camouflaged with the surrounding stone.

Amber swore.

"I bet they're dotted along the length of the tunnels," Connor said softly. "The fabric is thick enough to conceal the crystal, but not so thick as to blind it. If Celos was watching, he'd still be able to see us through it."

Jacs looked at him in alarm, and he added, "They hid one in my chambers the same way."

"What do we do?" Theo asked.

Jacs looked past the worried faces of her group at the menacing city of Alethia. They were so close. But if Celos knew they were coming, then she was leading them all into a trap.

"We may still have the upper hand," Yves suggested.

Jacs shook her head. She wasn't going to have another mass failure on her conscience. She couldn't afford to lose anyone else, and they had lost so much the last time they came unprepared into Celos's city. No, if her time with Amber had taught her anything, it was when to try another day.

"He might not even know we're here," Connor said.

"We retreat," she said sternly. "We retreat, regroup, and try again."

"Right," Amber said. "You heard her, everyone out, let's go back the way we—"

A scattered chorus of "Father Celos" drifted across the abyss from hundreds of hooded sources and cut her off. As Amber's command died, a breath-held silence stretched between heartbeats.

"Welcome, Your Majesty," a deep voice boomed across the chasm, echoing around the stone walls and reverberating inside her head. The sound seemed to be coming from everywhere all at once, spouted from hundreds of hidden amplifiers held by hundreds of hooded pawns.

As one, the figures peppering Alethia's exterior halted and turned to face the tunnel Jacs's group now huddled inside. A swarm of silent sentries stood frozen like statues.

"You're just in time," the disembodied voice echoed.

Amber shoved Jacs roughly behind both her and Yves a split second before everything erupted into motion. As one unit, the hooded men poured out of every tunnel and alcove and swarmed toward Jacs's group in droves, materializing out of the stone in numbers Jacs couldn't fathom. Behind her group, farther down the tunnel, the sound of swishing cloaks and soft, padded footfalls grew louder.

Jacs's Queensguard targeted the Sons emerging from deeper in the tunnel, while the Canaries struck at the hooded men marching across the bridges and platforms. Jacs, Connor, and Theo stood in the middle of a protective circle, safe for all of ten seconds before half a dozen shorter hoods charged through the crowd, followed by a hooded man the size of a bull. The smaller hoods knocked her guards aside, and the bull swept Jacs up and away.

In arms much stronger than her own, Jacs was hoisted onto a burly pair of shoulders and carried unceremoniously across the nearest bridge into Alethia. Her captor, like many of the other Sons, had his hood up to conceal his face, and Jacs hoped that it did not affect his ability to cross the bridge safely. She squeezed her eyes tightly shut as they crossed the chasm, and only opened them again once she heard her assailant's footfalls echo off the surrounding passageway on the other side.

Her view was limited to those behind her, and she saw that the distraction of her capture had left her friends open to attack. Connor, Theo, and Amber were now also restrained, as hooded figures dragged them to follow Jacs. Amber, Jacs saw with satisfaction, was unleashing all her years of training on the brutes. They'd wrapped a purple cloak tightly around her limbs to restrict her arms and legs, but as Jacs watched, Amber managed to land a hearty kick to her carrier's stomach, drop to the ground, and kick the legs of another hood out from beneath him. Clamoring to her feet, arms still tightly bound, she lowered her head and knocked the wind out of a third with the force of her skull. Reeling backward, she pushed off the wall and shot a foot squarely into the groin of a fourth.

"Release the Queen," she growled.

As if emboldened by their captain's display, the rest of the Queensguard and some of the Canaries began fighting back with renewed vigor. Groans and thumps echoed down the corridor and Jacs saw Yves spin the cloak off Amber with a playful flourish, setting her to rights and landing in a stance to press his back against hers as they faced their next opponents together.

Jacs squirmed in the hood's arms, flailing her limbs and torso against his might. She felt his arms tighten around her, willing her back to a stillness that she granted him just as suddenly, letting all tension dissipate from her limbs as she fell across his shoulders like dead weight. Surprised, he made to shift his grip to better hold her. In his moment of confusion, Jacs drove her elbow into the fleshy part of his throat. Retching and gagging, her captor staggered into the nearest wall and Jacs landed a kick just below his rib cage. Retrieving a dagger from its concealed sheath in her boot, she held it against the flickering pulse in his neck.

"You heard my knight, release me," she ordered. Breathing heavily, he held her tightly around the waist and did not let go, his face still shrouded by his hood. Impatiently, Jacs ripped the hood back with her free hand and gasped.

"Phillip," she breathed. "Phillip, let me go."

His eyes, clouded, held no recognition.

She couldn't believe it, wouldn't believe it. Phillip was not a traitor. She knew him. She knew his heart. "Phillip, let me go," she said again. With an alarmingly distant gaze, he stood motionless against her blade. Shakily, she withdrew her dagger. He did not move. His brow furrowed heavily, and he clenched his jaw tightly, but otherwise he did not react at all.

Amber and Yves approached and felled him quickly. Yves caught Jacs as she dropped from his grip and dusted her off as her feet found the ground. Amber glared down at Phillip.

"Told you he was a rat," she spat.

Hoods flooded the passage. Jacs saw Connor and Theo huddled together behind their guardpairs. A hood grasped Connor from behind and he drove the heel of his wrist into his assailant's nose. The hood cried out, blood seeping through his fingers as he stumbled backward clutching his nose.

"We need to retreat," Jacs said, gaze darting between the unresponsive Phillip and the bridge marking their escape. It swarmed with hoods. As she watched, more of her Queensguard barreled across its length to get to her side. Chiv. Ryder landed a kick, and the force sent a hood toppling over the side and into the darkness. Chiv. Ryder reached for the Son's hand too late. He didn't even scream. Jacs shuddered to think how she would get their small group back across safely.

A sudden, unified movement caught her eye as the surrounding hoods simultaneously rested their palms on the golden pommels of their weapons. *Golden?* The inclusion of such finery on a pawn's blade struck Jacs as odd.

"You disappoint me, little Queen," the same deep voice echoed through the passageway, freezing everyone in their places. Jacs noted with a start that it was coming from the Sons, or more specifically, their weapons. She seized Phillip's sword from his belt. It was a simple blade with a hollowed-out gold sphere in its hilt. "You are a guest in my halls and yet you bloody my Sons?" Celos's voice leaked from the pommel and Jacs dropped the sword in disgust. He continued, "Let me put it plainly. Allow my Sons to escort you to me, and you will have the opportunity to say one last goodbye to your beloved inventor. Put up any more of a fuss, and she'll be an empty shell by the time you reach her."

"Master Leschi," Jacs breathed. "He has Master Leschi, everyone stand down." Queensguard and Canary alike haltingly lowered their fists and sheathed their weapons.

"Jacqueline, I must advise against—"

"Amber, I can't—"

"I know, but you jeopardize the whole mission—"

"I can't lose her."

"—for one woman."

Jacs shot her a look and saw she was in earnest. Somewhere in the recesses of her mind, she knew Amber was right, knew that to obey Celos now likely put them on a back foot they might never recover from, but none of that mattered. *Say one last goodbye*, he had said. How much time did they have left? Amber seemed to read something on her face, for she bowed and tapped her wrists together, commanding the rest of the Queensguard to stand down. Nearby, hoods took up positions next to each of her women but did not appear interested in restraining them once they'd ceased fighting.

Crouching low over Phillip's prone form, Jacs slapped him hard across the face and said, "Phillip! Your mother, he has your mother, we can save her! Snap out of it and help us!" Grasping his shovel of a hand in hers, she wrenched him to his feet.

He staggered upright, eyes still glazed, and said simply, "I will take you to her."

"Jacqueline, I don't like this," Amber muttered. "You're not holding out on us again, are you, Yves? What's going on?"

"Honestly, Chiv, this is new territory for me." He waved a hand in front of Phillip's face to no effect. "It's eerie, isn't it?"

Connor shoved his way through the now docile hoods to reach Jacs, Theo following close behind.

"We don't have a choice," Jacs said when he was within earshot. "I can't lose her. And if it's my fault we do, I would never forgive myself." At her words, something ugly flickered across Phillip's stony expression and was quickly quashed. "Besides," she gestured around them, "we're caught either way. We might as well optimize our situation."

Amber sighed, shoulders slumping. "Fine. We have your back. Let's hope we get lucky in there."

"My dearest Chiv, don't forget you're traveling with the Canaries. Luck follows our heliotrope wings," Yves said cheerfully. "Let us walk boldly into this trap then, shall we? It's been a while since I've seen Father. I hope my absence hasn't caused him displeasure."

"Lead the way, you brutes," Amber said to the surrounding hoods. As if waiting for her signal, they all lurched into movement, Jacs and her retinue fumbling to keep pace with their steady, uniform march.

More than once Jacs tried to catch Phillip's eye, but he held a firm gaze straight ahead, and aside from the muscle tensing along his jaw, showed no deviation of expression. Voices from her past continued to whisper in her ear, but she could not allow herself to listen. They would not serve her for whatever was about to happen next. She threw up the walls in her mind, flexing her mental defenses like a new muscle: one she recognized from her dealings with the Griffins but she hadn't noticed before.

Weaving their way through Alethia, Jacs had the distinct impression they were passing directly through its heart. They barely turned left or right, and any bend in the route tended to be counteracted by a bend in the opposite direction farther down. She glanced around at the marching hooded figures guiding them toward Celos. *So much for our ambush,* Jacs thought bitterly. But she would see Master Leschi again, and they would figure a way out of this mess. They would come up with a plan. Celos was just one man with an army of twisted minds, but theirs wasn't true loyalty. She could turn the tides in her favor. She had to.

All too soon they stopped in front of a large stone door. From the corner of her eye, Jacs saw Yves don his hood and signal for his Canaries to follow suit. Suddenly she was unsure which men were hers and which were Celos's.

A Son knocked once, and the door swung inward on silent hinges. Jacs held her hand in front of her face to shield her eyes as a blinding white light burst from the room. It took Jacs longer than it should have for her to make sense of what she was seeing. A *balloon?* she thought. *No, an airborne warship.* A dark, warped perversion of her design.

Somewhere to her left, Yves flipped Connor's hood up, clamped a rough hand over his mouth and dragged him struggling and kicking into the crowd. A hooded Theo cried out a warning but Druine slapped a hand over his mouth and pushed him closer to Jacs, away from the retreating Connor.

Before Jacs could react, before Amber could half turn her head to see what had happened, a deep, silky voice cooed from within the room.

"There she is." Celos stood, dressed all in white, with arms out-stretched in greeting, a nasty twisted iron crown perched on top of his head. "Our little Queen. I've so longed to make your acquaintance. Come in, come in, we mustn't loiter in doorways. I have someone here who is dying to see you."

At his feet, a lone figure lay very still.

34

BIRDS OF A FEATHER

Connor fought bitterly. He was granted one last view of Jacs's wide eyes before he was ripped from her and swallowed by a sea of purple cloaks and rough hands. No one made a move to stop them. All hood-shaded eyes were vacant and staring toward the bright white light beyond the door. Two broke away from the horde to follow them and assist in his kidnapping. One grabbed his legs after a particularly violent kick almost brought Yves to his knees. The hood who now gripped him firmly around the ankles carried him as though he weighed nothing.

The Queensguard had been entirely unhelpful. Those who noticed him were either reluctant to leave their Queen or unsure what was happening. To their eyes, one hood was simply forcibly restraining another hood.

Regardless of the reason, they did not pursue him down the passageway.

"Stop fighting, you pain-in-the-neck prince, I'll release you as long as you promise not to draw attention to us, deal?" Yves growled. Connor nodded furiously, and the dancer signaled to his accomplice to set his feet down and release him.

Connor bolted. Drawing a deep breath, he yelled, "JA—" before Yves caught up to him and seized him roughly around the middle, clamping a clammy hand back over his mouth.

"So predictable," he muttered and dragged Connor farther away from Jacs. Connor threw his weight against Yves's grip, and the dancer staggered. The trailing hoods did their best to help. One was dripping wet and his boots made soft squelching noises with every step he took. Thomas. Members of the Canaries, then. Not Celos's men. If there *was* a difference at this point.

"Once we're clear, I can explain in more detail, but just know we're doing this to help her, so stop squirming. Come on," Yves said.

More curious now than outraged, Connor obeyed and let the dancer lead him through the winding side alleys of Alethia. Two Canaries followed closely behind. The alleys were empty. After several minutes, they stopped in front of a deep fissure in the wall and Yves shifted a few fallen slabs of stone in a well-practiced manner, then pushed Connor through with him. Blinking in the gloom, Connor tried to make out where they were.

"We need to go back," Connor said firmly.

"No."

"I'm not playing, Yves. Either we go back together, or I go back alone, but I'm going back to help her."

"To return is to hand yourself over to the jailer. If that is your desire, be my guest, but it won't save our fair Queen."

Connor glared at him and crossed his arms. "I suppose you have a better plan?"

"Naturally."

The two additional Canaries, Bertrum and Thomas, squeezed their way into the tiny room. They looked around with interest but made no comment. Connor, eyes now adjusted to the dim light, took in his surroundings. The quarters were cramped and held only a narrow bed and a shelf containing two small roughly carved stone bird figurines. The walls, however, were alive with color. Every inch was decorated with the bright motley plumage of more birds than Connor could name, let alone imagine. "Where are—"

"My room when I lived here. Or, at least, the room Father didn't know about."

"You painted—"

"Your Grace, while I'd love to regale you with the intricacies of my gripping and tumultuous life story, now is not the time."

"Right. What are we doing here?"

Yves took a breath as though to collect his thoughts and then launched into a rapid-fire explanation. "Life in Alethia is baseline horrific, but a few very new things are happening here now that add a whole new meaning to the word. The fact that Celos took us to the rift chamber is the least of our worries given whatever was making my brothers look so empty behind their eyes. No, for us to stay would have left too many mice in his trap. His focus isn't on us at the moment, so we have some advantage. *Obviously*, I would have attempted to save Her Majesty, but Celos wants her, so he would have caught on very quickly had she suddenly disappeared. She is safe as long as Chiv. Everstar is with her."

"Why are you risking your neck to help her?" Connor asked.

Yves rolled his eyes in exasperation and said slowly, as if to a child, "Because none of it exists if he wins! The seaside cottage, the galas, the music halls, the peacocks, the chandeliers, the honors, none of it. We needed a chance. I grabbed you because I knew you'd do whatever it took to save her, or that you'd at least thank me for the opportunity.

"Now, the rift chamber has two entrances and backs onto the void. One entrance, the one we would have utilized, is a no-go for obvious reasons. The other is a bit tricky to get to as we would have to go right past Father's quarters. Even with his eyes elsewhere, there's no way he's left his room unguarded. We may have to face a number of brothers to get past. Once clear, we would have to time our approach to when we would be most effective, as there are only four of us, and likely dozens of my brothers waiting for us within the rift chamber."

Connor held up a hand. "Wait, the room opens up to the abyss?"

"Yes, to the void itself. But entering from there is near impossible."

"But not entirely . . ." An idea sparked in Connor's mind. He bit his thumbnail as Yves waited for him to continue. "And we could feed two birds with one scone . . . but it would be risky."

"I beg, finish a thought, Your Grace."

"Right, I have an idea," he said, a giddy smile breaking free of his anxiety. "And trust me when I say, we are about to make history."

Yves glanced at Bertrum and Thomas. They all looked skeptical but willing. "Do enlighten us."

35

MIND OVER MATTER

Jacs instinctively felt for Connor's hand and, not finding it, grasped for Amber's and gripped tightly, knowing that to act rashly would be to play right into Celos's hands. He stood, fingers splayed and arms held open in welcome, waiting.

Everything inside her screamed to rush to Master Leschi's side. Why was she so still? Was her chest moving at all? Was she too late? No, she had led her team knowingly into a trap, she would doom them all to act thoughtlessly now.

"We can still win this," Amber muttered next to her. "Two points of exit, avoid the abyss at the far end, likely half a dozen more hoods inside, and potential to work with the balloon and Griffins. You've always had a knack with them. We can still win this, Jacqueline. Just don't lose your head."

It wasn't until Amber mentioned the Griffins that Jacs took in the rest of the room. The perverse balloon loomed over Celos and Master Leschi like a silent specter. Indignation flared in her chest to see the design she and her mentor had so lovingly perfected transformed into this monstrosity. Below the airship, a small army of pure white Griffins stood frozen in place. Heads bowed and stock-still, they could have been statues had Jacs not noticed the subtle rise and fall of their chests and occasional shift of their wings. Their faces and necks were wrapped in iron bridles with a rose-gold ring suspended in the center of each of their foreheads, just above their beaks. Within their maws were barbed bits, and Jacs noticed the corner of one of the Griffins's beaks dripping steadily with thick, dark blood from where the bit had broken flesh. Each bridle extended down a Griffin's neck and was secured in place by an armored chest piece that wrapped around its shoulders.

She hated to think what Celos had in mind for them and turned her attention back to the man behind the poison. He looked more charcoal sketch than flesh and blood. His white suit was immaculate; a black cloak hung from one shoulder. His white-blond hair was slicked back beneath the twisted iron of his crown. The only color on his person at all appeared to be the reddish-gold link chain around the base of his crown, a matching, larger ring set into the middle spike above his forehead.

"I've come willingly, Celos. Now make good on your word."

"Of course, Your Majesty. Come say goodbye to your inventor. You're just in time."

"You will retreat ten paces and I will keep a guardpair by my side."

"Naturally, naturally, little Queen. You are a guest in these halls. Come, come, her light is dimming as we speak." Celos's tone was light and almost kind, but like a bite into a rotten apple, the sweetness bordered on decay, its outward allure hiding something foul. His smile

quivered with a hungry excitement that never met his eyes, which were
pale gray and calculating. He stepped back and beckoned her over.

Leaving Theo, her Queensguard, and the remaining Canaries in
the corridor, she crossed the threshold into the chamber. Amber and
Chiv. Ryder fell into step behind her and it took all of her self-restraint
to slow her pace as she approached Master Leschi. With one last look
at Celos, she dropped to her knees at the inventor's side and felt for a
pulse. Master Leschi's red-rimmed eyes were closed and her brow was
furrowed as though she were working through a particularly complex
equation. Her hair was plastered around her face with sweat, the rest
a dirty mess tied up in an imitation of her usual messy bun. She wore
a tatty green tunic that fit her awkwardly in places and had far too
few pockets to belong in an inventor's wardrobe. The relief at seeing
her again threatened to overwhelm Jacs, but she fought to keep her
emotions in check.

"Master Leschi?" she whispered, the name catching in her throat.
"Master Leschi, please, wake up. I'm here, I've come to save you, and
it stands to reason that I can't do that if you don't wake up." Her
attempt at the banter they used to parry fell clumsily from her lips
and she shuddered an inhale. The stone beneath her was slick with a
dark liquid, and it soaked through the knees of Jacs's leggings. But she
wouldn't believe it to be Master Leschi's. Just a dampness of the stone
and a trick of the light. That's all.

A pulse, faint as a butterfly's wingbeat, stuttered against her fingertips.

"Oh! See, you're going to be fine, just fine. I'll figure a way out of
this, and we can chat about how I could have done it more efficiently
afterward."

Jacs's eyes scanned her quickly for wounds. The darkest shade of
red seemed localized under her ribs on her left side.

"So much has happened since I flew away on our balloon. I have
so much to tell you, and—and you have to meet Connor! You would

like him. And I can show you the palace. Th-there's a library bigger than our town hall and the city c-clock, it's gold plated. The dome on top is an architectural marvel, and you can meet the minds behind it. They would have so much to learn from you. I still have so much to learn from you. So please don't leave me. Don't leave me to figure it out on my own. I can't . . . I can't." As she felt her composure slip, Amber rested a comforting hand on her shoulder.

"Jacqueline," Amber said softly. "Jacqueline, it's too late."

"No! No, she just needs rest. Don't you, Master Leschi? Y-you always knew which problems I needed to figure out on my own. So, I'll take it from here, shall I?" The longer she looked at Master Leschi's pale features, the bolder the dark thoughts in her head grew. An ache filled her heart and clouded her mind, but she ignored it, she had to ignore it.

Every problem craves a solution. So let's find our solution, she thought, drawing Master Leschi's hand to her lips. The movement seemed to stir something in the inventor and her eyelids fluttered open. Her eyes swam in and out of focus as she squinted up at Jacs.

"Jacqueline?" she whispered, voice hoarse and faint.

"I'm here, Master Leschi. I'm here."

"Jacqueline. You need to . . . I—"

"Hush, save your strength."

"Forgive Phillip. Destroy the crown . . ."

"I'm going to fix this; you're going to be okay."

"Forgive . . . me." Master Leschi's pain-warped features twisted into a grimace. With a trembling hand, she reached up and cupped Jacs's cheek in her palm. "My dear girl. I'm so very proud of you." Her eyes fluttered shut once more, and Jacs fumbled again to find her pulse. It was there. Just.

"Master Leschi, please."

From ten paces away, Celos sighed. "Goodbyes are so bittersweet, are they not? I hate to cut this one short, but I'm on a schedule. You see, by the end of this hour, you will bow to me, little Queen." Eyes boring into Jacs, he placed two fingers against his temple.

Jacs reeled. "I will never bow to you," she spat, feeling an almost gentle pressure against her mind at the same time. The sensation was vaguely familiar. Reflexively, she drew up the walls of her mind with the snap of a slamming door. The probing recoiled.

Celos flinched and studied Jacs with an almost gleeful curiosity before he shifted his attention to the open door. "Phillip! Come finish what you started."

"Finish?" Jacs asked. She felt Amber's fingers tighten on her shoulder.

"Well, yes, he did a poor job the first time, then had to rush away to fetch you. But I can't very well have him not learn from his mistakes."

"No one comes near her," Jacs declared, standing slowly and glaring at Celos. Amber's grasp shifted from her shoulder to her elbow.

"Interesting, you seem to think you have authority here. No, my sweet, this is my city. Ah, here he is, Phillip, finish the job properly this time," he said and offered Phillip a bloodied blade.

Jacs looked at Phillip in horror. "You did this?"

A muscle tensed along Phillip's jaw, and his fingers clenched and unclenched at his sides, but he did not look at Jacs, nor did he reach for the dagger.

"Answer the little Queen, Phillip."

"Yes," Phillip said through lips that barely moved.

"You!" Jacs gasped, the pain in her heart threatening to drown her.

"Jacqueline," Amber said, uttering her name like a warning.

Forgive Phillip. Destroy the crown. Master Leschi's words echoed in her mind, and she snapped her eyes back to Celos. She didn't know if she could obey her mentor's first instruction, but she could try for the second. "Get the crown," she muttered to her knights, and planted herself between Phillip and Master Leschi. Louder, she declared, "You can try."

Phillip, teeth clenched so tightly Jacs could almost hear them crack, made no move toward her.

"Kill her," Celos whispered, a forefinger touching the crown just above his temple. His voice had an eerie quality to it now. Like silk rustling over stone. A blankness returned to Phillip's gaze, and he jerked an arm upward reaching for the offered dagger, his legs moving him steadily closer to Celos.

"Now!" Jacs barked at her knights. They sprang at Celos as one, and Jacs launched herself at Phillip. She had his arms behind his back in three swift movements and reached to her belt for her leather strap. Out in the corridor, her Queensguard flew into action, grunts and cries of pain bleeding into the chamber as they fought to restrain and detain the hoods.

"Fight back!" Celos growled at his Sons as the knights drew nearer. Immediately, Phillip broke free of her grip and rounded on her, his fist landing a blow to her stomach before she could recalibrate. She doubled over, winded.

"Why!" she screamed at him.

"Sons! Defend your father! And you two," he pointed a finger at the quickly approaching knights, "freeze." At his command, Amber and Chiv. Ryder staggered. Jacs saw their jaws clench and Amber, eyes blazing, managed a few extra steps forward before Celos's will overran hers too.

Tripping to a halt, muscles taut and straining against the fight now raging within their minds, they stood immobilized. Jacs felt a trickle of fear run down her spine.

Phillip approached her with that same vacant gaze, shouts from the corridor growing louder. Above the sounds of battle, Jacs heard Druine's distinctive cadence as he barked, "Lordson, stay behind me!"

Celos took two steps toward the frozen knights.

"Little Queen," he called above the cacophony, "no one else need suffer if you simply submit to me now."

Phillip loomed over her, obscuring her vision. "Never," Jacs said as she stumbled away from him, repositioning herself in front of Master Leschi.

"Phillip, stop," Celos commanded, toying with his dagger as Phillip stopped in his tracks. "You know," he said to Jacs, "I can force you. But it's so much more meaningful if you do it without my help. We could be a powerful team, you and I." He lifted his forefinger to his crown.

Jacs was aware of a pressure building behind her eyes, something forcing its way into her mind. The sensation mirrored her experience with the Griffins. Like an opposing side of the same coin, it was and was not the same. Where the Griffins pulled, ripped, tore thoughts from her mind, this was different: a pushing, shoving, punching sensation. Summoning the mental walls she'd built from her experiences with the Court, she focused on keeping whatever it was at bay. The pressure built until she had to close her eyes against its assault, but she did not allow Celos to gain ground. Did not let him in.

"Submit."

"No!" Jacs cried out. The pressure was almost unbearable.

Suddenly it disappeared and Jacs staggered forward.

Celos observed her with a look of impressed amusement on his face.

"Interesting," he mused. "I wonder . . . If you won't submit to me, maybe you'll submit to one of your own. Knight,"—he again pressed his finger to his crown as he locked eyes with Amber—"attack your Queen."

Jacs looked from Celos to Amber in horror. "Amber, whatever he's doing, you have to fight it."

Amber turned slowly on the spot, vacant eyes fixed on Jacs, and sunk into her fighting stance. A roaring filled Jacs's ears, and all at once her world descended into chaos.

36

MARIONETTE

Amber had been sixteen. On track to making a name for herself and eager to prove she was only just getting started. A celebratory drink had turned into several, and all at once a night with a linear timeline returned to her the next day as disjointed snapshots. A raised toast. Cheers from a crowd. A hand on her thigh. A lingering smile. A laugh at a joke that was not funny. All warm memories preserved in flashes in her mind. All but one. One she had never been able to make sense of. She had been so eager to impress. Had she really risked her future for the favor of a knight she didn't remember? A flash, a moment of dishonor as she broke into the palace armory and stole the sword of Sotera. The memory was fragmented.

She came back into her body to find the sword in her hands and realization dawning on her wine-fogged mind. Hurriedly, she replaced the sword and fled. The break-in had been reported, the culprit never found. Nothing had been stolen, so the search was quickly dropped. That night she had found her limit, crossed a line with which she would never flirt again. The actions simultaneously belonged and did not belong to her.

Here, now, in the Griffin army room with a white-haired brute wearing an ugly, twisted crown, she felt something similar. Something else seized her limbs and claimed her actions for their own.

"Attack your Queen," a voice echoed inside her mind and consumed her. Amber felt herself reduced to a tiny window behind her eyes as her awareness of the rest of her body retreated. She was now a voyeur of her own life. Free to watch but not touch. The only sensation was a barbed agony scraping through her synapses. She couldn't focus long enough on anything while the pain captured her attention. Something else moved her limbs into a ready stance, and she saw fear flash across Jacqueline's face.

Her arms came up and she pounced. Freewheeling in her own body, she had no control as her shin connected with Jacqueline's calf. Her fist swung around, colliding with Jacqueline's forearm as she blocked it at the last minute. With a twist and a thrust, Amber's elbow came down and collided with Jacqueline's shoulder. The queen cried out and Amber's fingers caught her wrist as Jacqueline threw a wild punch in her direction.

"Submit, little Queen," Celos commanded.

"No! Amber! Fight it!" Jacqueline shouted at her as she twisted just out of range of Amber's next blow.

Amber pushed against the edges of the tiny box her consciousness had been squeezed into, phantom daggers dragging through her mind. As her fist angled for Jacqueline's ribs, she threw her will against the movement and saw her arm slow before colliding. Satisfaction coursed through her. So, she had some control, but would it be enough? Her fist found its mark and Jacqueline doubled over, staggering backward.

She tripped out of the way of Master Leschi's prone form, lost her balance, and toppled to the floor. Jacqueline lay sprawled at Amber's feet.

Breathing heavily, Amber's body stood above Jacqueline. Inside her mind, she roared, fighting against her cage. A crack formed at its edges. Too small to break through. Not enough to stop it as Amber's knees pinned Jacqueline's limbs, her fingers wrapped around the Queen's throat.

37

MEETING MELINOE

It was all wrong. The farther he fled from Jacs's side, the more Connor doubted his plan and his ready trust in Yves. Far from perfect, it had sounded good in the confines of the little bird-covered room. Now, as they raced deeper into Alethia, Connor couldn't keep the doubt at bay.

"This better work," he whispered.

If anything, it was a relief to hear something outside of the voices in his head. The deeper they traveled, the more he felt the Undercourt's power.

He couldn't shake the feeling that he was repeating a pattern, his racing feet taking him farther from Jacs's side. Just like before, when he was carried away to safety in a balloon while the people who needed him fought for their lives far below.

"Your Grace, any plan is better than no plan at this point, so just trust that we have luck on our side," Yves said. They quickened their pace.

The tunnels were eerily empty. They encountered no one as they sped through each winding alley. Last time they were here, pockets of hooded men were everywhere, but now? No one. As if reading his mind, Bertrum asked, "Where is everyone?"

"I doubt we want to know," Yves said. Approaching a fork in their path, he hesitated, then headed right. "I think it was this way."

"No," Connor said, skidding to a stop. "No, I remember this part, we went left."

Yves raised an eyebrow. "Then lead on, Your Grace."

It took another few minutes, but sure enough, they entered a corridor facing two large stone doors Connor remembered well.

As if sensing their approach, a Griffin roared from beyond. The sound ricocheted down the tunnel, deafening. Connor's eye was pulled inward, and suddenly he was seven again. He hovered, uncertain, in the doorway and watched as his mother, curled in the dark at the foot of her bed, sobbed as though her heart would break, a portrait of her brother clutched to her chest. "He was all I had left," she choked out through her tears.

Connor shook his head and returned to the present, heart hammering.

"Depths," Thomas muttered, the fingers of one hand gripping at the roots of his hair.

"Keep your wits about you, lads. It's about to get worse," Yves said with mock cheer.

"Hoods up, just in case," Connor said. All four hid their faces and they came to a stop in front of the doors. Connor hesitated with his hand hovering over the talon-shaped handle. "Here we go," he breathed. Throwing his weight behind it, he pushed the door open.

Griffins cried out from below. The sound, a perfect blend of lion's roar and eagle's cry, crashed around his ears like a landslide and reverberated inside his rib cage.

Again his eye was drawn inward by a formidable force, and he was back on his horse, waving to a smiling crowd, gold glittering around him from carriages and livery. In his memory, he spied a large, colorful bird perched atop an oddly shaped hat. *Look at its feathers!* he exclaimed to his mother. She laughed, riding just ahead of him, her golden hair putting the sun's rays to shame.

The parade stopped.

Level the Upper, came the dreadful chorus.

He spied the hooded figures as they stepped out of the clock tower. A bow drew, an arrow flew, and suddenly there was too much blood. Jumping from his horse, guardpairs materializing around him, he rushed to his mother, catching her as she fell. His father helped him lower her to the cobbled street. Despite his pleading, her eyes slowly lost focus. Her hand fell limply to her side.

Connor bit down on the inside of his cheek, hard. He had to stay in the present. Amber had been right; nothing could be gained lingering in a past he could not change. Sweat beaded his brow as he struggled against the Griffin's pull. He opened his eyes and focused on the room before him. They stood at the entrance, on an upper balcony overlooking the Undercourt's den. From his vantage point, he could see their large, dank nest filled with golden eggs.

Two Griffins stood guard at its perimeter, their gold-tipped feathers almost translucent and appearing to glow with the silvery white luminescence that lit the room. Purple scry crystals grew from the ceiling and emitted no light of their own. Three more Griffins were scattered around the chamber, heads bowed in dreary resignation. One walked in aimless circles. The scene was almost identical to his last visit there, except now there were no hoods present, and there were far fewer Griffins than before. But they could be hiding. Connor whispered an order to be on the lookout for both hoods and extra Griffins. No one responded.

He focused on his small group, each seemingly paralyzed by their internal battles. Connor gripped Yves's shoulders and shook him but received no response. Not knowing what else to do, he slapped Yves hard across the face and hissed, "Snap out of it."

The dancer blinked several times, and focus stole back into his eyes. Clapping Connor on the shoulder, he said, "Right you are, Your Grace. I'll get Thomas, you're on Bertrum."

Connor nodded and delivered a similar blow to Bertrum. "We need you to focus, they'll trap you in your own head if you're not careful."

"Y-yup, can do, Your Grace," the man stammered.

"Okay, follow me and keep an eye out for hoods. There might be more Griffins lurking where we can't see," Connor repeated, unnerved at the near-empty chamber. He kept his fist clenched and focused on the sensation of his fingernails digging into his palm. To focus on this small external pain seemed enough for the moment to keep him from being pulled into his internal nightmare.

Scanning the perimeter of the upper balcony, he spotted a staircase leading to the floor below. Steps light, he led the way and hurried down. Another roar tore through his mind, and he missed a step, his body suspended for a moment before crashing the rest of the way to lay in a heap at the foot of the stairs. The pain from the fall drew him out of his next memory: the vision of Jacs, bound and injured, being led away from the second task flared for a moment. Her terror-soaked words filled his mind: *Find Connor . . . I've done nothing wrong! Please, Cornelius, you know me.* The vision faded, and he got shakily to his feet.

Of the dancers, Yves was the first to come back to himself, and he helped the other two down the rest of the stairs. Connor was thankful Yves made no comment about his tumble and merely straightened his cloak for him, dusting off his shoulders.

Understandably, their entrance did not go unnoticed by the Undercourt Griffins, and all but the two Griffins guarding the nest approached warily. Iron chains shackled each of their legs and clinked as they moved. Each, Connor noticed, was bridled with a cruel iron muzzle. Dark streaks stained their white feathers. Dried blood depicted where the manacles had cut into their soft flesh. A wave of revulsion and sorrow washed over Connor. This was no fate for the lowliest of beasts, let alone their Queendom's most divine creatures.

"Esteemed members of the Undercourt. We've come to free you, and to ask for help," Connor said gently, fighting another pull on his mind as the Griffins approached. They stalked toward him like cats approaching a sparrow.

At his words, distrust flared in the eyes of the nearest Griffin, and it tossed its head proudly, shackles crashing together, a fresh wound trickling blood below its eye.

"I know you have no reason to trust us," Connor said, palms up and open.

"We should have taken the cloaks off," Yves muttered unhelpfully.

"You have every right to hate us. Men have hurt you, so why should we be any different?"

"I'd make your case quicker, Your Grace," Yves said in his ear. The Griffin continued to approach.

"—but I promise we are not the same as the men who imprisoned you. We are here to help. We fight for a Queen who rode with your sister court. A Courtier Queen who fights your jailer as we speak."

Another roar, another memory ripped to the forefront of his mind. He was huddled in the bottom of a burning basket, the sounds of war echoing below him as he floated to safety.

There's too many of them! Dryft's cry reached him from far away. He hurled a log at her attacker and barely slowed the brute. He could have helped; he should have stayed behind. They died for him. For a coward in a basket.

"We can help you!" Connor screamed through the memory. "Please! Let us help you escape. Don't you want to see an open sky again?" Like a receding tide, the vision drew back and faded. "Search my mind, confirm I'm telling the truth," he said. Yves hovered to his right and Bertrum held a shaking Thomas to his left. "And please, until you've proven to yourselves that I'm on your side, stop tormenting my friends. If afterward you're unconvinced, do with our minds what you will."

"Hang on—" Yves began but broke off at a look from Connor.

Like a weight lifted from their shoulders, the Undercourt removed its presence from their minds. The visions vanished, the voices stopped, they were free. Bertrum slumped over with relief, and Thomas barked a startled laugh. It was like waking from a dream: every sight, sound, and smell could be experienced in its entirety. With the Undercourt's fog gone, Connor could see again.

They were surrounded by three blood-streaked, iron-shackled, male-loathing Griffins. Even if they had wanted to escape, they had most definitely missed their chance. Connor swallowed, mouth dry, and kept his eyes on the Griffin directly opposite him.

Dropping slowly to one knee, he bowed his head and waited. Behind him, the Canaries followed suit. Connor forced himself not to flinch as the Griffin snapped its beak and growled deep in its throat. Eyes lowered, Connor saw its taloned forelegs enter his field of vision and felt the sharp prickle along his scalp as the creature ran its beak through his hair.

The Griffin exhaled a forceful puff of air and placed its beak against Connor's forehead. In a flash, images, thoughts, and memories rushed between them. All that had happened since his last visit to Alethia, his conversations with Jacs, her promise to the Court to save the Undercourt, the failed attempt by her army to infiltrate the catacombs, the vision of her standing outside Celos's chamber. A wave of recognition hit him, and he got the impression the Griffin remembered Jacs from before, had touched her mind and sent her a plea for rescue. An overwhelming sense of relief flooded his thoughts.

"She heard you," Connor said. "She is trying to help you, but she needs us."

Focusing on the thoughts he was sharing, he formulated his plan and presented it to the Griffin. He sensed a hesitancy, a reluctance to trust, and an impatience to be free.

They remained locked in a silent battle of thoughts. Connor pleaded his case as best he could, until finally, the Griffin relented upon a single condition.

It withdrew its beak and waited, ancient eyes gazing at him expectantly, pinning him in place.

"What does it want?" Yves asked in a reverential whisper.

"I need to be judged. If I am deemed worthy, they will allow us to ride with them, they will help us save Jacs."

"And if you're not?"

"Run," Connor whispered.

"Your Grace, no! We hold the keys to their freedom, they need us. You don't have to do this—"

"They won't help us without it."

Connor bowed his head again as, gently, the Griffin pressed the dorsal portion of its beak to his chest. He barely had a chance to take a breath before his gaze was forced inward and he plunged deep within himself.

Falling, tumbling, twisting, he plummeted for what felt like an instant inside an eternity. An invisible force wrapped fists around his heart and mind and pulled him deeper. Unable to scream, unable to resist, unable to think, he crashed into a circular stone chamber. Floor, ceiling, and walls were made of the same smooth slate, their surfaces unbroken by door or window. A large mirror was the room's only addition. Taller than Connor and pitch black, its surface shifted eerily, as if reflecting the movement of clouds in shadows.

Where am I? Connor opened his mouth to speak and found he did not have a voice. The thought instead echoed around the room. Standing in front of the mirror, he realized he had no reflection. He existed in this place as an observer only. Moving closer to the looking glass, he tried to identify something familiar in the shifting shadows.

He saw himself, not as he was now but as he had been. In the mirror's clouded surface, he was five years old, his cheeks still rounded with youth. Leather armor that was much too big for him hung from his tiny frame; a rusted sword dragged the belt from his hip. He looked ridiculous.

His five-year-old self tried to pull the sword from its scabbard only to get it caught in his belt, and he fell over. Tears welled in his bright blue eyes.

You could have saved me. His mother's voice echoed around the room, just as her reflection solidified from the swirling smoke within the mirror world and came to stand behind his young self. Her face shifted. Like a flickering flame, her features changed, cycling through the face of his mother to Iliana Dryft's to Masterchiv Rathbone's. *You could have saved me,* the specter said with each new face. His mother's face returned, and she glared down her nose at her son.

If you had been stronger. The words dripped with scorn. Connor saw his reflection reach for his mother. Her lips twisted in a cruel smile as she watched him struggle under the weight and within the folds of his uniform. She turned her back on him, her figure dissolving into smoke.

Mother! the real Connor cried, *I'm sorry, Mother! Come back!*

His younger self reached for her, stumbling in his oversized boots, his little hand outstretched to catch the back of her cloak before it disappeared.

Don't bother, boy! his father's voice startled the little Connor to a standstill. *Let the Council get away with more murder, eh? You could have stopped them, you know.* His father appeared from the mist, twice as tall and looming over his little son.

The boy's oversized armor disappeared, sword vanishing from his hip, and the royal advisor pin materialized on his chest. The symbol, a crossed quill and sword within a golden ring, dripped with fresh blood. Slung around his shoulders, a blanket of a cloak almost engulfed him.

If you had been wiser. His father shook his head in resignation, regarding the boy at his feet with the same expression as if he had stepped in a particularly mucky puddle.

Father, I didn't know! Connor called into the mirror to a reflection that paid him no heed. With a disapproving sniff, King Aren spun on his heel and disappeared. Connor's little self stumbled to his feet and tried to follow. His cloak snagged and wrenched him backward.

Loved you? A man who disappears the moment I need him? Ha! Jacs's voice, now derisive and shrill, came next. Connor beat at the mirror with his formless fists, willing himself into the reflected world. His young self wiped his tears and stood on shaking legs, trying to locate the source of the voice. A heavy crown appeared on his head. *I could have loved you,* Jacs continued, and she finally formed from the swirling eddies of smoke. Dripping with jewels, she looked every inch a queen. Just like his parents, she towered over little Connor, whose eyes were now obscured by the lopsided crown. Crouching low, she lifted the crown off his temples and sneered, *If you had been braver.* From the mist, Lordson Theo Claustrom appeared. Laughing as she dropped the crown back on young Connor's head, she happily looped her arm through Theo's. Connor lost his balance under the weight of the ill-fitting crown and lay sprawled at their feet.

The swirling mist grew thicker, and more people began emerging from its depths. His parents reappeared, then Iliana Dryft, Masterchiv Rathbone, the Council of Four, Edith, Chiv. Everstar, Yves, Master Aestos, Lordson Hector, faces from his past, faces from the palace, faces of people, living and dead, until the mirror was filled with twisted, sneering, smirking faces circling around the little boy. Their voices layered over one another, forming a cruel chorus: *If you had been wiser.*

If you had been quicker. If you had been braver. If you had been kinder. If you had been stronger.

If you had been better.

If you'd been enough.

You're not enough.

The little boy curled in on himself, and Connor screamed, pounding weightless fists against the mirror's surface. The people vanished as gradually as they had appeared, and finally the little boy in the mirror was left alone. All alone. Was that his fate? He screamed again, the sound piercing his mind. With a sudden lurch, he felt cold stone collide with his knees. His palms hit the straw-strewn cave floor and he was slammed back to the present. His whole body shuddered, wracked with sobs.

He couldn't shake their voices, couldn't shake the image of himself, a sad little boy, a disappointment, a joke. The room was very still, all within waiting on him. To do what? Let them down again? Why should he bother? Why rise when he knew he was never going to be good enough? The world was not made for him, the world did not care about him. His father had been right all those months ago when they'd stood in his study and he'd calmly told Connor the truth about the Contest. Why try? Far easier to despair in the futility of it all. None of it mattered anyway.

High above him, the Griffin snarled menacingly and gnashed its beak. Connor began to curl in on himself, lowering his head to the floor, when his own words came back to him, spilling from his lips in a hitching whisper: "If none of this matters"—he opened his eyes—"at least my actions will."

Sitting back on his heels, he planted one foot, then the next, and rose shakily to standing. The Griffin observed him a moment longer, and like the dawn breaking, its demeanor changed. It clicked its beak in satisfaction and roared. Extending one clawed foreleg, it sunk into a reverential bow.

"Your Grace? Are you okay?" Yves hurried to his side and gripped his shoulders tightly lest he fall. "You're white as a sheet."

"It worked," he breathed.

"That's—"

"I was enough."

"Enough? Of course you—you just put your life on the line, and ours too for that matter, but it all worked out, so I suppose that doesn't—"

"Yves?"

"Yes, Your Grace."

"Just give me a minute."

"Right. Men, give the advisor space to breathe, let's find the keys to these shackles, shall we?"

While the Canaries hurried away to find keys, Connor stood, waiting for his heart rate to slow. The Griffin surveyed him steadily. With a subtle jerk of its head, it beckoned for Connor to approach. His palms prickled but he did as he was bid and stood very still as the Griffin placed its beak against his forehead again. This time, a name entered Connor's mind, sharp and expectant, as though in introduction: *Melinoe*.

Clearing his throat, Connor replied, "Well met, Altus Melinoe, I am Cornelius Frean, royal advisor to Queen Jacqueline Frean."

A gentle cooing purr issued from its throat: *Courtier*, it corrected, causing Connor to smile despite himself. He tentatively placed a hand on its feathered neck.

"Thank you," he whispered.

38

THE QUEEN AND THE TYRANT

She was dying. Dying at the hands of her most trusted knight.

Choking. Her brain screamed for more oxygen; her body flailed beneath the slight but powerful woman who had sworn to protect her. The look on Amber's face was void of any emotion, almost serene as her fingers squeezed tighter around Jacs's throat. The only break in the mask was the muscle working along her jaw as she clenched her teeth. Celos had taken hold of her, diluting her true abilities by using her as a puppet. That was likely the only reason why Jacs had lasted so long to begin with. Not that that was any comfort now.

Her fingers scrambled against Amber's grip. She was running out of time, there was so little air left in her system. Darkness appeared on the edges of her vision and began to close in around her until all she could see were Amber's eyes. Her empty, vacant eyes. As her own began to close, she saw something flicker within Amber's. A shout came from her left. Her Queensguard must have fought their way through the hoods at last and breached the room. More puppets for Celos.

Jacs couldn't let that happen. Lungs burning, heart bursting, she dropped her hands from Amber's, wrapped them around the knight's shoulders, and pulled downward, tugging Amber toward her like she was pulling her into an embrace. In the split moment the knight's grip loosened, Jacs sucked in a desperate gasp of air. She brought her knee up but collided uselessly with the leather armor covering Amber's torso, then drove her thumb into the soft flesh of her underarm. Like clouds dissipating, focus returned to Amber's gaze and suddenly her hands vanished from around Jacs's neck. She fell backward and rolled off her, scrambling away from Jacs.

"Forgive me," Amber pleaded, horrified, before rounding on Celos. "Snake," she snarled. "BRUTE!"

Jacs, spluttering and coughing, staggered to her feet, rubbing a hand across her throat. Glancing around, she took two breaths to consider her surroundings. Dozens of hoods were fighting against her Queensguard and the Canaries near the room's entrance. Given they all wore purple cloaks, it was tough to determine which side was winning. All she could tell was they had yet to make much ground toward the center of the room. She caught a glimpse of Theo's pure white hair as he ducked behind Druine. A Son lunged for the dancer and landed a slap before Druine spun around and drove the Son back. Celos stood, relaxed, beneath his airship. The wall of silent Griffins stood behind him, and Phillip and Chiv. Ryder flanked him, all immobile for the moment. Master Leschi lay at Jacs's feet. *Don't look. She'll be fine.* Amber charged Celos, features warped with fury. Jacs had never seen her break composure like this before. Not during battle.

"Amber, wait!" she croaked.

The knight skidded to a halt and half turned to face her, still keeping Celos in her sights.

Jacs drew herself up. "Celos, are you such a coward that you would have my own knights do your dirty work? Would you honestly have your victory denoted in history as a knight's treason? Because that's all the historians will see. Are you so used to hiding that even face-to-face you'd rather cower behind women far more honorable than yourself? Leave their minds alone. Your fight is with me."

Baring his teeth, Celos snarled. "You dare call me a coward?"

"The only threat you pose is through the borrowed strength of others. Alone you are nothing," Jacs said, walking steadily closer.

"Jacqueline, what are you doing?" Amber muttered as she drew level with the knight.

"If this goes sideways . . ." Jacs hissed, then with a flat palm, drew the pointer finger of her other hand through her middle and fourth finger.

"No—" Amber began.

"That's an order."

Amber scowled and hesitated only a moment. "Understood."

"I know all about you, Celos," Jacs said. "It's little wonder your heart is so twisted."

"You know nothing."

"I know you suffered the fate of most Lordsons. You were a pawn in your mother's plans for power. I know the only brave thing you've done in your life is defy her. You ran away for love, didn't you? And look how that turned out. I've met your paramour, Lady Claustrom; her affections are as fickle as a Lowrian sun shower. Or did you think you were different? Special?"

Celos scoffed. "So young and naïve you are, little Queen. What do you know of love?"

"I know you've lived a life devoid of it. I know it's nothing without trust. Or else why would you need to go to such lengths to secure fealty?"

"Love has nothing to do with fealty. Fear is where true loyalty lies. It is the only reliable way. My Sons fear me, that makes their loyalty unwavering."

"Yet you resort to controlling their minds. Why?"

"Their thoughts are mine already."

"A jailer is only powerful if the cell doors hold, Celos. What will you do when your prisoners find the keys?"

"Jacqueline," Amber ventured in warning, but Jacs did not turn around. Celos's face was impassive except for a slight tremor at the corner of his mouth.

"You are so like Bruna," he drawled. The mention of her mentor's name struck Jacs like a slap. "But I was quick to tire of her banter too. Submit. I will not ask again."

"Never."

"Fine," he snapped and placed his finger to his crown. The pressure behind Jacs's eyes returned and she gritted her teeth against it.

"I won't let you in."

"You don't have a choice. I have such plans for my *King*dom, and you will not be the reason they fail."

The pressure built until it was almost unbearable. Jacs was vaguely aware that she had dropped to one knee. The steadying presence of the stone floor felt rough against one palm, her other hand clutched at her head. She forced herself to her feet again. A Queen did not bow to a tyrant.

As though caught in a landslide, the world seemed to cave in around her. The weight of the mountains crashed against her mind. A moment of weakness, a chink in her mind's armor, and suddenly he was everywhere. Pain lanced through the space between thoughts. Colors distorted as two perceptions fought to make sense of one reality. Sounds clamored between four sets of ears. Smells evoked different memories as his mind aligned with hers.

She struggled against him, but he already had a chokehold on her thoughts. And Jacs knew how to combat a chokehold. Rather than struggle against his barrage, she changed tack and attempted to pull his mind to hers, to draw his thoughts from him. She felt a shocked resistance, but his guard was down, and he was untrained. He had not anticipated anyone snatching at his own thoughts, and unprotected, they rushed at her. A cacophony of sound and a blurring of images assaulted her senses, threatening to drown her. In an instant, she understood.

She saw a life of powerless disappointment laid at her feet. Passed over by his mother as a child. *Three children: an heir, a spare, and a pawn,* she joked with her tea group, unaware he was listening. *But a clever pawn indeed. Little Lancelyn has caught the eye of Dame Claustrom.*

Sent to a finishing school to become the perfect genteel. *Cunning little boy. His schemes will not be looked on favorably by any promising Dame. I suggest he leave matters of politics to the women,* his headmaster had remarked to his mother. Both spoke about him as though he had not been in the room.

Forced into an arranged marriage with a dull Dame from a tiny county. *Dame Claustrom accepted a much more promising match, but I know you will make Dame Finette a fine genteel. Lynnhaven is lovely in the fall,* his father had promised. His mother had apparently been too disappointed in his failed efforts with Sybil to look at him.

Then finally, finally seen for the potential he possessed by a traveler in a dank tavern. *You are wasted in the world of women; I can show you a place where you can be free. The Kingdom of Alethia awaits.* That was where his true life began.

How easy it had been to rise through the ranks of disillusioned and lost boys when no longer held back by a mother who only saw him as a bargaining chip. No longer Lancelyn, he forged himself anew as Celos. He was quick to seize control of Alethia, and then it was only a matter of time before he began to mold it. His Kingdom of shadows. He had seen how gold brought power, so his first task had been to steal eggs from the Court of Griffins. Once the two fledglings had hatched, his Undercourt was secured. Recruitment had been his next goal, and steadily the number of his Sons began to grow. Some had tried to flee in the beginning, not convinced his life was to their taste, but once he had harnessed the power of the Undercourt, defection rates dropped to zero.

He was the balm of this corrupt world. He would save the forgotten and powerless. No one should be made to feel like a chess piece, moved around by unfeeling hands. At the mercy and whim of others. He knew the true path; he would guide his Sons to a better life. No mother or Queen would ever dare to control him or his Sons again.

For that was where the true power was, wasn't it? At first, he had thought it would come from gold, but even with overflowing coffers, he was not granted the level of power he craved. No. True power lay in control. Control the thoughts, control the actions, control them all. His Sons had faithfully spread his message throughout the Lower Realm, his words ringing in the hearts of Lowrians. Their minds were open to him, and soon he would own them.

After that, it was only a matter of time before the Upper Realm was his too. Bruna had been instrumental in the last phase of his plan. He would unleash his fleet, traveling high above the two realms, and use the amplified power of the Undercourt's crown to secure the hearts and minds of his subjects. The realms would be his, Sybil would be his, and together with their son, with his Sons, they would rule the Kingdom of Frea.

A vision filled Jacs's mind, so vivid it felt closer to a memory than an idea. Celos, standing at the bow of his airship, crown shining atop his brow, soaring across the two realms watching the masses kneel before his waves of power. He was so close.

Jacs struggled against Celos's thoughts. She could not see past the torrent of images and impressions coming from him but felt an undercurrent of alarm that was separate from her own.

"Get. Out," Celos said vehemently through gritted teeth. She felt him retreating and seized her chance: in an instant she had thrown the defenses up around her mind, ejecting him completely. A welcome emptiness followed in his wake, and she rested her palms on her knees, breathing heavily.

"That's your plan?" she said. "You hated having no control as a child, so your solution is to control everyone?"

"You—" Celos spat, advancing toward her.

"Celos, I'm sorry for what happened to you in the past. I'm sorry it drove you here. But past hurts are never an excuse to hurt others. You will pay for your crimes against these men. You will pay for your crimes against the Undercourt Griffins."

"Phillip! Bind her. Knights, stand down, the little Queen is mine," Celos ordered, finger pressed to his temple. Phillip lurched into motion as Jacs darted toward Celos, eyes fixed on his crown. She launched herself at him just as Phillip reached her, wrapping an arm around her waist and trapping her arms at her sides.

"Phillip! Let me go!" She fought within his grip to no avail.

Celos stalked closer. "I gave you ample opportunity to join me, and you have refused. You leave me no choice," he said. Placing both forefingers to his temples, he commanded the fighting crowd near the entrance: "Sons! Queen supporters! Come watch your Father's triumph." After a moment's hesitation, the sound of battle subsided, and dozens of vacant-eyed, hooded figures turned and marched toward Celos, forming a semicircle in front of him where he stood with Jacs, Phillip, Amber, and Chiv. Ryder. Master Leschi lay to Celos's left. Her chest barely rose and fell, but it moved. That was enough. All eyes were on Jacs—so many empty eyes.

Celos turned his attention back to her with a satisfied smirk. He stood too close, gray eyes boring into hers. Over his shoulder, Jacs saw Amber's face contort, her serene expression gaining focus.

"Let's try this again. Listen closely. You have failed. Your guards are no match for my Sons, and all obey me now." He gently pressed his dagger into Phillip's hand. Phillip studied its hilt for a moment, jaw clenching, curling and uncurling his fingers around it. His eyes shifted from the blade to Master Leschi as she groaned softly, a crease forming between her brows. "Kill her," Celos whispered.

Before Jacs could stop him, Phillip flicked his wrist and flung the dagger point-down into his mother's chest. The sound was soft. Gentle. A gasp followed, and a final breath was caught in Master Leschi's throat. Its release marked life's close.

In the echoing silence, Celos continued mildly: "Your mentor is dead. Your friends have turned on you. No one is coming to save you. If you value what's left of your life, you will bow to me."

The weight of Phillip's arm disappeared from where it had held Jacs, and she registered faintly that he'd fallen to his knees beside her. A ringing filled her ears, and all she saw was the blade hilt lodged in a too-still chest. Such a little thing to fell her everything.

"Bow to me," Celos hissed.

"No," she said, her voice sounding weak to her ears. Celos was right. Her plans stopped here; she couldn't outnumber him, couldn't overpower him, couldn't get the crown from him. All she could do was resist, but for what? And what would be the fate of everyone who followed her down here? She'd lost so much. What else did she have to give? Who else could she afford to lose?

Horror silenced her tongue. Denial held her in place. Grief's rage roared through her veins as she watched Celos bend down and rip the dagger free. As he straightened, he grasped the hem of Jacs's cloak and tugged. She stumbled toward him on leaden feet. With a fistful of fabric, he took his time wiping the blood free from the blade, eyes hungry for Jacs's every shift in expression. Using the blade tip to lift her chin, he leaned in close to her ear.

"Submit," he whispered, the word a gentle caress. For the fourth time, a pressure descended on her mind.

She closed her eyes. Her knees buckled.

A Griffin's roar echoed far below.

39

FLOWN AND FALLEN

Connor whooped with terrified delight as the Griffins bore them upward through the black space between Alethia and the surrounding walls of stone. As though shooting up a giant chimney, they climbed higher. Four of the five Griffins rode free, the one left behind having stayed of its own volition to guard the nest until their eggs could be safely rescued. White feathers shone with a faint golden light in the pitch darkness, and Connor felt as though he were riding a star through the constellations.

A tiny whisper of doubt tickled the back of his mind. There was an undercurrent of viciousness to the Undercourt Griffins that scared him. But they were on the same team now, and he just had to hope it stayed that way. Pushing that thought aside, he set his sights ahead of them in the darkness. They had a Queen to fight for.

Yves clung to Connor, gripping his waist painfully. He had appeared much more comfortable with hanging on to Connor than navigating a Griffin of his own. Thomas clung similarly to Bertrum, who had rolled his sleeves to his elbows and steered his Griffin with white-knuckled intensity.

After sharing thoughts of their desired location, the Griffins had needed no further prompting. They galloped through the air with purpose. Leveling out after several minutes of steep climbing, Altus Melinoe banked to the left and followed the curve of Alethia. A glowing white patch up ahead grew steadily larger. Almost there. He could just make out the gaping hole in the city's structure. The sounds of battle met his ears. The clashing cries of pain and triumph grew steadily louder the closer they flew, until a sudden silence fell.

His gut clenched. "Faster," he urged in the darkness. Altus Melinoe roared. The sound was amplified as it ricocheted around the abyss. Drawing level to the ceiling of the glowing-white rift chamber, the Griffins roared again and angled themselves into a dive. Behind him, Yves's curse was lost in the wind, and they sped toward the ground.

Through squinting eyes, Connor was able to make out the scene rushing into focus below. A half circle of hooded figures stood before a kneeling Jacs, a prone figure, and four standing people Connor had a split second to recognize as Chivilras Everstar and Ryder, Phillip, and Celos himself, crowned in twisted black iron. A circlet of bloodied gold glittered against the dark metal.

Celos spun around with a look of fury and raised a forefinger to his temple. All at once, Connor felt his awareness retreat inward. As though being forced inside himself, he saw his fingers clutching feathers he could no longer feel. He screamed, but the sound never left his throat. White-hot pain seared through his mind and consumed his thoughts.

Barely able to focus, Connor registered Altus Melinoe growling deep within its chest, and a new presence bullied its way into Connor's head. Wedging itself between Celos's will and Connor's consciousness, Altus Melinoe battered Celos back. The two struggled within Connor's mind.

In the physical world, Altus Melinoe landed heavily on the ground and shouldered its way between Jacs and Celos. The latter took several hurried steps backward. Melinoe braced its talons against the stone with a roar. Gradually, Connor felt Celos's influence peeling away, and he returned to himself. Sensations returned to his fingertips; movement came back under his control.

Celos slumped as if he'd run a mile. "Filthy beast," he swore. Clenching his fist, he placed it against the ring embedded in his crown, opposing forefinger pointed at the monarch. The Griffin braced itself against his will as if fending off a buffeting wind and leaned toward him. To his right, Connor saw the three other Griffins land and adopt similar stances. As one, the small Court began to push Celos's powers back. Gaze scanning the crowd of hoods, he noticed a few of the boys blinking and shaking their heads. Below the airship, bridled and frozen in place, a wall of Griffins remained. Despite Celos's snarls, despite the growls of the freed Undercourt, they didn't react.

Jacs rose to her feet.

"Perfect timing," she said to Connor. She too glanced around the surrounding hoods and turned triumphantly to Celos. "What did I say about keys, Celos?"

"No!" Celos roared, both hands now clutching his temples. A couple of the hoods staggered, but more and more seemed to be waking up from whatever trance they had been under. Connor fumbled to dismount, desperate to get to Jacs's side. Yves jumped gracefully to the ground and helped him down. The world seemed to move in slow motion. His feet touched stone, toes bending as he pushed off, and he half turned from Celos toward Jacs.

With a curse, Celos reached for Chiv. Everstar's shortsword as the knight grabbed for it two heartbeats too slow. Wrenching it from her scabbard, he lunged for Altus Melinoe. "You bow to a boy, but not to your master?" Celos snarled. "Then you'll bow in death!"

Jacs's eyes widened, and she launched into motion, closing the distance between the two. Celos advanced and made a vicious thrust at the Griffin's chest. The sword slid home in Jacs's.

Connor screamed.

A ringing filled his ears as sound erupted around him. The four Undercourt Griffins screeched, the sound shaking the stone walls and ceiling. Dust and rubble showered the people below. He raced to her side, ripping the sword from her body and cradling her in his arms. His hands fumbled over the wound, willing it closed, willing the blood back in. An unbroken denial poured from his throat.

Chiv. Everstar dropped to her knees beside him. Phillip, Theo, Chiv. Ryder, and Yves, all would-be protectors, crowded around them. Too late.

"Help me!" Connor pleaded with them. "Stop the bleeding! Please!" Red to the wrist, he grabbed for Chiv. Everstar. "Save her!"

"Connor . . ." Jacs said softly. He stroked stray strands of hair from her face, taking care to straighten the thin golden circlet from where it had become dislodged when she fell.

"It's okay, you're okay, you'll be—" his voice caught. He cupped her cheek in his bloodied palm. There was so much blood. It soaked his tunic, spilled across the stones, and the pain in his chest was enough to convince him it might be his. If only it were his.

Jacs blinked up at him, eyes fighting to hold focus. Her fingers gripped at the fabric of his sleeve and her lips struggled to form words.

"Connor, get them . . . get them out." She coughed, crimson staining her lips and trickling from the corner of her mouth. The grip on his sleeve wavered and he caught her hand as it slipped from his arm.

"Jacs, please," he begged.

"Promise me."

"Jacs—"

Her eyelids fluttered but she held his gaze a moment longer. "Yours . . . always," she managed as a flicker of fear passed across her face. Connor held her tightly, vision distorted and unable to breathe.

"Forever," he promised. "Always and forever, I'm yours, Jacs."

The fear that had flared in her eyes vanished, replaced by warmth, light, love. It shone from her as her last heartbeat ricocheted against Connor's desperate fingertips.

"It looks like I've won, little Queen," Celos said above the din. He appeared shocked and out of breath but triumphant.

The four Griffins tossed their heads in outrage. One reared on its hindquarters and slashed the air with deadly talons. Fingertips at his temples, Celos closed his eyes and Connor felt pain rip through his mind again. He bowed over Jacs's body and clutched her to him. All around, hooded figures dropped to their knees. Phillip groaned to his right. The four Griffins roared in dissonant protest as they huddled against the blast.

"I've dallied here long enough," Celos declared, gaze sweeping over the crowd. "Come, beasts. It's time I claim my throne."

Celos stalked toward his airship as the row of bridled Griffins crouched, readying themselves for flight. Canaries and Queensguard remained huddled on the floor, and the four free members of the Undercourt gnashed their beaks against the invisible force Celos leveled at them.

Almost leisurely, Celos mounted his airship, alone on the open-air platform save for two hooded Sons who stood ready to control the furnace. At a barked command, a handful of Celos's Sons released the six tethers keeping the airship grounded. As it rose steadily into the air, Celos glowered down in triumph. With his fingers to his crown, he commanded the bridled army of mind-controlled Griffins to rise. The rose-gold rings glittered on their foreheads as they took to the air beneath the balloon. Six of their number, tethered to the airship with chains, guided the balloon out of the rift chamber and into the chasm that would lead them to the Upper Realm. The remaining army flew in a protective circle around the balloon.

It was over.

They had failed.

And worst of all, he had lost Jacs.

As though walking through mud, the four unshackled Griffins approached the fallen Queen and formed a protective circle around her.

Too late, Connor thought bitterly. He fumbled for her hand. It was so cold. Her eyes were vacant, staring past his shoulder at nothing. *I'm always too late.*

A low keening started from Altus Melinoe and spread around the Undercourt. The steady wailing of a broken heart. It almost silenced the painful tearing Connor felt throughout every corner of his mind. But Celos's will was stronger, and Jacs's most trusted protectors remained huddled around her fallen body. Unable to look up, let alone stand, such was the agony within their minds. One by one, Chiv. Everstar, Chiv. Ryder, Yves, Phillip, and Theo placed their palms reverentially on Jacs. The four Griffins bowed their heads, beaks lowered to rest on her forehead and chest.

Connor noticed as if from far away a change in the white light of the room.

The gold-dusted feathers of the Undercourt began to glow.

40

RENAISTRE

In times the realms have long forgotten when the age of woman was but a seed in history's soil, the Court of Griffins ruled all. With talon, beak, and wing, they ruled the skies, and all beneath the clouds fell under their domain. Had women accepted their place alongside the beasts of the land, there need not have been as much bloodshed, but the race of woman could not be subdued as easily as the deer and rabbits. Women wanted to raise cities, dam rivers, dig deep beneath the earth. They wanted to shape a land that was not theirs.

The Court was displeased. As village gave way to town, and town grew to city, they watched in outrage as towers cut into their skies. As the natural courses of rivers were diverted for irrigation, as forests were cut down for farmland, as mountains were hollowed for mining, the ire of the Court grew. It was not the natural way of things. It would not be tolerated.

War raged between woman and Griffin and numbers dwindled. Heartbreak and loss tore minds apart, until finally a day of negotiation was demanded from both sides. The Queen of womankind met with the reigning monarch of the Court. Together they negotiated the peace treaty of Court and Crown. Griffin and womankind were vastly different. Each side feared they would never find a common ground on which to stand.

A bridge was the surest way to connect two sides, so it was a bridge they forged. Not one of brick and mortar, but of flesh and blood. An ambassador for the peace between races. A living embodiment of the treaty, whose heart and soul was sworn to protect. Sworn to defend. Sworn to uphold the promised peace. Both races called upon the ancient magic to bind the first Queen of Frea to the Court of Griffins. Thus, the first Alessi was born. A woman forged by Griffins to join the Court in the skies with wings of golden light. Half her heart belonged to Griffin, half to woman, her soul bound between land and sky.

The gifts of her new form were designed to combat all that had torn the two races apart. Fear's hatred had divided the Queendom, and her eyes now clearly saw fear's inky grasp. Her gilded heart burned to vanquish it. With her glowing shields she vowed to protect the minds and bodies of her subjects. With her speed and flight, she promised to defend the highest mountains and farthest borders of her Queendom.

The treaty held true and over the centuries that followed, the need for an Alessi dwindled. It was enough that a human Queen honor the treaty of her foremothers. It wasn't long before knowledge of the Alessi and her role in the Queendom's history faded to legend. For it is only in times of great strife that the Court and Crown need forge another.

Jacs felt the slash before the pain of it tore through her. Like fire, like ice, it burned through her synapses, rending her asunder. Then everything stopped. She hadn't had time to think, to plan, to react. She became pain, then nothing. Ripped from her body, she soared. Floating in an empty forever. Time ceased. Breath ceased. All fell silent in an instant.

Suspended in a deep nothingness, she saw a golden face materialize. Shifting in an endless flux, a thousand faces in one smiled. The smile of a goddess she didn't believe in. A Griffin's roar echoed through the ether, and the Goddess's smile elongated, becoming a Griffin's beak. Words she'd never heard from a source she couldn't name filled her mind and wove through her being. The deity rested its beak on Jacs's chest.

She braced for the onslaught of memories. Braced to face the depths of her heart as she had twice before. Instinctively, she closed her eyes and clenched her fists. All her awareness narrowed to the point of contact between beak and sternum. The feeling of falling and flying blended as they seized her senses, and the vision dropped her in the middle of an ancient battlefield.

The slain and twisted bodies of Griffins and armored women lay in spiraling patterns at her feet. Gold-dusted feathers slicked and clotted with blood littered the spaces between like grotesque confetti. Two women nearby reached across the churned-up earth to clasp hands and hold tight as they loosed their last breaths. To Jacs's right, a Griffin, feathers still mottled with youth, nuzzled its beak against the cheek of its fallen friend. Realization stole into its eyes and it threw its head back, releasing a cry to the skies.

The vision rushed past her and she now stood atop Court's Mountain. A heavily bandaged Queen stood before the equally battle-worn monarch, Altus Thenya. The Queen's retinue huddled nervously in her wake, watching each twitch and flicker of movement coming from the Griffins. Straight backed and proud, the Queen stepped forward and lowered her head. Altus Thenya bowed in turn and placed its beak between her brows. Four more Griffins stepped forward and formed a circle around the Queen, placing their beaks against her sternum, temples, and the space between her shoulder blades.

As one, the members of the Queen's retinue and guard approached and placed their hands on their Queen's shoulders, palms resting over her heart, fingers stroking her hair.

The gold dust of the Griffins' feathers began to glow. Its radiance filled the Court's mountain-top chamber, blinding all. The light raced across the realms and with it, so did Jacs's vision. She caught glimpses of the life held within. Snapshots of love, fear, connection, separation. A Griffin soared the updrafts near Parima, delighting in the sensation of the wind buffeting its course. A farmer in Sennuik halted her plow and stooped to pluck a wildflower from its path. With a shy grin, she spun and presented it to her husband, who placed it carefully in the brim of his hat. A circle of soldiers wrestled with a thrashing Griffin. They'd bound its wings with ropes and taunted it with swords and jeers. The Griffin roared, and a man emerged from the shadows. With a cry of rage he threw a brick at the nearest soldier and bent to retrieve another as the women turned to face him.

The visions flickered faster. A girl pulled from a bramble patch. A young Griffin attempting its first controlled dive. An old woman sharing her scone recipe with her wide-eyed grandson. An ancient Griffin visiting a memorial grove with its fledglings, necks bowed in respect for the fallen. Moments of division left its subjects isolated, fearful, and vulnerable. Moments of connection shone like division's balm. Citizens banded together, their individual weaknesses diminished by their unified strength. Differences offered variety, variety of skill, of experience, of perspective. The diversity made them stronger.

The rushing stopped, the golden glow subsided, and Jacs's vision returned to Court's Mountain, where the first Queen stood alone. Members of the Court and the Crown surrounded her in an unbroken circle, mouths and beaks open in shock and wonder. From her shoulder blades sprouted two wings made of golden light. Her eyes reflected that same golden glow.

Sourceless words wove around Jacs's heart: Thus, the first Alessi was born.

Her vision faded to black, then the darkness shifted. Threads of golden light shot through its finality, becoming life's ellipses.

Her vision brought her back to the Alethian chamber, and as though she were looking down from above, she saw her blood-soaked body. She lay at the center of a glowing circle of Griffins, her friends and loved ones clutching her close.

The sourceless voice spoke again, and this time Jacs saw the face of the beaked Goddess swim between her and her lifeless form. Young Queen, you would have given your life to protect your people. You sacrificed your life to protect a member of the Court. The peace treaty between Court and Crown is threatened once more. The hearts and minds of womankind and Griffin will be twisted against one another without an ambassador, a protector, an Alessi. For it is only in times of great strife that the Court and Crown need forge another.

Jacs plummeted into her body.

A sensation exploded through her from the inside out, reaching her fingers and toes and somehow further. She felt a tickle on the tip of her nose and a fuzz in her outer extremities spread back inward. An echo. Toward the fissure in her chest. The burning wound numbed, and the pain subsided. Sinew knit. Flesh mended. Her eyelids fluttered open.

She blinked up at a crowd of familiar faces who hastened to withdraw from her. All but Connor, who held her tight with a fear-stricken face.

"It can't be," he whispered.

"What happened?" Jacs asked. The pain in her chest subsided completely and she felt a warmth along her shoulder blades. An uncomfortable prickle danced along her spine. With Connor's help, she got shakily to her feet. Everything appeared blurred, as if she were looking at it through a filthy window. An inky film hung over the crowd, which took another hasty step away from her.

"Jacs," Connor said in a reverential whisper, "you have . . . you're an . . ."

"What?"

"Alessi."

At the word, the four Griffins roared in triumph and rays of golden light burst forth from between her shoulder blades, forming the outlines of wings. The women and men around her fell to their knees, and as Jacs watched, the Griffins followed suit. Feathered heads bowed low over bent foreleg.

Alessi? Jacs thought, bewildered. A deep understanding ran through her veins. *Alessi.* She spread her awareness to fingertip and toes, then further, to explore the edges of her new limbs. The wings of light extended behind her. Not substantial, not imaginary, they existed in an in-between realm.

Flexing them again, she looked up and saw the airship disappearing far above her, half a dozen Griffins guiding its course, and dozens more circling it protectively, almost obscuring it from view. Up. Up to darken the dawn of the Upper Realm. Toward her Queendom. She had seen Celos's plans, she knew what he intended to unleash upon the two realms. She had to stop him.

Returning her gaze to the crowd, she noticed an inky film clinging to each individual's head. Tiny black smokey tendrils drifted up and away, following the airship's course, connecting them all like a thousand tiny strings.

How had she not noticed it before? She turned to Connor. The thin, smoky tethers clung to him too. She waved her hand through them, but they didn't shift.

Connor.

With a shaky laugh, she threw her arms around him and he clutched her to his chest tightly. Closing her eyes, she buried her face in his neck.

"I thought I'd lost you," he whispered.

Pulling back, she kissed him, not caring who saw. "Never again." Elated, she felt determination thrumming through her veins. She looked from the airships to Connor, her gaze following the dark strings. The Griffin Jacs had saved clicked its beak meaningfully, capturing her attention.

Shaking her head as if to clear water from her ears, she said, "It's not over yet. Celos can't be allowed to spread his poison. We have to work together. I need any woman or man unafraid of heights and any Alti willing to ride with a human to step forward."

All four Griffins stepped forward. After a moment of reshuffling, Amber, Chiv. Ryder, Connor, and—to Jacs's surprise—Theo stepped out of the crowd. He had a battered look about him, shoulders slumped and eyes averted from the Queen and her advisor. Positioning himself next to an available Griffin, he lifted his chin as though challenging any who would deny him the flight. Everyone else stood still or took a few hurried steps backward. The task was insanity with wings, and it was no wonder that there were so few volunteers.

Jacs seized Amber's fallen shortsword, still crimson with her blood, and balanced it in her palm. To her right, Yves presented his sword to Amber, who accepted it with a nod of thanks and stepped to Jacs's side. They needed weapons, anything, to cut that balloon down and free the Griffins from their bridles. She noted that the Sons who had ambushed their party had swords hanging from their belts.

"You men," she ordered, careful not to associate them with Celos, "my soldiers need your swords. Let your first free actions be ones that defy Celos's tyranny. Lend us your weapons."

A number of bewildered hoods hastily handed over their swords and daggers to Connor and Theo. Chiv. Ryder accepted a dagger and added it to her belt beside her shortsword. Satisfied, Jacs stalked toward the rising airship.

"Let's finish this," she said. "Fly true, and strike for Celos. The Griffins are not to be harmed but find any way you can to hinder their progress and free them from those bridles. Protect each other. If you can, make sure the two men aboard survive. Celos will have no more innocent blood on his hands, and I want none on yours either. Everyone ready?" She saw her small assault force clamber onto the backs of the Griffins. Would it be enough? She'd soon find out. "Let's go!"

She didn't know how her body knew what to do, but as unconscious as breathing, as easy as laughing, she launched herself into the air. Her light-spun wings struck down forcefully, bearing her higher. Leading the charge, she shot up through the abyss, rising through the deep canyon in pursuit of the airship.

Emerging from the depths of the earth, she spread her wings in the breaking dawn, sword brandished high. The Upper Realm spread out beneath her, and she took her bearings. She had emerged from the dark green forest surrounding the entrances to the Catacombs of Lethe. With the shadow of the Lower Realm to her right and the glittering Azulon Sea to her left, she figured she now hovered above the northern tip of the forest she had entered all those months before for the second task: the forest she had sent the bulk of her army into before they had become trapped in the catacombs.

Straight ahead were the ancient peaks of Court's Mountain. Had she really climbed to the top with a golden egg strapped to her chest and a broken wrist? It felt like a lifetime ago. Nestled at the base of the mountain near an expansive black lake was a city. Jacs recalled the maps she'd studied of the Upper Realm. From the looks of it, Celos's army was heading for Springbank.

In the distance, the ship soared a mile above the treetops, flying parallel to the ground. Its lift was controlled by the two hoods tending to the furnace, and six bridled Griffins guided its course. Each wore a tar-black chain attached to the chest pieces of their harness, its length stretched out taut between the flying creature and the balloon. Four flew at the helm, and two steered from the back. All flew in an eerie unison, deftly steering the great balloon toward the nearest city.

The rest of the bridled Griffins reorganized their formation as they neared the city's outskirts. Where before they had circled the balloon like synchronized wasps, now they fanned to the left and right of it, stretching out like the wings of an enormous beast with the balloon at its center. For a moment, Jacs thought the line of Griffins was also connected by chains, but on second glance it appeared that the same thick black smog that had encircled the heads and shoulders of her friends was wrapped around each bridled Griffin too.

"Do you see that black smoke?" Jacs called as Amber flew alongside her.

"What smoke? From the city?" Amber called.

"No—"

"Jacqueline, that's my city, that's Springbank, we have to stop Celos before he reaches its borders."

"Agreed." She surveyed her team. Four freed Griffins, their riders, and her. Would it be enough?

"The balloon is relying on those chained Griffins to navigate, let's break them loose and strand Celos in the wind," Jacs said. A chorus of determined yeses met her ears and she led the charge. They had to make up a lot of ground, or more accurately, a lot of sky. Luckily, the balloon was a slow-moving monster. They were faster.

Against the dark green of the forest below and the blushing pink of the dawn sky, the sleet-gray and soot-black airship stood out like a stain. The army of pure white bridled Griffins glittered like gold-dusted diamonds in morning light. Jacs could have almost called the scene beautiful if it weren't for the darkness spreading from the central balloon along the line of bridled Griffins. The glow of the new day's masterpiece was blotted by their dark forms.

With his head start, Celos flew miles ahead, and Jacs felt a trickle of horror run down her spine. Were they too late? She set her jaw. Wind roared in her ears, making them ache as she burst forward.

Closer and closer Jacs flew. Celos's airship had now reached the first row of houses on the city's border. Jacs's fleet closed the distance. Closer and closer still, the city's edge crept toward them far below. Jacs could just make out early risers already walking the streets. Whatever she was going to do, she had to do it soon. Celos's airship blazed ahead, but she was almost level with the rearmost Griffin.

Got you, she thought. With a burst of speed, she tore through the sky toward the Griffin. To her left, Connor spurred his Griffin to follow, and she saw Theo close behind. Chiv. Ryder and Amber took the outer edge of their formation on either side.

She was close enough to peer into the open-air hanging platform to see Celos's back where he stood at the bow, elbows slightly bent as he gripped the railing and stared at the city that lay at his feet. His white-blond hair caught the dawn light.

The balloon was shrouded in an inky black smog. No, the smog was *coming* from his ship. From him. As she watched, she saw him press a raised finger to his temple and a billowing black cloud oozed from his crown, gathered around the large gold ring in the center of his balloon, then spread to the left and right, connecting to the gold rings on the foreheads of each flanking and chained, bridled Griffin. The line of Griffins extended far out on either side of the airship, almost spanning the length of the city's borders entirely. The black smog thickened and darkened, almost solidifying in the space between crown, airship, and Griffins, then fell to the earth below.

Like a black waterfall in slow motion, it plummeted to the city streets, a falling curtain smothering the unaware citizens. The effect was chilling, a thick wall of black spewing from Celos's crown.

Everything below Celos's line of smoke quickly became ensnared. Faces from the city below turned upward, then as the smog encircled their heads, the people of Springbank dropped to their knees before Celos.

"Hurry!" Jacs cried and charged toward the nearest chained Griffin. It didn't appear to hear her approach, nor did it flinch as she landed on its back. Hurriedly, she studied the clasps of the Griffin's bridle, and noticed with dismay that it was soldered onto the creature's head and shoulders. No buckle, strap, or loose link existed, and she cursed. The chain connecting it to the balloon protruded from its metal breastplate and was similarly welded in place.

Amber's Griffin flew alongside her.

"It's no use," Jacs called above the rush of wind and cold morning air, "they're welded on."

"Plan B then?" Amber roared and sent her mount into a dive toward the next tethered Griffin. She barreled into the creature, forcing it to jerk down on its chain. The airship jolted violently in response. The smooth black curtain wavered. From the platform of his airship, Celos's head snapped around, his eyes narrowing at Amber, then widening in alarm to see Jacs on golden wings shoot toward him, sword raised.

He barked an order at the nearest Griffins in the line flanking the airship and they immediately dove to intercept Jacs. The wall of smog flickered and sections of it dissipated as the line of Griffins broke rank and chaos consumed them. Although the smog wall was patchier than before, it was still intact. As it fell, it flared and unfurled at its base, ensnaring the minds below and spreading like an infection through the streets.

It was as though they had thrown a rock at a hornet's nest. One minute Celos's Griffins had flown alongside their guiding comrades in uniformed serenity, the next they were a flurry of gnashing beak and thrashing talon, all targeted at Jacs and her fleet. Heavily outnumbered, Jacs was just thankful that many remained in formation to sustain the thick black curtain.

Jacs swooped below an oncoming Griffin and saw Connor and Theo scatter as another Griffin charged at them. Amber roared off to her left and swung her sword at the chains tethering one of the bridled Griffins to the balloon. A deafening clang echoed through the dawn sky and her mount wheeled around in midair to give her another clear shot at the tether. Chiv. Ryder flew off to try a similar tactic on a different Griffin.

Mounted and bridled Griffins alike clashed and sprang apart. Talons locked and beaks snapped, but Jacs was relieved to see all riders remaining seated for the moment, and all swords were aimed at chains rather than their mind-controlled opponents.

She caught Connor's eye and saw him brandish his sword like a knight, banking around the airship's curve and slicing at the chains tethered to another bridled Griffin.

The sudden motion tore a weak link free. Connor bellowed in victory, the cry shifting to one of alarm as the now freed Griffin shot toward Connor's mount, a roar ripped from its beak. Connor's Griffin hugged its wings close to its body and dove out of the way, missing its opponent's claws by a hair.

Sharp beaks glittered like daggers in the dawn light as they flew at the fleet, doing all within their power to halt Celos's advance. Their roars shook the earth far below.

Unfortunately, Jacs's newfound powers didn't appear to include additional strength. Despite her efforts, she found hacking at the chains a fruitless endeavor. Celos, attention now directed their way, sent a wave of darkness toward them.

Submit, his voice echoed in the peripheries of her mind, but she did not let him in. With a force of effort, she pushed back. A golden glow burst from her temples and bullied the darkness away. Jacs blinked, shocked. The smog retreated, and no matter how many veins popped out on Celos's forehead, he couldn't advance against her golden aura. There was a cry to her left from Chiv. Ryder, and her concentration wavered. In the split second of distraction, the darkness encroached, winning back some of the sky it had lost.

Jacs bared her teeth, focused her mind, and pushed. Every wall she had built around her mind to protect herself she now wielded as a blunt force shoving the darkness away. This she could use.

She scanned the bridled Griffins, all under Celos's control. Wings beating downward, she targeted the balloon and drew a deep breath and closed her eyes, visualizing her golden mental walls, her golden shields. How far could they extend past her mind? How far past her body? A theory was only as good as its proof, so it was time she found some proof.

Eyes snapping open, she focused on the chained Griffin directly below her, its head and shoulders engulfed in Celos's dark smog. No sooner had she tried to concentrate than a bridled Griffin charged at her, screeching. She dove out of the way and acted on instinct, pressing outward with her mind and enclosing the attacking Griffin in her projected aura. It stopped in midair. The darkness that had encircled its head and shoulders dissolved and it shook its head, taking in its surroundings with wild eyes. With a roar, it dove at the balloon below it, talons outstretched to slash at the canvas, and a Griffin still under Celos's control flew at it and knocked it off course. The two creatures clashed and tumbled through the sky.

Celos, puppeteering his army while maintaining the curtain of darkness that continued to spread through the city below, snarled up at Jacs and sent two more Griffins her way. She rolled to the side and plummeted below the height of the platform. Her mind whirled. Was she strong enough to stop the blackness oozing over the town? Should she take control of the bridled Griffins instead? What was the best course of action? No, she needed to stop Celos. All the rest would follow.

She looped around the back of the balloon, avoiding three Griffins as she went, and called to Connor and Theo. Amber and Chiv. Ryder were busy taking turns deflecting Griffin attacks and hacking through another chain.

"Cover me. We take Celos," she called to the men. Immediately, they steered their Griffins to either side of her. With a burst of speed, she drew level to the hanging metal platform. Celos's features were set in pained concentration and Jacs saw the inky smoke clearly billowing from him in waves. With a humorless grin, he pointed his forefinger at Connor and sent a pillar of darkness toward him.

"Their minds are mine!" Celos roared at Jacs. The smog wrapped itself around Connor and his Griffin. Immediately, Jacs saw them falter, saw Connor's eyes glaze over. A split second later, the blackness engulfed her too. It was the same pressure as before, the same earth-heavy weight pressed against her eyes.

Submit, Celos's insidious cadence hissed.

She was ready for him; her mind radiated a denial that flung his presence from her in a burst of golden light. His inky smog retreated in its wake. Instinctively, Jacs threw out her hand toward Connor. She couldn't define this new power she held within her mind, but her whole being became suddenly focused on shielding him, shielding his mind, and protecting him from Celos's corruption. Like an extension of her hand, her golden aura soared between Celos and Connor, severing the smog's hold. She flung out her other hand toward Theo and watched gold trump black as he too blinked away Celos's influence.

Radiance collided with pitch in an explosion of wills. Celos's eyes widened, and gradually, the darkness retreated.

Connor twisted his Griffin to the left and together they ripped the chains free from another harness. With only two bridled Griffins leading the balloon onward, Celos's airship barely crawled forward. Snarling, Celos barked an order that was lost in the sound of battle and the roaring wind, and a bridled Griffin seized the dangling tether in its talons and resumed guiding the balloon onward nonetheless.

Celos stood, clutching the banister, face contorted in rage as he saw Jacs's shields pry three nearby Griffins' minds from his clutches. She was directly in front of him now, Connor and Theo hovering on either side.

"Celos!" Jacs cried in a voice of thunder. "You have tormented the minds of men and Griffins and corrupted the peace between our realms, between Court and Crown. You will pay for your crimes!"

"You!" Celos screamed.

His lip twisted, then his eyes darted over her left shoulder and his mouth fell open in shocked recognition. He looked as if he'd seen a ghost.

"Theodosius?" he whispered. "My son . . . Theodosius!" He reached for Theo with his unringed hand. The outpouring of inky black smog vanished abruptly. The effect on the bridled Undercourt Griffins was immediate. The swarming onslaught ceased. Time appeared to stop. Everyone held their breath as the Griffins reclaimed themselves.

Jacs spun, her own shields dissipating, to see Theo's look of bewildered fear. In the moment of their distraction, two bridled Griffins raced toward Celos. One tore him from the deck of his airship, while the other ripped the crown from his head, leaving trails of blood to spill into his eyes from its aggressive claw marks. The crown crumpled within the first Griffin's talons.

As the crown dissolved into dust, the Undercourt Griffins roared their outrage into the sky. The sound was deafening. Jacs clapped her hands over her ears and saw the rest of her team do the same. She watched in horror as the bridled Griffins snatched Celos and soared back the way they had come, back toward the abyss of Alethia.

"Wait!" Jacs cried and flew after them. Connor's Griffin collided with her and knocked her off course. She reeled and regained her bearings but was blocked by three bridled Griffins. Diving to avoid them, she was stopped in midair by a fourth Griffin from the Undercourt. Every remaining Griffin was now focused on preventing Jacs's pursuit of the screaming Celos. Despite her efforts, the Undercourt would not be denied the right to exact their own justice.

The minutes dashed by, and finally Celos was too far from her to be heard above the wind. With a roar, the majority of the bridled Griffins turned and followed their retreating kin. In moments, the only remaining Griffins were the ones still chained to the balloon, and Jacs's team's mounts.

In the sudden stillness, Jacs looked around. Two hoods still cowered beside the furnace beneath the balloon. A mile below, the people of Springbank were struggling to process what they had just felt and what they were still seeing. A few people screamed. Jacs hurried to calm the crowd and flew to land on the roof of the bell tower in the center of town.

"Fellow Freans!" she called above the rising din, sending a surge of light and power through her wings. The golden halo that surrounded her limbs flashed and ignited across windowpanes. How to explain what had just happened when she herself was still reeling with the implications?

"The Queendom is safe! The Griffins and my soldiers have saved our lands from an evil that threatened to consume us all. What you just felt will have no lasting effects, and you can rest assured more will be explained to you in the following week."

Jacs saw more confused and scared faces than she knew how to handle and was saved further explanation by Amber, who had followed her with her Griffin. She raised her hands above the crowd and roared enthusiastically: "Long live Queen Jacqueline, the Griffin-forged conqueror! Our winged Queen has saved the realms from tyranny! Rest easy knowing your hearts and minds are safe! Long live the Queen!"

"Long live the Queen!" the crowd cried back, relief washing over many faces and excitement coloring still more.

"Long live our Alessi!"

The crowd roared in wonder and disbelief.

In an undertone, Amber muttered to Jacs, "Let's leave them on a high before they start to ask questions. We can send more information to Lord Barnaby to distribute in the coming week. Now let's give them a show and go."

With a grateful nod at her knight, Jacs launched into the air, doing her best to display the full glory of her wings and golden halo to the awestruck crowd. She returned to the balloon, where Chiv. Ryder had dismounted her Griffin to join the two hoods on the platform. She was speaking to each in a low tone. Connor and Theo were inspecting the chains of the remaining three Griffins and hurried to join her. Taking a steadying breath, Jacs struggled to suggest next steps.

"Let's take this monstrosity back to Alethia. We can unhook the remaining Griffins there and decide what we want to do with it," she said. The mounted Griffins soared to the free-hanging chains and gathered them up in their talons to help pull the airship back to Alethia. Back to the chasm, where Jacs was hopeful they could bury this perversion of her designs for good.

She hovered above it all, slow, steady wingbeats keeping her airborne. Light shone from her shoulder blades, rivaling the rising sun's rays.

It was over.

Womanning the airship was simple, and she controlled the furnace's blaze to aid its descent down the chasm and return to the rift chamber in the heart of Alethia. The Griffins steered the balloon deftly, and she touched down in front of her Queensguard, the Canaries, and the remaining hooded men. A broad smile spread across her face, and she raised a fist triumphantly.

"Men of Frea! Celos has poisoned your minds and hearts for too long. You deserve to walk in the sunshine and breathe lungfuls of fresh air. I can't imagine what you've been through, trapped in the darkness as you were, and I know that freedom has been too long in coming. The road to healing will be arduous, but I promise you we will walk it together."

"For Frea!" Amber called from the back of her Griffin.

"For freedom!" her knights and Canaries replied. The former Sons joined in the cheer until the chamber was awash with sound. Jacs caught sight of Connor. His grin of triumph and relief was mirrored in every face. All traces of the Undercourt's darkness and Celos's control had vanished.

Whooping in celebration, face shining like a light, Connor cheered: "Long live Altus Jacqueline! Griffin-forged Queen! Alessi of Frea!"

She spread her arms and her wings flashed a bright, searing white as she flew from the airship to land on solid ground once more. At her unspoken command, the wings dissipated. While no longer visible to the eye, Jacs could feel them, ready and waiting to unfurl.

Connor dismounted his Griffin and hurried to her side, pulling her into a tight embrace. To her left, Amber offered Yves his sword back and he threw it aside to embrace her instead. All around her, Queensguard, Canary, and Son were embracing one another, tending to wounds, seeking out missing friends, and reclaiming themselves.

Jacs pulled away from Connor and sought out Phillip. He was where she expected him to be, and she rushed to join him beside Master Leschi. The terror of her last moments was frozen on her face and Jacs's breath caught in her throat. Deep lines carved valleys around Master Leschi's eyes and mouth, and her cheeks were sallow, her hair limp. Fear had warped her features into a grim mask. Jacs gathered Phillip into a tight hug, stroking his back as his frame shuddered with sobs.

"It's my fault," he croaked.

Tears prickled the corners of her eyes. Jacs shook her head, it was a moment before she could talk past the lump in her throat. "No. No, Phillip. It wasn't your fault. She knew it wasn't your fault."

"I couldn't protect her."

And I couldn't save her, Jacs thought. She had been so close. Master Leschi had been alive an hour ago, and now? How could the difference of minutes be so irrevocable? Phillip continued to sob as he clung to his mother's body, and Jacs felt a hollowness consume her. An echoing tone reverberated in her mind, and she clasped Master Leschi's cold fingers. She had been so close! It couldn't end like this. The Griffins had brought Jacs back. What if . . .?

If her mentor had taught her anything it was the power of a what-if. Placing a hand on Master Leschi's forehead and the other over her heart, she closed her eyes and took a steady breath through her nose. The hollowness in her chest terrified her, and she focused her attention on the new sensation that had spread through her body. She felt the root of her wings, felt the new power pulsing in her veins. There. With the same pressure she used to defend against Celos's force, she pushed the power beyond herself, toward Master Leschi. A brilliant golden light burned against her closed eyelids and Phillip uttered a strangled cry beside her. She felt her wings unfurl and extend, felt a warmth roll through her and crash beyond the borders of her skin like a wave breaching a bank.

"Come on," Jacs muttered, opening her eyes.

A golden glow enveloped Master Leschi's form and Jacs watched the marks of Celos's brutality dim and smooth. All the tension that had creased her eyes and brows vanished. The grime and grease of months spent below ground dissolved and she appeared now as though she had just bathed and dressed.

Hope flared in Jacs's chest, and she waited for her mentor's eyelids to flutter open, waited for the blush of life to bloom in her cheeks. The seconds passed and, impatient, she shook Master Leschi's shoulder.

Phillip fumbled for her wrist and felt for a pulse. He met Jacs's gaze and shook his head.

The hollowness in her chest filled with an aching pain so sharp Jacs's hand flew to her breast as though to search for a bloodied blade tip. Detaching itself from the remaining members of the Undercourt, Altus Melinoe approached Jacs silently.

"Please," Jacs begged the Griffin, knowing she was asking more from a Court that had already given enough.

The Griffin shook its head sharply and pressed its beak against Jacs's forehead. A rusted and worn image entered Jacs's mind, as though she were inspecting a battered and forgotten coin for an inscription the years had long since stripped away. A young Griffin leaping into the air to catch a coveted star. It flew and flew, and as Jacs watched, she saw it grow older and older, youthful vigor maturing into an ancient monotony. Centuries passed as the Griffin ascended, and still it did not get any closer to the star it so desperately wanted.

The image dissipated as Altus Melinoe retreated, a tinge of regret staining Jacs's mind.

All powers, all beings have their limits, it seemed to say. *Some things will forever be beyond your reach.*

Jacs's gaze returned to the now peaceful face of her beloved mentor. A golden glow clung to her. It streaked her hair and dusted the laugh lines around her eyes. All the horror that had etched her features was gone, replaced with a calm serenity. Phillip stroked the hair from his mother's face. With her head on his lap, eyes closed, covered in Phillip's cloak, she looked as though she were simply sleeping.

41

FAREWELLS AND FUTURES

Word of how their Alessi Queen vanquished Celos's darkness spread quickly from the onlookers in Springbank to the further reaches of the Queendom, and Jacs returned to Basileia to an awed reverence. While her subjects would never know the extent of the damage Celos wrought, to see her fly in on wings of light leading two Courts of Griffins drew citizens from their homes in droves. Voices clamored over one another in taverns and market squares to tell the world where they had been and what they had seen the day Altus Jacqueline returned to the palace.

Everyone wanted to be present for the birth of the legend, to be a part of the living myth, and in no time at all bards were spinning songs about their Alessi's triumph with varying degrees of accuracy. The fateful morning when Celos almost blackened the Queendom became known as the Dark Dawn. After decades trapped beneath the earth, the Undercourt had wasted no time taking to the skies the moment they finished with Celos's punishment.

The Court had sent Altus Hermes as their ambassador to connect their two courts, and as far as Jacs knew, nothing permanent had been decided. What she did know was that the Undercourt had no desire to fall under the Court's den and rule, so the next step was to determine how a second court of Griffins fit into their Queendom. Last reports indicated Altus Melinoe had sent scouts to the far side of the Lower Realm's basin and was investigating a possible den in the mountains there.

Jacs's role as an Alessi was also new. She was still discovering the extent of her abilities. Her glowing wings and mind shield had come as naturally as breathing when she had needed them to face Celos, but Jacs was a woman of science. Instinct and intuition were all well and good, but if she could, she would discover the exact limits of her abilities. The shape of her powers. Maybe with more data, she could better understand why she had been chosen to bear them in the first place. Her new powers thrummed through her veins and tickled her between her shoulder blades, a constant reminder of that night. Every inhale and beat of her heart were laced with the power's warmth. It had saved her. The Undercourt had saved her. And through her, it had saved her Queendom.

After a lengthy meeting with both Courts, Jacs's determination finally won out and they agreed to train her in all they knew and remembered of the ways of the Alessi. Their records went much further back than the records of Woman. Of course they did; Altus Thenya had been there from the start. Gleaning any personal information from the monarch, however, was out of the question while the two Courts were in negotiations, and she doubted the snow-white Griffin had time to attend her lessons. Altus Hermes, to Jacs's delight, had accepted its role as her mentor in the matter.

While she assumed her standing with both Courts was stable, she also knew how quickly politics could shift. As Connor counseled, maintaining relations with the Courts was a top priority. Besides, the additional benefits afforded her by the Courts were well worth it. As their equal, she could now vouch for people to fly with either Court without needing to prove herself worthy. She would not miss that ordeal.

It was all happening so quickly and involved matters she could have never dreamed of as a simple farm girl picking bean bits from beneath her fingernails. Jacs felt acutely that she was balancing on the precipice of great change, but she couldn't stop to bask in the ripples of celebration that scattered across her Queendom when so much lay ahead. Her heart was still so heavy that the last thing she felt like doing was celebrating.

Her first priority had been to broadcast Celos's defeat throughout the Lower Realm using his own system of crystals and mirrors. She knew that recovering the trust of the Lowrians would be a bumpy road, but the best she could do was start with honesty.

So little was known about the extent of Celos's mind-corrupting influence on the hooded men that Jacs had been hesitant to send them all home without first making sure they were fit and healthy enough for her to do so. Infirmaries across the Upper Realm offered their vacant beds to these men, and rehabilitation was well underway. Reports came in daily about the importance of sunlight, walks in nature, regular sleep schedules, and a healthy diet in the men's recovery, but across the board it became apparent that what most of them craved was a purpose and a sense of belonging.

Master healers were continuing to work on how best to pull the pieces of their minds back together, while Jacs had enlisted a small task force to locate each man's family and set up supports within their hometowns for them to return to. She knew they still had a long way to go, but it was a start.

The harder work was making sure justice was served, and those who had committed crimes were identified and given the chance to atone. Jacs was still unsure where to draw the line of culpability and had begun the mind-numbing process of working it out with the leaders within the justice system. How far can a puppet be blamed for the actions of the puppeteer? They were all shaded areas of gray she knew would take a long time to sift through. In her heart she knew that punishing Phillip would not bring him peace, would not bring her satisfaction, and would not bring Master Leschi back.

Master Leschi's funeral had begun as a private affair. Phillip hadn't said much in the time since, and Jacs had forcibly kept herself too busy to dwell on the ache within her heart. So many lives had been lost since she had donned the crown, but she never imagined a world without Master Leschi in it. A part of her clung to the fantasy that, if she just returned to Bridgeport, just walked the well-worn route to her mentor's wonky two-story workshop, she'd ring the doorbell and see her, rushing to greet her with messy hair and a theory to test. The world was a much smaller place without her.

As the Bridge had been destroyed, and Jacs's engineers were still making sense of her scribbled schematics, Jacs pled favor from the Court, who generously obliged. Jacs's mother, Maria; Phillip; Connor; and a guardpair consisting of Amber and Yves rode with the Court to the Lower Realm.

Their arrival was met with cheers from Bridgeport citizens, who rushed to welcome their Queen, their Alessi. Once Mayor Odette had discovered the nature of her visit, however, the mood of the town quickly changed. Everyone had known Master Leschi. While her ideas had been eccentric at times, and though she may not have always been well loved, she had been universally respected.

The entire town followed Jacs to the memorial grove to pay their respects and give her mentor the sendoff she deserved. A long, winding line of mourners with lanterns held aloft looped its way from the town.

Smatterings of conversation flitted down the line and Jacs caught snippets of memories shared between friends.

"I remember one time she said she'd hang a line for my laundry—you know I'm not so nimble on a ladder anymore—and when I come back out to see how she was getting on, I see a newfangled contraption that I can raise and lower at will and rotate with a crank. I tell you, I was the talk of the town with my new clothesline."

"A quick fix was never her style."

"No, that phrase didn't exist in her vocabulary. It was a better fix, a revolutionary fix, or no fix at all."

"She set us back five minutes though; that threw my bread bake time off and I burned the day's loaves."

"Didn't she come to you the next week with a bread timer?"

"Oh yeah."

"Revolutionary, she was."

The memorial grove grew on the outskirts of Bridgeport along the banks of the river. People gathered on both banks and spread throughout the whole forest. Phillip, white knuckles clutching an urn, scattered Master Leschi's ashes beneath a rosemary tree that Jacs planted. They made sure to plant her tree beside Florence's willow.

Long after the mourners had said their goodbyes and departed, Phillip and Jacs knelt side by side in front of the little plant. Jacs's guardpair, Amber and Yves, stood a short distance away, whispering to one another now and again, but for the most part were silent. Connor had taken Maria for a walk through the memorial grove and every so often Maria's delighted laugh wove its way through the evening air to Jacs. The sharp, spicy scent of rosemary tickled her nose and brought forth a wave of longing for sunny days spent in a workshop filled with ideas and prototypes.

"I'm so sorry, Ma," Phillip whispered into the scented stillness.

"Phillip," Jacs said, frozen hand clumsily grasping his, "she wouldn't want you to blame yourself."

"I did it. If it weren't for me——"

"*Celos* did this. Celos did this and no one else. He was too power-ful; you didn't have a chance."

"You fought back just fine."

Jacs shook her head. "I had practice. I'd encountered the Griffin's power a handful of times before. It's not the same, you had no train-ing, and Celos had been weakening your mind's defenses for weeks. There was nothing you could have done."

"Doesn't matter. Doesn't change anything. Doesn't bring her back. Doesn't stop this bloody pain in my——" he gestured vaguely to himself.

Jacs sighed, "I know."

"I . . . I miss her." His voice broke.

"I miss her too," Jacs said as tears rolled down her cheeks.

She pulled Phillip into a hug, and they clung to one another. The rosemary's scent wove itself around them in the cool night air. It tick-led her nose and, even in her sorrow, Jacs found the corners of her lips lifting in an almost smile as a thought intruded upon her pain.

"That bush is her to a T," Jacs mumbled into Phillip's chest. "You know it spreads like wildfire? Soon the whole town will smell like rose-mary. Every new idea will have her stamp on it." An image popped into her mind of a town overrun with the herb, and her mentor's glee-ful laugh echoed in her ears.

Phillip chuckled; the sound rumbled in his chest against Jacs's cheek. "I can hear her voice in every student's ear already, *rosemary for memory, and for queen's sake, keep reading!*"

Jacs snorted and soon tears of laughter raced their sorrowful sis-ters down her cheeks. Breaking apart, Jacs wiped her eyes and met Phillip's gaze. "What will you do now? Will you stay in Bridgeport?"

He looked away and scrunched his mouth to the side.

"You can join me in the palace, until you're ready to decide? And you can come visit Master Leschi's tree whenever you want. I'll make sure of that. I'll likely join you," she added quickly.

He clamored to his feet and pulled Jacs up with him. Casting a lingering look at the little rosemary plant and the shining golden plaque, he nodded. "Okay."

Jacs looked around them at the darkening woods. "I'll give you a few minutes alone," she said, rising to her feet and brushing her split skirts. Phillip nodded gratefully and turned his attention back to his mother.

Rubbing her arms against the evening air's chilly caress, she beckoned Amber and Yves to follow her as she walked deeper into the memorial grove. She knew exactly where her mother would be and made a beeline for her father's tree: an apple tree, sister to the one in their yard, out of sight of the river.

Connor sat with Maria on a bench beneath the magnificent tree. The bench had been a gift from Master Leschi to Maria shortly after Jacs had begun her apprenticeship with the inventor. Florence Leschi had made it himself. Jacs approached slowly, not wanting to disturb the pretty scene she had stumbled upon. Connor's head was bent to listen as Maria told him a story that involved a great many hand waves and gestures.

"Oh, the man could make me laugh, but some days I swear I wanted to strangle him!" she said, her smile broadening as she glanced up and saw Jacs watching them.

She beckoned her daughter over eagerly and patted a spot on the bench beside her.

"Hello, Plum! I was introducing your beau to Francis."

"He sounded like a wonderful man," Connor said warmly, rising to kiss Jacs's cheek as she approached. With his cheek against hers, he muttered softly in her ear so only she could hear. "She's been fine."

Jacs squeezed his hands in thanks and murmured, "Give me a minute with her, I can meet you and Phillip by the entrance."

"Of course, take your time. I'll wait for you outside the Stroppy Mule. I want to catch Mayor Odette to discuss the clock tower memorial." Another kiss and he politely excused himself as Jacs sat next to her mother beneath her father's tree.

"That's a man worthy of your heart, Plum," Maria said, nodding toward Connor's retreating figure.

Jacs looped her arm around her mother's still too-frail frame. "You were right, Mum. One worth fighting for."

"So, you figured it out?"

"Of course."

"That's my girl," Maria said, resting her head against Jacs's shoulder. A sudden breeze ruffled through the few remaining leaves above, dislodging one.

It fell in a twirling spiral onto Maria's open palms where they rested on her lap. She closed her fingers over the leaf with loving tenderness. Jacs looked up and saw the leaves and branches waving merrily down at her. The sound of a lone fiddle resonated for a moment in the wind. A half-heard harmonic wove in and out between bough and branch.

Jacs's small group walked through town, leaving the rowdier townsfolk to toast Master Leschi in the Stroppy Mule, where Connor had joined them as he said he would. Phillip led the way, while Connor helped Jacs support Maria down the cobbled road. Amber and Yves guarded their rear flank, eyes ever watchful despite the deserted streets. Maria had taken on the role of tour guide and kept a running commentary for Connor's benefit as they passed all her familiar haunts.

". . . and here of course is Bruna's home. The only two-story building on the street, you'll notice, and you will not be surprised to hear that she was on the committee that decided the height restrictions of different residential buildings," she said with a light laugh. Jacs, eyes transfixed on her mentor's crooked house, missed a step and stumbled.

Yves, a half step behind, deftly caught her hand and set her to rights without drawing any attention to the misstep.

The house was just as she remembered. A low overgrown fence outlined the lot's perimeter and kept an assortment of statues and contraptions at bay. A handful of grandmother clocks in various states of disrepair with succulents and ferns growing out of them scattered the front yard, and a large brass telescope hung at ease in one corner. The house, though structurally sound, was all comprised of odd angles.

Phillip had stopped at the gate and seemed frozen in place.

"Go on, lad, let's send her off right," Yves boomed in a voice that appeared to shake Phillip free of his reverie, setting him in motion.

Soon they were through the gate, up the steps, and across the threshold. Everything was in its proper place. It looked as though Master Leschi had just stepped out for a pot of Upperite water. After settling her mother safely in one of Master Leschi's book-strewn chairs, Jacs enlisted Connor's help to make tea, realized quickly he had never made a pot of tea in his life, and sent him to locate a bottle of wine from the cellar as Yves took his place with the kettle.

Phillip, with a few muffled curses, got the music maker working and sent a pleasant tinkle of sound through the main room. Amber located glasses, and Jacs, in a moment of over-delegation, took a second for herself and tiptoed upstairs to the workshop.

A lump formed in her throat. Her gaze scanned the worktables, prototypes, schematics, and notebooks of their years together, and she drew a shuddering breath.

It was a room full of more questions than answers. A room full of promise and intrigue.

She saw the outlines and models of her hot-air balloons, saw the three clocks labeled *Yesterday*, *Today*, and *Tomorrow*, the scale that weighed names against objects, the warped mirror portholes, the scales and rulers, protractors and compasses, and dozens and dozens of writing tools.

Closing her eyes, she felt her mentor standing beside her. Heard the echo of her voice thrum through her heart. It was a comfort and an ache. The bittersweet torment of a love lost but not forgotten.

"Jacs?" Connor's low voice interrupted her thoughts as he climbed the stairs behind her. She turned to him with tear-streaked cheeks and attempted a smile. Without a word, he drew her to his chest.

The minutes passed and finally Jacs pulled away.

"Ready?" he asked.

"Ready."

Together they picked a path through the bookstacks lining either side of the stairwell and joined the others for a toast in the main room.

"To Master Leschi!" Jacs said, glass raised high. "The defender of the line between genius and madness. May her legacy inspire us to always think outside the box!"

"To Master Leschi!" chorused the others.

Connor held tight to Jacs's hand and kissed her lightly on the cheek. The warmth of his palm grounded her in the moment as the room filled with the sound of clinking glasses.

42

UNANSWERED QUESTIONS AND THOSE THAT CRAVE RESOLUTION

Three days after Master Leschi's funeral, Jacs sought an audience with Theo. Connor had offered his company, but she had insisted on the private meeting. The chill of winter's wind cut through the grounds and rattled the windows in their frames, making the thought of an outdoor stroll unpleasant.

She was to meet him in the small room above the conservatory and had a few moments to collect her thoughts while she waited for him to arrive.

The cozy room was smaller than Jacs's bedroom in Bridgeport. With the ceilings and walls comprised entirely of windows, it contained a low table and two curl-up-in chairs, a wicker basket filled with folded blankets, and a low bookshelf with half a dozen titles, all with damp-warped pages. The air was humid and smelled sweetly of the little vase of fresh lilac perched on the bookshelf. Four columns of orchids burst with color from their small woven hanging pots, dangling from the ceiling at even intervals along the windows.

She had wrapped a thick woolen blanket around her shoulders and stared out the foggy windows with her gaze turned inward. The gentle trickling of the fountain below kept her company until Theo's tentative footfalls on the iron spiral staircase brought her back to the present.

"Good afternoon, Your Majesty," Theo said as his head appeared above the top step.

"Theo, thank you for coming," she said as she rose to her feet, indicating the empty chair for him to occupy. He obliged, and she poured them each a cup of tea. Her guardpair that afternoon, Chivilras Ryder and Fayworth, made themselves a vigilant part of the décor.

"You wanted to speak with me?"

"Yes, how are you? How have you been since Alethia?"

Theo gnawed at his lip before answering. "That's quite the question, Your Majesty. I find I don't know where to start. But I am well in health, and am happy with the outcome of that day, I swear to you."

Jacs cocked her head to the side as she considered his last statement. She knew she had to tread carefully, sure of the evidence, but unsure how much to bring to light. "Why is it important you swear that to me? I have no reason to doubt your loyalty . . . do I?"

Theo could not meet her eye.

"Is there any sinister reason why Celos reacted to seeing you the way he did? His distraction bought the Undercourt their opening to end him and to destroy his crown, but did you know he would react to you in that way? Had you met him before?"

"No! No, of course not. I have no affiliation with him. None. He must have known me by my mother's description, that's all. She's the only one who calls me by my full name . . . How else would he have known it? Brovnen is my father. Brovnen. I don't know why Celos called to me like that. He must have lost his mind when he realized he was failing. He was mad. Tried to turn me into one of his followers. One of his Sons. You saw him. He was trying to trap my mind . . . He was desperate by that point. Desperate a-and mad—"

"I see." Jacs cut him off and let her statement hang in the air. He shifted uncomfortably beneath her steady gaze. To see him look so distressed brought her little joy, and she was hesitant to push the matter further. Why whip a long-dead horse, when she knew?

She knew.

And given his reaction to her question, he knew too. He ran a shaky hand through his white-blond hair. Such a distinct color.

"Your Majesty, my mother is a traitor, and my father . . ." His voice broke and he cleared his throat. It took him a few moments before he finished. "I am not my parents."

Jacs studied him shrewdly. "No. You're not. And I trust you will spend the rest of your days proving it."

"Of course! Of course, Your Majesty."

"Then let's leave that where it is, as it is," she said gently. "Trust is hard earned and easily lost. I will give you the same chance I extend to most. You may do with that chance what you will. But I have another matter to discuss with you."

He sat awkwardly, waiting for her to continue.

"Theo, you deserve the truth. Over the past weeks, I've enjoyed our time together. I've grown to respect you, seek your counsel, and consider you a friend. I made a promise to you, and you have likely been waiting for a proposal. You mentioned before how much you have come to detest waiting, and I apologize for being the source of your uncertainty. I'm going to ask you a question, and I want you to be honest with me."

"Okay . . ." Theo's apprehension seemed only to increase at her words.

"What is it you want?"

"What do I— That is also quite the question."

"There's no rush, the tea's still hot," Jacs said kindly, and as if to emphasize her words, she settled back into her chair and crossed her legs comfortably.

Theo eyed her as if suspecting a trap and let his gaze wander out the window. "What do I want? You know, I rarely get asked that. Even with regard to little things, like what to have for supper." He placed his steaming cup on the small table between them and scratched his jaw. "I know what my sister wants, I don't know what she said to get you to agree, but I know she hoped to see me sit beside you as King."

Jacs said nothing.

"But I'm not blind. I see how you are with Cornelius. Even when your affections are subdued, likely out of politeness for me, I'm not an idiot. While I never expected a love match, I also never desired to interrupt one. I've seen the outcome of that . . ." His voice trailed off and he finished his thought almost to himself: ". . . and I never want to suffer my father's fate."

Jacs noted a tightness around his eyes, and he blinked rapidly to dissipate the emotion that had sprung to their edges.

"I understand," she said softly, "and I would hate to be the cause of your suffering. I can't change how I feel, and you deserve an honest heart."

"Thank you."

"So, what is it you want? Would you like to return home? I could arrange a powerful match for you. Or . . ." She paused, watching how her words sparked first alarm then intrigue in his features. The boy really did wear his heart for the world to see. "I have a different kind of proposal. The role of Queen is one I'm still learning to wear and, as you likely noticed that day we walked in the garden, is one that can be overwhelming. There are very few people who are able to bring me the calm you did that day and on days since. I know moving forward

I am going to need people I trust around me. In the months to come, I will be compiling a new Council made up of women *and men* who I trust to aid in ruling this Queendom. So far, the Council is small, consisting of Courtierdame Lena Glowra. You've already shared various areas of policy and law that you are invested in setting straight. Would you be interested in taking on a role of Councilor?"

Theo stared at her slack-jawed. Apparently, he had been prepared for many things, but this had not been one of them.

"Councilor? But what happened to my sister? Isn't she on your Council?" he spluttered.

Jacs shook her head. "Your sister was to be a member, yes, but I spoke with her this morning, and it seems carrying the dual role of Lord and Councilor is more responsibility than she can comfortably shoulder. Given that your mother is now under house arrest and awaiting trial, it seemed fitting she return home. She has agreed to step down. She will likely be returning to Hesperida in the next few days."

Theo looked suddenly wary. "Did she know you were going to offer me a seat on the Council?"

Jacs selected her words carefully. "She knew I was to make a proposal to you this afternoon. I never specified the nature of what that proposal would be, but assured her it would elevate your and your family's status. She may be surprised by some of the details."

A knowing smile spread across his face. "Ah . . . well, I'm sure I can talk to her. She's always been stubborn, but I've never failed to make her see sense when needed—it'd be a shame to start now. We can consider it my first act as Councilor."

"So, that's a yes?"

"Yes."

Jacs beamed. Setting her teacup down, she extended her hand across the space between her and Theo, who, after wiping his palm swiftly down his trouser leg, shook it gladly.

Once Jacs had bathed and changed and had a moment to breathe while her hair was arranged carefully by a giddy Adaine, she found Connor in his room. He was chatting merrily with Edith and beamed as she entered.

"Connor, can I borrow you for the evening?" she asked. Edith hid a knowing smile that Jacs hoped Connor didn't notice.

"Of course."

"Excellent, I thought we could go for a walk, so I'd bring a—"

"Here you go!" Edith said, cheerily presenting Connor with a ready bundle of cloak, gloves, and hat. Before Jacs could finish her sentence, she had also retrieved his winter boots, which had been polished to a high shine.

"—cloak."

He raised an eyebrow but accepted them without comment and allowed Edith to settle the cloak around his shoulders before pulling on his boots. "Whoa, I could use these as a looking glass," he remarked mildly.

His valet busied herself with smoothing a crease and did not reply. Jacs felt her heart rate pick up speed but kept her face neutral.

"Ready?" she asked and offered Connor her arm. As they left the room, Edith flashed her a grin and waved her crossed fingers at her behind Connor's back.

They walked across the palace grounds, frosted grass crunching beneath their feet, and chatted idly about the different towns they had visited. White puffs of frozen air floated about their heads as they talked. Jacs forced herself to remain focused on the conversation but noticed her mind had wandered more than once, and she'd missed what Connor had said. Step by step, they walked farther from the palace and toward the forest. The evening sun lingered in the west, casting a golden glow across the grounds. As they entered the shade of the trees, Jacs retrieved a lantern from the base of a large rowan and lit the candle within. Connor shot her a sidelong look as they began tracing a familiar route.

"Feeling nostalgic today?" he asked when it was clear they were headed toward his oak tree on the edge of the Cliff.

"Something like that," she replied. "We haven't been back since the first time we met. Before I knew who you were to me."

"That seems so long ago," he said softly, helping her duck under a low branch. The sound of the river filtered through the trees. Jacs marveled that it was still flowing. This time of year in the Lower Realm meant ice and snow. She had to admit, it was nice not being quite so frozen.

"So much has changed," she said.

"Has it? In what way?" he teased, pulling a smile to her face.

They emerged from the trees and the oak tree came into view.

Connor stopped in his tracks. "Jacs . . ."

She spun to look at him, butterflies erupting into a flurry of motion within her chest. Decorating the branches of their oak tree were dozens of brightly colored lanterns fashioned in the shape of balloons, each with a little flickering candle hanging within. The light and the colored glass of the balloons cast a glowing rainbow of color into the branches, reflecting and shimmering on the leaves. It looked like a dazzling stained-glass window.

From the lowest branch, Jacs retrieved a slightly different balloon. This was one of her original designs, waxed canvas and all. Beneath it, in the place of the candle-filled basket, hung a little box in the shape of a boat. Holding the balloon gingerly between her palms, box swinging beneath, she walked back to where Connor stood rooted to the spot.

"Connor," she began, furious that already her eyes were prickling. She had been rehearsing what she wanted to say for the past week. She'd had a speech, she'd even practiced where to pause, and now, looking into his bright blue eyes with their little crinkles in each corner, she was at a loss for words. Keeping her voice steady, she continued: "Connor, I love you." Her mouth had gone dry, and all coherence disappeared from her mind. Her heart hammered in her chest. This wasn't like her. She *always* knew the right words to say.

He took two steps toward her and covered her hands with his, one on each side of the balloon.

Taking a breath, she tried again. "Connor, I love you. With all my heart, with every piece of my soul. I . . . no, wait I can do this. Give me a second." A shaky hybrid between laugh and sob burst from her, and she gave the little balloon between them a tiny shake. "I can't imagine my future without you in it. I can't imagine ruling as Queen without you as my King. I—" tears blurred her vision and colored her words, but his steady gaze gave her the strength to keep going, "—I want you by my side and in my heart always. Yesterday, today, and forever. Will you marry me?"

Connor smiled, his eyes shining with tears of their own and replied, "Jacs, I'm yours. Forever. Yes!"

All the nervous energy that had built up around her heart exploded in a clamor of laughter and sobs. Once her ring slid snugly onto his finger, he pulled her into an embrace that felt like home, new adventures, and all the thrilling messes that lay in between.

43

SWAN SONG INTERRUPTED

"Not bad, Turner, you might be able to best my mother in a fight with reflexes like that," Amber teased.

"I've sparred with your mother, Everstar. That's a compliment." Andromeda rolled out her shoulder and winced as she settled into a defensive stance. Amber noticed her slight flash of pain and stood straight, flexing her fingers and shaking out her fists.

In the span of heartbeats that she lowered her defenses, Andromeda winked and struck for her abdomen with a speed that took Amber by surprise.

"Oof!" Amber groaned as the wind left her lungs and she landed on her rear. Her mouth fell open. "You tricked me!"

Limping only slightly, Andromeda offered her arm and pulled her upright. "I deceived you honestly. There's a difference."

"Dishonorable combat. I fear the Canaries are a bad influence on you." Amber smirked, dusting herself off.

"Aren't you responsible for training them?"

"Touché, but they don't learn all their tricks from me," she conceded, glancing toward the other side of the practice grounds, where Yves was currently adding what he liked to call *flourish* to her *straightforward* teachings.

The winter sun was high in the sky and provided little warmth despite its cheery rays. Small puffs of frosted air erupted from the mouths of women and men dotted around the arena. Most of the women trained in pairs or groups of four, decked in the training kit of either guard or knight, but the men still preferred to train as a troupe in their silks and linens.

So far, the Canaries had proven themselves a successful trial program, and Amber had a meeting in the battle room later that afternoon to discuss what inviting men to train as guards could look like. It was a slow start, but if her opinion could come around to the idea, she didn't know a woman alive who would be able to reject it for long.

Gaze scanning the arena, her eyes fell on the approaching figure of Dyna Flent.

Andromeda noticed her a moment later and said quietly, "I'm just going to get some water; I'll give you a minute."

"Thanks, Turner," Amber muttered. Andromeda walked away after clapping her roughly on the shoulder.

"Hi," Flent said.

"Hi."

They hurried to fill the following silence and talked over one another in a flustered rush.

"It's good to see—"

"How are you do—"

"You first," Flent offered, tucking a curl back into her headband.

"How are you feeling? Master Epione said there was no lasting . . . er . . . I mean to say that she mentioned you were going to be fine when I happened to run into her," Amber scrambled to clarify.

"I got a clean bill of health yesterday, ready to resume service."

"That's great news."

"Yes. And I'm to be transferred next week."

"Transferred? Why? You don't have to . . . Is it because of—"

"No. It's not about that. I'm going to start my knight training. I'll be transferred to Llynhaven for my first placement; then, once the Bridges are replaced, I'll head down to the Oldfrean Bastion in the Lower Realm. I get the feeling training across both realms will come in handy when I reapply for a position within the Queensguard once I've received my knighthood." Flent said, crooked smile lighting up her somber features.

Amber shifted her weight between her feet and scratched the back of her neck. "You're wise in that regard. Well, I wish you the best in your training and look forward to seeing your application come across my desk. Truly," she said and stuck out her hand for the guard to shake.

Flent took it warmly. "And who knows, maybe I'll be interested in something a little more long-lasting by then."

"What do you mean?"

"You don't court guards, remember?" she said and before Amber knew what was happening, Flent pulled her in for a one-armed hug. Lips close to Amber's ear, she finished softly, "But you said nothing about knights."

The familiar scent of jasmine and orange blossom made her head spin. It was a moment before propriety caught up with her and she pulled away from their embrace. She saw Flent was blushing. The back of Amber's neck felt hot, and she fumbled for something to say.

"I'll see you around, Everstar," Flent said, tapping her upturned wrists together twice.

"Yeah, I'll see you," Amber managed before Flent spun on her heel and walked away across the practice grounds. She watched her go, a mixture of uncertain emotions coiling themselves around her navel.

Sand-scrunched footfalls approached from behind, and Amber turned to see Andromeda approach. "Told you she was trouble," she said.

"I hate how often you're right," Amber grumbled and accepted a proffered waterskin.

"What did she want?"

"To postpone her troublemaking," Amber said with forced bravado. "How are you feeling, want to call it?"

Andromeda's gaze darted from Flent's retreating figure to Amber's face and she nodded, dropping the matter.

"Great, I have to check in with Yves but will see you this afternoon?" Amber said.

"Yes, I'll walk over with you from the barracks. I have a checkup with Master Epione if you need me before then."

The two knights shared a salute. Andromeda retrieved her waterskin and headed for the bathhouse, while Amber marched over to where Yves had just dismissed his men.

"To what do I owe this honor, Everstar?" he said with a flourish.

"Thought I'd see how you were getting on."

"Oh fine, just fine. We were refining our blocking today. Turns out some of the drills you showed them this morning align closely with choreography from our past performance in Bregend of Percival Bairden's *Pearls in the Mist*. So, it was just a matter of footwork and timing to pull it all together."

Amber didn't quite know what he meant but had watched his progress from afar and trusted his process was getting the results she was after. "Excellent. Honestly, Yves, I didn't think you had it in you."

"You underestimate me."

"Apparently so. Will I see you this afternoon at the—"

"Of course."

"Right," Amber cleared her throat. Her eyes surveyed Yves's retreating men as they fooled about in post-training relief. Each wore a different shade of smile, shoving and laughing with one another. "You've really put your heart into training these men. But . . . don't you have a seaside cottage to decorate?"

Yves, who had been unwinding his wrist wraps, shot her a sidelong look. "Ah yes, Swan Song Cottage. She awaits with bated breath for her master to grace her halls and fill her with splendor. My new ship, the *Encore*, awaits as well, moored in the harbor until I unleash her on the open seas."

"I see."

"However, I have been known to keep the ladies waiting. I fear I simply cannot leave my men in your—make no mistake, very capable—hands until I am sure they will fare well without me. I would hate for them to feel abandoned and, as a result, be the cause of their lacking luster and dimming sparkle. No! You deserve their best performance, and at this time, I must resign myself to the fact that my presence is still required."

"Right," Amber said, hiding her smile behind a stoic facade of professionalism. "So, no Swan Song Cottage."

"Alas, not yet."

"Because your men need you."

"The encores are ceaseless."

"Yves, you sacrifice too much."

"I know."

"Your men are lucky to have you."

"It's true."

"As am I."

"Of course, you—" Yves cut off and shot her a look, taken aback. "You? You surprise me, Chivilra."

Amber winked at him. "Just like to keep you guessing."

The morning's levity gave way to afternoon's gravitas. Amber fidgeted in her mourning uniform, thankful to have Andromeda by her side. Their walk from the barracks was a quiet one, but silence with her was never awkward, and Amber enjoyed a moment in her thoughts. The pathway was dotted with pairs of knights, guards, and Canaries (Amber would have to start calling them SHIELD again soon but couldn't deny that their stage name was sticking), some of whom saluted in greeting. Her stomach fluttered uncomfortably.

As they wove their way past the palace gardens, Andromeda said suddenly, "You ever think about doing something else?"

"Like, if I weren't a knight?"

"Yeah."

"Nope."

Andromeda smirked. She still walked with a slight limp, and Amber slowed her pace to give her time to breathe. "Me neither."

"Not even after you were used as target practice?"

"Maybe for a minute. It wasn't the most glamorous of lows, needing someone else to bathe me, but no. All those arrows did was show me I need to work on increasing my agility."

Amber shook her head. "Ah yes, it was definitely your lacking dexterity that got you shot through with arrows."

"One can always be quicker."

Two bare rowan trees stood like sentinels on either side of a mossy stacked-stone archway. They passed through it and fell silent once more. The air held a chill, and a reverential stillness settled around their shoulders. Unlike most memorial gardens in the bigger cities, this garden was not walled off with stone; its borders were outlined with a holly hedge. A forest of memorial trees and bushes grew throughout the garden, where, in its center, an enormous woven sycamore monument towered over them all. It dated back hundreds if not thousands of years and was said to have been planted in the age of the first Queen shortly after the treaty of Court and Crown had been signed. It was the size of a cathedral. Each window between the woven trunks was filled with plaques commemorating fallen soldiers across the generations. Well out of reach of human hands, golden fragments of eggshell and gold-dusted feathers were embedded in the bark to honor fallen members of the Court.

Both Amber and Andromeda paused to crane their necks, taking in the sheer size of the woven trees. Scanning the gathering crowd, Amber spotted Yves with the rest of his men. They all wore dark red or purple silk with black arm bands wrapped around their upper arms. Yves even wore a mourning veil. The rest of the Queensguard stood not far off, all dressed in their mourning uniforms, black polished leather breastplates gleaming in the dying light of the day. Flent stood with a cluster of guards and nodded in solemn greeting.

Amber sought out Jacqueline and found her standing with her mother, Cornelius, her two Councilors Lena and Theo, Anya, and the Lowrian boy, Phillip. She wore a simple black split-skirt gown, her only adornment a thin gold band that circled her temples. She gave a little nod when she noticed Amber, face grim.

A small dais awaited Amber at the base of the sycamore, and she walked with Andromeda toward it, feeling her throat tighten. At the base, Andromeda clapped her on the back, shared a salute, and moved to stand with the rest of the Queensguard. Amber took a breath, took a step, then the next, and turned to face the crowd.

"Good evening," she began. "I am a woman of few words, so I chose the best ones with which to honor our fallen sisters. Masterchiv Cassida Rathbone was a soldier the likes of which we will be lucky to see again in this lifetime. Honor, bravery, and loyalty she had by the wagonload, and in all her years of service to the Crown, she only ever unsheathed her blade thrice. Her prowess on the battlefield was matched only by her competence within the battle room. With her guidance, countless lives were saved, many threats diffused before crossing the threshold to war. Freans, Austerians, and Nysans alike have reason to respect her name, and she alone can be cited as prolonging the peace with Auster's King after a dangerous miscommunication was resolved by her lending the man her boots. Luckily, they were the same size, or we'd likely be speaking Austerian right now."

A smattering of laughter flickered through the glade, and Amber waited for it to settle before continuing.

"Every battle has its casualties, and our mission as soldiers is to save as many as possible. May we all strive to embody all that Masterchiv Rathbone stood for. May the women who fought and died alongside her and within the catacombs live on in our deeds, in the lives we continue to save, and in the peace we continue to uphold. I ask you now to take a minute of silence for Masterchiv Cassida Rathbone and Iliana Dryft, who fell protecting the life of Cornelius Frean. For Faline Cervah, Miera Jaenheir, Reesa Gideon, Jolene Sendar, Kiera Blunt, and Lauren Dalia, who fell in the battle of the catacombs and whose actions have reportedly saved over a dozen other women who also became trapped underground. And finally"—she glanced over at Jacqueline—"for the honorary member of the Queensguard, Master Bruna Leschi, who raised and trained our fair queen, fell in the battle of Alethia and who, in her last moments, provided Queen Jacqueline with crucial information regarding how to defeat Celos. Her actions saved countless lives across both realms and preserved our way of life as we know it."

She bowed her head as silence expanded within the garden. Dry leaves rustled among the boughs overhead, and a raven *quorked* from somewhere deeper in the trees. The hanging memorial plaques clinked together softly as a breeze disturbed them. When she lifted her head, she saw Jacqueline's eyes shining with unshed tears. Cornelius gently took her hand in his.

Clearing her throat, she said, "Let us live our tomorrows with these women's virtues in our hearts and guiding our actions. Let their mistakes forever be viewed with compassion and stand as lessons from which we may learn. Let their triumphs be the signposts that lead us to brighter futures. Soldiers, we thank you for your service. May you rest now, in peace." With her back now turned to the crowd, she offered a knight's salute to the hundreds of names immortalized on the sycamore. The nine new plaques shone brightest in the evening's amber glow, standing out like stars in a new constellation.

44

MASTER MOIRA'S MASTERPIECE

"And you're *sure* this isn't bad luck?" Anya asked from atop her stool. They were in Lena's chambers, days after the memorial, in the shafts of sunlight filtering through the picture windows. A fire crackled merrily in the grate to keep winter's chill from the air, and Anya's cheeks were flushed pink from either its heat or embarrassment.

"Darling, no!" Master Moira exclaimed. "It's bad luck to see each other on the wedding *day*, and even then, it's only the moments before one sets foot on that aisle that are of ill fortune. This is well before. Besides, I always add an extra little sparkle to each ensemble as a surprise on the day. A sparkle for all to see, and a secret sparkle for you to find after the ceremony." Master Moira punctuated her last statement with a tinkling laugh. Lena, with fingers covering her eyes, bounced a little on the balls of her feet in anticipation.

"Okay, okay, can I look now?" she asked, unable to wait any longer.

"Yes," Master Moira decreed, and Lena dropped her hands. Anya stood, arms crossed self-consciously, in a high-necked gown with a full skirt of floral lace. The dress itself clung in odd places, but even so, Lena's breath caught in her throat.

"Oh, Anya," she breathed, hands clasped in front of her heart.

Master Moira prompted Anya to spin with a wave of her hand. "Give your fiancée the full effect!" Anya shot Lena a pleading look and did as she was bid. Lena struggled against a wry grin.

"I don't see why we couldn't have started with you, Lee."

"Tush! Your beloved is still mending. Standing in a constricting garment full of pins is the last feat of endurance I would wish upon her. Juliana! We're missing something. Of course the floral lace embellishments are divine, but we don't want you to become lost in them, Ms. Bishop. No, you are to be a rose among daisies, not some common dandelion. Maybe it's the hue I'm loathing. We don't want to wash out the bride. Or is it the neckline?" Master Moira stood back with her chin resting on her crooked forefinger. It was a shock to see her immobile.

Juliana hurried closer and adjusted the neckline with a few expert folds.

"No! Incinerate it! I hate every stitch! This dress must make dear Lena weep with joy to see you in it! We got a gasp, that's all! Not even a mild sniffle. No! It will not do. I must go away to think. You may step down. Remove it, destroy it. We begin again, Juliana."

Juliana's face fell, and she nodded, helping Anya out of the gorgeous garment. Master Moira pinched the bridge of her nose, her other hand dithering about her waist, her brows furrowed with concern.

"No, don't destroy it. It will remain in the graveyard of dismal ideas for me to mourn the loss of my ingenuity."

Lena placed a hand on hers gently. "Master Moira, I've always thought Anya looked best with a sweetheart neckline."

Clapping her hands together, Master Moira exclaimed, "Sweetheart! For the sweethearts! Of course! Juliana! What are you doing removing the dress? We still have work to do!"

Anya narrowed her eyes playfully at Lena as the dress, which she had halfway escaped, was pushed back down over her head.

Lena hid a giggle and rocked smugly back and forth on her heels. "And what do we think of a cape?" she suggested, knowing she was pushing her luck.

"No cape," Anya said firmly.

"A cape! Heavens, that opens a number of possibilities, do we envision one shoulder, two shoulders, across the body, half length, full length . . . Call for cakes, dear heart, the muse is with us."

Lena hurried to relay the message to the serving boy standing by the door, feeling Anya's eyes on her back the whole time. She would likely pay for this later, but she was having far too much fun for it to matter right now.

The next half hour passed in playful dress-up until Master Moira held up her hand and said decisively, "Yes. We have made a start at least. Leave the rest with me. We'll be in touch. Come, Juliana, *now* you may remove the garment. See the difference between ongoing and complete? Dear Lena, I look forward to seeing you soon. Ms. Bishop, keep making our girl happy. Adieu!"

Calm returned to the room, and Anya rounded on Lena. "*A start? We made a start?*"

Lena dissolved into a fit of giggles and helped Anya down. "Your face! I can't!" she managed.

"You fox!" Anya exploded incredulously, deftly leading Lena to the cushioned window bench as she winced over her wounded side. The laughter sent a prickle of pain through her that she purposefully tried to ignore. But she couldn't hide anything from Anya.

"And when she started suggesting live flowers—" Lena said, lowering herself onto the velvet gingerly.

Anya crossed the room and retrieved two goblets of wine from the refreshment table, still shaking her head.

"Which would need to be sewn in, while I'm wearing it, on the day *five hours* before the ceremony. Five hours!"

"I thought you were going to throw your teacup in her face at one point."

"I almost did, but she took it away to measure my fingers. Why in Frea does she need my finger measurements?"

"For elbow-length lace gloves, perhaps?" Lena suggested innocently. She accepted the proffered goblet, and Anya took her place beside her.

"Live flowers, honestly, I'm surprised she didn't consider having a dove sit on my wrist as an *intriguing statement piece*," she said in her best imitation of Master Moira's singsong cadence.

"Now that's an idea, should I call her back?"

Anya shot her a look to make sure she was kidding. "Just you wait till your fitting. I'm going to suggest headdresses, bell sleeves, the works."

"A just and fair punishment, I concede."

Anya planted a swift peck on her cheek.

"I hardly think I deserve that after what I just put you through," Lena said.

Anya arched an eyebrow mischievously. "Well what I had in mind might rip your stitches, so it'll have to do till you're mended."

Blushing, Lena grinned and tapped her other cheek with a pointed finger, happily accepting the kiss that Anya planted there shortly after. Anya pulled back, her eyes searching Lena's face and her smile deepening the dimples in her cheeks.

"What is it?" Lena asked.

"Nothing, it's just good to see you laughing, Lee."

45

DISCOVERING ART

Connor didn't know why he was so nervous. For the third time since arriving outside the room, he wiped his palms down his trousers. His mouth was dry. He adjusted his collar. Trying not to pace, he walked from one side of the door to the other. The thick plush of the intricate Nysan rug striping the length of the hallway muted his footfalls but did nothing to lessen their weight. Sunlight streamed through tall arched windows dotted along the corridor.

Years ago, in the summers, Connor's mother would remove the glass panes, opening the hallway up to the elements. The warm floral-soaked scents wafted in from the gardens like long-awaited guests. Occasionally chickadees would fly inside, filling the vaulted ceilings with their song.

Today it was cold, quiet, and empty.

The glass windowpanes sat firmly in place with the odd spider's web denoting their permanence. Beyond the doorway lay his mother's studio, a room he'd been in once or twice while she'd been alive. It had been his mother's sanctuary and one he had always been reluctant to invade. Since her death, he'd had it closed up and hadn't had the courage to investigate.

Clearing his throat, Connor hesitated at the door, then eased it open. He blinked into the gloom and watched the dust motes swirl and settle.

Unlike the hall stretching away behind him, this room's arched, vaulted windows were blanketed in heavy velvet curtains. Thin white sheets draped over every piece of furniture, shelf, and countertop, depriving the objects within the room of definition. It was a room full of vague shrouds of various sizes.

Near the far window, five covered easels stood like off-duty soldiers. A concealed canvas perched on each. The only source of light came from the far end of the room where one curtain had been pulled back halfway. The gap of exposed sunlight was just wide enough for a man to stand in. Which a man did.

At the sound of Connor's entrance, the man turned, his silhouette of sharp lines and angles a direct contrast to the pale shrouded blobs marking territory between him and Connor. Between father and son.

"Hello, Father," Connor said softly.

"Ah! Cornelius, m'boy. Good to see you."

"It's certainly been a long time," Connor said, ashamed of the bitterness that had crept into his tone. He hesitated halfway across the room, standing beneath a dusty chandelier.

"That it has. A lot has happened. A lot has changed. You've kept yourself well, I trust?"

"Well enough. And you?" The banality of their exchange sent a ripple of irritation down Connor's spine, but there were steps to this dance that needed following.

His father nodded slowly with hands clasped behind his back. He'd always been an imposing man. A man of certainty. But now the kyphotic curve of his spine mocked the remnants of his conviction. An embodied question mark. He looked so small. The dowager King cast his gaze around the room. A sadness laced the creases around his eyes. "Oh, son. I don't even know how to answer that question."

Connor crossed and uncrossed his arms. To the depths with decorum. "How could you leave me?"

"Nor that one."

"It was a mess. We almost lost everything Mother worked so hard to create. I needed you."

"You did just fine without me."

"That's not the . . ." Connor stopped himself short as his voice began to rise, as he heard the whining of a petulant child break from his chest. He would change nothing by bemoaning the past. His gaze landed on one of the easels. "Are you back for long?"

"I think so."

"Good."

"Is it?" his father asked. Doubt and shame flickered across his face, and Connor was struck with how lost he looked. This man had been a mountain.

"Yes," Connor said stiffly. Watching his father shift his weight from one foot to the other, Connor felt something rough within him crack and flake away. In five long strides, he crossed the room and pulled his father into a rough embrace. "It's good to see you."

Connor felt the warm weight of his father's palms on his back as he haltingly returned the hug. Both pulled away, clearing their throats.

"Your mother loved this room," his father said. He pushed back another curtain, allowing more light into the studio. Connor drifted toward the nearest easel and lifted the corner of the white sheet that concealed the painting. A few splotches of color assaulted his eyes and he pulled the rest of the sheet off with a startled laugh. Beneath was what had to be the worst painting he had ever seen. As though a child had described a sunset to an artist who was blindfolded and riding on horseback. A mess of color and odd horizon lines.

His father, drawn to Connor's laugh, looked over his shoulder and studied the painting with a grin. "She always was a dreadful painter," he said fondly.

"Was she? I don't really remember her painting."

His father nodded. "It was her quiet time. She wasn't one to share her work," he said delicately. His subsequent pause and subtle gesture at the depicted mess only emphasized why no piece from the late Queen had ever graced the palace galleries. "And you wouldn't believe it, but she took lessons and everything. No matter the tutor, this was the typical result." With his forefinger, he traced one of the stuttered brushstrokes that might have been a cloud. "I think it was one of the things I loved most about her. She was so talented in so many domains. Benevolent queen, caring friend, loving mother, wonderful wife . . . terrible painter." They both laughed. "I asked her once why she liked it so much. I mean, she was in here every other evening and always returned paint-spattered with lifted spirits. She just said, *It makes me smile.*"

Connor cocked his head as though this would bring the subject into sharper focus and grinned. "It makes me smile," he muttered to himself. "I like that."

"Lately I've realized the wisdom in it. Sometimes a smile feels impossible to find, and she was ruling a broken Queendom laced with a level of corruption I still can't wrap my head around. If a handful of ruined canvases was all it took, no wonder she painted so many of them."

Connor nodded, unsure what to say. His gaze scanned the clashing hues and wonky lines. The world needed a few more smiles in it.

"She also said it was good for her to be rubbish at something. Kept her humble," his father added.

Connor snorted. "Then we thank you, brave canvas, for your service to our late Queen. For keeping her from pride and tyranny."

"Your sacrifice was not in vain!" his father chuckled, clapping a hand on Connor's shoulder as they fell against each other, laughing. One by one, father and son pulled back the sheets hanging over the easels, delighting in the shambles beneath.

"She just never improved, huh?" Connor chuckled as they studied the collection.

"Not in the slightest. I think, if anything, her mistakes simply became bolder."

"Well, is a mistake really a mistake if it's on purpose?"

Like the slow gutting of a candle, his father's mood shifted, his grin slipped, and he became thoughtful. "That's exactly the kind of thing she would say," he said softly, turning to look at Connor. It wasn't until he felt his father's eyes on him that Connor realized he'd not looked at him properly since he'd walked in the room.

Outside, the sun was setting in a manner entirely separate from the late Queen Ariel's painted interpretation. The golden sheen lacing the palace grounds retreated to the horizon where the sun lay, gently gathering the last of its rays.

For a moment, his father's sunken cheeks took on the blush of the remaining reds. His gaze held Connor in place, and when he finally spoke, it was with the solemn respect of a man addressing an equal. "The Queen . . . Jacqueline, wrote of your actions. She told me all you've done to save our Queendom. To save your mother's legacy. Your mother . . . well, I just know she'd be so proud of the man you've become. *I'm* so proud of the man you've become. You made it matter, son. All of it."

46

TAKING FLIGHT

S omehow, the following months passed by in the blink of an eye. Jacs was thankful for the small support team that traveled with her throughout the Queendom. Leaving the palace in ruins had been difficult, and she wouldn't have felt half as comfortable if not for the support from the beginnings of her Council of Four, Lordson Theo Claustrom and Courtierdame Lena Glowra, and the return of the dowager King Aren, who was quickly proving himself an effective advisor despite his proclaimed retirement.

Adaine had spent an entire bedridden week planning Jacs's itinerary down to the minute and through sheer force of will alone seemed to have mended enough to accompany her. Despite her heavily bandaged leg and the need for a serving boy to push her around in a wheeled chair, she was by Jacs's side. Jacs was thankful, for she had missed her valet's cheerful presence. Twelve Upper Realm counties and eight Lower Realm regions later, Jacs had finally completed her tour of the Queendom. As the five Bridges were still under construction, she had enlisted the help of the Court to deliver her retinue to the Lower Realm.

In each city, she held an audience with the lord or mayor, spoke to the people in the city hall or town square, and spent days mingling with the locals, visiting local businesses, and hearing the citizens' complaints and concerns. Of course, a citizen never came to her with a compliment. No one ever wanted to talk about the things that were running smoothly. A serving boy wheeled Adaine in Jacs's wake, keeping a half a pace behind as she sat hunched with her pen poised to write each of Jacs's comments down. By the end of the tour, Jacs had a small library's worth of notebooks to sift through.

The major event in each location was always the revelation that Jacs had been anointed by the Undercourt as an Alessi. Citizens clamored over themselves to catch a glimpse of their winged Queen and, even though she performed twenty separate ceremonies and should have gotten the hang of it at some point, each one filled Jacs with nerves. She was still getting used to the implications of her elevated status. The little farm girl milking a grumpy cow seemed so distant from who she had become.

One constant she was thankful for was Connor. He kept her sane, and with him she was able to keep a piece of herself sacred as well. She could give the realms Altus Jacqueline Frean, Courtier Jacqueline Daidala, or even apprentice Jacqueline Tabart, but Jacs was Connor's. Jacs, he kept safe.

"Here," Connor said softly, retrieving her simple gold circlet from its velvet cushion and blocking her well-trod path to place it on her head. They were finally back in her chambers. Jacs was preparing for a meeting with the Courts and hadn't stood still for the past half hour. Adaine had given up trying to chase her around the room in her wheeled chair and had called for reinforcements. Edith and Connor hovered around the nervous Queen with light chatter and well-timed bobby pins.

Jacs paused midstride to lower her head so that Connor could straighten the golden circlet, and he caught her hands in his. The band of his engagement ring pressed gently against her knuckles and calmed her for the moment.

"Breathe," he said. "It's going to be fine."

She met his gaze and nodded, feeling the tightness in her chest relax minutely. "Right, you're right. I just need my crown, could you—"

His eyes crinkled and he kissed her forehead. "You're wearing it, Jacs."

"Right."

A messenger creaked the door open and whispered a few words to the awaiting Adaine.

"Your Majesty, they're set to arrive in ten. The Council and Queensguard are in place."

"Right," Jacs said again, steadying herself with a breath. "Let's not keep them waiting." Clasping Connor's hand in hers, she nodded her thanks to Edith and Adaine and strode from the room. Chivilras Ryder and Fayworth detached themselves from their posts at either side of her door to follow a short distance behind.

The throne room was awash with midmorning light that filtered in through windows and the open arches surrounding the bottomless belvedere high above. Together, Jacs and Connor walked the length of the room, passing her Queensguard, members of the Queen's SHIELD, the dowager King, her Councilors—Theo and Lena—and Anya. Jacs stopped short of the throne and waited below the dais. With a reassuring squeeze of her hand, Connor took two steps back to stand behind her.

The room held its breath. In the still morning air, Jacs picked up the sound of wingbeats and bowed her head as five Griffins dove through the oculus in the ceiling and landed lightly in front of her throne. The first three: Altus Thenya, Altus Riesa, and Altus Hermes—monarch, mate, and messenger of the Court—landed and lifted their gaze to the circle of sky above them, waiting. Soon after, the last two Griffins arrived: Altus Melinoe and Altus Zagreus, monarch and mate of the Undercourt.

"Welcome, esteemed members of our dual Courts," Jacs said. The others in the room sank to their knees out of respect, and she did the same. Altus Hermes approached and ran its beak through her hair gently. Pulling back, it placed the dorsal blade of its beak against her forehead and pressed a thought at the threshold of her mind. She lowered her defenses and let it in. A series of impressions floated into her mind's eye, and she smiled to feel a golden thread of hope woven through each one. Knees still digging into the throne-room floor, she felt herself soaring high above the Upper Realm, launched from the Court's den high on Court's Mountain. In her vision, the air rushed through feathers that did not belong to her and a roar of pure unbridled joy erupted from her borrowed beak. Banking to the left, she saw the Lower Realm stretching away toward the horizon, the mountains in the distance cutting it off from the rest of the land.

The vision shifted, and she had flown hours in a matter of heartbeats. The mountains on the far side of the Lower Realm's basin were now directly before her, and she saw that the ghostly white Undercourt Griffins had joined her. The tips of each of their feathers glittered with gold dust. Her mind's eye fell on the ornate openings to a dozen or more caves circling the outside of a stone spire high in the far mountains. The openings were arranged with such care and precision and were decorated with such intricate detail that they could not have been forged by nature alone. Each cave was open to the elements with strategic awnings and windbreaks offering shelter without smothering the inhabitants. A feeling passed through her, and she understood. After decades spent buried below ground, the Undercourt would never again be hidden from the sky. Abruptly, the vision disappeared and was replaced with a question, an invitation, a summons.

Altus Hermes stepped back, and Jacs blinked eyes that were her own once more. She stood slowly and surveyed the members of the Courts. "We would be honored."

The Griffins stamped their taloned forelegs in approval. Altus Melinoe and Altus Hermes crouched low as the rest shot upward through the hole in the ceiling. Jacs turned with a broad grin to Connor.

"They've finished their new den."

"Excellent! When will you return?"

"*We* will return before Upper sundown."

Connor's eyes sparkled. "We?"

"Of course, Courtier Cornelius. I want you by my side in this." In two short steps, she stood before him with mischief on her lips and lowered her voice so that only he could hear. "If you can keep up. I'll even give you a head start."

"You're on."

Jacs closed her eyes and summoned her wings with the same innate ability she'd had since she first attained them. Connor threw a hand up to shield his eyes as a burst of golden light erupted from her shoulder blades. Her ethereal wings extended outward to fill every corner of the throne room before settling at an appropriate length.

With obvious self-restraint, Connor walked toward Altus Melinoe and paid it all honors as he alighted on its back. Jacs rolled her shoulders and flexed her wings experimentally. Their eyes met, Connor winked, and Altus Melinoe launched itself into the air.

"Chiv. Everstar, I'll need a guardpair willing to fly with Altus Hermes."

Amber stepped forward and nodded, her gaze traveling down the line of Queensguards and Canaries. Many had taken a voluntary step backward, including Chiv. Turner. Yves, however, bounced on the balls of his feet, a sly grin plastered across his features.

"With me, Lightfoot," Amber said gruffly. With a flourish, he bowed low and practically skipped along behind her to the Griffin's side.

"My crystals," Jacs called and a moment later, Cyrus appeared with a small black leather pouch containing a purple and a blue scry crystal, as well as a handheld looking glass decorated with golden trumpeting flowers. "We will return before Upper sundown," Jacs announced to the room. "I will check in every two hours, Cyrus, so have a scryer watching and listening."

"Of course, Your Majesty."

"Ready?"

"Ready," Amber called from Altus Hermes's back.

"Let's go."

Jacs watched Altus Hermes crouch low and spring into the air, following Altus Melinoe's path through the oculus. Jacs flexed her wings again and felt the ground disappear beneath her. She shot upward like an arrow loosed from its bow and darted through one of the stone archways of the Griffins' perch.

Sunlight danced through the golden light of her wings as though greeting an old friend. With a powerful flap downward, she rose high above the members of the Courts. Her palace shrank away beneath her, the Upper Realm unfolded itself around her, and far in the distance, the Lower Realm expanded before her. Cities clustered in pockets, interspersed between forest, plain, and river. She recalled her visits to each one, remembered the tasks that lay in Adaine's countless notebooks. All represented problems she had the privilege to help solve. She saw the scars of the destroyed Bridges dotting the edge of the Cliff and noted with pride the construction at each site. Her new Bridges would be up and running by year's end.

She led the formation across the realms, woven sunbeams bursting from her shoulder blades and buoying her up toward the clouds' mantle.

With arms outstretched and wings unfurled, she embraced her Queendom.

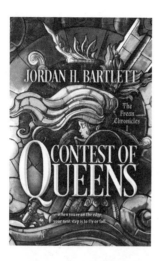

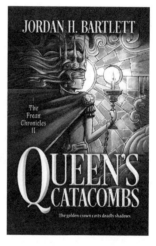

ACKNOWLEDGMENTS

What an adventure. It has been such a wonderful and humbling experience crafting this trilogy. When fifteen-year-old Jordan wrote "publish a book" at the top of her bucket list, she couldn't have imagined the road she'd one day travel to make it a reality, the incredible people she'd meet, the countries she'd write in, the research field trips she'd embark on, the panels, interviews, and events she'd attend—let alone that it would be three books, not one, that she would set loose in the world. It has been an absolute dream.

None of this would have been possible without Sue Arroyo and the CamCat team, or my wonderful editor Bridget McFadden. Thank you for taking a chance on this series and for making it shine so brilliantly.

A huge thank you to my parents, Cathy and Tim, for everything. You walk with me through the catacombs and help me into the light every time. And my brother, Josh, for everything else. Thanks for keeping me humble, and just know that I would fight a very large gentleman for you no sweat. To my far-reaching family that spans New Zealand, Canada, England, and Scotland: all the Highleys, Bartletts, Birds, Joneses, and Hollandses—thank you. A tree is nothing without strong roots.

My beta readers: Nikki Romano, thank you for your insight and wisdom. For discussing these characters as if they were old friends, and for exploring this world as if you'd traveled its roads and breathed its air. Laura Filipchuk, without your sharp eye and extensive knowledge of how exactly one wields a comma, this novel would be a spliced mess with a very sneaky plot hole. Thank you for bringing passion and care into all that you do, and for directing both into late-stage edits with every single manuscript.

My experts on speed dial: Dr. Jessie Breton, for our gore chats. Thank you for talking through the logistics of each owie, booboo, gash, and laceration. One of these days, I'll finally ask a question that fazes you, but until then, I hope you know I enjoy every bloody detail. Chivilra Celia Aceae, a real-life knight and my go-to woman for all things botany. You shaped the memorial groves (and made sure I knew the difference between a sycamore and a maple). Thank you for every moment I got to glimpse the world through your eyes, and chatting codes of chivalry with me while we conquered munros.

My wonderful friends. Rounding out a series that has been my heartsong for so many years wouldn't have been possible without a solid support system. So thank you Katie James for listening while I worked out plot and characters across Denmark, France, and Scotland, and for always knowing when the soup is good. Kate Rayner, for knowing the ache of having one foot on either side of the pond and helping me with not only Jacs's but also my own. Sonya Blade Englert, for putting the pictures in my mind on paper and painting life into Jacs. I don't know where or who I'd be without your advice. Conor

Furphy, for all the magic and helping me find whimsy on even the stickiest of writing days. Riley Eshenko, for doing the impossible and making this tech-wary author believe marketing is fun, and for always being up for an adventure (or happy hour).

My writing buddy, Victoria Schwab. I will forever cherish our shadow and sunshine year. And to the Tanifiki crew, it took more than coffee to cross this finish line; luckily you also had cake.

And finally, to you, dear reader, thank you for sticking with these characters to the end. This story can only come alive in your eyes. Thank you for every page you turned and every step you took with Jacs and Connor. May love guide your thoughts, your words, your actions, and may you seek to understand those still governed by fear. In all things, choose kindness.

Live magically.

ABOUT THE AUTHOR

Award-winning New Zealand-born Canadian Jordan H. Bartlett has lived on islands and has been surrounded by mountains—has fallen asleep to the sound of waves and train whistles. Growing up, home was the label given to family, not places, and stories of adventure kept her reaching toward the horizon. She grew up reading books about boys for boys and struggled to find that strong heroine she could relate to. While empowering female characters are more prevalent in recent literature, they are often found in worlds dominated by men. Bartlett wrote the Frean Chronicles to create a world asking, "What if," where females are the default gender.

Bartlett has studied the areas of children's literature and the role of women in literature throughout history. It is this affinity for fairy tales mixed with her desire to breathe life into compelling, unique, and ultimately flawed female characters in a world where they have not been tethered that she hopes to flip fantasy tropes and challenge gendered expectations in young adult readers—while keeping the levity of a fairy tale.

When she is not writing, Bartlett works as a speech language pathologist and is a certified yoga instructor in Banff, Alberta. Any other free time is spent hiking, biking, and kayaking in the mountains and lakes of her backyard. She has devoured literature all her life and is honored to add to the world's library.

Find other works, writing updates, and more information at
www.jordanhbartlett.com
and tune into monthly interviews with fellow authors
on Jordan's podcast on Spotify and YouTube:
Author Nook with Jordan H. Bartlett

If you enjoyed
Jordan H. Bartlett's *Queendom Come*,
consider leaving a review
to help our authors.

And check out:
Magic at the Grand Dragonfly Theatre
by Brandie June.

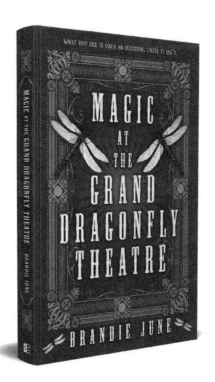

PROLOGUE

 IRIS

*By order of His Majesty, King Edmund IV, all Conjurors are to
immediately report to the Noble Guard for mandatory five-year military service
to aid in the war against the revolting colonies of Tsitonia.*

Military service for Illusionists and those without the Gifts remains voluntary.

I RIS HAD BEEN PRACTICING HER trick for weeks, and now she was
ready to show her uncle that she could also be a performer. She
dreamed of standing onstage instead of watching in the dark.
During the ferry crossing to the Isle of Ily, she pulled out her coin and
her mother's blue silk handkerchief, the one with her mother's initials
embroidered in gold, but the swaying of the boat made her drop the
coin instead of hiding it.

"I want to see the magic show!" Violet said when they reached the
docks, wriggling in their mother's arms.

"It's not a *magic* show. It's a show of *illusion*," Iris corrected with a six-year-old's sense of superiority.

"That's right, Iris," her mother said, as she set Violet down and went to hail one of Uncle Leo's shiny black carriages, the ones with large gold dragonflies painted on the doors.

"It's important you two know this is a place for illusions only," their mother said sternly when she returned.

"Illusions *and* wonder," Iris added. Her mother had helped her read some of the advertisement posters in the city. One poster depicted Uncle Leo pulling a rabbit out of a hat. In another, he was sawing a beautiful woman in half, but since the woman was smiling, Iris decided that it was nothing to worry about.

Today, she would tell Uncle Leo that she wanted to be an Illusionist like him.

Iris draped the blue silk handkerchief over the coin in her left hand. "Now Violet, blow on the handkerchief."

"Why?" her little sister asked. Violet was a smaller version of Iris with similar chestnut hair, hazel eyes, and a white lace dress that matched the one Iris was wearing.

"Because it is part of the trick."

Violet stared at the silk square, not sure what to make of it.

"Come on, Vi," Iris insisted.

Violet leaned over and blew so hard on the handkerchief that she flecked it with spittle.

"With that breath, I make the coin disappear!" Iris tried to move the coin into her sleeve, but it slipped, falling to the ground. Iris waved the handkerchief around, hoping the effect was mesmerizing as she quickly stepped on the coin.

"And voilà!" Iris said with a flourish, handing the coin-less handkerchief to her sister.

Violet took the piece of silk but wrinkled her nose at her sister. "You stepped on the coin."

Defeated, Iris lifted her foot and picked up the coin.

"You do the trick like *this*," Violet said. A coin appeared in her empty palm amidst a small wisp of white smoke that evaporated as quickly as it appeared. Iris could smell roses and smoke and her own hands tingled, as though something was heating the air.

"How did you do that?" Iris asked, her incredulity warring with jealousy. Violet hadn't been practicing for weeks to impress their uncle like she had.

"I don't know," Violet said, shrugging.

"Give that to me," Iris demanded.

"Stop that!" their mother said, so sharply that Iris froze. Their mother snatched the coin from Violet. "We don't conjure things, do you understand?" She bent down and held Violet's shoulders. "Understand?"

"Mommy, you're hurting me," Violet whined.

Their mother seemed to melt, almost crying as she quickly wrapped Violet in a hug. "I'm so sorry sweetheart. Your father was taken away because bad men saw him conjuring. I only want to keep you safe."

The sun was low in the sky as the carriage jostled them down a winding road to the theatre. Violet grumbled as their seats shook after hitting a jut in the road, but Iris grinned, knowing this was only the beginning of their journey.

The theatre came into view as they crested the final hill. The building was large and stately, reminding Iris of a palace. Today, the theatre was the perfect shade of butterscotch yellow, making it look warm and inviting against the sunset. Large pillars carved to look like giant stone dragonflies supported the massive domed roof and the great stained-glass windows of amber and green, illuminated by warm light from within. Enormous brass letters above engraved double doors declared that this was the Grand Dragonfly Theatre. Silver and gold stars and moons bedecked the theatre's walls and glittered in the fading sunlight.

"We've arrived," Iris called out in a majestic tone, trying to imitate the booming voice her uncle used when welcoming people to his theatre.

"We are late, so we must get to our seats," their mother said, quickly ushering the girls through a grand mirrored foyer and into their usual box.

Iris hovered on the edge of her seat, leaning as far as she could toward the railing of the balcony, even though all she could see were the thick burgundy curtains that hid the stage.

"Careful darling, lean over any further and you'll fall over the edge," her mother warned.

"No, I won't," Iris argued, but she scooted back a tiny bit to avoid a second scolding.

"When will the show start?" Violet asked.

As if on cue, the lights inside the auditorium went dark.

I could be anywhere, Iris thought and smiled. Her belly filled with happy butterflies as she anticipated the start of the show. With a flash of light and what sounded like a clap of thunder, the footlights along the stage flared to life, casting the stage in bright illumination as the curtain was pulled away. Iris inhaled the familiar scent of gas from the lights. The stage looked like an extraordinary palace. Gold filigree had been worked into the walls and incorporated in a magnificent throne embedded with rubies and sapphires that sat center stage.

A young boy wearing the regalia of a medieval squire entered stage right and walked to the throne with dignified purpose. Iris wondered if the boy had been made up with white lead paint, since his skin and hair were snow white beneath the bright stage lights.

"Your Highness, one of your subjects requests an audience," the boy said, his high voice surprisingly strong in the vast theater.

A sparkling puff of green smoke exploded in front of the throne, causing gasps of surprise throughout the audience. When the smoke cleared, a king sat upon the great golden chair.

"And which of my subjects comes to see the king?"

Iris recognized her uncle's voice right away. Uncle Leo wore a jeweled crown instead of his usual top hat and a richly embroidered doublet with a bottle-green cape.

The squire introduced a knight, who entered the stage and bowed low to Uncle Leo. As her uncle gave the knight a quest, Iris let herself slip into the story as easily as she slipped into dreams, living in the world playing out in front of her. Iris felt the ocean spray on her skin and tasted saltwater on her tongue as the knight saved himself from drowning after a tidal wave hit his ship in a storm. She held her breath when the knight fought a three-headed wolf that guarded a witch's hut, the wild animal onstage looking so real that Iris wondered if there really were wolves with three heads.

The audience booed when they saw the witch, a hunched woman clad in rags, a giant snake slithering over her shoulders. And Iris shrieked in delight when the brown phoenix the knight fought so hard for burst into flames, only to reappear golden and mirror bright. Iris cheered loudly when Uncle Leo rewarded the knight and welcomed him home.

As the actors took their bows, the audience applauded loudly. Iris stood, clapping as hard as she could. Tiny golden feathers no larger than Iris's pinkie finger floated down from the ceiling and the sisters reached out for them, managing to pocket a few of the small treasures so that they would remember this perfect night forever.

"That was incredible." Iris sighed, as the audience began to file out of the theatre.

"Indeed, it was," her mother agreed. "Now let's go see Uncle Leo." Iris's mother led the girls out of the auditorium. The woman who had played the witch stood in one corner of the lobby surrounded by audience members waiting their turn to pet the large snake coiled around her neck.

"Mrs. Ashmore."

Iris turned to see a strange man approaching them. His dirty trench coat and muddy boots clashed with the finely dressed patrons, and his beady eyes were fixed on Iris's mother.

Iris's mother stepped in front of Iris and Violet, shielding them from the stranger.

"I'm afraid you have me at a disadvantage," Iris's mother said. Her sweet voice had gone cold. Iris didn't know what was going on, but she wanted the strange man to go away. "I don't believe I've made your acquaintance," her mother added, but did not offer him her hand.

The stranger chuckled, a gravelly sound that scared Iris. "How thoughtless of me. Mr. Roman Whitlock."

Iris's mother stiffened and Iris thought she heard her mother say *bounty hunter* under her breath. Iris noticed that the other people in the lobby had stilled their chatter as they stared at Iris's family and Mr. Whitlock. Iris peeked around her mother's skirts. Several men in yellow and brown uniforms stood behind Mr. Whitlock.

"Now Mrs. Ashmore, it seems that your husband was not the only Conjuror in your family. I have reason to believe you are as well," Mr. Whitlock said. There were several audible gasps in the lobby. Mr. Whitlock licked his thick lips. "Which means you are charged with failing to report yourself for conscription." Mr. Whitlock was grinning, but Iris knew he wasn't friendly.

"What is going on here?" Uncle Leo had finally arrived, out of costume, but still wearing the thick greasepaint makeup. Iris sighed in relief. She was certain he could make the bad man go away.

"Business for the Crown," Mr. Whitlock said, puffing himself up. "You ought to stay out of it, Mr. Von Frey."

"This is my theatre and you are speaking to my sister," Uncle Leo said, stepping right up to Mr. Whitlock, even though he was almost a head shorter.

"And Mrs. Ashmore is a Conjuror. I will be taking her in to collect the bounty."

"You have no proof," Iris's mother said, but Iris could hear her mother's voice shaking.

The bounty hunter moved far faster than Iris thought a man of his size could move. Before she realized what was going on, Mr. Whitlock snatched her away from her mother, yanking her arm so hard it hurt. Iris screamed as his meaty fingers dug into her arm, but the sound was cut off as his other hand wrapped around her throat, squeezing the air out of her.

A blade appeared in her mother's hand, wisps of gray smoke evaporating as she slashed at the bounty hunter, a deep cut along his temple and down his cheek. He swore and dropped Iris. She fell to the floor, gasping for air. Everything hurt. She didn't want to move, but Uncle Leo was already picking her up.

"You don't touch my daughters," her mother said. Iris had never heard her mother so angry. Iris silently cried as she looked over at the terrible, mean man. The cut on his face was bleeding, but he only smiled.

"I love the smell of smoke and roses," Mr. Whitlock said, inhaling deeply. "Using the True Gift always leaves that smell."

"Enough!" One of the guards in the yellow and brown uniforms stepped forward. He wore more metals than the other guards, and for a fleeting moment, Iris thought he was going to help them. "This is not how we operate." He shot Mr. Whitlock a disdainful look.

"But Captain, you saw her conjure. She created a knife out of thin air."

"We do not go around choking little girls," the captain said. He pointed to another uniformed guard. "Give me the bone."

Iris's mother tried to back away, but two guards were suddenly by her side, holding her firmly in place. Iris reached out for her mother, but Leo held her fast. The captain was given a polished wood box, and he opened it to reveal a small finger bone. Iris's mother struggled against the men holding her.

"This will only take a moment, Mrs. Ashmore." In one swift movement, the captain pressed the bone into Iris's mother's hand, closing his hands around hers to force her to hold the bone. Iris's mother screamed and Iris smelled burning flesh.

It was over in a moment. The captain released his grip on Iris's mother's hand, picking up the bone as it fell from her mother's palm. The bone was still pristine and white, but the shape of the bone was burned into her mother's hand.

"See, I told you," Mr. Whitlock crowed, sick delight on his face.

The captain gave him a distasteful look, but nodded. "She is a Conjuror. You will be paid the full bounty, Mr. Whitlock." The captain turned to Iris's mother. "You are required to come with us."

The color had leached out of her mother's face, but she stood tall as she said, "Please let me say goodbye to my children." The captain nodded and the guards released their hold on Iris's mother, but they stayed close to her side.

Iris's mother looked to Uncle Leo with so much fear that Iris cried harder. "I'm so sorry," her mother said. Uncle Leo stepped close to Iris's mother, sandwiching Iris between them.

"I will figure out something, Lynnette," Uncle Leo said.

Iris's mother shook her head. For a moment, she leaned on Uncle Leo's shoulder, and Iris could hear her sobbing. When Iris's mother straightened, tears were running down her mother's cheeks. Iris pulled out the crumpled blue handkerchief and handed it to her mother. She gave Iris a watery smile as she accepted the piece of silk, silently wiping her face as she took long, deep breaths.

"I need you to take the girls," Iris's mother said to Uncle Leo.

He nodded vigorously. "Of course, Lynnette. Who do you want me to take them to?"

"No, Leo. I need you to keep the girls." Quietly, so that the bad men couldn't hear, her mother added, "You know what my daughter is. I need you to protect her."

Uncle Leo's mouth opened but no sound came out. Violet started crying so hard she hiccupped.

"Please Leo, keep my daughters safe. Someday, I will be released from service and I'll come back for them." Her mother's eyes were glossy with tears, but she did not look away from Uncle Leo.

"I would do anything for you and the girls," Uncle Leo said resolutely. Iris's unease swelled inside her, giving her a stomachache.

Gently, Uncle Leo set Iris down. Her mother wrapped her and Violet up in a tight embrace. "I love you girls so much. I need you to know that."

When the captain cleared his throat, Iris's mother reluctantly released Iris and Violet, kissing each of them on the top of their heads. "I must go now. Be good for your uncle."

Iris wanted to speak but had no words. Only hours ago, she would have given anything to live in her uncle's theatre, but now she regretted it. She didn't want her mother to leave. Violet sobbed. When their mother rose to leave, Violet lunged to stop her.

"Mama!" she cried. Uncle Leo held Violet back as she kicked and screamed.

Iris reached for her mother's skirts. "Please don't go without me," Iris said. "I don't want you to go."

Her mother bent down, so she was eye-to-eye with her daughter, "I love you and your sister more than I could ever say and I need to keep you safe. Right now, the safest place for you and your sister is with your uncle."

"I don't want to be safe. Not if you're leaving."

"But who will protect Violet if you come with me?" Iris blinked and looked up at her mother. "I will be back as soon as I can. Until then, I am counting on you, Iris."

"We don't have all night, Mrs. Ashmore," the bounty hunter said.

All eyes were fixed on Iris's mother. Her fists were clenched so tightly they turned white, but still she rose and followed Mr. Whitlock and the captain, a line of Noble Guardsmen trailing behind her. Then, she was gone, leaving Iris with her screaming sister and Uncle Leo.

Iris ran.

The courtyard was dark. Most of the carriages had left, making it easy for Iris to find the one her mother was in with the bounty hunter. The carriage was already moving as Iris raced outside. She ran after it, yelling for her mother, but her tiny legs were no match for the horses. Iris was crying, her vision blurry with tears. She tripped, skinning her knee bloody as the coach rolled farther and farther away. Everything hurt, and Iris screamed and screamed. But her mother never came back.

CHAPTER ONE

 VIOLET

Due to the continued resistance from the colonies of Tsitonia, service terms of Conjurors have been extended indefinitely for the foreseeable future.

By royal decree of His Majesty, King Edmund IV.

THE GRAND DRAGONFLY THEATRE a different color every day. Uncle Leo, known as *Leopold The Great*, insisted that guests immediately know they were in for great spectacle. Only in the early hours of the morning, long after even the most enthusiastic or inebriated patron had stumbled into a hansom cab, did the illusion fade and the walls of the theatre melt back to the traditional colors of wood and stone. But once Leo woke, often at a decadently late hour, the plain walls would once again be drenched in a gaudy splash of color. Today, the theatre was the deep mauve of rain clouds after sunset. After eleven years of living in the loud and lavish Grand Dragonfly

Theatre, Violet Ashmore sought peace and quiet wherever she could find it. For this reason, she had climbed the trellis outside her bedroom window and sat on the roof, legs dangling over the window ledge. In the predawn stillness, she could almost hear the ocean waves crashing on the shore of their island, the fresh air cold and salty.

She thought about changing the color of the theatre, going so far as to touch the wall, rough and cool under her fingers. The fear of forgetting to let her conjuring fade the way illusions naturally did after a day or so brought on anxiety that the Noble Guardsmen would discover her.

Less than a week ago, the Crown announced they were doubling the bounty price on Conjurors. The war with the colonies of Tsitonia was going poorly, and the Crown was desperate for more Conjurors to send overseas to fight.

She shivered and withdrew her hand from the wall. Technically only adults of eighteen or older were required to fight, but Violet knew that being fifteen wouldn't protect her from a war that had been going on for over a decade. Even children could be dragged away by the Noble Guard, kept locked up until they were old enough to fight. Violet was many things, but a fighter wasn't one of them. Just the idea of war made her insides squeeze tight with fear.

The sky was just beginning to lighten in the east as it groggily remembered what dawn should look like. Violet rubbed her eyes, trying to soothe the strain. She had been up for hours, writing by candlelight and savoring the sleepy quiet that was a rarity in theatre life. The ink was drying on the final pages of her script. She mulled over the story, her mind engrossed in the fantasy of magical moon princesses and star-crossed lovers.

"Are you up there?" A head of glossy auburn curls poked through Violet's window. Iris Ashmore looked up at Violet with large hazel eyes.

"Why are you in my room?" Violet snapped, her sense of calm evaporating.

"I hadn't seen you since intermission. I thought I'd check on my favorite sister."

"*Only* sister."

"And still my favorite. Why are you on the roof?"

"Because it was quiet," Violet grumbled, starting to climb down.

"Don't. I'll join you," her sister replied, ducking her head back into Violet's room before hoisting herself out the window. Iris was still clad in the thick crimson and gold embroidered robe she'd worn in last night's show.

"In that?" Violet laughed. Iris played the role of Captain Josephine, the Pirate Queen. The costume was fitting for commanding a motley crew of buccaneers, but hardly appropriate for scaling a trellis. Violet looked down at her more practical attire, a plain blouse and a split skirt, which resembled extremely loose trousers and provided her with more freedom of movement while still maintaining the appearance of a skirt.

"Why not? It's chilly." Iris shrugged and, with the same grace she used to dance across the stage, ascended the trellis and settled next to her sister.

Violet tamped down a flush of jealousy. Iris could make anything look effortless. Violet had been climbing out her window for years to watch the sunrise, and even in wide-legged skirts, she felt more like a scuttling bug. "Uncle Leo will never forgive me if you break your leg," Violet added, though Iris was already smoothing out her pirate's robe.

"Actually, one is required to break a leg before a show," Iris joked, giving Violet an affectionate nudge with her shoulder.

"You know what I mean," Violet said, her tone softer now. "I'm surprised to see you up this early."

"What do you mean 'this early'?"

Violet realized her sister was still wearing the greasepaint makeup from the night before. Iris's eyes were exaggerated with dark liner and her lips still bright with color. Violet sighed. "You've not been to bed at all tonight?"

"I'll be in bed soon enough. There was a party after the show with some of the more distinguished patrons. It ran longer than I anticipated," she said breezily with a wry smile.

"I don't envy you the late nights."

"I still think you should consider a life onstage. It's so much more entertaining than the box office."

"I don't mind selling tickets." Violet shrugged. She knew that someone with a sense for numbers needed to keep the finances in order, and she didn't trust anyone else to do it.

"You would be lovely on stage," Iris continued, looking over at her sister. "You have the perfect profile for it. Very distinguished."

"You only say that because we're sisters. Our profiles look exactly the same." *But not truly,* Violet thought. Her sister was the elegant grace that was promised on the large promotional posters around the city of Leitha. She, on the other hand, was a general mess onstage. Her hair refused to mold into delicate curls, demanding instead to frizz around her face, and she was so flat-chested that she would be forced to add stuffing to any of her sister's costumes.

"Besides, I hate being onstage. I don't know what to do with my hands." Violet's hands were perfectly capable appendages when she was writing or tallying the nightly accounting, but onstage, they suddenly became as ineffectual as two dead fish hanging from her wrists. The last time she had accepted a role, she fidgeted with her hands so much that the audience broke into laughter during a dramatic death scene. Lance had offered to glue her hands to her sides the next night. It had been mortifying. "I'm perfectly happy off the stage, thank you very much."

"Too busy writing?" Iris asked, her smug smirk jerking Violet out of an old fear and into a new one.

"You were snooping in my room!"

Iris pointed a finger at Violet. "It was right on your desk, Vi. That's hardly snooping."

Violet glared at her sister and crossed her arms. "You shouldn't be in my room at all." She kicked herself for not hiding her script. She wasn't ready to share her work with anyone, even Iris.

"Can I read it? I only glanced at a few pages. It was lovely. I want to know more about this Sea Prince. He sounds charming."

"No!" Violet cried, a flush creeping into her face. "Leave my things alone. Is that so difficult?"

"I meant no offense," Iris said, raising her hands in surrender. "Only trying to show my support as your adoring big sister." Iris grinned, wrapping velvet-clad arms around Violet.

"I'll let you know when I want support," Violet said, struggling to free herself from her sister's loving embrace.

Neither of the girls spoke for a few minutes as they watched the sun crest the horizon, a tiny golden orb breaking the dawn blue. Violet's frustration cooled. Part of her was pleased Iris wanted to read her story, even if Violet wasn't ready to share it.

"I can see why you like it out here. It is peaceful," Iris said, finally breaking the quiet.

"I thought you were allergic to peace and calm."

"I can handle some peace." Iris stifled a yawn. "And that's about as much as I can handle. I'm going to bed." She kissed Violet on the cheek before climbing down the trellis and pulling herself through the window.

Violet stayed on her perch, savoring the morning stillness. In a few hours, the theatre would come to life as the performers who lived there woke up while those who stayed at the village by the dock arrived with traveling bags full of costumes and makeup, and in Arabella's case, her snake.

Then the deliveries would start coming in. Ruth and Mary, two girls from the village, would bring fresh roses to replace the wilting ones as well as food for the troupe: meat pies, fresh cod, dumplings filled with artichoke hearts, and spice cakes. The cook, Nat, would create the finer delicacies for the wealthy patrons: caviar blinis, rosewater candies, whipped caramels, and miniature fruit tarts. He would hire several strong village lads to pull the cart of wines and spirits, fresh arrivals from Leitha. Violet needed to get the books in order and ensure that her cash till had enough smaller foil bills, gold crowns, and silver florins to make change.

Violet closed her eyes, reliving the final scene of her play, the one with the Moon Princess and the Sea Prince. She considered slight changes to the dialogue, perhaps different stage directions, and played out the scene in her head several ways before deciding to let the matter sit for a while. Sighing, she opened her eyes. Violet carefully climbed back through the window. She was about to head down to the cellars to see how many bottles of champagne they had for guests when she noticed that her script was no longer on her desk. Her stomach plummeted. Violet snapped open every drawer, knowing full well that it was useless.

"Iris!" she screamed. Forget telling her sister not to pry, Violet was going to get a lock for her door.

She flung open her door and sprinted down the hall to her sister's room, her slippers sliding on the carpet as she planned how to reacquire her script—with the use of threats and violence if necessary. Catching her breath outside her sister's room, Violet twisted the doorknob, but it did not budge.

When had Iris gotten a lock?

"Iris, give me back my play, you little thief!" Violet banged on her door. Her sister gave no answer. Violet pounded on the door more rapidly. "I am serious, Iris!"

"Sorry, I can't hear you. I'm asleep."

Violet let out a loud shriek of annoyance. "Cut the bollocks, Iris!"

"I am talking in my sleep," her sister insisted. Violet could hear the infuriating grin in her voice.

"If you don't open this door right now, I'm going to tell Uncle Leo." Violet cringed, feeling like a small child threatening to tattle to her uncle.

"Good luck waking him before noon." Iris began fake snoring so loudly that Violet marveled how it was possible for her sister to be such a great actress considering how unconvincing she was at this moment.

"I hate you."

"Love you."

"Argh!" Violet yelled, pounding on the door as hard as she could, but to no avail. She considered following through on her threat to tell their uncle, but he might ask her about the play and the embarrassment of confessing to Uncle Leo that she hoped to be a playwright was too much.

Out of options, Violet decided on drastic measures. She looked up and down the hall, ensuring no one was around. She opened her palm and concentrated on conjuring a key. She closed her eyes and focused on the details of a brass key: the metallic sheen, a long, slender body, and delicate teeth. Heat filled her hands as she felt the heft of metal. The air smelled of smoke and roses as wisps of white vapor dissipated from her palms. She examined the shiny brass key she had created. Violet tried to insert the key, but it jammed in the lock. She wanted to scream.

Violet thrust the useless key in her pocket and stormed off in a rage, stomping all the way to the box office where she began to viciously attack the accounting books.

Violet was halfway through adding up the recent order of port and brandy when she heard a loud knocking coming from the front of the theatre. Checking her pocket watch, she realized it was already eleven in the morning. Ruth had been due an hour ago to replace the roses and tidy the theatre. Violet made her way to the entrance of the theatre and swung open the doors of the Dragonfly Theatre.

"Ruth, you're late," Violet said.

But instead of Ruth, a young man stood in front of her. He was a scrawny thing and wore an ill-fitting suit that hung on his wiry frame. The material of his suit was fine if a bit worn. The bowler hat on his head sat at an angle that would have been jaunty if he didn't look so destitute.

"Who are you?" Violet blurted out.

Without a word, the boy dropped into a bow low enough that his hat fell from his head, rolling down his arm. He caught it with ease before settling it back on his head.

"Alexander Morgan at your service. Call me Alec." He cracked a smile, revealing twin dimples. Violet realized he was older than she first thought, probably Iris's age. His baggy clothes and thin limbs made him appear younger.

"Did Ruth send you?" Violet asked, wondering if the village girl had taken ill and sent this boy in her place.

"I don't know any Ruth."

"Then why are you here?" Violet asked, a bit too sharply. She didn't like being around strangers, especially when she was on her own.

"Because of this," the boy, Alec, answered, his smile never faltering. If anything, it widened as Alec held up a thick, cream-colored piece of paper. Violet could easily see the letterhead that Uncle Leo favored, a stylized image of the theatre surrounded by tiny stars in gold foil. "For I am to start work at your marvelous establishment." Alec extended the letter to Violet, who grabbed it and read it over quickly.

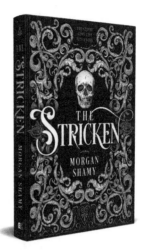
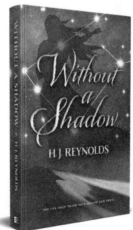

CamCat Books

VISIT US ONLINE FOR MORE BOOKS TO LIVE IN:
CAMCATBOOKS.COM

SIGN UP FOR CAMCAT'S FICTION NEWSLETTER FOR
COVER REVEALS, EBOOK DEALS, AND MORE EXCLUSIVE CONTENT.

CamCatBooks @CamCatBooks @CamCat_Books @CamCatBooks